HIDDEN
IN THE
WOODS

THE TRAGIC TALE OF THE MISTRESS OF ALL EVIL

M. A. KERSH

Dedicated to my wonderful children, whom I love and treasure above all things in this magical world, and my own dark darling, Pyewackit, who has always been there for me. I couldn't have wished for a better companion to complete my soul. Through every dark age of my life, she has been my shining light.

PROLOGUE

Your Excellence,

It has come to my attention that you have bestowed a curse upon the Rose Kingdom and that of the princess born to King Stefan and his Queen. Others, like myself, cannot deny admiring the glorious masterpiece you have cast, brazen as it was. Most like us, me above all, must keep our wicked ways hidden, which is why I have need to ask for your help. You see, I too have a princess in my kingdom. I am the queen, the fairest in the land, but with each passing year, the king's brat grows more beautiful. I want nothing more than to hold her bloodied heart in my hands and keep it as a trophy. As queen, I find myself unable to do with her as I would like. I want her tortured, slashed, and left an ugly mess. As our kingdom isn't far from King Stefan's, many have heard of your dark magic. I ask you to kill the princess to restore my rightful vanity. No one will trace her death back to me. I need someone I can trust and in exchange, I offer you my most prized possession, my magic mirror. It can show you anything you desire. There is no question it cannot answer, but be warned, for it will only reflect the truth. I hate that. Should you wish to comply, please send to me one of your ravens with your written answer.

Ever fairest,
The Evil Queen

CHAPTER ONE
THE STOLEN CHILD

The very spirt of celebration could be heard within the smallest home of the village known as Foolsgold on the first night of fall. It had been one year to the day since Hook and Ainsel had magically appeared on the doorstep of Mr. Smee's tiny house.

It had been the wish of the old man that had brought the two to his window on that starry evening. Hook didn't know what was more shocking; to find his old mate in such a horrid little home, or that he had somehow been brought to him. But the answer to such a riddle was simple... Smee's wish had been spoken louder than any other in all the world on that night, and it was that *exact* wish that had been strong enough to not only pull Ainsel and Hook from the ship, but to save them as well.

Fifteen years ago, after Smee's return with Hook from Neverland, Hook had given him a substantial amount of gold, and a most respectable recommendation, but alas, Smee could no longer practice medicine. The fears and nerve-racking tortures he had endured had turned themselves into permanent scars within his broken mind. His hands shook terribly, and all the drinking he had consumed to cope with all those years on the sea had made him ill, and the reputation he had gained being amongst the likes of Hook had made it utterly impossible to live a normal life anywhere. So, he decided to change his name to Geppetto and move to a private place where no one had ever heard of him.

It wasn't exactly the best town to live in, for the sort that lived there were that of fools and thieves. Though Smee had never been so ignorant as to live an extravagant lifestyle in the city, his weakness had gotten him robbed on more than one occasion. So, with what money he had left, he decided to keep well hidden within his small home. But with no one to talk to and no need to work for pay or profit, Smee decided that in order to prevent drinking himself to death, he would need some sort of distraction; a healthy hobby, perhaps. Then one day, a kind neighbor that lived beside him had one such suggestion, and it was this suggestion that would turn Geppetto's entire life completely upside down.

The neighbor's name was Charo Cherry, and he was a skilled wood carpenter. He taught Geppetto how to cut, shape, and design the most magical of carvings. Since Smee was a former doctor and a very skilled surgeon, the craft came quite easy for him. And just as he had hoped, the hobby did just the trick.

Throughout the next lonely years of his life, he learned how to make clocks, tables, cups, bowls, chairs, and other useful things for around the house. His favorite thing to make, however strange that it may be, were the cuckoo clocks. He knew his captain's hatred for them, but after spending so much time at sea and on the Lost Island, Neverland; never knowing what time it was, what day it was, or even the year, there was something about the constant ticking of a clock that was a soothing reminder of not just the time, but rather that he was finally in a still and normal world. Oh, yes, the symbol of the clock to Geppetto had become the complete and utter opposite of Hook's view. Time may be the cruelest element in the mortal world, but it was because of its ties to the human world that Geppetto loved. And so, it happened, that much of his life had become quite simple and wonderful throughout the following years of Hook's absence. Yet, the sad truth of his reality had become unbearably clear... he was nothing more than a lonely old man.

Since being responsible for the life of another creature had for so long been a matter of frantic pressure, Smee decided to start small. He went out and got himself a tiny goldfish. But as the ticking went by, and the beautiful fish was growing bigger and healthier by the day, he soon realized that taking care of her was not a matter of anxiety at all... it was a joy. Still, he found himself searching for something else; something *more*. So, next he found a cat; a tiny tuxedo kitten to be exact. He named him Figaro, and he was quite the cuddly companion. But if someone would have asked Geppetto what his favorite thing about him was, if there had been anyone to ask, it was how adorable the kitten was with the goldfish, Cleo. They didn't behave like friends exactly, but rather siblings. They both had such strong personalities; it was quite entertaining to watch them interact with each other. Even still, there was an aching void within him that he had not been able to fill. Then one day as Geppetto was using his imagination to carve his next piece of wood, he was surprised to find that what he had unknowingly created was the wooden puppet of a young boy. A tear fell down his cheek as he realized that what he was missing in his life was a child of his very own.

It was on that chilly night that he wished upon the very star that brought both Hook and Ainsel to him. Of course, Ainsel being a dear old friend, was most eager to help Smee, but such a wish was not so easy to grant. For bringing a child to life from wood meant making a changeling, and that would mean using dark magic. The magic that it would take to turn the creature into a real boy wasn't the hardest problem, it was the constant trouble that changelings caused. They misbehave terribly and have a tendency to attract other magical creatures of the darkest kind. It is not in the changeling's nature to do the right thing, but that is exactly what the wooden boy named Pinocchio would have to learn to do.

The journey to the right path was a difficult one, alright. A few kidnappings, an imprisonment by a gypsy puppeteer, and a trip to a faraway place corrupted by a touch of dark magic, known as Paradise Island; a place that transformed bad little boys into donkeys. Luckily enough for Pinocchio, he was not a real boy, so he was able to escape before the transformation took over his entire body. As bad as this was though, the worst was

4

yet to come as Pinocchio discovered Geppetto had been swallowed by a whale on his search for him. With a great deal of bravery and love, Pinocchio found his father and sacrificed himself to save him. It was this good deed that would seal the final piece of magic Ainsel would need to cast the spell that would transform the wooden puppet into a living, breathing child.

So, after a long and heart wrenching journey for the little puppet and his father, in the end, it was all worth it. Geppetto got his wish. Pinocchio had proven himself kind, truthful, and unselfish. He was finally a real boy. Geppetto had himself a son of his very own. But that wasn't the only cause for a celebration on this particular night. No, there was more happy news on the horizon.

"Thank you so much for giving me my precious boy, Ainsel. We will all be so eternally grateful, won't we, Pinocchio?"

"Oh, yes sir! I am grateful, miss. Most grateful! Thank you very much. We are a family now. Little Cleo!" He said kissing the small fishbowl. "And Figaro... Oh, Figaro, you are so sweet," he said cuddling the little cat.

Ainsel smiled, delighted to see such a happy family. It was in this precious moment, that she decided it was time to tell everyone of her own announcement. "Excuse me, James... Smee... I have something very important to tell you."

"What is it, my love?" Hook asked, with Smee's eager eyes popping up behind his shoulder. Ainsel smiled in a way that Hook had never seen before, making him even more anxious for her answer. "Ainsel, what is it?"

She gently pulled her dainty hand up to her belly and let a sparkling tear of complete happiness fall from her beautiful eyes. Hook rushed up to her, putting his hand over her stomach with hers.

"Is it true?" He asked with a hidden smile. "Are you?"

Ainsel nodded, giggling happily, "Yes! I am."

Hook scooped her up in his arms and kissed her in a passionate embrace. It was the kind of kiss that could bring tears to a child's eyes and hope to a hardened soul. Geppetto and Pinocchio clapped and cheered in delight to Ainsel's most wonderful news. But somewhere hidden behind the open window of such a joyous celebration was another face smiling; the most sinister and ominous of all smiles... the smile of Peter Pan. He had been searching for Hook and Ainsel for quite some time now, but the task of finding a roaming pirate and a fairy was a near impossible one. It wasn't that Hook and the Blue Fairy were hiding from him, for the pirate would have loved nothing more than another chance to defeat his devilish foe once and for all, but being shielded in the way that Hook was from the fae and all their powers had prevented such an encounter. Ainsel on the other hand was in no hurry to face Pan again. Though she didn't doubt James' protection, she couldn't help but fear Pan, nor could anyone or anything else in the Nine Realms. Even the Snow Queen herself feared his ever- growing power.

Nevertheless, the Gancanagh hadn't been able to find his prey, and his year of searching had only made his desire for vengeance grow. But now, on this very night, the generous act of bringing the little puppet back to life and transforming him into a real boy took the kind of magic that sent off a burst of energy—and that kind of energy; the kind that could only come from the pure of heart... Well, it didn't take long for a creature of the likes of Pan to discover where and *who* it was coming from. It was in that very moment that Pan too, felt as if his wish had been granted, for not only had he found his mortal enemy, he had come across the very gift that could deliver him a vengeance so deliciously sinister, that it was beyond anything he had imagined in his most malevolent of dreams.

The haunting gaze hidden behind the shrouded blanket of midnight shadows suddenly brought a strange imposing feeling to only one within the tiny house. Pan's sinister thrill traversed upon Hook's spine, raising every hair upon the nape of his neck. It was a familiar sensation akin to that childhood feeling when you sense danger lurking within the darkness under your bed. The vexing moment was short, but enough to stop Hook's breath. While Ainsel and the others never ceased their cheers of excitement, Hook found himself rushing to the creaking sound of the window. With a quick shove of force, the window flew open... but there was nothing there; nothing but the luminous stare from the full moon in the night sky above.

"James, what is it?" Ainsel said with concerned curiosity.

Hook shook his head, disregarding the feeling of hate and vile that gnawed at his stomach. "Nothing, love," he said looking up at the stars. "Nothing at all."

Ainsel let out a sigh of relief, "Well then, close the window, and come celebrate with us."

Hook smiled a fake smile, knowing that she couldn't read his mind, and though he was not one to normally hide anything from Ainsel, in this particular moment, he had never been more grateful for it. After all, she was right. Tonight, *was* a night of celebration, and he didn't want to do anything to spoil it, not for her, not for Smee, and not for himself.

Ainsel was going to be a mother, and he was going to be a father. Everybody was cheerful and happy, as they all should be. He was just being paranoid... *Right?*

His spiraling uneasiness grew like a fever as the surrounding sound of ticking echoed in his ears. "Mr. Smee..." Hook said rather calmly.

"Yes, Captain?" Geppetto replied. The words spouting from his lips as if no time had ever passed between them. And in all honesty, saying it brought an old smile to his wrinkled face.

"You and I are old mates, yes?"

"Of course." Smee answered, confused by his question.

"Yes. And I think it's about time I told you how much I cherish you as a friend."

Geppetto heaped in glee, "Oh, Captain, that is so..."

"—And that is *why* I think I should say that while I appreciate what a great carpenter you have become over our many years apart, I must warn you that if you do not turn off all of these damn clocks, I am going to have to destroy them."

Smee chuckled awkwardly, before racing about the house in his old clumsy manner.

"James!" Ainsel snapped, glaring at him with a shocked scolding tone.

Hook raised his hand, "What?! I mean... is he serious with all these? I cannot possibly think, let alone celebrate properly with all this relentless ticking!"

It was at that moment that the largest of cuckoo clocks struck the hour, unleashing two tiny wooden figures from inside and spouting off the loudest of cuckoos. Smee urgently raced to silence it, but the climbing volume of cuckoos came like a contiguous mountain of mocking to Hook's irritation. Ainsel and Smee both looked up to find the most hilarious look of utter annoyance on Hook's face. It was then that Pinocchio burst into laughter, setting off the others to do the same; each laughing and pointing at the pirate's exasperated expression. But as Hook looked into the eyes of his loved ones, not even he could resist laughing at that moment. As the three looked at each other, and over to Pinocchio and Catcher playing with Figaro, they each realized how important this night was. And it seemed that a good laugh between the oldest of friends, after all they had been through, was exactly what they all needed. They had done it. They had been through it all, and now here they all were to celebrate their

children, their survival, and their lives. A good laugh—
It was the perfect end to the perfect evening.

The following morning, Hook and Ainsel bid their dear friend their goodbyes and set off into the early morning. As they began to set sail into their future together, they stood in a happy and wonderous awe as the glorious sun painted its beautiful colors upon the water below.

* * *

While the ever-growing, ever-glowing Blue Fairy and the proud Captain Hook were sailing upon the Jolly Roger II, the lovers were both under the *very* wrong assumption that they were protected simply because they were on the water. But the dark truth that they were tragically and ultimately going to discover was that they were not safe at all, no matter what they did or where they went. The trouble was— neither Hook nor Ainsel fully understood the being that Peter Pan had become. The sadistic little welsh boy that feared the water was no longer that child at all. In fact, the young boy that he once was could barely be detected as anything more than a bitter fragment within his dark soul. No longer the boy that didn't ever want to grow up was now the Gancanagh, with powers that had grown to extraordinary heights. But more than that... so had his bitter hatred. And it was that very element that had raised him to the evil throne of which he dwelled. And yet, even with all his power, he remained a torn and tortured soul. Both feelings were wrought by none other than the man who was both his oldest friend, and his most loathed enemy.

Pan had lost everything because of Hook: his youth, his home, his best friend, Tinker Bell, his love, Tiger Lily, and most importantly— who he himself once was. The fact that he was the leader of the lost boys now seemed like nothing more than a cruel ironic joke. For now, it was he, and he alone that was completely and utterly lost. He still hadn't been able to find Tiger Lily, and though he had been a charming lover to many young unsuspecting women across the world as the preying Gancanagh, hunting and searching for the one that could fill the hole in his black heart— nothing had even been able to fill the void that caused him such terrible pain and sorrow. And while so much of him wanted to just kill Hook for all that he had done to him, Pan was no longer an impulsive little child. He knew by now that killing James would only bring him more loss. After all, Hook was the only thing left to tie him to the adventurous little boy he once was. That was the hardest part; missing that version of his former self; the Peter Pan that ruled Neverland with Tinker Bell at his side. Those years with her were the best he ever had. And they were gone; everything from his past. Everything that is, except for James Hook.

It may seem strange, but he felt that if he killed Hook, it would mean killing the best part of himself as well. Not to mention the very real fact that if he did, then he would have to live his miserable immortal life forever all alone, enduring the painful loss of his memories that would have died with Hook. And that, to

Pan, wasn't justice, not even for a villain. Death was too swift, too unjust. No, he wanted to do something much worse. He needed Hook to lose something he truly loved. Something that if it were ripped away, it would destroy everything within him. His heart, his mind, and eventually the very essence of his soul would die inside of him while he still walked the earth— as a living breathing corpse. Only when Hook had lost what he is and what he had always been, only then would it be the poetic justice Pan craved with his every being.

Up until that starry evening by the window, Pan had no idea what he was going to do when he found Hook. Sure, he fantasized about killing Ainsel and their unborn child right in front of him, but as Pan knew all too well, facing a tragedy was nothing new for Hook. He had witnessed the terrible death of the woman he loved as a mother, and though it changed him, it didn't leave him a destroyed broken soul. No... It made him stronger, more powerful, and dangerously focused. But after hearing the Blue Fairy's happy news— Pan had a new plan; one that would-be set-in motion on the very day that their newborn child took its first breath.

When the Grand Elder considered the incredible lengths that Pan could reach as a fairy all those years ago, beyond the swirling tunnel of magical portals, that first night on the Lost Island, not even the Grand Elder, in all his wisdom and power, could have imagined the depths of Pan's sinister potential as a magical being. But as it turned out, a child, opening iron windows and blowing on his magical pipes to steal the lives and souls of children really *was* just a matter of fun and games compared to what terrible evil that was to come next. When the Snow Queen took him as her right hand and taught him what it meant to take the souls unto yourself and not deliver them for the sake of the realm, what she didn't realize was that unlike the Unseelie Court, the Bear Prince, and the stolen lover of her sister, Draven, Pan was not loyal to anyone or anything but himself. In fact, Pan now considered himself entirely above her. He could do things that the Snow Queen could never hope to do. For even if she could leave her icy citadel, she didn't have the mortal touch one needed to be able to break the warding barriers for magical creatures, such as iron and the like.

And so, it happened that after spending so many years swallowing spirits and breaking the hearts of those who dared to love him, Pan no longer needed the Snow Queen. He no longer needed anything; that is— anything but the patience needed for time to serve its next cruel play against Hook.

Yes, Pan would take great pleasure knowing and watching as every day came to pass in the following nine months, for as they did, Pan knew that it was the time on the sea between them that let the Blue Fairy and Captain Hook believe that they were safe.

Yes... What a terrible fate it is to believe that time is on your side.

* * *

The next eight and half months went by fairly quickly, though not exactly pleasant. At least, not for Ainsel. Under normal circumstances, a fairy pregnancy would not have taken nine months to give birth, but since the baby was half mortal and half fairy, the pregnancy had been a most interesting and long one. Despite what Pan was thinking, Hook wasn't leaving all of their luck to the water. After all, surely if there was some devious intent afoot, then Ainsel would know about it. She would see it in her visions like she had always done before. But little did Ainsel and Hook know that when a fairy is pregnant with a half mortal child, then like most babies do whenever they are in the womb, it drained her. This baby wasn't just taking nutrients and other vital things that a baby needs, but also something else. It was taking some of her magic. The effect wouldn't be permanent of course. Once the baby was born, Ainsel's magic would return to normal. Nevertheless, the two proud parents were not worried, as a matter of fact, they were nothing short of elated. The day of delivery would be happening very soon. Little did they know, however, that the blessed event would actually be happening on this very evening, the first day of summer, Beltane Eve. This was no accident, for Pan himself had conjured the spell needed to make it so. Ainsel and Hook thought nothing of the timing, as they were too caught up in the excitement, like new parents should be.

Ainsel and Hook had summoned Smee aboard the ship for such an occasion, with the promise, of course, to send him and Pinocchio right back to their home once Hook knew that Ainsel and the baby were perfectly safe. At first, the charge made Smee a little nervous, being so out of practice, but it was Ainsel that insisted upon it being him to deliver their baby. And when the moment arrived, Smee was the perfect man for the job as usual. He talked Ainsel through it all; letting her know when to take her deep breaths and when to push. Hook himself, was rather worried and felt helpless in the situation, unable to do anything but kiss and praise Ainsel, keeping her hand in his all the while. The Blue Fairy's face dripped with sparkling sweat and her eyes burst with purple specks of determination.

Then finally, with one last push... a beautiful baby girl was born. Smee quickly cleaned her off before handing her back to her parents. Ainsel was the first to hold her; to gaze into her child's bright green eyes. She had the fairest skin one could touch, and the most enchanting features that had ever been seen on a baby. She was beautiful. She was perfect. And now, with her baby in her arms, and James standing above her, smiling as he caressed their little daughter's head, she realized that she had never been happier than she was in this moment. While Smee and Pinocchio proceeded to clean up, Ainsel smiled, looking up into her love's teary blue eyes.

"You did wonderful, my love." Hook whispered to her.

Ainsel giggled, "Thank you."

"How are you feeling?" He asked.

She sighed happily, "Just a little tired," she said slowly gazing over to Smee. "I'm sorry, but I don't think I can..."

Geppetto raised his hand, "Shush now... Don't worry about that now, my dear. I spent many years on the water, I am sure I can handle one more night. Get some rest."

Ainsel smiled and nodded in agreement. Hook reached down carefully to swoop up his newborn daughter for the first time. Gentle as he was, he couldn't help his nervousness. She was so small and the most precious looking thing he had ever laid eyes on. The baby began to coo and cry, but it was in that instant that Hook knew just what to do. With a little bobbing up and down, he slowly danced his way around the room, never losing his focused gaze upon her bright green eyes. He hummed her a little song as he danced, calming her slowly. Then suddenly, he bumped into something that stood behind him; something large. And the moment he did, he could hear what sounded like— *pouring rain.* The baby began to cry from the commotion, but it was the look of absolute horror that had blossomed within every face of the room that made Hook's heart race harder than it ever had in his life. The room went silent then, as if everyone within it no longer had the ability to breathe. A flutter of fear flared up in Hook's stomach as he slowly turned around to face the mirror within the room.

There, standing in the pouring rain behind the refection was a cloaked man in a vast forest. The dark green hood was pulled low over his face, leaving only his narrow nose and eerie smile jutting from within the oval of darkness. Before Hook had a second to comprehend what was happening, the hooded figure snatched the baby from his arms and turned to run out into the blanket of heavy showers beyond. In those splintered seconds, Hook jumped through the mirror, chasing after the hooded figure into the woods. The moment that his boots touched the forest ground, he heard the distant echo of Ainsel's throat tearing shriek of fear and desperation. The strange thing about this was that he could hear her long after the mirror had disappeared behind him. He didn't know why the hooded man allowed him to step across the threshold, but something about the timing of it all just seemed too perfect to be an accident. This question, this *feeling*—only grew as the rain suddenly stopped. The ground was not wet; the dirt was not muddy, nor could a single raindrop be found on a distant leaf. It was then that Hook realized that he too was completely dry. The rain had not felt like true rain at all. It was merely an illusion. It was the typical dark magic of the woods.

It all felt like a bad dream. The lively branches and twigs above moved and bent as if they were alive; each trying to snatch him; to rip him off the trail. Incandescent mushrooms littered the ground around the towering presence of knotted trees. The hooded man raced faster and had made his way into the gaping throat of darkness ahead of him, but Hook was too determined to give up. Something about this figure seemed familiar and yet, it was strange and terrifying.

The deeper into the woods they became, Hook realized that they were not alone. Hooting, howling, and laughing could be heard from what sounded like every direction. The darkness of the forest was swallowing him... and his daughter. Hook knew of the secret doorways that stood hidden in the woods; doors that led to the other worlds; the ones that few had seen, and even fewer had survived. Yet, *this* forest felt different. It was as if it had been designed somehow. The rural trail winded in and out of the trees, making it harder to follow, but perfect for those who wished to hide or disappear. It was a frightening place shrouded in shadows of hills and trees, but the worst was yet to come. The hooded figure suddenly began to chant in utter elation. At first, Hook thought it was only to taunt him; mocking him during his desperate chase... but he was wrong. This wasn't to taunt him; the chanting of the hooded man was a calling. The howling from the distance grew louder in that moment; each getting closer and closer until Hook could hear the movement of their bodies upon the fallen leaves. Still, Hook did not stop. He didn't know how much longer he could go on, but if he was running out of breath, surely the hooded man was too. He wanted to scream *Stop!* And, *let my daughter go!* But he dared not spare a single breath.

Suddenly a cold spike of fear suffused him as a pack of what appeared to be massive white hounds with red ears and piercing red eyes came racing through the trees on either side of him. With snarling jaws of large sharp teeth, they charged at him with deadly force. Like hungry beasts, they used their claws and teeth to dig their way into the meat of his flesh. Hook tried to fight them off, struggling and writhing in incredible pain, but never did he stop moving. This felt like it was going to go on forever; the running, the pain, and the sound of Ainsel's everlasting screams echoing off in the distance.

But then, the hooded man looked to be suddenly slowing down. It wasn't a lot, but it was enough to give Hook a spark of hope. The two made their way towards a massive hill. Just before the hooded man began to climb, he *whistled* out a little tune. The white hounds then dispersed, running back into the darkness of the woods. In his agony and confusion, Hook followed the cloaked man up the giant steep hill. With his last bit of desperation and energy, he finally reached the very top. The hooded man stood perfectly still in that moment. With the creature's back facing him, Hook couldn't see what the man was looking at. The woods went silent. The surrounding leaves and mushrooms that had previously been so lively, now cracked and withered away from the dying trees. Hook didn't understand, that is, until the hooded man slowly turned his face towards him.

It was *Pan*. The golden specks in his evil eyes were unmistakable. *But why had he felt so different? Why did he bring me here?* Hook reached for his sword, but it wasn't there. He hadn't been wearing it when the baby was born.

"Give me back my daughter, Peter!" Hook demanded in a weak breath.

Pan laughed in the way that only he could. "You are in no position to give orders, Captain!"

Hook looked around, knowing that he was right. "Pan, don't do this. She is just an innocent child. She has done nothing wrong. Please, just let me give her back to her mother, and you and I can settle this the right way. This is between us... Please."

19

Pan squinted, looking back and forth between Hook and the baby he still held in his arms. "This was *always* supposed to just be between us," he said as if speaking to himself.

Hook nodded with reason, "Yes."

Suddenly, Pan looked back up at him, "So are you saying that you are s*orry*?"

Hook looked instantly taken aback, "Sorry?"

"If this was supposed to just be about us... then are you sorry that you included the *others*?"

Hook paused, enraging Pan.

"Tinker Bell, Tiger Lily, Mr. Smee... even Ainsel wouldn't be suffering the pain she is- if it weren't for you *including* her in our affairs! So, I ask you again, Hook, *are- you- sorry?*"

Hook then took his first sigh of defeat as Pan's brutal truth rose tears into his eyes, "- Yes, Peter. I am sorry."

Peter nodded with a crooked smile, "Well... you may be lying, or maybe you are being sincere. *Maybe* you truly are sorry for taking everyone and everything I cared about, knowing full well that I would live forever with that loss. *Maybe* you are sorry about that. But *I*... will never be sorry for doing the same to you!" With that, Pan suddenly whipped through an invisible veil, tearing through it like a busted seam.

"No!" Hook shouted, his head thundering as he tried to reach it before it closed, but it was gone. The crushing moment came like a massive sledgehammer, obliterating his mind like an orb of fragile glass. He fell to his knees in despair. The blood from the hound's attack erupted from his flesh, dripping lazily unto the ground. With Pan no longer standing in his view, the dawning horror of what was truly happening robbed the breath from his lungs... From the top of the hill, he could see that the forest he had run into- was *endless*. There was no sun, no moon, no food, no life, and no *time;* just the everlasting woods below and the sound of Ainsel's screams that echoed through the dry air, reminding him of his loss and the promise he had broken to her. Pan had known all along that he would chase him. This wasn't just about stealing the baby. This was about bringing him here— to this place; the everlasting woods, where he would remain lost and alone, wallowing like a ghost forever.

* * *

Once Pan had made his way through the black veil of the everlasting woods, he flew to the realm of the Snow Queen. After all, if there was anyone who would appreciate his devious plan, it would be the one who lost her own daughter to the likes of Captain Hook. It had been many years since the pirate had taken the Scarlet Fairy's life, but not a day had gone by within the frosted realm that laid beyond the legendary wardrobe, that the queen hadn't ached for her rightful justice to be delivered. As Pan flew past the lanterns that stood amongst the snow and trees that sparkled with diamond-like icicles hanging from the branches, he always took the time to admire the captivating splendor of the land. Elegant fairy doors of all sizes and colors could be found high and low as you made your way towards the towering crystals of the Frosted Citadel. The chilled air and ground were cold, but something about this place was different. You could touch the snow with your bare hands, and it was as if you were holding glittering ice. It was soft and fell like a powder. Pan enjoyed watching some of the smaller gnomes fall right through it in the early mornings. Deer, owls, and gentle foxes could be seen throughout the enchanted forest that surrounded the court; each appearing more mystical than the last.

But as beautiful as the realm undeniably was, no one could forget the day the snow went red with blood; the empty houses beyond the ghostly fairy doors that had been left behind were forever heart-wrenching to pass. As Pan made his way to the tall doorway into the icy palace, all of the Unseelie Court followed behind him, eager to hear what he had to say. The Snow Queen found this behavior to be especially aggravating, but Pan had become someone to fear; someone to follow. After he discovered that he could devour souls the way that she could, he had never given her another one for her or her realm. She was locked away, banished to live within her citadel until she was powerful enough to wage war upon the Elders; a hope that was crushed the instant that Hook unleashed his wrath upon all those who served her. She had hoped that with Pan at her side, she could finally gain the amount of souls that she needed. But Pan decided to serve himself, just as he had always done.

Once he had gone from being a young boy to the beautiful and charming Gancanagh, the Snow Queen knew she was losing control; not only of him, but of her court as well. They saw him as a king; a being more powerful than anything they had ever seen before. He could do what no other fairy could do... he could break through all of the barriers that mortals could use to protect themselves. He was the perfect predator. And so, it was with a heavy heart that the Snow Queen decided to use her hypnotizing beauty and witting charm to lure him into the match of marriage. He could be king of the Third Realm and obtain the most desired of all creatures, Snow White herself. But to her utter amazement and humiliation, Pan turned down her proposal. The fact was— he didn't love her. And more than that, he didn't want to be king of the Third Realm, he was better than that. After all, even the Grand Elder was afraid of him. Not publicly of course, but he always had a reason or rather an excuse to not go hunting Peter down. Pan didn't care though. He no longer feared anyone or anything; that is the sort of thing that happens when you have already lost everything one can lose. Still, though he felt he owed the Snow Queen nothing, he knew that she was the only other one who fully understood his hatred towards Hook. He had taken her daughter from her, and now it was he who would bring Hook's daughter to her vengeful grasp. As he approached the queen's crystal throne, the sleeping baby awoke within his arms. With a single cry, the Snow Queen's eyes widened in utter shock. "What- is- that?!" She exclaimed in disgust.

Pan smiled wickedly, eager to answer: "This— is Captain Hook's new-born daughter; the daughter I just stole from his own arms."

"Really?" A sparkling light could be seen in the queen's lavender eyes in that moment. It was both a terrifying and beautiful thing to witness. She approached the child with the sinister gaze of a predator eyeing its prey. "And the pirate? How did you kill him?" She asked in thrilling elation.

"I didn't." Pan stated plainly. His gaze told her to not press for answers, but she wasn't one to take orders; not even from him.

"What?! Why not?! You promised me that if I..."

"I never promised you anything! You told me how you devoured souls simply so that you could show off your power. I took care of Hook! And it was a fate of my own design; one far worse than any death. It was justice! One that he will never escape from!"

The Snow Queen looked at him sternly— *murderously*. "Have you lost your mind? How dare you!"

A devious chuckle erupted from his throat, "Now see there... *that* is the part about you that I love- *the real you!* None of these phony charms of seduction, but rather the cruel cold-hearted queen that I see before me. I have always been a creature that respects very little, but one thing that I have always respected was someone strong and real. Though he was a real thorn in my side from the instant we met, James Hook was one of *those* people. He was never fake about anything,

24

even if he could have profited from it somehow. You— are a ruthless, merciless, vicious being! That is *what* you are! I do not care that you are a *queen*. I do not think you above me! So, if you want *my* respect, then be real with me, Snow White."

The queen looked as if she were about to explode, unleashing every inch of power she had upon him. The surrounding court of Unseelies could do nothing but gaze in fearful awe at the two figures of profound power and dominance; each unknowing what was to happen next, and terrified to find out.

"I know that you feel as if I have robbed you of something but understand if you will that this just the opposite. Don't you see? I have brought you your own body of justice. Kill the daughter of the one who took the life of yours, and you will finally be sated."

The Snow Queen lowered her gaze, easing her way towards the quietly cooing child laying in his arms. It was then that she saw the baby's face for the first time. Her emerald eyes were brighter than fresh spring grass; her skin was pale and fair; her cheeks were full, and yet had defining bones that flattered her face perfectly, and her lips... like two blushing pink roses barely bloomed. The very sight of her left the queen breathless. The snow that fell freely from the sky stopped dead, frozen in the air as her expression of jealousy reverberated within her stinging gaze. This was it... the moment she was going to kill the baby. She raised her hand; her long fingers spreading above the child's tiny throat, but the moment she touched her skin, something happened. A mark appeared on the child's forehead. It was the mark of a raven. It was there for only an instant before it disappeared, but it made the blood-thirsty queen seethe with uncontrollable anger.

"What was that?" Pan asked intensely.

"No!" The Snow Queen shouted. She tried to touch the baby again, but the mark stopped her. The queen writhed, stomping, and screaming for a moment before suddenly pausing as if out of nowhere. Pan didn't know what was going on, but something about the wicked look upon her face made his stomach knot with thrilling anxiety.

"Snow White, what is it? What is happening?" He asked.

"I cannot kill this child," she answered in a harrowing tone.

Pan stared at her with utter confusion, "Why?"

"Because it was my bloodline that was responsible for hers."

"I do not understand."

"She belongs to the Wood Witch. She is a magical creature that lives within the mortal world. The baby belongs to her. Once she is delivered to the witch, the blood debt will be paid. So, I cannot kill her, that is certain, but I realize now that you may be right about something. Maybe death is not the rightful vengeance. I have a better idea— one that if done correctly; will not only give me justice for my daughter, but something to soothe my longing thirst for revenge completely."

Pan smiled, "I like the sound of that."

She turned to him with evil determination, "Good, because I am going to need *your* help."

* * *

When the Snow Queen first told Pan of her vindictive plan, he had to admit, he was not all that thrilled; for most of the work would need to be done by him. But when he resisted the charge, the cunning queen wrought upon him the very real consequences of what would happen should he refuse... *Without Hook in his life, without the thing that drove him onward— what else did he have to do?* He had gotten his revenge, and yet the fact still remained that he had nothing and no one. Still, Pan needed another reason to do all that the queen asked of him.

And to his surprise, she gave him an answer. If he should succeed, then the queen would then have enough power to bring everything and everyone that Pan loved back into his life. He could be a little boy again. Tinker Bell would be alive, and Tiger Lily would be there to play with him as she had always done on the island. Pan was not one to trust the queen, but her proposition was just too tempting to ignore.

"How do I find this *Wood Witch?*" He asked, ready to move forward.

"She is hidden and ever-moving, but alas, since it was my bloodline that was responsible for bringing the child to her, then it is my blood that will be your guide." The Snow Queen snapped her fingers, bringing a silver vial emerging between her fingers. She stared at it with an intense gaze as the vial suddenly began to slowly fill with blood. The sparkling crimson within caused the vial to grow instantly cold, covering itself with glittering

27

frost. Once it was full, she handed it to him. "When you get to the mortal world, drink this. Only then will you be able to find her."

"What will she look like? This... *witch*?"

The Snow Queen laughed, "She is a witch, my dear, she will appear however she wants to. She has powers that we do not possess. Though since she herself *is* a descendant of our kind, she too has the magic that is born to the fae. I have heard that she lives a hidden life deep within the forest, luring unsuspecting victims to her cabin. She is a dealer of souls, or whatever it is she desires at the present time. She has lived so long that what she seeks has changed many times over the ages."

"But if she..."

"Enough questions!" The queen interrupted. "This child is hungry, and I have nothing for mortals here. So, if she is to survive, as I so desperately need for her to do, then you must leave now. Take this vial and go to her. Do everything that I have said. But heed my warning of caution. Do *not* upset the witch at any cost. And most importantly, do *not* underestimate her."

Feeling annoyed, Pan nodded in agreement and took the crying child into his arms and the vial of cold blood from the queen before turning his way out of the Frosted Citadel.

The path back to the mortal world was normally an easy one, but he found that flying with a crying infant attached to him was not at *all* pleasing. He rushed to a hidden ground by a nearby forest below. With no hesitation, he quickly opened the vial and drank the frosted blood of the queen. Its cold chill fell slowly down his throat like burning ice. It was almost too painful to breathe for a moment, but no sooner had the blood made its way inside of him, did he suddenly feel different. Within a mere moment, he knew exactly where to find the witch's current location. Without another thought, he flew high into the sky and headed near the sacred woods of his old mortal home, Wales.

As they drew closer to the elusive cabin of the Wood Witch, Pan couldn't help noticing the eyes that stared up at them. The crows: they were gawking at the baby. Her mark was now fully exposed on her skin, as if calling to them. They flew in circles, never losing a single gaze of the baby; the child that their mistress so desperately wanted. When the mark suddenly disappeared, the ravens left, all heading back to the witch as if to tell her of their sighting. Now on the ground, Pan could see why so many would get lost here; for these were no ordinary woods. The sun, though still fairly high in the sky, was invisible from inside the dense and sprawling forest of impenetrable fog. There was no path, nor tracks to help with direction; it was the perfect bewildering place to get lost, and if he hadn't the power to fly, nor the blood of the Snow Queen coursing through his veins, he knew that he could never have found her on his own. Even with the blood he had consumed, the aching thought telling him that he was lost, brought a most dreaded feeling of hopelessness upon him; a feeling that grew more intensely the closer to the cabin he became. As the murder of crows circled above him in the darkness, he realized that this consuming feeling was her. It was the first time he had felt the magic of witchcraft. It was imposing and strange. Still, he pushed through every instinct he had and made his way up the hill where the Wood Witch's rural cabin dwelled. The ramshackle old house appeared empty, decrepit, and abandoned. Pan looked to see if the mark upon the baby's forehead had returned, but it hadn't. Then suddenly, the loud caw of a large crow caused Pan to look up through the fog again.

The house— the cabin... It's changed. It appeared newly painted and the flickering lights of lanterns could be seen throughout all the windows. To a wandering lost traveler, it appeared warm and inviting. Pan reluctantly made his way to her front porch. With his first step upon the doorstep, the glow from the distant sun instantly began to slide down the sky so that the mysterious moon could take its place. Suddenly, Pan felt uneasy, not because he was near the very witch that even the Snow Queen deemed worthy of fear, but the vision of the endless oceans of green pastures that could now be seen through the disappearing fog. It suddenly felt as if he would be swallowed by the dense pasture of dark trees if he dared try to run off with the baby. But as he gazed out to the forest, he noticed something else. There were no other creatures in the woods; none except for the *crows*. There was an eerie feeling about it all, but there was no turning back now. He reached for the doorknob, which squealed and juddered, locked with disuse. It was stuck, at least that is why he thought it wasn't working. After a couple moments that left him wondering how he was going to get in or if there was anyone even there, the door suddenly proceeded to open all on its own. Feeling a little bewildered, Pan stepped inside the lonely cabin. A gust of humid air then assaulted his face; carrying the strange smells of a place that had been locked shut for who knows how long.

Once inside, he was greeted with a cracking deep voice. "Who are you?" She asked grimly.

Pan was struck with surprise, "Well... I- how did the door open? I thought it was jammed?" He asked.

"Well it wasn't as if you were going to give me the courtesy of knocking first. And in any case, the door opens when I *want* it to."

It was then that the baby sneezed, no doubt from the stuffiness of the surroundings. The mere sound of the child was enough to make the old witch spring up with the kind of boisterous cheer that one would expect from a mother. Brimming with excitement, the witch took the baby from his arms and squeezed her tightly like a lost treasure she had finally found.

She went into her kitchen and after speaking a few words that Pan didn't understand, she came back out with a bottle full of milk. The heavenly meal instantly calmed the hungry baby, swooning her off to a deep sleep. Then with a menacing giggle, the inside of the cabin began to change again. Gaudy jewelry, golden trinkets, brass ornaments, greenery, and even a baby cradle covered in silver ivy appeared. It wasn't full of pink bedding or even an inch away from being eerily enchanting in its appearance, but somehow, this witch was trying to make her home fitting for the little baby. It

31

was just as the Snow Queen had hoped; the witch wasn't going to devour her soul; she made this deal because she wanted a child of her own; one like her— *half fae and half mortal.* The witch had the baby she wanted now, and the debt was paid, but there was more; a tiny stipulation wanted by the Snow Queen. "I am pleased you are happy with your long-awaited payment, but I fear that is not the entire reason I am here," Pan said reluctantly. It wasn't fear that made him so, but rather how strange she was. *How could the Snow Queen respect such a haggard old woman?* She looked to be on the very brink of death itself. *Why not just take the baby from her?* It was all so odd and unsettling; akin to that feeling you get when you are waiting for something to happen, and the longer it takes, the stranger it feels.

She glared up at him suspiciously, "What is it you desire from me?" She asked.

"I wish to be permitted to come see the child as often as I wish."

"Why?" She asked in an almost oppressive way.

"Oh... I have just grown *fond* of the little thing," he said, trying hard to persuade her, and knowing full well that she wasn't believing it for a second.

Instead of answering his most peculiar request, she had a query of her own— "How did this baby come to find its way into your *possession?*" Her words sounded like a question, but Pan couldn't help feeling as though he was under some interrogation.

"I just took it from him," he said, unable to resist the gleam of madness that stretched across his smiling face.

The old witch cackled like a bird, "From James Hook? ...Very doubtful. Then again, I don't see him giving up his child to me willingly. I must admit, I had thought the debt owed to me- dead long ago. I never thought this was going to happen. This is most strange. I do not understand... How did this happen?"

"Let's just say— I have a history with the *father*."

Again, the nail-scratching laughter erupted from her lips, cracking them like clay. "Oh, dearie, I know exactly what you mean. I dealt with *his* father long before I met the one who... *Wait!* It was you! You were the one he was after all those years ago!"

Pan smiled, lifting his hands up in an arrogant shrug.

A small crow-like screech could be heard from her throat before she said her next words, "Ehh, what that boy went through to find you... well, let's just say it will be a legendary tale that will be told for many ages to come. The real question is, however— will it be the *true story* they tell?"

Pan looked at her unamused by her insinuation. "It doesn't matter anymore what people believe happened, because in the end, I won. I snatched the baby from his arm's mere moments after the Blue Fairy gave birth to her. The look of horror on their faces will be as immortally victorious to me as I am to the story itself."

This time, the Wood Witch did not laugh. Her bright green eyes went gray and empty, and her face chipped and cracked like aged stone. She appeared shocked and out of breath. Pan waited for her to say something, but it was as if all her energy went to her desperate attempt to suppress the heaviest of all tears. Not for her, but for the Blue Fairy. Pan then couldn't escape the overwhelming feeling of guilt that assailed her. She rose from her chair with the presence of an entirely different creature; one far fiercer than the old brittle hag she had been only seconds before.

"How could you do such a thing? You! You, evil little monster!" She shouted, pointing a long-crooked staff at his chest.

Pan was stunned, not only because of her words, but because he suddenly couldn't move. It wasn't that her staff was especially large or heavy, but for whatever reason, he was completely unable to move so much as a finger. As he gazed back into her eyes, he found that they were green again; as bright and vibrant as ever. The ratty gray of her hair had turned silver and seemed to shine. Her expression was livid.

"What are you talking about?! Get this thing off of me!" Pan shouted, choking on every word.

"What kind of creature would be so vile as to take a baby away from its mother in such a horrible way!?"

"You have struck many deals in your time, hag! Were you under the impression that the babies had no mother?" Pan replied in a most unruly tone.

The witch slowly twisted the staff within her deadly grasp, causing a terrible sickness to arise inside him. He felt ill, but that wasn't all. He was also suddenly in terrible pain. His muscles tensed and ached as if they were on fire, his tongue burned, his eyes stung, and his insides felt as if they were rotting away like they would within a corpse. He hadn't felt sickness since he was a boy. And now it felt as if he were being tortured from it. Vomit bubbled up from his stomach; the smell of putrid death lifting to each gasping breath. The mere seconds felt like hours, and it only got worse as the moments continued.

"I have never just taken a baby away from someone. When a parent comes to me and strikes a deal, I have always made sure the *mother* never knew of her loss. I replaced them with other magical creatures-changelings or even crystal children. I have never, nor would I have ever allowed a child- a *baby* to be ripped away from a mother in plain sight. I make deals, *exchanges*! Mortals ask and they take! It is a deal! What's fair is fair, but James Hook was not the one who struck a bargain with me. It was the red one who failed to deliver what I was owed, and now there is this unfortunate matter of a blood oath. James gained nothing from this. No, in *this* tragedy, they were given nothing but loss; the worst fate for a mother," she sighed regretfully. "But there is nothing we can do about that now. She belongs to me," she said placing the baby in her new crib. Then suddenly, as if lightning had struck, she shot a murderous gaze towards him. "As you well know, once a deal is made, it cannot be undone, but *you...* this kind of cruelty cannot be forgiven! I should kill you for this!"

With a choking breath, and blood running out from the sides of his mouth, Pan spoke with a burst of red spray, "You can't kill me," he said weakly, never allowing his stern face to falter.

"Ha! Why? Because you think you are the next king of the fairies? Please! I see right through the phantasm you would have everyone believe. The magic you have, came from the cost of others! But me... oh, my dear, you have *no* idea what I am capable of. But you, in all your stolen glory, do not possess the shield brought on by love and sacrifice that the pirate carried. I could not touch him, nor harm him in any way, but you... I could kill you more simply than I could a spider on my walls. There is more than just fairy magic in the Nine Realms, and if you believe you are the most powerful of them all, then you are as foolish as you are disgustingly *wicked!*"

Pan flinched under her murderous scowl of grimace. Her words seemed to echo with a force so strong, that he could feel them crushing him. If he didn't do something fast, he was sure that he would die. So, with the kind of desperation that one can only obtain through the grips of death, he pierced through his closing throat with a last plea. "Please... What can I do?"

It was in that moment that the tiny baby began to cry. The Wood Witch pulled the staff from his chest to attend to her. Pan crumbled with full force to the floor, gasping in painful splintered breaths. With bloodshot eyes, he fearfully gazed towards her as she scooped up the child gracefully in her arms. How strange it was that this woman; this *witch* that had only moments ago been a towering presence of horror, now stood sweet and smiling at her precious gift. Pan dared not utter a single word to draw her attention back to him. Instead he crawled with weak limbs back towards the door. A buzzing of smothering fear thundered throughout his body as if coursing through the absence of blood that she had stripped away from his veins.

He reached for the doorknob, but as he twisted it with what little strength his body could muster, a clench of hopelessness suffused him. The door couldn't... or rather *wouldn't* open. The words the witch had spoken upon his arrival echoed throughout his miserable dread in that moment. *"The door opens when I want it to."*

Terror burned in his mind as he once again fell to the floor. The witch then began to hum what sounded like a lullaby. A strange feeling filled the gloomy room then. The melody soon reverberated as if it was no longer coming from her lips at all, but rather carrying on... all on its own. Pan could feel it reaching into him. With nothing left, the exhaustion from pain and fear was soon nothing more than a fog of suffocating defeat. The lullaby slowly grew louder, and as if his eyes were being covered with heavy black drapes, he felt himself give in to the shrouding darkness of the legendary cabin.

CHAPTER TWO
JACK FROST

To his utter amazement, Pan rose from the closing darkness of death; but the feeling was not one of victory or even relief, for the afflictions the witch had cursed upon him had left him weak and frail. His eyes, though heavy, opened with a slow burning fog. There was a warmth next to him, drawing his sight towards what appeared to be dancing flames within a massive fireplace. Afraid he was about to be burned, he gasped with a dry choking breath, backing his body away from the fire before him. He bumped into something. A chill of fear crawled up his tingling spine as he heard the baby suddenly begin to cry. He had bumped into the silver cradle. His eyes quickly searched for *her*— for surely the Wood Witch had heard the commotion and would come for him. It was such a strange and terrible feeling- being so helplessly afraid. How something so simple as upsetting her precious child could become so terrifying was enough to rattle the very core of his being. He quickly tried to retreat into a dark corner; an effort as useless as a child hiding under their sheets for fear of the thing under their bed.

"So, you are alive, after all," said a distant voice.

At first, he didn't know who it was. The voice sounded so different. It was young and almost enchanting. Believing for a moment that there was indeed someone else there brought him to a sense of urgent desperation. A figure then appeared before him, and in the haze that still clouded his sight, he found himself groveling before a stranger.

"Please... you must help me. Open the door! Hurry, before she comes back."

It was then that the distant figure drew closer; the vision of silver hair with a purplish hue and bright green eyes within an almost portrait perfect face came into focus.

It was *her*. The Wood Witch, now appearing as vivacious and beautiful as a young woman. But those eyes were unmistakable. It was definitely her. Pan's eyes widened in shock.

The witch laughed in a gleeful menacing cackle. "You must forgive my appearance. I haven't been this *fresh* in quite some time. I guess I have you to thank for that."

"What... What do you mean?"

"Well after you crumbled like the weak creature that you actually are, I had time to digress my anger and think. I wondered to myself, what could possess a boy to be so cruel; so utterly foolish and disrespectful? And then I realized that while such evil as you are born, I also believe that it is the *power* that has made you what you are. So, I decided to teach you a much-needed, long overdue lesson; that no matter how powerful you think you are, what you take can always be taken away from you. With that in mind, in the hours of your near-death slumber, I took from you a great vast of the poor souls that you have devoured in your years of greed and wickedness."

Her words stole his breath from his weak body as he reached to his chest and limbs the way one does when they're franticly afraid that something might be missing. But with a single glance upon one of her ancient mirrors, the true horror of what she had stolen from him came to light.

"Oh, yes," she said as if suddenly remembering. "I felt it only proper to take a little essence of your own soul as payment for your arrogance."

Pan stepped urgently towards the closest mirror. He ran his fingers through his now white hair. His skin no longer embodied the touch of the sun, but rather looked livid and pale. His once golden eyes now shimmered blue like two freshly frosted ponds. But it wasn't his outward appearance that made it hard to breathe; it was everything *within*.

"It is strange, is it not? How we can take for granted what was born from our own soul, though not many know the pain of having what makes you- *you* ripped away. The boy who brought the sun... who carried with him the youth and joyous beauty of spring and summer is now gone. That is not who you are anymore. You are cold, cruel, and bitter, and for us immortals, time has a way of changing who we are. What you see before you is— your true reflection. What fae magic you have left will now only rise by the light of the moon." Then Mim sighed as if a bit displeased. "I fear that you still illuminate beauty, though now it shines through winter's charm. But the Gancanagh you are no longer. I daresay not even Her Majesty, Snow White would love you now." Suddenly she erupted with shrill manic laughter that seemed too menacing for her now beautiful appearance. It was unsettling, like seeing someone possessed. Realizing she had trailed off in a fit of amusement, she coughed and adjusted her tone back to its youthful lie.

"I apologize. It is only that I remembered my favorite part of this little lesson."

Pan's eyes widened in great anxiety. *"Little?* You have taken *everything* from me!"

Mim giggled to herself, "Now, boyo, not *everything*... you still have your life, do you not? But you are right, I suppose I shouldn't say little. But that is the price you pay when you cross a bored old witch as powerful as I. This next bit, however, is not for your disrespect towards me, but rather the heinous deeds that brought you here. I found as I pulled the countless souls that you have taken so heartlessly that I couldn't help but wonder why you would take so many souls unto yourself; and what sort of evil might befall us all if you continue. So..."

"What? What did you do to me?"

"Well, I thought it would be easiest if I just killed you, but then I thought of something better. You are no longer going to lure lost children looking for magic; you are now bound by this."

It was then with by a mere flick of her wrist that an old staff of curved dark wood came floating towards her, falling slowly into her youthful hand. "You too. Come on," she ordered sternly. Pan turned to see a glimmering lantern emerge from the hidden corners of her shadowy shelves. The lantern floated over and right there before their eyes, the lantern absorbed itself into the staff, causing the ancient wood to glow like an amber flame. "There now. It is ready."

Pan's turned up expression spoke louder than any spoken word could have. Still, he did not understand. "What is *that?*" He asked with unbearable disgust.

This is my traveler's staff. It can help guide anyone that is lost- home. Doesn't matter how far or what obstacle blinds them, this staff will light their way back to where they belong. This shall be your penance."

Pan could see he had no choice. It was a feeling that suffused him with such hatred that the floor beneath his bare feet began to freeze. With a breath of sharp frost, he asked the only question he could. "How long?"

Mim gave him a side-ways glance, "How long what?"

"How long have you bound me to this thing? How long will I have to do this?"

"I do not think you understand," she replied plainly.

"No, I do. You think by turning me into some servant for lost travelers, that I will have learned some lesson you are trying to teach in hopes it will change me. Well it will not work! So just name the mark. *How-long- will- I- have- to- do- this?"*

Mim shook her head, *"Tisk- Tisk- Tisk.* You still think this is merely some temporary punishment, but I'm afraid you still do not understand. This isn't your charge in hopes that it changes you. I *have* changed you. This is who you are now. You are no longer Pan. You wish to know how long you have to do this— until you cannot remember ever doing anything else. There. Is that clear enough for you? Let go of who you were. Don't worry, it gets easier over time. You will have many more names, many more stories. It is what happens when you are an immortal. You cannot stop it. You cannot go back."

"Not me. I will never change. You can change my appearance and even alter my abilities, but you cannot change who I am."

Mim chuckled, "It was happening before you even came to my door, dearie. You were once known as Peter. We've heard the stories, one way or the other. Then you were Pan, the sun of Neverland. Then after the island, the years flew by, and you became the legendary Gancanagh, the breaker of hearts, the stealer of souls. You see? You cannot escape it. People think time doesn't apply to the immortal, but time is far too powerful and clever. Instead of dying and being born again as a new person like a mortal, what happens to us is far worse."

"Worse?"

"Yes, because ultimately it is *them* that decides who you are."

"Them? ...Who?"

"The lives around you, the stories, the mortals, all of it. Every name that has been mine was given by someone else. Meanwhile the tales of all who you were before— go on haunting you. Peter is dead. Pan is dead. And now, the *Gancanagh* is dead. Accept it. For it is done."

Now Pan was mad. Feeling an overwhelming sense of rage, a force of adrenaline surged through him, regenerating his weakened body back to strength. With a single glance from his frosty glare, his look of fury upon his face struck her.

"Be careful, lad. You have been foolish enough to cross me once, I would advise not aggravating me further. Think not on revenge nor store a flicker of hope within some clever plot against me or what is mine. For as I said before, you have no idea what I am capable of. I have fought with the likes of *Merlin*, the world's most powerful wizard. So, believe me when I tell you how utterly *insignificant,* I find you. Truth be told, you would not even be alive right now if you did not have the Snow Queen's blood coursing through your icy veins. Nevertheless, if the baby had not cried out when she did, my power would have destroyed you completely a mere moment after your body hit the floor."

Though Pan huffed in dread and fury, he knew that she was telling the truth.

"Reach out your hand," she ordered.

44

Most unwillingly, his body did as she told, and once the staff was in his grasp, a latching sensation came over him. It was as if the staff had become part of his body like that of a leg or arm. And instantly, the idea of being separated from it was painful. It was bizarre in every possible way.

"There is one more thing before you go."

He could not hide his frustration any further. All of this: her, everything she took, everything he was and what he has now become... it was beyond overwhelming. It was crippling.

Within mere moments, Mim had grown irritated by his lack of instant obedience. "I will make a deal with you," she said in a sinister tone that crawled up his silvery skin.

"Have I not given you enough?" He asked harshly through his raspy breaths of winter cold.

She smiled, "Oh, do not worry, dearie, this isn't for me."

A look of confusion assailed him in that moment, "Then who?"

"The Blue Fairy, *Ainsel.* I have something I want you to give to her."

"*No.*" Pan said trembling.

A long pause rippled between them before he realized that he hadn't actually said the word out loud. He tried again, but it just didn't come. The truth was, he was petrified. When his voice could finally find its way through the spiraling rage and hate, the words that spilled out from his mouth with dripping disdain was—

"Is this the only way I am going to get through that door?"

With a wicked twinkle in her eye, she smiled, "Yes."

Pan closed his eyes in defeat. He lowered his head as three little words came out quietly from his blue lips... *"As- you- wish."*

The Wood Witch nodded, walking towards her wall of the extraordinary treasures she had gained over the course of her legendary life. As she sorted through the shelves of intricate pieces, it was as if Pan could see the vast sea of payments she had been given from the deals of her past. But it wasn't just material riches of the mortal world he could see, but also tokens of magic as well. There were so many, in fact, that a blanket of dust had coated most of them.

Finally, with the help of one of her dearest crows, she found the one piece that she had been searching for. Pan's eyes squinted, trying to see which one of her enchanted treasures she had decided upon. The witch used a nearby cloth to wipe off the soot of time.

It was some sort of magical terrarium. It appeared empty— at least it was before the witch's green eyes began to *glow.*

"Hidden I am
Deep in the woods
But now I do
What no witch should
Show the Blue Fairy
Where I dwell

Allow her to see
With this magical spell
Here within the glass
Let the dark forest appear
And when she is broken
Only then let her peer
As my rueful token
For all that she has lost
Let her not be alone
To pay the ultimate cost."

It was then through the thick amber-tinted glass that a lavishly detailed illusion of the dark forest appeared within the terrarium. The witch came towards him, reaching the enchanted trinket out for him to hold.

"Once you touch the terrarium, our deal will be bound by the strongest of magic. You will take this to the Blue Fairy and tell her what vision dwells within the glass. If you fail to deliver it, a slow curse of a most torturous death will be wrought upon you. And remember this... With a mere touch of my power, I almost killed you. Take this chance, for it will be my only grace of mercy!"

Pan let out a sigh of hateful frustration. He had never wanted to kill someone so badly in his entire life. It was pure bitter hatred. Swallowing such a feeling was probably the hardest thing he had ever had to do.

As he took the terrarium into his hands. Upon the touch of the scrolled ebony base, his body became instantly restored. The pain and weakness were gone. At least, it seemed that way.

The Wood Witch then made her way over to the rocking cradle that swayed magically back and forth like a ship on the water. She picked the happily cooing baby up, gazing into her beautiful emerald eyes, and with a mere tilt of her head, the door to the cabin was finally open.

Pan's heart raced as he made his way towards the exit, but before he stepped out onto the porch, the witch had one more warning for him. "The terrarium is meant for the blue one's eyes only... if *anything* should happen to her, the terrarium will appear back in my cabin, and you don't want to find out what I will do to you then, dearie."

"I understand," he said seething through his teeth.

"Good, then let this be the last time we meet, Mr... *Hmm?* We mustn't forget to give you a name."

"I respectfully refuse." He hissed.

"Now, now. I am the one who brought this new you to light. As your creator, I find it only proper that I name you. Besides, even if you deny me the pleasure, stories seem to spread best when they come from me. One way or another, in this land and the next, you will be known as— Jack."

"*Jack?* Why Jack? I've been named after the god Pan, and until you stripped me of everything I am, my name was legend. Jack. It is a name undeserving for my person."

Mim shook her head, suppressing a giggle. "Once again, the point escapes you. You have always thought yourself special, better than anyone or anything. With each escalation of title, your soul only became rottener. I can see that it is too important to you. *That* is why I chose such a name. It is a name for those with no name. It is plain, humble, mortal, and most importantly, it is completely and utterly *insignificant.* And yet, I think you will find that it is not the name that matters. They will know who you are, and who made you!"

With a brisk breath of murderous desire, he turned his back and made his way towards her door, wishing harder with every step for her immediate death.

"Do not come back! I do not know why you wanted to *visit* my child, but the answer to your request is *never!* She is *mine* now— my beautiful *Maleficent.*"

...The door closed.

* * *

Pan didn't tell the Snow Queen of his witchy encounter, at least not right away. He needed time to think of a plan. It didn't take him long to find the Blue Fairy. To his surprise, she was still on the ship. He watched her through the corner windows of the captain's former quarters.

There she sat, alone and utterly broken. Her face appeared to be the saddest he had ever seen. With a dull-witted expression, her fixed wooden-like face stared at the nothingness before her. One would almost think her dead, if not for the constant streams of sparkling tears that fell down her pale cheeks. All joy had been ripped from her spirit. Everything she was and cared for had been stolen away.

Her broken heart brought a crooked smile to Pan's shadowy face. It was just the vision he needed to see after his terrible nightmare within the cabin. How he wished that he didn't have to do what came next—the *deal* that had been magically bound to him. He was about to tap on the locked window, when the old ponderous doctor came into the dreary room.

He was carrying with him a tray of food and water, with an expression of desperation and hope upon his face. He wanted to comfort her. He reminded her of all the times that Hook had returned; that he was a creature of survival. He assured her that Hook would find their precious baby and come back from the frightening forest beyond the mirror. Still, the Blue Fairy didn't so much as blink an eye. For her, this time was entirely different than all of the last... and nothing, not even her dear friend Mr. Smee, could console her broken heart.

As the doctor left the room, leaving the tray and hope behind him, a tiny sniffle could be heard in the distance, and a single hidden tear could be seen under the round frames of his glasses. Upon the closing of the door, Pan was struck with an idea; one that if done right could turn this moment that supposed to be of the Wood Witch's design of remorse, could be twisted for his own advantage.

He tapped on the window, sending a glowing stream of music to her ears. In an instant, she turned in alarm. Their eyes met, and as if she thought him a dream, her eyes fell back to the floor.

He knocked again, this time louder and more aggressive. Shaken out of her deep haze of depression, she stood and made her way towards the window.

When she opened the latch, and saw his eyes, it was as if reality had crashed upon her. He may have looked different, but it was if the witch had painted his image from what he was within. She didn't know why he looked the way he did, and she didn't care. She cried out with an intensity of rage and sorrow with the likes he had never seen before.

"Where are they?!" She screamed flailing at him with her arms and hands. "Where is my daughter! Did you hurt her?! Tell me where James is, you monster! Tell me!"

"I have come to you in kindness, Ainsel. Compose yourself, or I might just take my gift with me."

She froze under his icy glare, unsure of what he meant. The mounting desperation that was painted across her face was so pleasing to him, that he paused with a smile; happy to make her wait for answers. It felt good having control again.

"...That's better," he said in his usual arrogant belittling tone.

She closed her watery eyes; a sad whimper expelling from her lips as she asked the question that ached her heart, "Are they dead?"

Savoring her torturous moment, Pan decided to pace the room, eyeing every cloth, painting, and chosen piece that had once belong to his unfortunate foe. "I'm sorry it came to this, Ainsel. It was not my intention to bring you into our affairs. But alas, it is the cruel fate at hand. Still, as a token to ease my contrite sorrow for you— I brought you this."

He reached into his cloak and pulled out the ancient terrarium. "What you have lost dwells within the domed glass. You may gaze into it whenever you are sad. Unlike my own, *your* loved ones are still alive, and you may gaze into the glass whenever you wish to feel close to them, but remember this... if you dare try to interfere again, I *will* know— and I *will* kill them. Do you understand me?" He asked in a stern cold voice.

Ainsel slowly took the enchanted piece from his hand and gazed into the terrarium. The glowing amber tinted glass was so thick that at first it was difficult to see anything within the distortion.

Inside was a tiny elaborate forest of the blackest trees surrounded by a moving fog. The fascinating details were lavish and yet were so that she couldn't get a clear picture of all that was inside at once.

She turned the base in her hands, staring transfixed at the very talisman of her loss. She stared mesmerized at the swaying leaves upon the tiny trees, but just as she saw the flapping wings of a crow, she suddenly heard the sound of the wind. But as a cold breeze touched her cheek, the sight of the open window stole her gaze.

Pan was gone, leaving the room ever empty once again. With heavy sorrow she closed the window, locking the latch before returning to her only solace left in the world...

Peering into the tiny forest beneath the glass where her lost loves were hidden.

CHAPTER THREE

HALF-LING

The next decade of Maleficent's life went on like a breeze and were the happiest that the Wood Witch had been in ages. She finally had the child she had been longing for. She was perfect to her in every way; enchantingly beautiful and clever. When the Blue Fairy didn't come around to see her lost child, the Wood Witch decided to never reveal the dark truth of her true parents to Maleficent.

Instead, she herself became the girl's mother. The likeness between them made the lie all the more believable. That wasn't to say that there weren't the rare occasions of difficulty. For Maleficent was a wild girl, in love with nature and had a spritely soul. From an early age, the witch could feel the infant's power. It was strong... very strong. Though many would find this to be a good thing, for a mother raising a boisterous child, capable of running off or throwing a tantrum, such profound power proved to be a challenge. Being a magical creature of astounding knowledge, the witch wasted no time in teaching her darling new pupil. Spells came easy for her, but like most children, she knew that there was something else inside her; something bubbling deep within her core. Though she was close with her mother, and enjoyed her ever-growing power of magic, the child often found herself lonely. So, it was on her tenth birthday, that she was given her most precious gift... a familiar of her very own— *a raven*. She named him Grip, but her mother always referred to him as Diablo- as he seemed to reflect Maleficent's unruly behavior. They were perfectly symmetrical in every way; a special bond that few are likely to ever find in a lifetime. And though Maleficent was able to conjure even the most challenging of spells on her own, she refused to do anything without her darling companion at her side.

With the cabin moving to the various woods within the world, Maleficent's greatest joys were when her mother would permit her and the willful raven to wander the mysterious forest. One night however, everything changed. The cabin had moved to an eerie dense forest. Maleficent, though still very young, could see from one of the windows that the moon was full and seemed bigger than usual. But that wasn't all, the moon... was changing colors. It would go from blue, then green, then pink, and red, and then it would go blue again. It was beautiful and brought a strange allure to the forest below it.

"Mother... Mother! Look at the moon!" She cried out to the witch sitting in her rocking chair. She stood and made her way towards the window. The moon above though enticing to Maleficent, seemed to stir a very different feeling to her mother. "I want to go outside. May I go? Please," she pleaded.

The witch gazed at her sadly, as if she were about to have to disappoint her, "No, my little witch. Not tonight."

Not understanding, Maleficent pleaded harder. "But—its— calling me. I feel it. Please."

"Not now, for I fear the Elle are out dancing tonight."

"Are they magical creatures like us?" Maleficent asked, feeling more excited by the moment.

"No, sweet thing, they are not like us. You must stay inside with me tonight.

"No! Please...We can go together, Mother!"

But the witch sternly shook her head, "No, Maleficent! I cannot. I must *always* stay in the cabin."

"But why!" Maleficent cried, now on the verge of a full-blown tantrum. "Why must we always hide? I never get to play with anyone!"

It was then that an objecting caw could be heard within the room.

"Except you, Grip!" Maleficent corrected herself.

Now feeling a swelling anger brewing inside her, the witch pointed her scolding finger, shaking it slowly in warning, "Enough! You will stay inside with me tonight, and that is the end of it. Now come, I will put you to bed and read to you from your favorite book."

Maleficent's green eyes glowed fiercely in that moment, tears welling up inside of them. Everything within her wanted to scream and fight, but she knew that once her mother raised her finger towards her, the fight was over. With her arms crossed and feet stomping, Maleficent and her raven made their way to her bedroom. Normally, this was a lovely end to her day. The raven flew to its large elaborate perch that sat on a small table next to her. The bed that had once been a small cradle, had grown with her. The silver ivy wrapped around its enchanted frame, and long blue curtains hung from its four pillars: each swaying as if under water. The effect had been one of Maleficent's own design in the passing years. Something about them always had a way of lulling her off to sleep, especially if the sounds of a storm could be heard rumbling through the forest. She had asked her mother many times if she could open her window but for some reason unknown to her, her mother had never allowed it.

As her mother read one of her ancient tales out loud to her, a moment that she usually treasured, she couldn't seem to take her mind off of the woods, and what mysterious creatures dwelled within them on this night. Once Maleficent closed her bright eyes, and her mother thought her asleep, the witch closed the book and left her room. Maleficent tried to sleep, but the overwhelming sensation of yearning curiosity began to ache inside her. As if it could hear her, the luminescence of the moon suddenly shined down into her bedroom, *calling to her.* The brilliance of its light caused her eyes to open. She slipped quietly out of her bed and slowly tip-toed towards the inviting window. Out in the darkness, she could suddenly see tiny twinkling lights. They were all different sizes and colors; each glowing and moving towards the center of the forest. They were so beautiful and strange. She could not help herself. She had to know what these magical creatures were and if they were anything like her.

Getting the attention of her curious raven, she turned to creep towards her cracked open door. She could hear and even see the silhouette of her mother's rocking chair, moving slowly back and forth, creaking by the fire. There was no way that she would be able to go out the window without her mother knowing. She had never disobeyed her like this before. She didn't know what it was, but something inside her needed to go into the woods. So, with the kind of nerve-racking reluctance a child has the first time they're going to try to get away with something big, she fearfully hesitated. But the overwhelming desire for answers had become stronger than that. She had to do this, that was certain, but for Maleficent, such a venture was not that simple. If she was going to go out the window, then her mother would have to be asleep... *deeply asleep*. And that would mean doing something that surprised even her; she was going to have to put a spell on her. Suddenly, as if he could hear her thoughts, the beautiful raven flew quietly into her dainty hands. And with a few strokes upon his feathers, a spoken whisper spilled from her trembling lips...

"Close your eyes
Soar into your dreams
And no matter what you hear
It's not what it seems."

A light green smoke then came from the ravens widening mouth, flowing ever slowly towards her mother. Then suddenly, the rocking chair went still. An overwhelming sensation of both thrill and guilt suffused her in that moment. A part of her instantly regretted it and wanted nothing more than for her mother to wake up so she could apologize, but as she stared at the chair, she realized that she wasn't going to wake up, at least, not right now. Then that feeling crawled up her skin once more; the feeling that was calling her out to the forest under the changing moon. And this time, she was going to answer. She opened the window and with one big breath of bravery, she jumped out into the forbidden night with nothing but the shadow of her darling pet behind her.

Making her way into the shady grove of trees, Maleficent could hear the whimsical sound of music. There was something so mystical about it, and yet as she tried to make her way through the bushes, brambles, and trees, it felt as if she were cutting through virgin forest. There were no tracks, nor was there even a trail on the ground. But it wasn't just the difficulty of shoving through the brush, it was the surreal illusion that the woods were growing darker the closer she came towards the twinkling lights. A strange and almost ominous feeling came through the chill of the air as she sensed that she was being watched. The imposing presence from the shadows was enough to make her pause fearfully.

"Who's there?" She asked, swallowing a lump of anxiety down her throat.

A movement shivered through the knotted trees, but still— no one answered.

Though she was a little frightened, she spoke out bravely, "Come out here. Show yourself! I can make you if I have to!" She said sternly.

After a chuckle that unnerved her, she could suddenly make out the vision of two eyes emerging from the darkness before her. Then suddenly, a young man stepped out into the moonlight that came through the cracks between the trees. He was terrifyingly beautiful. He had tousled silvery white hair, pale sapphire eyes that appeared to be speckled with ice, and a crooked smile that made her blush. The mere image of him was enough to leave anyone in awe. It wasn't just that his skin was grey like that of a corpse with no blood or life, it was that the feeling he illuminated carried the complete opposite.

At first, she didn't know what to say to him. For in some strange way, he felt familiar to her somehow. But that was impossible, of course. She hadn't met anyone else before tonight, and yet...

Suddenly her thought process was interrupted as he opened his mouth to speak, "Well, are you coming?"

"Where?" She asked taken by surprise.

"To the party," he replied with a voice most charming. "Come with me, I will take you there," he said, reaching out his cool hand for her.

As if swept away by his glamor, she took his hand without another thought in her head, and to her utter amazement, he carried her up into the starry sky and then lowered them back to the ground where an invisible doorway stood between two trees.

He turned to her and whispered, "Go on, Maleficent."

"How do you know my name?" She asked, but as she turned around, she found that he had disappeared from where he stood. But as her sweet pet perched himself upon her shoulder, she made her way into the twinkling party. There were three massive pavilions covered in the most vibrant of colored leaves and glittering moss. Umbrellas floated over the elaborate tables covered with lace tablecloths. Lanterns hung from the long-decorated limbs of the trees.

But what snatched her full attention was the dancing creatures that floated below. She gawked at their unbelievable radiance. Each moved in such graceful elegance, that it was almost eerie. Their costumes were designed with perfectly tailored fabrics that were sewn as if to frame each individual character; each so confident and utterly bizarre. But as extraordinary as their attire was, it was their wings that captured Maleficent's awe. For while the dancing creatures themselves couldn't really be described as beautiful, their wings were stunning and absolutely glorious for any eyes to behold. The striking colors of their hair and eyes appeared bold and almost unnerving upon their pale livid skin and boney sharp faces.

But just as she was about to leave, she saw the young man again. He was wearing different clothing, but it was definitely him. He smiled in a way that called her towards him. He stood by the tables that were covered with all sorts of exquisite foods she had never seen before in her entire life. He held up a fancy bowl that looked as if it had been hand painted by magic itself, and within it were bright round cherries. From the second she took her first bite; she no longer felt any fear. She felt happy. But just as he handed her a dainty cup filled with cold fresh cream to drink... the whimsical music that radiated with history and profound meaning grew silent. The dancing figures slowly turned to face the small intruder that stood meekly below them. Their grave stares seemed to burn upon her as one of the more extravagantly dressed creatures floated towards her with ominous oppression. She had long dark hair and a gaze that seemed both curious and unpleasantly surprised. "Who are you?" She asked, circling Maleficent like a leering vulture.

"I—I am- Maleficent," she stuttered, looking around for the charming man, but... he was gone again.

It was then that three glowing figures came from behind the winged woman's elaborate dress. Maleficent watched as they floated towards her. They were much smaller than the others and appeared to be as young as she was. One shined with the glow of red, the second green, and the third was baby blue. Each wore a pretty gown and hat to reflect the neon light that radiated from within them. Their pale features compressed into expressions of utter disgust and shocking disdain.

"Get out of here!" Demanded the blue one.

"Yes! You are not welcome here!" Screamed the little red creature.

Maleficent waited for the green one to spout off at her as well, but instead she pulled on the woman's dress the way a child does to a mother. "How did she get in here? Make her go," she whispered timidly.

"Yes, Mother! Make her go away! This is our celebration!" Screamed the red one again.

But the woman simply patted them, consoling their outburst, "Now, girls— don't get yourselves all worked up in a such a dreadful fret. After all, the filth of mortal blood does often find its way into our domains. But this one... Well, she is not just *any* typical human. Are you, little one?"

Maleficent shrunk under the revolted gaze that circled her. "I am no human... I'm a witch," she said bravely.

Her words brought about a wave of chilling laughter to the party; each creature bending and contorting with villainous glee. It was a moment that they would regret, for it was so that a spark within Maleficent was born that night.

"Poor baby halfling... how deliciously tragic this all is," the woman said.

"What is?" Maleficent asked.

"Why, to not know what and who you really are?" The woman replied in a mocking tone.

"I *am* a witch! I am a magical being just like you!" She shouted feeling smaller and uglier by the minute.

The winged woman scoffed and giggled most wickedly before turning her gaze down to her darling three. "Flora, Fauna, Merryweather..."

They each looked up, answering her in unison, "Yes, Mother?"

"*Tonight,* you have each been given your wands. Draw them— and show this little *witch* what true magic can do."

* * *

As the old legend goes... The first fairy was born when the sound of a laughing baby burst into a thousand pieces, but to the fae folk— such nonsense is beyond even Wonderland's proportions. The truth was that in the midst of all the magical creatures that wander the Ten Realms, be they the trolls that roam the rocky cliffs, the elves, goblins, and gnomes that like to work in the woods or scatter mischief about, the buttery sprites that like to dwell in abandoned sacred structures, and the likes of pixies that are born from the buds of blossoming roses in the winter frost. Not even the Elders could remember how the first fairy came into being, but it was on this very night that would be remembered forever as the night the *dark fairy* was born.

The three young fairies known as Fauna, Flora, and Merryweather wasted no time in obeying their mother's wish. For it happened that before Maleficent could even utter a single word, the glowing flashes of red, blue, and green were striking towards her; each painful blow blasted her with crippling agony.

Maleficent crumpled and screamed; at first out of fear, but when she heard the sound of her darling raven's caws of pain, her terror turned into rage.

Through her gasps of agony, she screamed out to him: "Fly home, Grip! Fly home!"

The raven did as she said, but Maleficent couldn't hear the sound of his flapping wings over the creature's laughter. It was then in the swarm of all the glowing blast that something truly magical happened. Whether it was because of the pain, the fear that she herself may die, or simply under the duress from their cruelty... somehow the seed of rage burst from inside her. "Enough!" She roared.

The striking cloud of all their power then faded away as the crowd of woodland fairies gasped in utter shock at the small child rising from the ground. Her long dark hair curled, flowing wildly behind her as two black horns emerged slowly from her skull. The green of her eyes glowed fiercely, radiating a profound power that frightened all of those that stood silent before her... all, that is, *except* for one. Beyond the darkness, hidden in the dense forbidden corner of the forest, the dark silhouette of her raven entered the open window of the witch's cabin. Flapping urgently, the magical familiar cawed and squawked until the charm upon the witch was lifted. She awoke from her chair, frantically racing to Maleficent's bedroom searching for her. Grip cawed loudly out to her. She turned quickly to see him perched on the window ceil— *the open window.* Her emerald eyes went wide with a mother's panic. "Maleficent! Maleficent! Where are you?!" She screamed out the window. A shrill terror struck her heart when no answer or sight of her beloved daughter came. When she gazed down to the twinkling lights in the distance, the absence of music felt like a silent clutch around her throat, robbing her of a single breath.

The raven squawked again, bringing her back to her crashing reality. She looked over to him, tears welling in her eyes for the first time in many years.

"What has happened... what have they done to her?" She asked, whishing a flow of purple magic towards him. In an instant, she could see what he saw— *and the last thing he saw*; the entire crowd of woodland fairies laughing as blasting magic struck upon Maleficent as she lay crumbled on the ground crying. The tears fell down the witch's beautiful pale face, cracking it for the first time since she had taken the souls from Pan. She reached her hands over her mouth in horror. She turned to sit upon Maleficent's ivy bed, her gaze still taken by the forest. The raven cawed at her, pulling on her heavy purple cloak.

"I cannot leave the cabin. That was the rules. I cannot leave the cabin. I cannot leave the cabin..." She repeated as if talking around in circles to herself.

It was in that moment that Grip flew out the window, back to Maleficent in fear that the witch would not be coming to help her. The Wood Witch watched as he glided through the trees. "If I leave, I will no longer be protected. But if I *don't* then she will... No!" She declared, arising from the bed, and reaching her arm out for the staff that came rushing into the palm of her hand. A burst of smoking green magic did then erupt, surrounding its mistress as she cast the very spell, she had sworn to never do...

Come, my dark darlings
Let us fly into the night
For if I am to leave this cabin
Let be without sight
Cover me with feathers
As black as midnight shadows
Make me as gloomy
As a fate hung in the gallows
If they think they are more gruesome
and grim than the likes of me...
Then let us give those fairies
A taste of black sorcery."

After a cackle most daring, the witch closed her eyes and bent back her head, letting the swarming cloud of magic engulf her completely. And within a mere moment of the smoky transformation, it all faded away, leaving only a great crow with green swirling eyes in its wake. With the squawking call from her beak, and the flapping of her feathered wings, the black crows came to their mistress, surrounding her as she flew out the open window... into the night to save her daughter.

Meanwhile, the youngest of the ravens had already reached the child. But when he found the center of the forest, it was not the twinkling lights and manic laughter that greeted his sight, but rather a surrounding of shock. The three fairies floated behind the winged woman: each spouting off in both fear and panic.

"What's happening, Mother?!" Fauna asked, pulling on the train of her mother's dress; her green wings fluttering with anxiety.

"Those horns! She looks absolutely hideous!" Screamed her blue tempered sister, Merryweather.

Though Flora was normally united with her sister's in both thought and action, she seemed more focused on her wand than Maleficent's new sudden appearance. Lightly tapping at first, and then harder as if with a tantrum, Flora hit her wand against her hand. "Mother! Something must be wrong with my wand! This ugly creature's magic should be no match for mine! I am a fairy!"

"And so is she," said a distant voice. The crowd of woodland fairies then parted, allowing Maleficent to see that it was the charming man that had brought her to the party. He stood upon a bit of frosted ground, smiling his crooked smile. "And I'd say that her powers are as impressive as are her achingly beautiful new features."

The charm of his words brought a tiny sparkle to Maleficent's eye, but also ignited fury within all the surrounding woodland creatures; each hissing with a hatred so profound that Maleficent knew she would never forget it.

"Impressive, you say? We'll see about that!" Declared the winged woman, raising her own wand with a murderous gaze. The other fairies followed suit; only this time, it wasn't for the sake of cruel entertainment... it was personal now.

Grip flew down to Maleficent just as the forest burst with the most extraordinary of fae magic. Every vibrant color known by nature clouded the very air between the trees. Their power knocked Maleficent back again, tearing and searing its way into her insides. Slices that came like that of a thousand of the sharpest blades cut and ripped her all over. The pain was intense, but it was upon seeing her pet's singed wings that Maleficent pulled him down from the darkness above and covered him and her face under her tattered cloak. But that's the trouble with magic; its damage can cause wounds that go far beyond the skin. Seconds then felt like hours. The blasts kept coming, and she could feel herself getting weaker by the second. Suddenly, the sound of squawking crows echoed like thunder in her ears. She raised her cloak to see the shadows of massive crows beginning to close in, fluttering into the tall form of— "Mother?" Maleficent uttered under her weak breath. It was then with one strong slam of the Wood Witch's staff that all the magic came rushing to the crystal orb upon its top. With the air now clear, all that was left were the fearful gazes and dropped jaws of the fairies. Whispers of various names could be heard like tiny echoes in an empty cave.

"Yes! It is I... By whichever name you know, though such trifles do not matter now. For like so many before you, I fear you will find yourself unable to tell this most horrific tale. She turned around, eyeing everyone that quaked in fear before her. "Ah, Tatianna, queen of the woodland fairies, where is *my* daughter?"

The winged woman spoke through panting breaths, "*Your* daughter?" She asked, closing her eyes, and covering her face as she realized the true disaster at hand. "Maleficent...?"

"Yes!" The Wood Witch declared! "Where is she?"

"I'm here, Mother," said the child laying on the ground.

With one glance upon her daughter's frail burned body, the Wood Witch rushed to her, touching her gently. But as her eyes traveled, observing every wound within and the scars upon her body, the witch began to huff slow and hard. It was then that Maleficent saw something in her mother that she had never seen before... an ancient fury rising like a fire in her eyes. She was in every way terrifying as she stood to face the ones responsible.

"Who dared harm she who is *mine*? Come forth and face me— Now!"

But no one moved.

Their cowardice brought the Wood Witch to laughter, "Oh, I was hoping it would come to this..." She tapped her staff again, this time bringing every guilty fairy forward. "Ah ha, so the truth emerges... you *all* raised your wands against one little girl! Well then, I would normally scold you for deplorably attacking one girl with numbers such as this, but I fear what I am about to do to all of you would also be seen as an unfair fight!" She said with an ominous cackle; the same that Pan had heard inside the dreary cabin. With the crowd having been forced to surround her, Pan took his only chance to disappear unseen.

"Please— have mercy, great one. For we did not know that this one belonged to you." The winged woman fretted.

But the witch simply shook her head, "It- should- not- have- mattered! This..." She said raising her hand bringing Maleficent flying into her arms. Mim looked down, examining her wounds. "These marks will never fade. She is fae touched now! And the damage you were willing to inflict upon an innocent makes your accidental target immaterial. For even a wretched creature such as yourselves know that if you use your magic, you must always prepare for the consequences they may bring."

The winged woman lowered her head, "Yes, I know. But before you do what you must, I ask you for something, though I know I do not deserve it."

The witch cackled again at such a notion. "What is it you dare ask of me now, after attempting to destroy the only life I treasure?"

The winged woman sighed a disheartened breath, "You are right, she was innocent, and I am a monster that attacked her for the sake of sheer vanity. But my own daughters only used their magic when I ordered them to. So please, I ask you in all your magnificence to show my daughters the example I so poorly failed to do. Punish us as you see fit but let them go." It was then that Tatianna called for her darling three once more, "Flora, Fauna, Merryweather..."

The three sisters came trembling out from behind her; each crying in dreadful sobs. The Wood Witch scowled at their ugly brat-like faces, and the darkness that was already spreading in their eyes. "Tell me, little ones, do you think yourselves better or more beautiful than my daughter?"

The three colorful fairies squirmed under her striking glare; each too fearful to answer.

"Ah, you're speechless, are you? Well then, allow me to answer. No! You are not! Even with the scars you have inflicted upon her, she will grow more beautiful by the day. And as far as powers go, my dears, know now that your magic can never hope to measure that of hers again. Now, I am inclined to let you live..."

The three fairies sighed breaths of relief before she spoke again.

"But just one more thing before I do... Maleficent?"

"Yes, Mother?" She replied weakly.

"What role did these unfortunate fairies play in the heinous acts against you tonight?" Her mother asked, knowing the question brought a feverish panic to the red, green, and blue.

Maleficent gazed at them, seeing a different side to their faces; now so scared and nervous. It was a nice feeling that she would treasure forever; the justice of it all. She made them wait before delivering her answer. "They were the first to attack me, but it was as the winged woman said, she *did* order them to do it. Even still, they were especially cruel to me. I could hear them laughing as they took turns hurting me," she whispered tearfully.

The witch nodded, "Ah, I see. Well then, my dears, I fear you *do* have a punishment coming. Though I am not one to harm children, wicked as some might be. Still, you have harmed my child, and should I not have interfered, you would not have hesitated in killing her. And for that, *you- will- suffer.*"

The three fairies burst into sobs, clutching each other as if it would be their last moment.

"The witch snapped, making them stop and look to her with a sharpened focus. "I will let you live, but your punishment will nevertheless be just! When you leave here, you will never again use you magic for evil. Never will you speak a cruel word, nor act unkindly. You will do only good deeds to make up for the most terrible ones you have scarred upon my daughter. Do you understand?" She asked sternly.

The three nodded eagerly, "Oh, thank you, great one. Thank..."

"But- remember, if you should ever betray your vow, you will *all* turn to dust!"

With a lump of terror swallowed down their throats, they nodded again and after a sad glance towards their mother, they turned to fly away.

"Wait, dears! For I fear that is *not* the end of your punishment."

The three turned around with dreaded surprise written upon their faces, "What else must we do?" Asked Flora.

"You will stay here and *watch* what happens when bad fairies cross the wrong witch!"

The balance of nature between good and evil can be measured in almost all things, whether it be luck, fate, karma, or other powerful forces- *most* are beyond any one creature's control. But then... there are *some* that can bend those forces as they please; the magical and god-like creatures of the Otherworlds. The trouble with such events is that they are not always fair. While some terrible string of bad luck may fall upon you *quickly*, it could take a *long* time before things go well again... And though for the most part- they do, time has proved in both life and death that this is *not* the case with curses. Such legendary forces have been around since the beginning, but what makes these afflictions so special is their devastating depth. The craft of a curse, if done correctly, should be in all manner a dark art. Whether it be verbal, written, pieces collected upon an altar, or bubbling potions thrown into a cauldron... Its power can be utterly catastrophic with intent and devious design. You could see the signs immediately, or it could be years before you see its effects, but no matter how it begins, there is only one force of light that is powerful enough to lift such darkness— *true love.* And though the legends of the rare few who have survived such a terrible fate have been told throughout the ages, too often does time forget the countless others whose end was not a happy one.

It was on this dreadful night, under the stars and ever-changing moon, that one such powerful curse was cast upon the woodland party of the Forbidden Forest.

Maleficent and the three sobbing fairies watched in horrific awe as the Wood Witch crashed her staff to the ground, releasing a burst of bright green flames to swarm the beautiful winged creatures. It was the pain that flooded over their bodies first, tearing its way into their insides.

At first, Maleficent and the three little fairies believed this torture to be the sole purpose of the spell, but as the cruel scorching flames crawled their way slowly back to the witch's staff, the image of the nightmare it left behind presented the true craft of her masterpiece. The moon above went bloodshot then; its intensity painted upon the everlasting suffering below. The once whimsical bell-like music now sounded slow and sad as a glowing chain formed in the air. Then— one by one, the former enchanted figures that wore silky cream-laced attire were dragged up to the links by their limbs.

The three fairies gasped in horror as they laid their eyes upon the humanoid bodies dangling in the air. They were *gray*— almost clay-like in color; each bald and completely naked. Their bodies and faces no longer held any characteristics, but rather just appeared smooth like blank dolls, void of any expression. Their eyes, once so vibrant were now gone, leaving only dark hollowed holes within their sharp bony faces. The sound of the chain clinked as it slowly dragged them forward; each haunting figure painfully twitching and shaking.

"Why are they doing that?" Flora asked fearfully.

The witch gleamed upon her handiwork as she answered: "Well, they are dancing, of course! And they will never stop."

A sudden scream of shrieking horror pierced the air as Fauna pointed up to the next blank body that came contracting in the cursed procession. It was their mother. Like the others, the green flames had burned away her every essence. She had no hair, no eyes, no mouth, but upon her smooth bald skull, there laid a sharp copper-leafed headdress; each crowned piece appeared jagged and broken, slicing its way into her skin. Such pain would bring any creature to a wailing cry, but the wooden-fixed expression upon her blank face remained— forbidding even a single scream to escape.

Though the nightmare had been cast as an act of protection and justice by her mother, the majestic torment had sparked something dark within Maleficent as well. She had never seen such profound power and respect. But there was nothing more glorious than the marks of despair painted upon the three fairy's faces that had before been so cruel and pitiless. With devastating sobs, Flora, Fauna, and Merryweather turned away, making their way into the woods, leaving their home, mother, and kind to the imprisoned limbo splintered within the twinkling forest.

"Remember your vow, dearies! You may never use dark magic again, lest you turn to ash and I take your wands as treasures to add to my collection!" The Wood Witch called out, her cackling laughter thundering throughout the trees. When the fainted glow of red, green, and blue faded away with distance, Maleficent and Grip were left alone with her mother and the crows under those that hung from the cursed chain.

Maleficent then looked to her mother with a smile, but she quickly realized from the scolding glare of her mother's darkened eyes that the moment of protection was over.

"Come, *Maleficent*, let's go home."

There it was. The way she said her name whenever she was in trouble. It was a tone that all children know and dread to hear. In all honesty, in the midst of all that had happened tonight, she had nearly forgotten the spell she had cast upon her mother so that she may climb out the window.

But she was safe now, and like all mothers are after the sheer panic of worry is gone, like a calm after a raging storm, there is only the dreaded feeling of what consequences was to come next... a feeling that was only made worse by the silence that filled the air with every step they made side by side, back to the legendary cabin at the top of the hill. Once inside, the tense silence came to a halt as her mother approached the windowsill. With a grave expression she raised her arms to close it. Maleficent and Grip looked to each other in aching anticipation; each trying to keep a calm demeanor, but as the witch turned to face them, she found the young raven's feathers all in a frightful fluff. She closed her eyes for a moment, shaking her head in frustration.

"Blast it all! Go to your perch, Diablo!" She commanded.

The nervous crow did as she ordered and flew shyly to his spot next to Maleficent's bed. Now the focus was on her and her alone. She didn't know if it was because of her mother's terrifying performance or simply because of the gravity of what she had done. After all, she had not only disobeyed her mother, she had used magic to do it.

Finally, with a racing heart and suffusing adrenaline, her mother broke her silence, "Maleficent— how could you do something like this? Don't you realize what could have happened? You deliberately disobeyed me!"

"I'm so sorry, mother, but..."

"I give you a familiar, and you dare to use him against me! What were you thinking?!"

"I wasn't! I mean, it was like I couldn't help it! The moon, the music... it was like it was calling me, controlling me! I had to go to the woods! I don't know why, but I had to!"

Seeing Maleficent so frazzled left the Wood Witch with nothing but a digressed huff as she made her way back towards the rocking chair. The warmth from the fireplace grew as her presence ignited the flames once more. Feeling the skin upon her face crack like stone, she slowly waved her hand in front of her face, a glow of magic discreetly bringing her visage back to its youthful beauty. She stared at the dancing inferno, soaking in the final moments of Maleficent's childhood innocence. She had questions now, and she couldn't deny her the answers any longer. The truth was that Maleficent was right; there was a force within her that she didn't understand... A magic half born from the Nine Realms. The time had come for her to tell Maleficent the truth of who she really was. But was the Wood Witch ready to tell her who *she* really was?

"Mother?"

The Wood Witch turned to her, offering a dreaded smile, "Come, child, come sit with me by the fire. We need to talk."

There comes the hour in every parent's life when they must bestow a cruel truth upon their child. For many, such an occasion means shattering one's belief in magic... but in the twilight hours by the fire, the Wood Witch and a young Maleficent were having a far more devastating discussion. For while most children feel betrayed and lied to about what they formerly believed, for Maleficent, she had also been lied to about what she truly was.

"...What do you mean I'm a fairy?" Maleficent asked.

"No. You are only half fae," the witch corrected. "A *descendant* like me."

Maleficent turned up her face, remembering the words of the woodland queen, "Wait! That horrible winged woman in the forest called me a filthy halfling! What does that mean? What is the other half of me?"

The Wood Witch sighed, "I fear that you are half mortal, my dear. That is why they treated you so wretchedly, and why you do not mirror their *appearance*."

The words of her mother stung her like the minced wounds the creatures had inflicted upon her body. She suddenly remembered how they looked at her, how utterly ugly and unwanted they made her feel. "So that is why they hated me?"

The sadness in her eyes as she touched the marks upon her skin, melted the unyielding heart of the witch in that moment, "I'm sorry, lass, but I'm afraid you will find that all the fae of the Nine Realms will never fail to bluntly and cruelly prove their hatred towards you. I tried to protect you, but I underestimated the amount of fae magic that courses through you. But there is no use hiding it now... for your powers have already begun to blossom inside you. I can see the green sparkle in your eyes and the glow of moonlight glittering upon your skin. And now you have these glorious horns that erupt from your head like a crown upon your wild dark hair... you look beautiful, my darling."

But Maleficent shook her head with great sorrow, "The fairies from the forest didn't think so."

"Well, of course, they *did!* Why else do you think they would attack you so violently? The fae folk are vain creatures, darling. But in their attempt to destroy your beauty, they created something else. You have a great power within you, child, and with my help... you will not be half mortal- you will be half witch and half fairy; a creature with more magic than all the fairies, scary and otherwise could ever hope to possess."

A tear fell from Maleficent's face then, "But I still won't have wings."

The Wood Witch smiled, lifting Maleficent's chin, "Don't you see, my love, by the time I am done with you... You won't need them."

* * *

As in every case of utter turmoil, even the victorious survivors are worn, weary, and scarred. Though the Wood Witch's performance of destruction within the Forbidden Forest of woodland creatures had inflicted a legendary curse of everlasting pain upon her enemies, her mere presence would prove to cost her as well. She had broken a rule... the *only* rule. She had left the cabin, and in doing so— she had lifted the very veil of her protection. No longer would the cabin move like the whispering winds of the hidden corners of the woods. Instead it would stay upon the hill that overlooked the cursed grounds of dancing dolls below. There was only one thing she could do now... the one thing that could keep her as lost as her unfortunate victims that crossed her path... she would have to use the magic of the ancient four. Only then could she hide her home and her precious child from those that would surely come to destroy her.

After sending Maleficent to bed with the heart-wrenching gravitas of her new identity, it seemed that the witch had forgotten one important detail to bestow before rushing off to her secret room of ancient books and potions that lay beyond the narrow staircase of her secret passageway behind her shelves of vast treasures. For with every turn of the aged pages, the young fae-touched halfling began to drift off to sleep, making her way into the dangerous world between... the same place that had tormented her true father many years before... the Dream Realm. From the clouded darkness of her slumber, she emerged into a clearing of the most ethereal vision of woods she had ever seen in all her life. The trees were bare and yet glimmered with dangling crystals that shined hues of green, blue, and purple. The tranquil silence of snow falling lured her towards a lovely little gully where she found a frozen pond shining in the moonlight. Beams of her Luna's glare came through the towering trees, illuminating the shadows of each dancing snowflake that fell around her. Having only experienced the forest caught between the death of summer, the air thick and clouded by ominous mist, the ground covered with dead leaves that crunched under her feet within a distance so far from any edge of the woods, she had never felt the sunshine upon her skin, nor felt the cool touch of winter in such a wonderous way as this. The magic of nature was absolutely intoxicating. Suddenly, from within the center of the clearing, there did emerge a magnificent trellis, covered in shimmering ivy that twinkled like silver lights. And below its finely crafted roof, appeared a large table. Upon it, there was a long-laced cloth of exquisite design and various feast of sweet fruits and glasses of glowing wine. The last thing to appear was a fancy hand-painted teacup. As she leaned in, eyeing its lovely appearance, a lovely thick cream began to suddenly fill its empty void. But it wasn't just cream that filled the frosted teacup in that moment, it was that splintered spark of memory that chilled the bones, as white as milk.

And then *he* appeared. With eyes like the wilderness and silver hair that shined by the light of the moon. His smile was both devious and yet terrifyingly charming. "Why do you look so surprised?" He asked.

"I, I just do not underst—"

"Well, I thought it best to pick up where we left off at the party. I believe it was with a cup of cold cream, yes?"

"Yes, I suppose it was," she said sullenly; her eyes drifting off in memory. With a sigh she spoke again, "Last night was so terrible."

He smiled, shaking his head, "No! You were magnificent! If anything, I would say that you were the life of the party. And those horns..." he said eyeing them as if struck by the beauty of a golden crown. "you are absolutely striking, Maleficent."

His words brought blood to the pale skin of her cheeks then. "Well, I am just happy my mother showed up when she did."

Pan looked a little confused, "Your mother? — Oh, you mean the witch?"

"Yes! She is my mother, and if she hadn't come to my rescue, I don't think I would still be alive. Come to think of it, why did you bring me into the party? For if what my mother said is true, then even *you* must know that they would hate me."

Pan nodded, "And just how was I to know that?"

Maleficent looked at him sternly, "Well for one thing, I do not have the wings of a fairy."

"Well neither do I, but that is the beauty of this place... its magical, and with the kind of power that Slumberland holds, you can have anything you wish. That is, once you know how to control it."

"Anything?" She said timidly.

"Yes, and this world is only one of the Nine Realms of magic. Why, I was even once like you; burdened with the blood of a mere mortal, but now- I have the powers of any born fairy... and more. Look." He whispered, raising his arm towards her back. With a single glance, Maleficent's heart fell; there upon her back were two large wings, both absolutely magnificent in size and purple in color. Tears came to her eyes as he suddenly raised the teacup to her lips.

"Drink the cream, Maleficent. Stay here, and I can teach you what it means to be powerful. You can have wings, you can have my friendship, and most importantly... you can be someone that no one would dare wrong again.

Maleficent looked up, circling her vision around the beautiful forest. She thought by the time she met his eyes again, she would have an answer, but when the moment came, all she could say was... "I'm sorry, but I do not know you. My mother told me not to trust *any* magical creature. I do not even know your name. How could I possibly stay here with you? No, it's not right. Sorry."

He smiled slyly, "I thought you might feel this way, and I am pleased. So... a clever beauty it is then, how interesting indeed. Well fear not, for I may be just a stranger in the woods, but do not mistake me for an enemy. I am your friend. My name, I'm afraid is of little meaning. Just call me Jack. This world is yours to visit whenever you slip away to Slumberland. If you should ever need me, that is where you can find me. But we must keep it a secret."

"A secret? ...Why?"

"Well until your powers grow, I think it best to keep our visits private. For like you said, the fae do not like your *kind*."

Maleficent's face fell again, "Oh."

"Fear not, Dark Fairy. I expect we will see extraordinary things from you." It was then with a cheeky smile that Maleficent woke to sound of the birds singing their morning song, but as she looked out her window, her sight was not greeted with the glorious glow of the calling moon, but rather the gloomy fog of darkness that would forever hide her lonely home.

CHAPTER FOUR
ONCE UPON A DREAM

ost believe magic is powered by the rule of three, but this is merely modern age foolery. For like most beliefs, it was a story twisted from a long-forgotten past that had carried its way into an entirely different tale all together... one rooted from none other than the three fates— *past, present, and future.*

But like most beings, the three fates craved more power. Then, on a night of many deaths, in their typical fits of glee, the fate of the future thought of a way to bring them the glory they so eagerly craved. They could bear daughters that could rule the four elements and the four directions of all. They all agreed, and with a charm of mischief and a most incredible force, it was then that the first three witches were born into the ten realms. They were born just after the legendary division between the magical creatures and the mortals they hated. The witches were to rule the Nine Realms from the corners of the north, south, east, and west. And they were to control the elements of fire, water, earth, and air.

But like all things in life, the balance of light and dark magic had to remain equal. So, when the three fates each bore their own child, a single void was left to fill. It was then that they sought the help of the Erlking, the one true king of the fairies. With a promise unknown to the world, the fates struck a deal that created a being that would hold the power of all three of them, as well as the fae magic that the Erlking possessed.

And so, the four were born. The witch of the south was born from light and contained the strength of good magic, and the witches of the east and west were both born from the darkness, consumed with enough black magic to devastate the greatest of lands and rot the purest of heart. But the witch that was born from the fates *and* the Erlking was the most powerful of them all. She was to be the ruler of the north, and her name was Nimueh.

The other three sisters were equal in match. The witch of the west, Delora, was vile, envious, and *wicked.* The witch of the east, Crimson, was beautiful, alluring, and incredibly vicious. And finally, there was Glinda, the good witch of the south. Each contained features and powers that were most striking and profound, yet the enchanting characteristics and magical prowess of Nimueh were beyond the depth of her resentful older siblings. With a good heart and a touch of fairy darkness, she quickly found herself an outcast amongst her sisters. Even the fates treated her strangely.

The fates had believed that with control of the four, they would have the ultimate rule over all the lands. But the Erlking had tricked them. For the balance of the four sisters wasn't a balance at all. The halfling had been created in both dark and light, and with more power than they could hope to control. Fearing what the Erlking's true motives were in her design, they decided to use their powers to destroy him. They hoped that by doing so, it would obliterate the fae powers within Nimueh and bring the order of balance to the four.

But on the dreaded night of the Erlking's death, the three fates had destroyed his vessel, but in doing so- they forced his darkness to spill out, spreading like a disease across the land. The terrifying evil that had once consumed the king's soul, now threatened to destroy them all.

The three sisters tried with all their might to stop the dreaded curse wrought by their mother's mistake, but it was no use. For a single touch of the king's black magic was enough to *change* them... cursing them forever.

There was only one way they could stop it. Only the daughter born of the fates blood and the Erlking's fairy magic had the power.

To save the Ten Realms, both magical and mortal alike, Nimueh would have to take all of his darkness unto herself. But taking in such magic has a way of tainting a soul, no matter how good it once was. Even Glinda's kind heart had been changed. The balance of the four sisters was now completely destroyed. Not only had the king's death given Nimueh more power, it had changed the three sisters as well:

88

each suffused with more malice and envy than ever before.

With the fairy king's kingdom empty, and in need of a crown, the war of the witches began. Nimueh did what she could to deny her sisters the throne, but their blood thirsty desire could never be sated. They each knew that as long as she was alive, the crown could never truly be theirs.

Nimueh knew she couldn't kill her sisters, for if she did, she would also be killing the small bit of goodness that was left inside her. So that meant only one thing... She would have to hide. But with the amount of magic that she now possessed, such a notion would prove to be impossible. She would need to divide her magic into three parts and hide them amongst the lands.

But that wasn't all. Before the king's death, she had fallen in love with a powerful wizard. She knew if her sisters discovered their relationship, then they would surely find a way to kill him, drawing her out in a battle that could destroy the lives and lands of those around. So, she and the wizard made a pact. That they would forever appear as enemies, and even battle for the sake of spying eyes. They would never reveal their true feelings, but also never truly harm the other. Their love would have to forever become the illusion of hate, until the day came when they could change their fate. Until then, she would hide, alone in an unrelenting agony that would never lift.

All there was left for her was time... The marks of the passing ages cracking on her skin like ancient stone. But through it all, in acts of both true love and betrayal, the once most powerful witch of the north was now a lonely old mother that stood hidden in her cabin within the dark shadows of the Forbidden Forest.

Upon the brittle pages of the ancient four, the hag now known as Madam Mim read the incantation she needed to cover her little home, keeping it hidden from those who would surely discover the devastating curse that had been cast upon the woodland fairies.

"Call to the whispers of the wind
Twist the waves and curl the sand
To each and every realm there be
Hide the cabin from all who see
Keep thine self from the sun that I hate
Until the hour I can change my fate
Keep the tree of my love always near
To lose them both I cannot bear
If I should stay till the end of time
Then let my sacrifice be my crime
For I fear the worst is nearer yet
Keep the darkness from my pet."

At this, she closed her eyes as if whispering a wish...

"With this spell I will hide us
From the south, the east, and the west
For I know more than anyone
That the wicked never rest."

From the words of her magic spoken, she brought down a few of her dusty potions kept upon the various floating shelves. Then with a snap of her long fingers, a giant cauldron did then emerge into the dingy room of her ancient enchantment.

* * *

She twisted and pulled the corks from the chalky aged bottles, the weak pop from their lids brought a wrinkled smile to her face. In truth, it had been some time since the need for such drastic measures had been called for. Though a large part of her hated its cause, the intoxicating feeling from such power always managed to bring about a most sinister pleasure.

But the high from her magic quickly emptied like the spilling potions from her bottles as the images of her distant sisters appeared from her memory.

How long before they know of her curse?

How long before they came looking for her?

And how long would it be before she had to tell Maleficent of the grave danger, she had put her in?

Her thoughts of them swarmed her frantic mind like a deadly storm raging over a ship. She didn't even know if her sisters were still alive. After all, she had merely hidden the broken pieces of her father's soul in three enchanted objects.

True, she had taken one of the three with her, and had kept it safely tucked away within the lonely cabin... but if one of her sisters found a way to capture two of the magical pieces, they would have all they needed to find her. Only then could they capture the third piece and seize the crown that would give them the most desired kingdom in all the Nine Realms.

What if they had already found them?

Suddenly, a loud squawk came from one of the dusty corners filled with cobwebs.

She glared up, moving the purple smoke from her cauldron with a mere wave of her hand. It was one of her crows staring down at her.

"Oh, don't you look at me like that... I cannot help it! I have to know. Yes— I do. I have to know what they are up to."

The crow squawked again before flying to her shoulder as if comforting her. She petted him gently as she came out of the hidden room beyond the bookcase.

With a look of purpose and dread, she opened the nearest window. She lifted a finger and twirled it slowly. It was then that a storm began to rage in the woods, and everything went dark.

Then it happened. A deadly force suddenly appeared like the god of chaos had come to strike the Forbidden Forest with an unholy wrath.

A terrible vortex came to life from the tip of her finger, the twirling of wind began to spiral out the window until a magical twister emerged. And though it was barely beyond her reach, the raging winds of the tornado never touched the hidden cabin.

She looked to her darling pet upon her shoulder and with a tender touch, she picked him up and held him out.

"Go, my darling, to the land
 Where life's color was first born
Go, my pet, to find the three
That I have dared to scorn
Show me through your eyes
What they plan to do
And in the city where they dwell
See if they have the two
Look for the red-sand hourglass
And the ruby slippers that shine
See how close they think they are
To taking what is mine
Venture fourth, my darling
And please forgive my cause
For where I have to send you
Is the great land of Oz."

At that, the crow flew out into the twister, allowing it to carry him to a land far away. The air in the woods then went back to its original state as if the storm she had conjured had never happened at all. It was done now. He was gone. And though her pet had the skill to be silent and as crafty as the night, she couldn't help fearing that her darling might be spotted. But just as her thoughts were beginning to spread over her again like a wildfire for the soul, she heard the sound of Maleficent's door opening and her little feet coming down the hall.

"Mother?"

The Wood Witch quickly closed the window, locking its latch at such a speed that it proved most suspicious.

"Yes, my little witch... what a glorious morning it is! How did you sleep?"

Perturbed by her mother's unusual behavior, Maleficent peeked her eyes towards the window of aged glass.

They hadn't moved. Outside lay the same forest they had been in the night before. The sound of her mother's voice muffled in the background as if caught in a blur as she made her way towards the window. There, off in the distance, behind the shadowed lining of the tall forest trees, stood the young man from her dreams. Maleficent's eyes widened in great surprise as he smiled at her from the distance. The sun shined upon his glimmering eyes that mirrored the wood's wild spirit. He slowly raised his finger to his mouth, reminding her of their encounter and that it should remain, above all things, a secret.

It was then that the loud voice of her mother snatched her back to attention, "Maleficent!"

She turned to her mother, gulping with anxiety, "Yes?!"

"I asked you how you slept?"

"Oh! I... erm..." She paused, looking back towards the trees, but he was now gone. "I slept fine."

Her quickened answer also seemed suspicious, but before the witch had the proper chance to question her further, Maleficent spoke again.

"Why hasn't our home moved, mother? Why are we still here?"

The witch sighed, grabbing her small hand, and bringing her to her chair by the fireplace. "I fear after last night's events, the cabin *cannot* be moved."

"What do you mean? How long will we stay here?"

"Maleficent, I broke a powerful barrier to get to you last night. It was one that cannot be made again. I did all I could to keep the cabin hidden, but it will never again move beyond these trees. We are now bound to the very forest that I cursed in the twilight hours of the woodland party. It will not be long before the creatures beyond the veils come to the scorched grounds that I have burned. Those within the Nine will come to seek its power. The journey I took to protect you from the dancing Elle put us both in great danger. I have cast a cloak upon our home to keep its image invisible to those with sight beyond these ancient walls. Only here can we be lost and hidden."

"But I..."

"Listen, we both broke the rules last night, and for that... here in the Forbidden Forest is where we will both remain."

Maleficent was shocked, overwhelmed with questions that felt flooded with fear and guilt. "But what if we..."

"Enough! There is nothing more that can be done. What happened... happened. Time will move on, and so should we. Now come with me. I have much to show you."

Maleficent nodded, silently following her mother's reluctant steps towards the bookshelves of magical treasures. With a wave of her hand, the dust of age blew away, and the first book of dangerous enchantment began.

Time may be short and cruel for mortal beings, but for a creature that could live forever, it was guilt that would prove to be the cruelest fate of all. Maleficent and her mother never talked about the stillness of the cabin again. Instead, Maleficent became the greatest pupil of magic there ever was. She learned all she could of witchcraft, dabbling in both the dark and the light powers of magic, but that wasn't all. Her mother also taught her how to tap into the fae power that bubbled inside her. Maleficent worked hard, becoming more powerful everyday... all in a secret hope that she could fix whatever it was that she had broken.

But at night, when the moon was high and the wind whistled it's song between the thin branches of the trees, Maleficent would lay her dark crown of horns upon her pillow and dream of the man that waited for her beneath the beautiful moonlight; each time with more alluring temptations that became harder and harder to resist.

Maleficent often felt uneasy about the secret she kept hidden from her mother... but like so many children when they are young, they fear the repercussions that would come from the truth. After all, it was her mistakes that kept them in the forest, and her mother had already done all she could to protect them. She didn't want to make things worse. For if what the fairy lad said to her was true, speaking of their meetings out loud in the real world would only put them in more danger. So, with each and every day that passed, Maleficent treaded carefully; never knowing who might be listening. And though she adored her precious raven, Grip, she dared not even tell him of her secret.

Over time, the secret grew into something deeper. For no matter how powerful she became, there was only one thing that her magic couldn't conjure... a love.

Loneliness is a dangerous thing. It can cloud the mind and poison the soul. Maleficent knew her mother loved her, but it seemed that the rule she had broken had also broken something between them. With a sorrow most desperate, Maleficent spent every waking hour mastering everything within her mother's books... but no matter how much she learned or how much she tried to please her, the distance between them only seemed to grow over the years; a feeling as silent and dreary as the cabin itself.

* * *

As the years passed, the only solace left for the forlorn beauty was the charming man of her frosted dreams. To her, it wasn't only his sugared words or his desirable appearance that had made it so, but rather their unique bond that he had offered. With him, she wasn't growing up in the darkness of a lonely cabin that was hidden from the world... she was with someone that made her feel special. He would always tell her how beautiful he found her, gifting her with glittering dresses and the most extraordinary treasures of jewels and silver. But no matter what he gave her, she never wore anything other than her black fierce gowns, made by her own design; each with long sleeves and a tall collar that spread out like narrow wings. None of it was flattering to her appearance, but she just couldn't stand the ugliness of the scars the fairies had inflicted upon her. Instead she hid as much of herself as she could, but there was nothing that could hide the astonishing beauty of her face.

The two of them talked about many things, but soon she realized that she had nothing left to offer; for her secluded life within the cabin was nothing more than a gloomy fate. But the man in her dreams spoke of the most incredible lands and skies. He told her countless tales about the many wonders of the Nine Realms: the lands, the castles, and the kings and queens that ruled them. He spoke of the sun that shined in the spring, and all the silver seas. And then one night, she asked the question she had never dared ask in her youth. She asked about those who surrounded her own world; the very creature that consumed half of her blood. She asked about *humans*.

"Jack, what about mortals? Why do fairies hate them so much?" She asked covering her face, ashamed of her appearance.

He smiled, carefully taking her hand into his... This was it. This was his chance. With a mask of painted pain and his manipulated art of deception, he planted yet another dangerous seed within her. "It is not just the fairy kind that despises them so... it is *all* of the magical creatures of this world and those beyond the seven veils. I too have always loathed them... even when I was one, myself. They are terrible, ugly, destructive, cruel beings. Their lives are short, and yet they do not know how to truly live. Come to think of it, there is nothing I like about them."

Maleficent suddenly couldn't wait to wake up; for this was starting to feel like a nightmare. "You mean, you hate *all* mortals?" She asked sadly.

"In truth..." He spoke in whispers, gazing around them as if someone might hear him. "I have only met one of mortal blood that proved different. Though I would never admit it amongst the creatures of the Nine... nor can I at times even admit it to myself, I *have* met one such being that..." He paused, looking down with a sigh of great resistance.

Maleficent's heart raced inside her chest then, pounding hard like a drum that stole her breath. A fluttering of a hundred butterflies flew rapid in her stomach as she opened her mouth to ask: "A being that-what?"

Pan slowly looked up, his eyes gleaming with an alluring sparkle. He appeared sad and broken, turning to her in a desperate attempt to unburden his dark secret. "I have found the one that *completes* me. The rare soul that mirrors that ever so delicate balance of exitance. The one that drives the passion of the heart, giving and taking both a profound love and extraordinary level of hate. I found the one being that changes you, moves you, pains you... and without that one person... I fear I could no longer exist."

Tears welled up in Maleficent's emerald eyes in that moment. Consumed with his vulnerable charm and a searing doubt brought from her mother's constant warnings of fairy trickery, she stood from the rock where they sat side by side and faced him with such fierce power, that the winds of her dreams swirled around her. She knew what his words meant... and in truth, she had grown to feel the same way for him over the years. Still, she had to be sure. She had to know if he was being truthful. So, there, within the woods of beautiful moonlight, she spoke the only words that could bring her the answer she needed to know. "Through all these years in the twilight hours, I have come to meet you with a trusting heart, but I have also known for all these years that I should not. If your sweetened words are true, then you alone will have my melted heart, but before I give it freely... I must... yes, I must be sure."

Pan nodded with a smile that seemed to dance upon her spine. He slowly stood, bringing his face before hers, his gaze of love weakening her knees. "Go on, then."

Maleficent closed her eyes, and after a deep sigh, she opened them, revealing their fierce glow.

> *"Speak nothing false,*
> *Nor curve a single word*
> *Should I then believe*
> *What I've already heard?*
> *Magic, show me the truth*
> *Twine each lie in thy throat*

And if thou prove dishonest
Turn thee into a goat!"

Maleficent shouted, releasing a burst of green smoke. The flames slowly rose, covering him from his feet to the top of his head. She waited in aching hope, to not hear the shrill cries of pain. And just as she wished, down came the flames, revealing only that smile that took her breath away.

"Why do you *witches* always feel the need to turn people into ridiculous animals?"

Maleficent giggled in relief, rushing into his arms. "So, you did mean all of those things!" She exclaimed with pure joy.

He nodded with a cleverly sly brow, "I meant every word, Maleficent. I should hate the blood that runs through your veins, but I have found that it is your very blood that brings me here night after night. I watched you grow with such beauty and power... and though I never imagined it could be true; I believe that the very key to my happiness lives within you."

Tears fell from her eyes; their blissful pleasure dropped upon the glittering ground as he took her hand in his and placed the other upon his shoulder, and with a wink of his eye... a most enchanting music filled the air. With each and every note that came, he carried her higher into the air. And the two slowly twirled, moving gracefully to her given song. It was Maleficent's first dance... but it was also tragically, to be her last. For the cruel morning would soon come, and on that gloomy day, everything in her entire world would change forever; left with a twisted fate, painted by the blissful lie that had been disguised as true love... and the dance that would prove to be nothing more than an illusion; granted by the man who said he loved her- *once upon a dream.*

* * *

Once again, the master of mischief, be it by sun or moon, had used his deceiving charm and malevolent skills of strategy to completely bewitch his new prey. Having so carefully chosen his words of passion, Maleficent now had no doubt in her mind that he was in love with her. Much like Hook, Pan knew that though Maleficent's own feelings towards him had been rather transparent, she would still act with great caution. She had used her power of magic to measure his honesty; a fact that considering the amount of years he had put in to gain her unyielding trust, left him feeling quite impressed. She was Hook's daughter alright. This had been a brutally calculated game of strategic design from the beginning, and Peter Pan had always thrived in such challenges. But now the time had come to raise the stakes and reap the rewards for all his years of malicious effort. This victorious trickery felt like yet another win against Hook, and thus left him with such profound arrogance that he couldn't bear waiting any longer. *But was it too soon? How far was Maleficent willing to go for true love?*

As the morning approached and the dance of enchantment had come to an end. Maleficent found herself in a dreadful state of unusual sadness. "I wish I didn't have to wake up. I wish we could always be together," she whispered, laying her head upon his shoulder.

A sinister smile spread across his beautiful face as he held her tightly in his arms. "There *is* a way."

Maleficent raised her head and looked at him with hopeful eyes, "How?"

"Come with me to the Nine Realms."

Maleficent's eyes widened in disbelief, "What? Jack, no. I cannot."

"I know that you fear the world beyond these woods, but I swear before all the gods, the stars, and the moon that brings us together, that I will protect you. I can no longer bear the agonizing hours with us apart. But now that I know of your love for me, it has given me the courage to ask you the question that I never dared ask: Do as I did... and strike a deal with the fae. If you do, then you can have everything your heart desires, and *I* will be with you."

"But how can I? I mean... what about my mother?"

"If you make a deal, then the fae will no longer hate you, and then you and your mother will thus not be confined to the tight walls in which you are bound now. You can be free. Don't you understand, love? Your mother will thank you for what you've done."

Maleficent turned away, unsure of such an action. She had never left the cabin during the day. She had never seen the world beyond the darkness of the trees. She knew her mother would be furious once she discovered her absence. Her mind told her to say no, but her heart longed for the truth that could only be learned outside the secrets that dwelled within the Forbidden Forest. There were so many things she did not know; things that she felt she could never ask her mother. The distance that had grown between them had grown increasingly painful. Maybe this *was* the way to atone for her grave mistake... Or this decision might prove to be even more tragic than the last.

Like so many times in the past, her thoughts of doubt were swept away by the words of the silver-tongued devil that stood behind her: "Maleficent, please. I thought you said you trusted me; that your heart was mine," he said in a sad tone.

She rushed to him in assurance, "I do. I do. It's just..."

"Don't you see? This is the only way!" The longing gaze of his sparkling eyes seemed to melt her in that moment. She now realized that to say no would mean hurting him, disappointing him, or worse— losing him.

With a sigh of retreat, she said the words that he had never ceased loving to hear: "As you wish. Upon the late hour that she sleeps, I will run out into the woods. Meet me there and I will go with you to the Nine Realms." He smiled victoriously in return, and with a snap of his fingers and a wave of her hand, the two disappeared from the dream. The following day came and went as it always had before. There was plenty of reading and practicing the divine art of witchcraft as she always did. Her mother read to her of the many creatures of the realms and whom to fear. But when the distant sun set from its place in the sky, and the moon rose to take its rightful place amongst the twinkling stars, the Wood Witch retired to her room to sleep. Once Maleficent knew that her mother was in a deep sleep, she quietly rose from her own bed, eager to rush into the dark woods. But just as she reached the window, a swallowing feeling of guilt came over her. *The window...* If only she knew how often its frame led victims to a most unfortunate fate. Maleficent did something that not even *he* predicted. He had thought himself too high and the love for her mother too low. He hadn't counted on Maleficent leaving any clue to where she had gone, and luckily for him, she could leave very little insight as to where exactly she might be going.

Dearest Mother,

I pray you not worry about me. I have gone beyond the hidden veil of the forbidden forest, but you needn't fear my safety. I am bringing Grip with me, and should I get into trouble, he will come back and tell you where to find me. I hope that in my efforts, I may bring back news with the power to mend what I have broken.

Your little witch.

Under the weight of one of her favorite crystals, the written parchment laid out upon the table as she and her darling pet made their way out into the grey fog on the other side of the window. Running to the lands scorched by her mother's curse, Maleficent waited anxiously for Jack to appear. The moment came shortly, and just as it had been before, all her fear floated away. He came towards her and without a single word between them, he sprinkled a bright purple dust that seemed to fall upon her like glitter. He looked into her eyes and with a sly smile, he wrapped his hand around hers and lifted his staff into the air. And then, just as she had always wished, she began to fly. Maleficent loved the feeling of flying; there was just something so amazing about it. It wasn't about the magic or even power, as she had so much herself. Flying was different. It was special, beautiful even. How she longed to be such a creature; to not be covered in scars but rather gifted with wings. The two of them flew high above the tallest trees and into the mysterious beauty of the starry night.

"Where are we going?" Maleficent asked suffused with adrenaline, both from excitement and fear.

"Through the stars there is a portal; a gateway to the Nine Realms."

"Which one are we going to?"

He smiled, "The Third Realm... we will find many fairies there; ones that I believe will help us."

"Who are they?"

"They are known as the Unseelie."

Maleficent gasped, "My mother has told me of the Unseelie Court. They are..."

"I know what they are, Maleficent, but I think you will find a great company with those that are willing to bend the rules. Such a fairy dared to make a deal with me once upon a time. Let us hope one takes the same chance on you."

But hope was not the feeling that was now surging through Maleficent's person. No, what she was feeling was something entirely different. She was afraid, and though it was the kind of fear that spread through the body and mind like a poison, Maleficent dared not spill a single word. She said she trusted him. He *would* protect her... *right?*

Once the three of them made it into the blasting surface of the legendary second star to the right, he felt thrilling malice as he led them into the third veil edged with chilling frost. The burst to the other side was one of incredible force and one that stole Maleficent's breath. The bitter cold crept through her long gown and onto every inch of her skin. Unlike the comfort that was born from her dreams, the freezing air seemed to burn. Yet, like so many before her, Maleficent's gaze completely enthralled in awe.

The beauty of the glittering snow, the winter branches of the trees covered in icicles, and the tiny doorways of the homes that belonged to all of those who lived there. Little men with long beards and tall caps could be seen walking upon the snowy white hills, and up within the sky were little fairies glowing in such vibrant colors that they shined upon the ground with the reflection of beautiful jewels like rubies, sapphires, emeralds, and even gold; each complimenting each other.

As Jack brought her closer, she saw their faces. They weren't beautiful like the woodland fairies. In fact, they were painfully wretched to look at. With solid black eyes, sharp boney features, and skin so pale and livid that they appeared lifeless, the tiny creatures appeared most frightful. Yet each and every one of them possessed the large glorious wings that Maleficent so desperately longed for. They turned their dark gaze towards her; each stare flooded with a hate so intense that it even made her darling raven cringe.

"They don't want us here, Jack. We should leave," she whispered in a cold breath of inner terror.

But he did no such thing. Instead, he showed his bravery and approached one of them. She was small, pale, and bright yellow. Maleficent shied away from the creatures blackened gaze, focusing instead on the short dress made of yellow leaves and golden stitched cloth. And upon her feet were two jeweled shoes that shined like sunshine.

She turned her sight to him as he spoke: "I know how this must appear, but I swear that I bring the half-ling here not out of provocation, but rather out of love. I have seen what power she possesses, and I know that if she could live here amongst us, she would prove worthy of her post. I should like you to listen to her wish, and consider..."

The Yellow Fairy then rapidly raised a golden wand to his face, making Maleficent gasp. "How dare you try to coerce me into an act of treason! Do you think me a fool- like that little green one of yours? Ha! And just where is that treacherous friend of yours now? —Oh, that's right! She is dead!"

His expression changed in that moment, the blood rushed to his face and his pale glassy eyes of winter seemed to burn, each flickering like flames. After a huffed breath, he slapped her wand away from his face and snatched her person in close. "You- go- too-far," he said in a terrifying tone that sent chills up Maleficent's spine.

But the yellow fairy leaned in ever closer, seething through her tiny pointed teeth, "No, sir. It is *you* that has gone too far!"

Suddenly, he and Maleficent were snatched from the ground by a giant monstrous bear. Maleficent screamed as the creature tore her from Jack's arms and dragged them through the blistering snow. His grip was painful and strong, for no matter how hard she tried, no manner of strength, nor any range of magic could remove his claw that carried her.

"What are you doing? Where are you taking us?!" She screamed. But the snow was so fresh that it was like being pulled though a freezing powder. The beautiful ice that appeared like shining diamonds was now burning her, swallowing her.

She had been moved so roughly that she couldn't see where he was taking them, or what he was going to do. This went on torturously for what felt like hours, but just before her tired body went limp, and her long-suffocated breath began to falter, Grip had started his own attack. Flapping, clawing, and pecking with brutal force against the bear's eyes, the bear had no choice, nor any way to defend his face if he did not let them go. Maleficent and Jack both dropped from his painful hold, each gasping for breath. Once their eyes met, he rushed to her.

"What is happening? Where are we?" She asked fearfully.

He looked up; the answer to such a question towered above them. "The Icy Citadel."

Maleficent opened her eyes to find a wonderous palace of crystals. Suddenly, a man came, lifting them to their feet.

"Let go of us! I demand you set us free! We have done nothing wrong!" Jack shouted.

The tall masculine man didn't look at him, but rather just answered his demand plainly, "But you had been treasonous in thought, and if you had gotten your way, you would have been treacherous in deed. I must take you now before Her Majesty, where she will decide how to judge your betrayal."

"The queen?" Maleficent spoke softly.

The tall man looked down at her, though he had not done so when addressed by Jack. His eyes were not black like the others, but rather sweet and almost kind.

110

"Yes, mistress, I will be presenting you two to the *Snow Queen.*"

CHAPTER FIVE
MISTRESS OF ALL EVIL

hen the massive doors to the palace opened, the tall man escorted the two of them into the castle. Grip quickly flew inside before the doors closed behind them, leaving the giant bear growling in pain on the other side. So many things were happening now. And with each step, Maleficent drew closer to the amethyst throne. Upon the seat, sat the notorious Snow Queen. She was tall like the queen of the woodland fairies but appeared far more magnificent. She had an aura of such majesty that it demanded unquestioning respect. A long purple rug that shimmered like silk and edged in golden thread led them all the way to the foot of her throne. And on either side, there stood those of the Unseelie Court; each with an icy stare that Maleficent couldn't escape. Their whispers were like chilling echoes that had the ability to cloud the nervous mind. She looked to her love; his face was still stern with bravery. Even after being dragged through the snow, he still held his head high. She loved how strong he was, how utterly unafraid. When they reached the steps below the throne, the Snow Queen slowly rose, standing before them. Then, with a loud tap of her staff, the whispers within the court fell silent. Maleficent thought she would feel better if they stopped, but as it turned out this was worse. She looked around. The walls, though not transparent on the outside seemed to be completely transparent from the inside. And from the angle of the queen's elaborate throne, it appeared there was nothing that happened beyond the palace walls that *she* could not see. The queen herself appeared even more beautiful than the realm around her. Her gown carried a train of silver and diamonds. The design and intricate work upon her front were so exquisite that Maleficent knew no mortal could ever hope to create such a masterpiece.

The Snow Queen bent down, lifting Maleficent's head. "No. Could it be...? Draven!" She called out.

The tall man that had escorted them inside rushed to her. "Yes, Your Majesty?"

"Lift my veil! I want her to look me in the eye!"

Maleficent's heart raced as the tall man rushed to the queen, slowly raising her glittering white veil of lace and dazzling pearls. Within that moment, when the room was as silent as snow, Maleficent saw the queen's face. Her eyes were lavender, and her skin was bright and fair. The twist and curls of her long silvery hair were covered in freshly bloomed white roses. Maleficent had never seen anything more beautiful. It was as if she had been painted by some maestro of the divine. Still, there was something terrifying about her. A fact made even more unsettling by the alluring vision of her. Like the sirens Maleficent had learned about in her mother's teachings, she saw the queen as a person that no creature, godly or other could possibly deny.

The queen stared down at her; her expression dripping with utter disdain. "*Ah*, it is you! I can see it in those pretty little eyes of yours, the ocean that storms within your soul. Try as you might to hide behind your long dark gown and emerald beauty, there is no mistaking it. I know who you are! Why have you dared come to my kingdom?" The queen asked.

Maleficent was stunned. She didn't know what to say or how to answer. She opened her mouth to speak but felt as if the bitter cold choked her very breath. She must have taken too long to answer, because the queen huffed and slammed her staff against the floor with impatience.

"I ask you again, and this time I demand an answer... what are you doing in the Nine Realms? *Here* in *my* kingdom?"

Maleficent looked to Jack, but he said not a single word. She thought he must be looking to her to be strong; to be as brave as he was. "I... know that I am half mortal and therefore do not deserve your kindness. We came here for your mercy and hoped that one within your court would be willing to change that which you hate inside me. I wish to become wholly fae and live here within the Nine Realms amongst beings of magic and great power like yourself."

The Snow Queen scoffed, laughing at her pitiful, worthless flattery. "Wait! You think I hate you simply because you are half mortal?"

114

Maleficent paused, "Well… *yes.*"

The queen laughed again, only this time it seemed to ignite an explosion of whispers from the fairy court around them. The queen sat back down upon her throne, tapping her fingernails along the side of her staff as if in deep thought. The moment was tense. The queen stared at her, leering at her in an awkward silence. Finally, she lifted her gaze to the court, quieting them once more. Then with a sneer that seemed to bring a chill to the palace, she spoke again: "You have come here to make a deal. I believe you. But how did you get this traitor here to bring you? Did you bewitch him?"

Maleficent looked to Jack again. This time he spoke, if only to defend himself. "She did no such thing. We have come here together for *love.*"

The Snow Queen suddenly looked disgusted. "Then you are a fool! For I do not think this creature is capable of love. She has clearly used you as a pawn to gain our power and territory over our sacred realms."

Maleficent moved forward, "But I do love him, Your Majesty!"

Her sudden objection did not sit well with the queen. "Impossible! You forget that I know who you are! A creature bred from a traitor and a monster!"

Maleficent again looked bewildered, "I do not understand, Your Majesty."

The Snow Queen then nodded, smiling ever slowly. "Yes, you have made that quite clear. Well, allow me to enlighten you. I speak of your parents, child. But though I detest your treacherous mother, powerful as she is, the hatred I bear towards you comes from your *father.*"

"Because he was mortal?"

"No!" The queen shouted, her stern voice echoing off the crystal walls. "Because of what he did to me, the life he took from me and those of my precious realm."

"What?! No, you must be mistaken, Your Highness."

"There is no mistake, half-ling. Come here, and I will show you the pain your blood has caused me," the queen said swirling the top of her staff. A giant crystal did then appear before Maleficent. Fearing what would happen if she did not, she stood from the floor, approaching it with great caution and unbearable curiosity.

At first, the giant crystal within the Icy Citadel was clear, almost transparent, but as Maleficent leaned in closer, an image slowly began to appear within its center. It was a man. He had long dark hair, and bright blue eyes. He was entering the frosty realm from the top of a hill. His presence was oppressive and threatening as he inched forward. Upon being spotted, he charged in on all the small creatures that walked upon the snow innocently unaware. Before they had a chance to act or defend themselves, the man slashed through them with a sword.

Maleficent gasped, placing her hand over her mouth in horror. Within mere moments, the glittering snow was covered in blood. But the massacre was only the beginning. With a trail of enormous carnage behind him, the man entered the palace. Maleficent couldn't hear what he said to the queen, only that after a few heated words, a red fairy appeared as if by force. The fear upon the fairy's face was nothing short of a panic most defeating. The queen tried to stop him from leaving, but it was no use. Maleficent's eyes welled with tears as the man ripped the wings off the tiny creature.

The fairy's cries of such torturous pain brought water to the queen's lavender eyes. The image then faded away, and Maleficent's knees buckled to the floor.

"*That* is your father! Hook! He is a monster that took my daughter's life as well as the lives of many in my court. Only now is my realm's beauty beginning to shine again. But the blood he spilled all those years ago feels as fresh today as the day he unleashed his wrath upon my kingdom. I had heard that he fell in love with a fairy and had his own child. And now, here you are... standing before me with the blood of my only daughter stained upon your hands. I have waited a long time for my revenge; to get justice for my kingdom. And now I can!"

Grip squawked, ready to flee for help, but Maleficent shook her head. She couldn't bear the thought of her mother trying to come here. Even if they did survive, she knew that she would never be able to forgive her. Maleficent could do nothing but cry, desperately pleading, "No, please don't kill me. I had no idea. My mother never told me about him."

"I think you will find that the *witch* has kept a great many secrets from you."

"Will find? You mean... you aren't going to kill me?"

"Oh, no, child. For while I would love to kill the daughter of my enemy, that wouldn't be enough to console my broken heart."

"What are you going to do?"

The queen smirked, pleased by her fear.

"Please believe me, I would do anything to take it all back."

The Snow Queen's eyes sparkled in that moment. "I know... and that is *exactly* what you are going to do."

"How?"

"You came here to make a deal and make a deal you shall... *with me!*"

Suddenly, she pointed her staff towards Jack, unleashing a powerful blast upon him. He instantly screamed, collapsing in crippling pain. Maleficent tried to run to him, but before she could move an inch, the tall man grabbed her by her arms.

"Please stop! What are you doing?" She cried.

The queen pulled back her staff and the magic faded away. "If you truly do love this traitor and want to keep him alive... Then you will go back to your hidden cabin and find the spell that can bring a soul back from the realm of the dead."

Maleficent was shocked and confused. "But... my mother has been teaching me magic all my life, and I have never seen such a spell before."

"As I've already said, you have many secrets to uncover. Believe me, she has more magic than you can possibly imagine. Look in the hidden corners of her lies and I am sure you will find the power I seek. If not... then your little love here will die a most dreadful death. And believe me, dear, losing love will leave a hole in your heart that you can never hope to fill again."

Maleficent looked to Jack, at his weak body. "Yes, Your Majesty, I will do as you command."

Maleficent turned, as if to walk away, when suddenly the queen spoke again: "I am not finished."

Maleficent turned her head, afraid of what was to come next.

The queen smiled, "I will need a child."

"A child?" Maleficent asked in horror.

"Yes, one of *noble* blood."

"How?"

"It has come to my attention that King Stefan is on the verge of losing his kingdom in what will be one of the greatest wars of this era. And he has already tried to summon one of us to aid him. I also happen to know that his queen is *pregnant.* It is my wish that you use the fae power that courses through your veins and the skills of your mother in such matters, to make a *deal* with the king. Prideful kings have always put their power above their children. I have no doubt he will accept the deal. When he does, you will bring her to me. Then, with the spell that belongs to your mother, I will have a proper vessel for my daughter's poor soul."

Maleficent couldn't believe what the queen was asking. "A child. I, I just... don't know if I can."

Suddenly, a blast came from the staff again, striking him again with unbearable agony. He screamed, begging and pleading for Maleficent's help. Tears streamed from her emerald eyes as she thought of what to do.

"My love! Please! Save me!" Jack cried out in wailing terror and pain.

"You better give your answer soon, I don't think he will last much longer," the queen said playfully. "Then again, maybe you *are* more like your father than you thought. For *I* would never let someone I loved suffer through the pain that you see before you."

Maleficent closed her eyes, but it was no use. The wailing screams echoed in her mind. Finally, with a breath that she would remember for the rest of her life, she uttered the words the queen had so longed to hear: "Alright. I will do it!"

The blast stopped, and the queen stood, walking down the stairs towards her. "We have a deal then?"

"Yes," Maleficent whispered in defeat.

"Good, you must be off then, dear, you have a lot to do."

"But..." Maleficent countered, pointing to Jack.

"Oh, he will be staying here with me until you return with *all* that you have promised me."

"But then how shall I return home?"

"I will take care of that. When you open my castle doors, you will find the Forbidden Forest on the other side."

"But I cannot fly like him, how am I to ever find my way back here?"

"The queen's expression turned cold with irritation, "If your father, with nothing but mortal blood

120

coursing through his veins could find his way into this realm, so then can you. Now go, and do *not* fail me."

At that, Maleficent walked down the narrow rug to leave, and upon opening the towering doors, she saw that the queens magic had worked. Grip flew through first, and in just a few steps, they were finally home, in the Forbidden Forest where her mother would be waiting for them. Only she was not bringing the good news she had hoped to deliver to her mother, but rather an explosion of desperation, fear, and questions. But this time... she would need some real answers.

Once the doors to the palace were closed again, the Icy Citadel suddenly felt so unbelievably hot that the entire court of unblessed ones feared that it might just melt around them. Water began to trickle down the frozen crystals; cracks within the ice growing deeper by the second. The crowd of Unseelie fairies circled in fear; each turning towards the source of such power.

"Stop this, Pan!" The Snow Queen shouted, reaching her arms out to unleash a chilling frost from the palms her hands. The blast of winter cold rushed towards the walls of her castle in an attempt to counter the magic of his sunshine before he took down the palace completely.

"Have you lost your senses?! How dare you have your brain-washed minions treat me that way! That was not what we discussed!"

"Don't be a fool, Pan! It had to be convincing!"

"There was no need! I had her!"

"No! You're wrong!"

The wave of extraordinary heat then began to fade; his magic slowly pulling back towards him. "What do you mean?"

"Oh, how your arrogance blinds you! Why, I could see it from the second she arrived in this land."

"What?! What did you see?"

"Hesitance! Doubt! Uncertainty! She reeked of it! She was never going to make the deal we needed simply out of love; just to be with *you!* No, it had to be something *more*, something tragic and dire. She *needed* to see you suffering, to see you in pain. She *needed* to believe you were going to die because of her! Guilt can be a powerful thing, and I acted on it. Don't you see? The plan was changed because it had to!"

Jack squinted his eyes in fury and frustration. A moment of pause and consideration caused him to look down. His body ached. His throat still ached painfully from the excruciating breaths he had so desperately fought for. And the lingering ice from the queen's staff still singed like fiery embers blazing within his insides. But through it all, wretched as it all was, there was but one offense that he could not abide — nor forgive. He slowly raised his gaze back up towards the queen. "You may be right. Maybe the plan *did* have to change. I applaud your *thrilling* performance of hatred towards me... How fortunate we all are that Your Majesty can think up such an elaborate scheme so quickly. I must say that you and those in your court acted most convincingly. One would almost think you had planned it before I arrived."

The Snow Queen smiled slowly, "I am grateful for your flattery. Though I must say that *your* performance is also to be congratulated. Those screams —consumed with such utter agony. *Mmm...* Why, I almost felt sorry for you."

Jack nodded with a sinister smile. With an eerie pace walking up and down the floor, he snapped his fingers, manifesting his knotted staff. And with a mere twist of the wood upon the icy ground, the Yellow Fairy he had spoken with earlier, suddenly appeared; his hand instantly gripped tightly around her throat. The queen rapidly rose from her throne. "Tisk... Tisk... Tisk," he uttered in a hiss that echoed like a ghostly snake. "Your plan worked, Snow White, I will grant you that. But there was *one- rather- large- error*, I'm afraid. One that I intend to rectify right now."

"No, stop!" The queen commanded, but it was too late. With a simple blow from his blue lips, the Yellow Fairy screamed, freezing by his breath. Once turned into a mere statue of ice, he swung his heavy staff to smash her like glass. The court barely had the chance to gasp before the broken shards from her tiny body fell within the palm of his hand. The crowd of fairies turned away; each covering their mouths of silent cries as he brushed away her remains like dirt.

"I want all of you now to listen to me very carefully! *Never-* think to bring up Tinker Bell again, nor anything from my past that is of no business of yours. Should your *queen* command this of you in the future, remember this moment. For it will be your only warning!"

At that, he turned his sight towards the queen once more. She huffed in a fury so cold that there was not a single breath unseen within the palace. "You have made your point, Pan! Enough."

He chuckled to himself, "Good! Then we can be perfect friends again!"

The queen slowly sat back down upon her throne, her eyes glowing bright and fierce with stinging frustration. "Indeed," she said seething through her teeth. "What shall we do now?"

"Now all we have to do is wait... *Wait*—for my *beloved's* return."

* * *

Though Maleficent and Grip had made their way back into the Forbidden Forest, they found themselves completely unable to find the witch's cabin. With each moment that passed, Maleficent felt a terrible panic start to rise inside her. She had never been lost before. Never. *Had her home been moved? Had her mother left her behind, angered by her disobedience? No, she wouldn't do that. She couldn't... Right?* Her mind raced with endless questions; each more dreadful and toxic than the last. She wanted to believe that her mother had been truthful about the cabin, but with very little explanation about her secrecy, she couldn't help but wonder. But that wasn't the only poison that seeped through her troubled mind, nor the most crippling. The Snow Queen had set ablaze many embers of burning doubts. And it seemed that against all her efforts, every step Maleficent took within the woods, the more lost and afraid she became. She desperately sought the image of her mother's crows, but there was only that of her own, Grip, and not even he could guide her home. She looked for the smoke that so often came from her mother's chimney, but the trees were much too high for her to see. The fog started to feel as if it were full of ghosts and even though the woods were empty, it seemed as though there were hidden eyes watching her every move. It was utterly unnerving, but Maleficent knew she couldn't give up. She tried to remove the fog with her powers, but it had been made by her mother's magic; an element used to keep their home a secret. But try as Maleficent did to pierce it, the fog only thickened.

It was then that hysterics set in. The queen could be torturing Jack in her absence. *If only she hadn't agreed to go. If only he had forgotten her and left her to her lonely solitude. If only he hadn't fallen in love with her... then he wouldn't be in such danger. It was all her fault. She had put her mother in jeopardy, and now the boy she had promised her heart was being held captive... Why did this keep happening? Why was she so dangerous to love?* The passing hours had left her body weak, but her questions had left her soul truly lost. It was the key she needed to unlock the hidden path that would lead her home. The witch's cabin finally appeared. With a deep sigh of relief, Maleficent ran to open the door. It was dark inside. Everything was covered in dust, like no one had been there in years. A sudden squawk of a crow startled her. It flew to a hooded figure sitting within a dark corner of the room.

125

"Who are you?" Maleficent asked, raising her hand, ready to attack the person who had intruded her home. "What have you done to Mim?!"

"Maleficent?" The hooded woman lifted her head, removing the cloak that hid her face.

It was her mother. Maleficent gasped at her appearance. She looked old; her skin now grey and cracked like ancient stone. Her long silver hair that once shined with a tint of the purest purple now appeared thin and as brittle as her bones. Maleficent felt her breath fail her as she watched the witch stand from a creaking chair. She looked like a complete stranger. Now all that was left of her mother lay within her bright green eyes. The rest was only that of a haggard old witch. "What... What happened to you?"

"I thought... I thought I had lost you forever. Where have you been, my darling girl?"

Maleficent paused, unsure of where to begin. "I-I was with the fairies."

"Are you hurt? Did they harm you?"

"No, but..."

"But what?"

"I went to the Snow Queen's realm."

"The Snow Queen!? Why, Maleficent!?"

"I was taken there in hopes that one in her court might- make a *deal* with me."

The Wood Witch was stunned, "How could you do that? Have you completely lost your mind?"

"No! I did it for true love!"

The Wood Witch's face cracked with anger, "What do you mean- *love?* With whom?"

Maleficent felt a tremble of fear as she answered, "He is a fairy lad."

Mim's eyes widened with rage, "You mean to tell me that you have put me through this hell because you allowed yourself to be lured away by a fairy!? Have I taught you nothing?"

"No, it's not like that! I trust him. We have been meeting in my dreams for years."

"Excuse me!"

"There was no harm in it. It was innocent. I didn't mean to fall in love, but I did. And he loves me. He said that if we are to be together, then I should make a deal with a fairy in hopes that I could live in the Nine Realms with him instead of..."

The Wood Witch nodded in pained understanding, "—instead of *here* with *me.*"

Maleficent looked down.

"Well where is your *love* now? What could have possibly gone wrong in such a noble quest?"

Maleficent looked back up at her, unamused by such a tone. "You know perfectly well what went wrong! Our mission was doomed long before I got there!"

"You should never have attempted to go there in the first place!"

"I wouldn't have if you had told me the truth!"

The witch's heart sunk, "What truth?"

"The Snow Queen told me everything!"

Mim gulped, shaking her head in denial, "No, you cannot believe what she says. She is a liar! They are all liars!"

"Stop it! I know the truth now. I saw it in her magic crystal. She is not the liar! You are! Enough of the secrets!"

With a sigh of great sorrow, and tears rushing to her eyes, the witch sat back down upon her chair.

Her silence seemed to swell Maleficent's anger like a ruthless fever. "You cannot do this to me anymore! Sit there upon your chair, not speaking, not answering me. Don't you see what your secrets have wrought? What terrible pain you have caused me?"

Still the Wood Witch did not answer.

"If you persist in your cruelty, your *silence*, then I can no longer convince myself that you love me?"

Mim hastily raised her gaze towards her, "Of course, I love you. I would rather die than hurt you! I only kept the truth about your parents from you because..."

"What did you say!? My *parents*?"

The Wood Witch closed her eyes. She had said too much. But that's the trouble with lies. No matter how good their speaker intended, once they crumble, all will be revealed.

"Within the Snow Queen's crystal, I learned the truth about my mortal father; the blood he spilled upon her realm and the hatred her Majesty bears towards me. She holds my love captive in her castle, promising to kill him if I do not return with the magic you've kept hidden from me. Am I to understand that amongst all the demons that torture me, I now find that *you* are not really my mother? —Answer me!" She screamed.

"Yes, Maleficent... I am not really your mother."

Maleficent huffed with rage, "Then who is?"

Mim stood once again; her frail body weakening under the power of her gaze, "She is a fairy, a *good* fairy. Your father, well, I cannot lie and say I liked the lad, but I *will* say that he had a good heart... deep, *deep* down, that is."

"And just why did these *kind-hearted* parents abandon me? Why was I raised here in the darkness with *you?*"

"Oh, no, Maleficent, it wasn't like that! You were taken from them."

"By whom? You! Was I just another one of your deals?"

"No... Well, yes. You were taken from your parents by another, but I confess that it *was* a blood debt made by your grandfather that brought you to me."

"My grandfather! Wonderful! What a family! I can't hear anymore! Just tell me where the magic is that the queen seeks so I can save Jack!"

Mim's heart was suddenly struck with crippling horror and shock, "*Jack!* Is that what you said?"

"Yes!"

It suddenly felt as if she were going to explode, "Oh, Maleficent, no! He is an evil trickster! He is the one who took you from your parents!"

Now Maleficent was annoyed, "Are you serious!?" She seethed. "Your desperate reach of a lie not only hurt but offend me! He loves me! He is the only one who loves me!"

"Don't be a fool, child. That demon creature does not love you! You have been deceived. I cannot imagine what he is planning, but darling if you concede to his wishes, I fear it will only bring you great pain and a broken heart."

Maleficent huffed through her nose like a raging dragon, "Enough!"

"No, you must believe me."

"Believe you! Are you mad?! I will never believe another word that spills from your mouth. Why, even your appearance was a lie. Even now, the truth is cracking through your lifeless skin! You look like a corpse; something vile and too wicked to be alive. You mean nothing to me now! Just give me the spell! It's the least you could do!"

Her words caused tears to fall freely upon the witch's stony cheeks; not for herself, but for the bitter pain that she had caused. "I am sorry, child, but I can't do that."

"What! Why?"

"I would do anything for you— if I thought it would make you happy. But if what you wish is to put my magic in the hands of the two most evil souls that exist, then I fear I cannot do it. I won't. They are using you. And they *will* betray you."

In a huff of rage, Maleficent charged the wall where the witch's staff stood, gripping it tightly within her grasp. With possibly the greatest weapon of magic, she pointed its end against its master. "If you don't give it to me, I swear before all the gods that I will kill you!"

Mim shook her head, looking upon her daughter with pity and despair, "I'm sorry, dearie, but the answer is and forever will be— *no.*"

Maleficent's body then burst with green flames; a fire so powerful, one would almost think it came from hell itself. Her rage had turned into a deadly inferno. She raised her hand, ready to unleash it all, "Defend yourself, witch! Cast your worst against me!"

But the Wood Witch simply smiled, shaking her head. She wouldn't fight her. "You'll learn one day that I do this to protect you. I love you." At that, she opened her arms and closed her eyes.

The next moment was one of tragedy. Maleficent blasted her power upon the woman that had raised her and watched her burn within the scorching flames of her fury and bitter hatred. The witch never screamed, but rather happily set her final gaze upon her. The two stared into each other's eyes, all the way to the end. As Mim's ancient body broke apart from the cracks and fell to the floor in dreary ash, Maleficent's unflinching eyes glowed fiercely. A flicker of fear did then pierce her. The witch's body, like a bottle that had broken, that which had been held inside would spill, even if it only be a single drop. It was green, bright green; a smoke that moved quickly towards her. Maleficent backed up, inching closer and closer to the door. She reached behind her, desperately seeking the knob, but it would not turn. Instead, the smoke thickened, rising up before her. A stir of a thousand whispers could be heard but not understood as it moved. Maleficent froze, utterly afraid. She was cornered. She tried to raise her hand; to use her own power to cast it away, but as she opened her mouth to speak her demand, the smoke charged into her throat, smothering away her very breath. In the next moment, she was writhing in utter agony; her body convulsing violently. She dropped the staff and fell to the floor engulfed by the darkness of death. By all vision, the young half-ling appeared dead, with no sign of breath or pulse. Grip urgently flew down to his mistress. But as he bowed his head in devastation, a sudden glow did then appear inside her. The raven's gaze widened as the fluorescent green slowly coursed its way through her spidery veins, moving ever closer towards the silent heart. Watching with fretting spirit, Grip squawked as the glow spread its way into Maleficent's core... And it was in that moment that a strong beat came from the heart, and the emerald eyes of his mistress awakened— each shining with more power and magic than anything the worlds had ever seen.

* * *

When Maleficent arose from the floor, she stood a different person. She was still herself, but with a little something more. Her mother's soul had intertwined itself with hers. She had heard of stealing souls before, but this was not that. No, something else had happened here. Though she did not yet know why, it seemed that in this case, the soul had rather taken control, forcing its way into its chosen vessel. Without hesitance, it had swarmed her. And within mere minutes, it had changed her completely. Maleficent raised her hands before her face. She couldn't see it upon her fair skin, but inside—she could feel her mother's power surging through her body, mind, and even her soul. Suddenly Grip landed upon her shoulder, squawking inquisitively at her new condition. He knew his mistress was still inside her, but there was something about her that frightened him somehow. For though her body stood plainly within the room, the presence of her power felt as if she were a giant taller than any mountain. Maleficent smiled at him, petting his head gently, "It is alright, my pet, it is me." Her voice calmed the raven. He closed his eyes under her gentle touch. Grip wasn't alone in such comfort, for now... She was surrounded by her mother's crows, each eyeing their new mistress.

The haunting gaze they set upon her seemed to unveil the severity of what she had done. She had killed the witch who couldn't be killed. *But why did Mim let her? She could have stopped her if she wanted...* It didn't make sense. And now, in the destruction of the Wood Witch's ancient vessel, her soul had forced its way inside her. *What was she going to do now? What about Jack?* Maleficent suddenly began to panic. *How was she going to find Mim's hidden magic now?* She raced about the cabin, tearing through every room, every shelf, every book, but still she could not find the spell that the Snow Queen desired. With sweat that poured down her face, and her frantic breaths of anxiety climbing, Maleficent studied every written word upon the witch's books and scrolls.

The next torturous hours soon passed and the light from the moon rose into the darkened sky.

Maleficent closed the last of Mim's books in despair. She had scoured every inch of the cottage. There was nothing left, nothing untouched. *Where was it?* With the cabin is utter disarray, Maleficent stood alone. In her impulse, she had destroyed her only chance to save her love and pay penance for her father's terrible crime. She had failed. It seemed that in her death, Mim had gotten her final wish. Maleficent would have to return to the Third Realm empty handed... *Or would she?* It was then, in her moment of bitter frustration, that Maleficent suddenly realized something. She may not have found the Wood Witch's spell, but she had something better- *her powers.* If the Snow Queen didn't release her love, she would just have to take him from her. With a smile most wicked, Maleficent reached out her hand, bringing the tall powerful staff into her grasp. "Come, my darling," she called to Grip as the cabin door flew open. "Let's fly!"

The Wood Witch may have lied to Maleficent about many things, but she was right about one thing... once she had enough power, she wouldn't need wings to fly. Like a whirlwind of a deadly storm, her body disappeared within the air. Within mere moments, the void of a black hole appeared within the snowy realm. Her presence was enough to completely shock the entire court. The fairies, the gnomes, the elves, they all fled to the Icy Citadel. They didn't know what was happening; only that something about her had changed. She walked upon the glittering frost with oppressive force. The long-tattered train of her black gown cast a growing shadow of darkness upon the land behind her.

Step by step, Maleficent made her way towards the palace; with a sinister grin and a fierce glow that burned deep within her eyes. Soon the realm appeared empty; each creature hiding within the castle. Still, she took her time, walking at a slow and eerie pace. For though it was but a taste of it, she found that she *enjoyed* their fear. No longer would they look at her like some ugly weak thing. No longer could they think themselves above her. No longer would she have to be afraid. She may still be an outcast amongst them, but it was now because they were below her. And therefor, she reveled in every single moment of their terror.

"What is going on?" Pan asked hurriedly.

"It's Maleficent! She's back! Disappear! Now!"

He didn't understand what was going on, but he did as she said. With a twist of his staff, he was gone, and not a moment too soon. For it was then that the doors of the Icy Citadel flew open and a murder of crows came swarming through. The tiny black creatures screeched and squawked, flapping their feathered wings in aggression. The Unseelie Court ducked in fear, each fluttering to their queen for protection.

The Snow Queen stood from her throne, angered by the chaos exploding within her beautiful castle. "Enough!" She screamed, slamming her staff to the icy ground. But still, the crows never stopped. The entire palace was filled. It was as if every crow of the mortal world had followed her here. But how? All of the court screamed, looking to their queen for help. "I said! — Enough!" She said slamming down her staff once more, this time with more force.

But still... the crows did not listen.

Suddenly, above all the sounds of the panicked fairies, above all the fluttering and flapping of her darling's wings, above the words of frustration that uttered from the queen's breath, a wicked laugh did then roar. It echoed through the chilly air, getting louder and louder by the second. It sounded like it was coming from everywhere; a *sound* that carried such terror that it made blood run cold.

A thunderous clap of Maleficent's staff then struck the floor, and all the crows were finally called to a halt. Like two massive curtains of blackened feathers, a dashing division revealed their new mistress. The Snow Queen gazed upon the crows that covered the palace walls in darkness. The white castle was now shouted in black, and it left the queen incandescent with rage. "What is this!?" She asked. "How did you..." Suddenly she saw it- the Wood Witch's staff in the Dark Fairy's hand.

Maleficent smiled at the queen's gawking gaze, slowly twirling the staff within her grasp. "You look surprised to see me, Your Majesty."

Snow White composed herself before her subjects, "I, I hadn't thought you would arrive so soon after our meeting. But fear not, I am most pleased by your return. Have you brought me the witch's spell? I am eager to hear how you were able to obtain it— along with *other* things."

"I'm afraid my dear mother was not willing to aid me in my mission you so graciously bestowed upon me. She offered no token of love, but rather decided to feed me more of her poisonous lies. It was most tragic, actually— for in my anger towards her, I- *killed* her."

The Snow Queen's breath felt as if it had been suddenly ripped from her body. "You lie! You don't possess the power to do such a thing! It's impossible!"

Maleficent smiled, "The old woman was brittle and weak from the grief that weighed on her conscience. She accepted her fate willingly, believing that with her death, I would have no way of saving my love from your icy prison... But she was wrong. I admit that in my impulsiveness, I destroyed the only person who could hand me the magic you desire. I tried to find it, but alas, I could not. At first, I admit I was distraught, but then I realized I didn't need the spell or King Stefan's princess to get Jack back; I will simply just take him by force."

The Snow Queen went red with rage, "You're serious! You really killed her! Do you realize what you have done?! You have not only failed me, but you have unleashed a darkness upon us all!"

Maleficent turned up her chin and squinted her eyes in suspicion. "What are you talking about?"

The queen scoffed at her ignorance, "I speak of the witch's soul, you, fool! Mim's vessel was the only thing keeping the Erlking's black magic from spilling over the lands like an evil poison. She has spent all her life trying to contain it— and *you* set it free!" Maleficent looked down at her hands, feeling the power surging inside her. The Snow Queen grew uneasy with her pause. "What? What is it?" It was then, as Maleficent looked up with her emerald eyes; each glowing with the magic of the ancient witch, that she finally understood. "*No!* It can't be!"

Maleficent smiled wickedly, "Yes... Mim's soul now lives within me. *I*—hold all the power now!" The Unseelie Court gasped in fear as she rose her hands above her. "Now give me back my love or I'll cover your little white realm in darkness."

But the Snow Queen slowly shook her head, "I'm afraid your wrong again, little girl. You may hold a piece of the powerful four, but let me tell you what I have... I have the love of your life hidden!"

The surrounding court, though loyal, were getting a little anxious. For beneath their elegant tone, there swells a dark and deadly current. Maleficent scoffed at her poor play, "I'll find him."

"You can't."

"And why is that?"

"Because despite your heinous acts, you still have mortal blood coursing through your veins; a fact that prevents you from dwelling within our magical realms. You'll go mad before you find him. Not that it matters-really."

"What do you mean?"

The Snow Queen smiled, "Well, I speak of *my* charms, of course. With a mere twinkle of my eyes, I can make your love fall hopelessly in love with me. Touch my realm, and I will make you watch as he pours his heart into my hands."

Maleficent suddenly felt seized by shock, "No, you wouldn't dare!"

With a sinister chuckle uttered from her cold breath, the queen sat back down upon her throne. "Oh, sweetheart, I took my own sister's true love from her when she refused to give up her power and banished her to a world full of mad creatures. And I love my sister! What do you think I would do to you if you cross me?" Maleficent squinted her glowing gaze, huffing through her nose with fury. The vision of her frustration brought the queen a sensation of pleasure she hadn't felt in years; not since Hook had taken her happiness away from her. "Don't let the glittering frost fool you, my dear. There can only be one queen of darkness— and you're looking at her. If you wish to get your true love back, you will give the power of the Madam Mim to me!"

Maleficent gripped her staff tightly in her hand. She loved Jack, but did she love her power more? It was question that would prove to be the hardest she would have to answer. But at the end, the word that came from her crimson lips were: "Never."

The Snow Queen shook her head, Fine! Keep your power! Go live your wretched lonely life within the mortal world. But be careful... For the power you now have inside you will be hunted, and there's no little cabin for you to hide in anymore. The legendary three *will* come for you! And as for myself, I will take great pleasure adding Jack's loving heart to my treasured collection." The crowd of fairies within the palace then drew their wands, each glowing by the colors of all imagined beauty. They inched closer, with eyes most menacing. Maleficent turned her gaze, seeing the court closing in around her. "Get rid of her and call the three!" The queen commanded. "Now that the witch is dead, I will get my daughter back by some other means."

But before the Unseelie fairies could reach her, Maleficent struck her staff against the frozen ground, blasting them to the walls. She looked back up to the throne once more and pointed upon it with her staff's end. "Don't sick your pathetic ruffians upon me, Snow White! I'll go back to my world, but what you forget is this... The vessel you need is to be born within my realm, beyond your grasp!"

The queen quickly rose to her feet, "You leave her alone. I will not have her taken away by your filthy blood again! She is mine!"

"Oh, you'll never get your hands on her! She'll die by my own design! If you think you are wicked, you haven't seen anything yet! So, let it be heard by one and all, that when it comes to true evil, I am the Mistress of it all!" At that, the crows came, and in a swirl of darkness, Maleficent disappeared, leaving only the sound of her cruel laughter to haunt the Icy Citadel and the screaming queen she left behind.

When Maleficent reappeared within the mortal world, she was stunned to find that the Forbidden Forest had completely changed in her absence. It was bright, green, and lively. The fog had disappeared, and the darkness had been evaporated by sunshine. The once pale birch trees that reached high into the sky were now thick and bursting with vibrant leaves. The bushes below them were covered in delicious berries and blooming flowers. The light that shone like beams between the trees seemed to glow upon the forest. It was as if she had entered the world that had lain within the realm of her dreams. It was beautiful and yet something deep inside her hated it. She raised her hand before her face, trying to block the sunshine from her eyes.

"Find the cabin— now," she commanded her pets, but even the crows didn't fit in these woods anymore. They flitted through the air, frantically searching for the hidden cottage of the old witch... but it was gone. It seemed that it and the Forbidden Forest from which it formally dwelled had disappeared, and in its place, there stood the charming existence of the dreamy woods that was filled with enchanting brilliance. Just as her anger was swelling like a fever throughout majestic land around her, she saw something off in the distance. She had never seen it for herself before; she only heard about it from her mother. But now, without the foggy hills and dreary darkness, she could finally see King Stefan's castle. It stood tall and glorious beyond the trees. The flags marked with a rose flew proudly in the cool breeze from the top of the towers. It was then that Maleficent remembered what she had vowed before the entire Unseelie Court. *The princess would be born soon... but could she go through with it? Could she really kill an innocent child?*

The Snow Queen on the hand was not taking any chances. To her, Maleficent had proved that she was not the easily manipulated chess piece that they thought she would be but had turned into quite the worthy

141

adversary. Being the daughter of Hook, the Snow Queen didn't doubt her new evil ambitions. She would have to act fast if she were going to be able to secure her daughter's future vessel, but that was not the hardest obstacle in her way. She would have to find Mim's ancient magic that was hidden within the elusive cabin before Maleficent could get to it. Luckily, she knew exactly where the little cottage was... where it had been since the night the Wood Witch scorched the forest ground. If only Maleficent had listened to her mother said. She told her that the cabin couldn't be moved; that it could only be hidden. But Maleficent hadn't counted on the beautiful illusion that now covered the Forbidden Forest or who had been the one to put it there. In truth, the answer to such a riddle was shining down upon the trees. If only she knew about the truth about the mischievous sunshine and the deep seed of doubt that ached inside her. If only...

CHAPTER SIX

THE THREE FAIRIES

The news of the Wood Witch's passing didn't take long to spread; nor was her killer kept a secret. But the first to learn of Mim's demise was none other than the three little fairies she had cursed on the night of the woodland party. Flora, Fauna, and Merryweather were older now, though not much bigger in size. Each were only about a foot tall and wore a hat and formal gown that matched their magical glow. For years they did the witch's bidding, only using their power for good. But despite all their efforts, they had never found something to fill the void of losing their kind, their mother, and most importantly— their ability to indulge their cruel nature.

They had gone before the Elders many times seeking their help; hoping they might help to restore their home within the woods, but no one would dare step in the Forbidden Forest; not if it meant crossing the wrong witch. Then as fate would have it, the very forest that held their cursed kind upon the scorched bit of earth had been *changed* by something very, very, powerful. The three fairies had been outcast, pitied and rejected by all others within the Nine Realms; their mark cast by the witch had not only taken them away from their mother, it had left them utterly alone.

The Snow Queen had heard of their tragic encounter from Pan when it happened all those years ago. Up until now, she had merely thought of them as stupid misfits. But now, as the only creatures that hated Maleficent as much as she did, she saw them as the perfect pawns to use on the board. But first things first... She would have to send them a proper invitation. She sent a message in a white whispering light, summoning each of them to her castle. It was an invitation they couldn't refuse. For though they were afraid of her, they each knew that if they didn't appear, she would send something far less polite after them.

Without delay, Flora, Fauna, and Merryweather made their way towards the Third Realm, and into the Icy Citadel that belonged to one of the most dangerous creatures alive. Upon entering the tall crystal doorway, the three small fairies nervously floated towards the frosted throne. They had never seen the Snow Queen before, and she was quite an intimidating vision to behold. The sisters each took a deep breath as they approached her.

"Hello, my little dears. Thank you for coming."

Flora and Fauna looked at each other anxiously before answering, "It is an honor to be here, Your Majesty."

The Snow Queen then turned her gaze to the one fairy that didn't respond. "What about you? Aren't you happy to be here in my castle?"

Flora and Fauna nervously looked at their sister. They shook their heads; their eyes widening in fear. Merryweather had always been too spunky for her own good.

"It is not exactly like we had much of a choice in the matter. Let us just skip the pleasantries, shall we? What are we doing here?"

The Snow Queen smirked, "Tisk- Tisk- Tisk... Oh, my dear, we wouldn't want to stop being polite. After all, you are not here by my capture. You were invited; a gesture I only offered because you three are the daughters of a fellow queen. Though the other within the realms have not treated you with the respect that you deserve, the loss of your mother does not change what you are— *fairy royalty*. We are practically family, you and I."

"Really?" Merryweather said sarcastically. "Family?"

"Merryweather, stop it!" Flora said sternly.

But the blue pixie did no such thing. "No, Flora, I will not," she said looking back up at the queen. "You say we're family! Then why didn't you help us? We came to your realm once before... Do you remember that? We came through the veil, but no one in your court would help us! You wouldn't even see us! Now, all of the sudden we are treated like royal guest. Something is up, and *I* for one would like to know what it is."

Fauna suddenly felt like she was going to burst with panic, "We're so sorry, your Majesty. Please forgive my sister. We..."

But the Snow Queen raised her hand, silencing her instantly. "No, she is right."

"What?" Flora asked.

"There is a reason I have called you here. There is something I want you to do, something that will serve you as well as myself."

"And what is that?" Merryweather asked with a snotty tone.

"The one responsible for the curse that was cast upon your family, your mother- is going to try to destroy my one chance to get my daughter back. I need your help to stop her."

"Why should we?" Merryweather replied.

"Because if you do, I will lift the curse of the Woodland Party. You could have your realm back, your *mother* back."

The little blue pixie huffed in defeat. It seemed the Snow Queen had said the magic words she needed to hear. There was nothing she or her sisters wouldn't do to get back their family under the twinkling trees. "What do we have to do?"

Fauna shook, "We cannot fight her. The witch's curse..."

"If you do exactly as I tell you, you won't have to fight her. Do we have a deal?"

The three sisters looked at each other once more before answering bravely, "Yes, we will do as you command."

The Snow Queen nodded, "Good. Now here is what I need you to do— King Stefan is losing the war. The crops and land around the kingdom are failing. His reign has tragically befallen a terrible span of misfortune; all by my own design."

"Yours? Why?" Merryweather asked.

"Because I needed him to be desperate, willing to do anything or give up anything to turn his luck around. I need him to make a deal; one that would deliver me his newborn princess."

The three fairies looked at each other in disbelief, "I don't think we can..."

"You said we should skip the pleasantries, so here it is... I *order* you to go to King Stefen's castle and make the deal with him. Give him his glorious victory, restore his kingdom, and in return, you will take the newborn princess. Make sure she belongs to me! Do you all understand?"

The severity of her tone made the three sisters quiver. Even Merryweather didn't hesitate in her answer. "Yes, Your Majesty."

* * *

The Snow Queen had been right about the darkness within Maleficent. It was indeed spreading. And though she allowed her explosive anger to get the better of her, causing her to act impulsively, much like her own father, she also has her mother's kindness that sparkled like a star within her heart. But even the brightest of twinkling stars can burn out. As Maleficent made her way towards King Stefen's castle under the beautiful rays of sunlight, a growing uneasiness began to befall her. The reality of what she had promised to do had already begun to haunt her soul. Sure, she hated the

Snow Queen for what she had done, but maybe she could prevent the queen from getting the child by other means; one less cruel. The Snow Queen had counted on the king's misfortune. But what if it were naught. Surely, the king and queen would then have no need to sacrifice their daughter for the sake of their kingdom. Maleficent had never met any humans, and while she had never heard anything good about mortals and their ways, she wanted to believe that the parents would want to keep their daughter. It was this hope that clinched its way around what good was left within the Dark Fairy, and though the king and queen didn't know it yet, it would be this very decision that would frame the future of the Rose Kingdom, be that of glory or shrouded in a terrible darkness.

As Maleficent drew closer to the castle bridge, the standing guards, both above and below gasped in fear upon facing her frightening appearance. But though their eyes looked upon her curved horns and a black gown that trained long behind her, it was her terrifyingly beautiful face that stole their breath; for her eyes shined with that of the ancient witch.

It was her, the witch's killer. They tried to raise their horns, sending out alarm, but no sound did then emerge. The confused men tried again, but not a sound came. Instead, the guards were stunned to find that the bridge was lowering. The men looked amongst each other, but no one had a hand on the lever. It was her. She was moving it. Their fears mounted as the reality came clear... *Magic is here.* Each of the guards ran inside, urgently announcing to the court of their coming visitor. As Maleficent made her way into the castle, all within the palace gasped in horror upon seeing her menacing allure. The nobles parted as she walked into the throne room towards King Stefan and his sweet wife, Queen Leah. The royal couple tried to remain calm as any rulers should be, but there was something about her. It wasn't just that her eyes were glowing green and she had curved demonic horns that came from her head. It was the shadow that spread slowly behind her, growing to monstrous proportions. There was a terrible ominous feeling that came from it, like pain, sadness, and overwhelming anger. Maleficent couldn't help but gaze at all those that stood in awe around her. She had never set eyes upon a mortal before this moment. They were odd, ugly even. Each had different hair, eyes, shape, and height, and though they all were dressed in what should have been a most elegant fabric, colorful and refined, they instead all looked as drab and dreary as the castle walls around them. The men looked frumpy and frail, plagued with the fate of fatigue and misfortune. The women were no different; though due to their vain nature, they hid under their striking makeup and drowning themselves in the overpowering scents of perfume. It seemed that even the rich had fallen with the unfortunate fate of the gloomy land. For Maleficent, the humans were almost too wretched to look upon. And yet, as she turned her sights to their widening eyes, she could see that unmistakable gaze of judgement and disgust. Nevertheless, she approached the royal couple with a sharp smile and left the monstrous shadow behind her. "Greetings, Your Majesties."

"Who are you? How did you get in here?" King Stefan asked fiercely, reaching his hand out to his pregnant queen.

"Fear not, King Stefan. For I come here today to offer you a peaceful alliance. One that will benefit not only you and your kingdom, but also your future princess."

Queen Leah stood from her throne in alarm, "What do you mean? What of my daughter?"

"If you truly mean us no harm, then announce yourself before your betters properly," King Stefan commanded.

Maleficent couldn't help but laugh, "I'm afraid you are dreadfully mistaken, sir, you are *not* my better."

"Then you are royalty?" The queen asked.

"Of course, she is not! She's not even human!" King Stefan exclaimed harshly.

Maleficent cringed trying not lose her temper, "It is true, I am not mortal. I am a fairy."

"Liar! You are no fairy! Do you think me a fool? Do you think I do not know what truth lies behind those legendary eyes? You killed the Wood Witch! Don't deny it!"

The court gasped in fear as she rose her hands. "I deny nothing, nor have I lied. I *am* a fairy. I am also a great sorceress. And while *what* I am should be of great importance to you, you should also understand that I am not here as a threat, but rather to help you and *your child.*"

Before King Stefan could utter another word, the queen stepped towards her bravely, "How?"

"I know that Your Majesty has sought the help of my kind to restore your kingdom to its former glory. It is no secret that your fortune and land have suffered. You are losing the war. Your coffers are empty, and your people are sick and starving."

"Have you come to help us?" The queen asked.

"I have. I will return your kingdom to glory, restore all your riches, and bring life back to your land. Your people will be healed, your crops will grow, and your reign will be named the greatest of this era."

"And in return?" King Stefan asked suspiciously.

"I happen to know that Your Majesty has sought the help of magic to aid you in these desperate times. I also happen to know that you would be willing to give up your precious princess to ensure the future of your kingdom."

"What! No! We would never..." The queen looked to her husband, but with a single glance of his grief, she knew it was true. "You! How could you? Our daughter!"

The King stood from his throne fiercely, looking down at her with a stern scowl. For though he loved her dearly, he could not abide being scolded or shamed in front of his entire court. "Enough! I am king and I will do what I must to protect the crown! We can always have more children, but I only have one kingdom!"

Queen Leah fell to her seat in dismay, tears falling down her pale cheeks.

"Do not fret, Your Majesty, for there is another way, but you have to do exactly what I say."

Queen Leah looked up in hope, "Yes, I'll do anything to keep my child, to protect her. What must we do?"

"I will give you all that you wish, and all I ask in return is that you never, *ever* deal with a creature of magic again. No matter what! Never! Do you understand me?!"

Queen Leah smiled and nodded rapidly, "Of course, yes, we will do as you command! Won't we, husband?"

Stefan slowly sat back down upon his throne. He couldn't help but feel suspicious of such a noble deed. Still, he knew he couldn't deny his wife in her fragile state. The child was his only bargaining chip after all. He looked out the nearest window, at all the devastation that laid below. "How do I know that you will do as you promised? How do I know that you won't just disappear and then I am stuck with no way to deal with another?"

Maleficent smiled and shook her head, "Why, King Stefan, are you saying I look untrustworthy?"

Queen Leah rushed to her feet once more, "Oh, no..."

But Maleficent simply smiled and clanked her staff against the castle floor, and from the orb at its end came a green smoke that filled the air.
"From the seas to the sands,
I call all magic to this land
Green the grass

Let thou roses bloom
Bring glory to the King
That dwells in this room
Bring color and riches
To one and all
May your army be vast
And never fall
Feed the hungry
And heal the sick
May your crops
Grow full and thick
Fill the wells
With sparkling water
And let your rule
Never falter
With these gifts
Comes a small price
That you dare not dabble
In magic twice

...Do you accept my deal with thee?"

Both the King and Queen nodded in fear.

"Then from my lips, so shall it be."

It was then that the smoke swarmed around her
and her darling crows, and like the swirl of magic that
brought her to the castle grounds, the smoke carried
her and her shadow out into the air. The king and
queen rushed to the windows, as did their fellow court,

and from their view from up above they watched as the green smoke turned their dreary land into a glorious kingdom; one full of life, and of course, beautiful roses of red and white.

* * *

Sometimes it seems that no matter how hard you try, there is always something or *someone* that gets in your way. It wasn't that the three fairies weren't fast, they were, but as it turned out, they just weren't quick enough. By the time Flora, Fauna, and Merryweather reached the Rose Kingdom, it wasn't covered in the dreary misfortune that the Snow Queen had cast upon it. Instead, the three fairies were confronted by an overwhelming vision of beauty and charm.

"What happened here?" Fauna asked.

"How should I know, Fauna? Did you forget that we've been together this whole time?" Flora snapped.

"Don't yell at her, Flora. We can see what happened here... What we don't know is *how*. What are we going to do now?" Merryweather asked.

"What do mean?" Fauna asked feeling confused.

"She means how are we going to make the deal with King Stefan now?" Flora answered with a tone overwhelmed by stress.

"We have to tell the Snow Queen!" Fauna said in a shaky voice.

Flora and Merryweather knew she was right. At that, the three sisters flew down into the nearby forest and gathered beneath the trees. In a perfect triangle they brought their wands together. And from their glows of blue, red, and green came a magical orb. Then in unison, the sisters uttered the words they dreaded to say...

"Into the magical nine
Guide us into veil three
Beyond the frost
Show us the queen."

Suddenly, the glowing orb turned ice cold and the vision of the crowned Snow White emerged within. "Who is this? Who dares summon me?" She screamed, sending chills up the sister's spines.

"It is us, Your Majesty, Flora, Fauna, and Merryweather. Something has... Something has happened," Flora stuttered fearfully.

"What could have possibly gone wrong? I sent you to do a very simple task! I have set everything up for you to make the deal! So, go and make it!" She commanded harshly.

Fauna suddenly felt as if she was going to bust out in tears. She tried to speak but couldn't seem to get a word past her quivering lip. Merryweather hated seeing her poor sister in such a frantic state. "Actually! Your Majesty! By the time we got here to do our *simply little task*- we found that the kingdom is not in the devastated conditions that you promised!" Merryweather yelled back.

"What?!" The Snow Queen snapped.

"You heard me! It seems it is Stefan's kingdom that is *perfect*- not your plan! What do you expect us to do now? For it appears the land has reached its glory... all without *our* help."

The orb cracked like frosted glass from the queen's rage as she walked towards her magic crystal to see for herself. But as she gazed upon King Stefan's castle, all she saw was a radiant kingdom void of a single hope or desire. It was glorious, absolutely glorious. "It took me years to cause such destruction. My strength weakened from turning the winds of war against the king. I've wrought absolute devastation upon his land; merciless droughts, wreaking his ships, and even casting plagues that led to thousands of deaths. I rot their food and poisoned their waters! Do you understand how hard this all was? How many days I've slept in need of restoring my strength. I used the full reach of my powers to do this! All so that I could get my daughter back! How could it all suddenly be so... Wait! This is Maleficent's doing! It has to be!"

Flora, being the most sensible of the group, spoke up, "Well, we clearly cannot make a deal for this child. We will just have to find another. We needn't lose our heads."

"Yes, that's all we have to do; just find another baby!" Fauna said gleefully. "We can do that!"

"No, you idiots! It has to be *this* child! This baby!" The queen roared.

"Why?" Asked all three sisters.

The Snow Queen sighed at their insolence, "Because the vessel I need must be born upon the magical soil of the Rose Kingdom. It is where my sister and I were born. There won't be another first- born princess born within the kingdom for many ages to come, and I cannot wait any longer! I won't! One way or another, this child must be mine!"

"Well I don't see how?" Merryweather spouted. "It is not as if the king will make a deal with us now."

The Snow Queen huffed with frustration, "If you cannot make a deal for the child, then you are just going to have to steal it!"

"Steal it!?" Merryweather screamed as if shocked.

"How, Your Majesty?" Flora asked. "We cannot use our powers for evil. The Wood Witch may be dead, but her magic is still very much alive. The curse she laid upon us all those years ago still hinder us even now."

"Then you three are going to have to do it without magic! But you are going to do it! Because if you don't, I promise to cast a curse upon you something so torturous- that it will make what happened to your family look like a gift!"

"But how would we even get into the palace?" Fauna said, biting the tips of her fingernails.

"You three are known across the lands as the fairies of good deeds! Surely, you can figure something out! Now go! Do what you must! Am I clear?"

"Yes, Your Majesty," the three answered in unison.

"Good. Because the next time you summon me, it had better be with my daughter in your arms."

With her last words spoken, the orb fell to the ground and shattered like broken glass; each piece still glittering from the frost. The three fairies looked up at one another, though none uttered a single word. They didn't need to. For each of the sister's knew what must be done. And they also knew that before they could fly an inch above the forest, they were going to clean the icy glass that laid broken upon the ground; they were woodland fairies after all. Keeping the forest clean and beautiful was in their nature, so leaving something as horrible as glass upon the ground was completely out of the question. But with a few little zaps from their wands, the broken shards were turned to flowers, and the fairies were on their way.

* * *

The first night after Maleficent's return to the mortal world, she was faced with a terrible realization; one so harsh that it couldn't even be softened by her recent victory. It hit the very same moment she left the palace. Where was she going to go? She had lost her home. On one hand, she was free. She could finally travel the world with no walls or mother to restrain her. But on the other hand, if what the Snow Queen said was true, then being out in the open was a dangerous game to play. *She said that I am to be hunted... But by who? Where?*

It was an unnerving feeling not knowing who might be lurking behind every corner, every tree, and shadow. Odd as it might be, the only comfort Maleficent could find with such overwhelming vulnerability was darkness, secluded darkness. But where? The answer she sought could only be found in one thing— her magic. With one last glance of disgust at the forest where she had been raised, she raised her staff and called out the words that would bring her to her future home...

"Take me to the darkest land
That looks out to the black sea
Take me to a lonely place
That eyes have never seen
And from its shadows present a castle
One that is strong and tall
For I am coming home
The great mistress of all."

At that, her crooked staff glowed fierce with power. But just before the green could pull her from the edge of the forest, she looked over to her darling pets. "I'm sorry, my loves, but a few of you must stay and watch over the castle. The Snow Queen won't give up in her efforts so easily. I have ruined her plan, but her ambition is strong."

The Dark Fairy's murder of crows obeyed and divided by her command. And with the same swirl of smoke that brought her to the Forbidden Forest, Maleficent disappeared. She didn't know exactly where she was going to end up, but it didn't matter because it was going to be a home, a castle within a land that now belonged only to her. Like the portals to the Nine Realms, Maleficent felt herself tunneling towards her destination, but it was not to be one of magic, but rather a place covered in darkness. At long last, Maleficent emerged upon the top of a rocky cliff. She could hear the sound of the crashing waves below her, but she could not see within the blanket of black that surrounded her. So, she lifted her staff, and called out to the clouds, "Move!"

It seemed that even the clouds feared her, for they quickly moved away, far beyond her sight, leaving only the sparkling stars that they had so enviously hidden until this night. The stars twinkled happily within the dark sky; each admiring their long-forgotten refection that shined upon the deep black sea. Beautiful as they were though, there was nothing more glorious than that of the full moon. Ever since she was a little girl, she had admired its magnificence. It was nice to see it from somewhere outside her locked window. Now, with its luminescence shining down upon the land, she could find her way to the castle that stood upon the top of the rocky mountain.

With Grip at her side, she made her way up the stoned steps that would take her to her new home. With each step she took, she could feel herself feeling more pleased with herself. *How quickly things have changed*, she thought. Her mind raced with flashes of everything that had happened: her mother, the truth about her parents, losing Jack to the Snow Queen, losing her home and forest... but more than anything- she could not help but question her kindness towards the king and queen. After all, humans were not to be trusted. Still, this wasn't just an act of faith, they were bound to the deal they struck. *Right?*

Her thoughts quickly began to twist and turn in her chaotic mind. On one hand, she had brought the entire Rose Kingdom to their knees with only a glimpse of her power, but on the other, she couldn't help feeling that she had gone too easy on the Snow Queen. She had taken her love and yet she had spared hers. Jack was, after all, still being held prisoner within the Icy Citadel, and the thought of him actually falling in love with the ever-desirable queen. Maleficent knew she had the power to do it. Ugh, it was too frightful, too unbearable to think about. *If only I could find the witch's books of magic, I could use one of her spells to find him! There must be a way! There must!* Her thoughts seemed to suffuse her all the way to the top of the mountain; all had made the journey utterly exhausting. By the time she reached the doorway to her dark castle, Maleficent had barely taken her first step in before she collapsed. But before her tired body could hit the hard-rocky floor, a swarm of her crows came to her aid and carried her to a massive bed in a nearby chamber. In truth, Maleficent hadn't thought of such things before her arrival, but Grip, her darling familiar, had. The loyal raven hadn't near the same power that his mistress did, but they had always been connected.

After placing her upon the thick feathered bed, Grip took his place at her side, upon a wooden perch that came up from the ground beside her. At long last, the Dark Fairy took her rest, but the dream world would prove to be far different than she remembered. There was no sunshine that would be there to greet her, for there was no longer her love that had always been there to brighten her sad dreary life. But from the darkness of her slumber there came a painful clash. It felt as if memories were trying to fight their way into her mind. But they came like flashes; too many and too fast did they storm. And through it all there was a voice that came too; one familiar and yet too distant of a whisper to understand. Maleficent desperately tried to slow everything down, but like in all dreams, she learned that they can quickly turn into a nightmare. Sweat quickly began to pour down her head as the chaos mounted within. The colors, the memories, the voice, it was growing, racing faster and faster until finally Maleficent woke in a frightful scream. The overwhelming swarm of pain, memories, and magic expelled from her like a sickness then.

When it was all over, Maleficent felt as if she hadn't rested at all. But that's how it is with nightmares. They are vivid, terrible, and worst of all— they linger.

Grip rushed to her in alarm. Seeing the worry in his deep onyx eyes, she pat his head. "It's alright, my darling. It's over now. It's over."

The raven didn't know what had happened or what she was talking about but took comfort in her assurance. As Maleficent weakly rose to her feet, he made his way to her shoulder. His sweetness made her smile, however faintly, as she slowly walked out of her bed chambers and into a vast open room within the castle. There, just as she had cast, was a magnificent throne. It sat alone within the dark room, but as she sat upon its seat, she saw before her a large open window. There was no glass, nor a lock upon its frame, only the rocky edge of her castle. And out beyond the palace walls, she found the most beautiful sight of her life. It was the deep black sea, moving constant and serene. The smell of the salty waters brought a calm to her heart. And though there was nothing else within her castle, not a bell, book, or candle... she suddenly felt like she had everything she would ever need. If only her love was there to share it with her.

The moon and the stars still shined as if not an hour had passed. It seemed that she had found her own corner of the world. By her magic, she would live in darkness; a place where the sun would never rise. She felt it was the only way to be close to *him,* and the dreams they shared under her Luna's shine; before everything in her life turned into a nightmare.

* * *

Though the three fairies knew they had no choice in the matter, they couldn't help but worry about how they were going to accomplish their wicked charge. Before they could emerge from the forest, they needed to decide how to properly enact their plan. Of course, Fauna was the most nervous of them all. "What are we going to say? What are we going to do? Are we *actually* going to try to steal a baby?"

"You heard the queen, Fauna! We have to!" Merryweather screamed.

"Calm down, you two! We may not like it, but we must do as she says. And let us not forget that if we succeed— then we will be in the Snow Queen's favor. We will be the ones that delivered her what no one could! Her daughter! Don't you know what that means?" Flora asked excitedly.

But both of her sisters merely looked at her with annoyed confusion, answering together, "What!?"

"We will no longer be the *three little fairies* everyone pities- we will finally have the respect we deserve. The witch's curse won't matter anymore! We will be famous amongst the Nine Realms and maybe even get our mother back! The Snow Queen said that if she gets the old witch's spell books, she will have the power to restore the Woodlands, and I believe her!"

The very thought brought a smile to her sister's tearful faces. But as Merryweather turned her hopeful gaze back up towards King Stefan's castle, her frown returned. "Well, that was a very *inspiring* speech, Flora, but somehow it failed to answer our question! How are we going to get *into* the castle, and get a new-born baby *out* of it?"

"Well... I am glad you asked." Flora said in an arrogant tone.

But Merryweather was in no mood for her sister's righteous manner. In fact, she was getting quite annoyed, "Flora! That's all we have asked! Repeatedly!"

"Fauna's shaky voice suddenly jumped in, "Now, now, Merryweather, calm down. If our sister has thought of a solution, then we should by all means hear what she has to say."

"Fine," Merryweather uttered under her breath.

Flora huffed with frustration, but she was too excited about her idea to let her sister's temper ruin it. "In her angered words, the queen gave us the answer.

164

She said that we are known across the lands as the fairies of good deeds. She's right! So that is what we will use. We will arrive to the palace offering blessings upon the child. They won't suspect any threat. And when nightfall comes, when everyone is asleep, we will very quietly, very carefully- sneak the child out through her nursery window."

Merryweather and Fauna looked at each other; each still suffused with worry and doubt, but their sister had always led them, and it wasn't as if they had any better ideas. So, they nodded in agreement. The plan was set. And from the edge of the Forbidden Forest, the three fairies flew towards the magnificent castle of King Stefan and his expecting queen.

The three didn't want to risk being turned away at the gate, so they used their magic to make themselves even smaller. So small, in fact, that they could have slipped through any crack of the wall or flown under any door. The hardest part was trying not to glow. It was just something that happened when using their magic and making yourself as tiny as a flea was no exception. Their best bet was to hurry inside the palace as quickly as possible. Once the three were past the castle gate, they needed to get into the throne room, but it was heavily guarded. Flora and Merryweather were quick and buzzed by the guards without notice. But like all of those who enter danger with nervousness and doubt, poor Fauna hesitated. Shaking before a standing guard at the doorway, her tiny green light began to glow. Merryweather and Flora turned in fright to find their precious sister floating in fear right before his eyes. The two gasped, afraid of what might happen next. But just as Merryweather lifted her wand, the guard waved his hand before his face, speaking in good humor, "That is odd. How did a firefly get in here? Shoo, bug! Shoo! Shoo!" The danger of his large swatting hand broke Fauna from her frozen state. She flew to her sisters, both taking a deep breath of relief as her light began to dim once more. Without a spoken word, the three continued forward, and within a few moments, they were there— floating before the thrones of the king and queen. The three sisters silently flew behind a nearby chandelier. The royal couple were speaking to someone, discussing matters of state. It seemed that all of the surrounding kingdoms had gone from enemies to allies; each wanting to honor and celebrate the coming princess. The most eager of all was none other than King Hubert. How strange it was to see two men who had just been the greatest of foes mere days ago suddenly behave like the best of friends. In truth, King Hubert had been thought to win the war, but now with his terrible loss of victory and only one heir to his throne, with his late queen dead and his age already so high, he was desperate to make a proper match for his son, little Prince Phillip. The pair could finally seal the alliance between the two most powerful kingdoms once and for all. And though King Stefan hadn't truly forgiven King Hubert for the devastation he had caused his land, he knew that Prince Phillip was indeed an excellent match for his new daughter. Even still, Stefan couldn't help but enjoy this moment of humiliation for his rival. And it gave him a glorious idea.

"I will agree to your proposal of such a match on two conditions."

Hubert was instantly insulted by his words, but smiled humbly before responding, "Of course, brother, what is it you wish from me?"

"It is not a wish, but rather a demand, I'm afraid. Your son may have my daughter's hand in marriage... If you give up your right to her dowry."

King Hubert was stunned, "But— That is not the proper..."

"And! — You must present your proposal and gift for the princess before all the surrounding kingdoms!"

"All of them?"

"Yes! All of them! I think it would put to ease to see you display such an act of loyal submission."

King Hubert's face went red with suppressed rage. For the events of late made no sense to him at all. He had been on the winning side of the war for years. Then suddenly, his ships fell to the fate of terrible storms, and his soldiers rapidly became too ill to fight. His most trusted and knowledgeable of advisers left him. And now, with no ambassador to make proper arrangements for him, he was forced to come in person to seek an alliance by marriage to his only son. He was utterly and horribly defeated. With a sigh of sorrow, he agreed, "If you seek my humiliation, then I will do what I must. I will give up my right to a dowry and present a gift to your daughter before the other lands, in front of people high and low, but I ask you most humbly to not defile my son's name in a shameful display. Hold a celebration for the princess once she is born, and on that day, before every member that appears in your court, I will ask for the betrothal of your daughter and my only son. Will you agree?"

King Stefan wanted to say no; it was queen Leah that spoke in her sweet merciful way, "I think that will do just fine. After all, we do not want our daughter's future husband to feel mistreated by his future in-laws. Do we, husband?"

King Stefan huffed in frustration but nodded in agreement. At that, King Hubert took his leave of the palace. A silence fell over the room then. Stefan turned to his wife with a look of anger, "What have I told you about meddling in my affairs? You are not my minister, nor my adviser. You are my queen and should behave as such."

Queen Leah stood from her throne, "I had to say something before you ruined our daughter's only chance for a proper marriage. Prince Phillip is not only the perfect age, but he comes from a long line of successful princes. Just because the fairy granted our wishes to restore our land to glory, what do you think might happen if the others discover how you came to such a turn of fate?"

"They are not going to find out! How could they? It's not as if more fairies are going to come to the castle. We have guards all over! As long as we honor the deal with that horrid creature, we will never need the likes of magic again."

The three fairy's eyes fell to dismay in that moment... That was until the queen replied, "I suppose you are right. That awful plague- I was fearing the worst."

King Stefan let out a sigh, angry at himself for yelling at her. Reaching out his hand, he caressed her face, "Don't worry, my dear, it is all over now. We are safe. And more than that, we will be celebrated by all of those who doubted us. Our prayers were answered. I have all that I desire."

The queen smiled under the grace of her husband's love. "Yes, I have only but one wish left."

"What is that?"

"That our daughter is born healthy and I survive after the childbirth long enough to embrace her."

It was then that the three fairies looked at each other. Instantly, Merryweather and Flora could see that it was Fauna who had an idea. The shock was too great. Neither of them knew what to say, but it didn't matter. For Fauna made her way out from their shadowy corner and sparkled towards the castle floor. Afraid to leave her alone, the two sisters of blue and red followed behind her; each floating as light as bubbles to the long running rug that led to the king and queen. It wasn't their glittering entrance that got the royal couple's attention, but the music. The sound that can only come from a magical fairy. As the three touched the floor, they each grew, not into their typical height, for that was still far too short, but rather the size of a young child. But even at four feet tall, their sudden presence frightened the royal couple. "It's alright, Your Majesties. We have not come to harm you," Fauna said sweetly.

The king rose to his feet and pointed to the door, "I am no longer in need of fairies! You three must get out here!"

"It was not your wish that brought us here, Your Majesty. It was your queens."

Flora and Merryweather looked at each with confusion; each not knowing what their sister was going to do or say next. But whatever she was planning, it had better be quicker than the guards that were heading towards them. The king looked to his wife, but she simply shook her head, pale and stricken with fear, "No, I don't... I didn't!"

"You did, Your Highness, when you said that you want your daughter to be healthy. — *That* was your spoken wish."

"My wife is almost at full term. Her words were merely the whispers of an expecting mother, nothing more. We have no need for your magic. The dark one granted all that we could ever hope for."

But Fauna did not turn, nor was she going to. And something upon her face kept her sisters still as well. It was certainty, and it was something that they had never seen on her face before this very moment. They didn't know what had gotten into her. It was like she had been possessed. "It is true that the Dark Fairy helped you and your kingdom reach glory beyond that of any other in this era, but there is one thing that she didn't fix, something she forgot."

The king sat back down upon the seat of his throne, reaching a caring hand out to his wife.

"What are you saying? What did she forget? You said it was my wish that brought you here. Is something wrong with my baby?" The queen asked suffused with worry.

"I fear that the Dark Fairy could not have foreseen the state of your child's condition. She will be born, but there *will be* complications. I am afraid that without our help, your child will be born with a terrible illness; one that will leave her body weak. She will grow to be ugly and deformed. It would be such a shame for King Hubert to find that his son is betrothed to one with such horrible afflictions. Your daughter will lose her match and will likely never find herself another suitor. Her short life will be a terrible one."

The queen cried into her hands. The king looked down to her helplessly, "I am sorry my darling, but you heard what the Dark Fairy said. We cannot make any deals for magic again. We swore!"

"We are the fairies of good deeds, Your Highness. You need not make a deal with us. We merely want to offer the princess our blessings. But if you do not want our help..."

"No! We do!" Queen Leah screamed with desperation.

Fauna smiled, "Good. We will come after the child is born. You can expect us on the day of your grand celebration."

King Stefan felt violated. "How do you know of our celebration?"

The three sisters giggled together, "No matter where you are, there might be someone listening. In the

171

mortal world, nothing is private. We are hidden, but that shouldn't suggest that we are not around."

"I will not abide spies! Magical or otherwise!"

"You may be a king among mortals, but to us- you are just another susceptible human."

"What do you mean susceptible?"

"Those like us, *good* fairies who are drawn to those who don't live by a strict set of moral codes: the greedy, the misery, and the hypocrites of your world. Think of us as the neighbors who are always right next to you, hidden in the invisible passageways of our realms. Only if a human is still and very quiet might they catch the image of a face somewhere in the walls, or a shadow that moves in the dark... But we *three*— we will *not* be a secret. We have heard your demands and seen your greed, but this is foolish," Fauna said sternly.

"First you spy, and now you dare to call me a fool?" Stefan huffed.

The queen quickly reached out to calm him, "Dear, please."

"If you truly thought that you hid the true means of your sudden grace of good fortune— then yes. It wouldn't be such a bad thing to let the other princes of the world know that you have magic in your corner."

That was it. Even Merryweather and Flora were impressed. Their twitchy little sister had managed to sing the song that both the king and queen needed to hear. They each knew that the king would not be able to resist making himself look even more powerful. And like so many mothers before her, the queen was willing to do anything to protect her unborn child. The royal couple agreed. After all, it wasn't as if they had struck a deal with the three fairies, they had merely brought blessings upon the daughter that would have suffered otherwise and shined the light of fae magic upon their kingdom for all to see. The three fairies left then; each with the promise that they would return on the day of the princess's grand celebration.

* * *

Energy is a magical thing. It is alive. It breathes, moves, and for those that can control it- know how dangerous it can be. When someone dies, their energy sometimes lingers behind. And sometimes, something so bad happens, that the energy of evil itself can be felt. At times, a mortal may think a place is haunted, that something bad is around them. But that shivery sense that crawls under the skin isn't always a spirit of the dead that is there, but simply the energy that was left behind. Every use of magic, however small, is like a burst of energy. And whether it is good, or it is bad— it calls out like a signature.

For most creatures, this fact makes it nearly impossible to hide. But throughout the ages, there had been one, only one, who had the ability to hide their powers from all— the Wood Witch. And though Maleficent hadn't realized it yet, she had used this same magic to create a place of her own; a place that was invisible to everyone else, even those with great power.

173

She didn't know who might be hunting her, but it seemed that it was her own mind that would prove to be her worst enemy. Having one of the ancient four's magic had not only become a gift- it had become a curse. When she was awake, it all seemed to be within her control, but in sleep- every scattered thought or memory that the old witch had over the course of her entire life, tried to race its way through her mind every night. But there was just too much: too many years, too many voices, and too many sad memories. It was not only impossible to process, but also torturous. Soon, Maleficent did everything she could to avoid sleep, to avoid the nightmares.

In the following days, every waking hour was spent gazing out at the stars. The constant crashing of the waves felt like she was surrounded by beautiful chaos; each splash that struck the rocky cliffs soon became as important as the pulse of her darkening heart. The mysterious sea felt more like home than all the years she had spent in the woods, and yet, she had never touched it; not once. For in Maleficent's eyes, the water was as far away as the brilliant stars that shined above in the dark sky. And though there were thousands reflected from the sea, there were only two that truly caught her eye. They twinkled brightly, side by side. She remembered what Jack had told her, back when her dreams were her own; that one of those stars used to lead to him. *But which one was it?* While Maleficent sadly stared up at the stars, she had no idea that there was someone staring back down at her. It wasn't the fairy lad who had stolen her heart, but rather the Blue Fairy who had been watching her from a torturous distance all her life from the inside of the witch's ancient terrarium. For many years, Ainsel had stayed away for fear of Jack's promise to harm her. But now she was more worried than ever; not for her safety- for she proved without a shadow of a doubt that she could take care of herself. No, now there was something else that consumed her with sadness— her daughter's unhappiness. It seemed the energy of Maleficent's bitter hatred and anger was enough to even reach the magical stars. If only she would speak a wish... the *right* wish. Like all fairies, Ainsel could sense her loneliness, her desire. A wish was bound to spill from her lips. There was nothing the Blue Fairy wouldn't do for her, but the question was- *what was the key to Maleficent's happiness?*

Ainsel wanted so badly to reach out and hug her daughter, to let her know that she wasn't truly alone, but she still feared what *he* might do. After all, Maleficent might be bursting with magical powers, but James was still within the shadowy world of Pan's creation. *Did she dare go against him now? Could she finally make contact with her beloved daughter?*

As it turned out, the power of the ancient four that Maleficent now had coursing through her had already brought her more than she imagined. She had used her magic to bring her to her perfect home, but what she didn't realize was why the Forbidden Mountain felt so safe, so hers. Fate had somehow dropped her right between the two worlds that once belonged to her long-lost parents... the stars and the ocean. It was on this night, however, that Maleficent found herself utterly consumed by her loneliness. Maybe it was the nightmares, maybe it was exhaustion, maybe it was chaotic thoughts that raced with regrets and hatred, but she could have sworn that she could hear a voice calling out to her. It was beautiful and alluring, but it was too distant to understand. It was then that she saw where this mysterious whisper was coming from. Her eyes widened as she saw the first star on the left twinkle brightly with each and every word the voice spoke. Maleficent rushed to her window, desperate to hear what the voice was saying. The waves were loud, too loud. She closed her eyes, trying to silence the earth. The waves that came from the Black Sea went still and the cold breath of air touched her cheek like a kiss. It was then that she heard it. *"Wish. Wish upon the star."*

The whisper opened Maleficent's glowing eyes. She didn't know who the lovely voice belonged to or why it wanted her to wish upon the star, but something inside her told her to trust it.

"Wish... Hmmm." She looked down to think. There were so many things she could think to wish for, but more than anything— she wanted to be back in her true love's arms. *But could it really be that simple? How powerful is the one beyond the twinkling star, and why did it want her to wish for something so badly?*

Maleficent didn't quite understand, but maybe it was a sign. It *was* Jack, after all, who spoke about the magic beyond the two stars. Maybe this *was* the best way to get him back. Without any further resistance, she

176

took a single breath, looked back up at the stars, and uttered the words she hoped more than anything to be granted, "I wish, I wish..."

Suddenly, the sound of loud squawking stopped her words. It was a distant crow flying frantically through the open window. It was one of her little lovelies she had left at King Stefan's castle. She reached out her arm, allowing him to settle himself upon her hand. "What is it, my pet? You look positively frazzled?"

The crow screeched loudly in reply, and just as it had done for many years before the Dark Fairy became his mistress, the raven turned his beak, and gazed into Maleficent's eyes, glamouring upon her the visions he had seen. At that, her sight tunneled through what appeared to be a portal back through time. And from the baby blue sky where her darling pet flew, she saw the sight that would make her blood boil. The Rose Kingdom was buzzing with activity; people high and low had come to the extravagant celebration that anyone had ever seen. Men marched with banners, horns, drums, each singing in cheer for the new princess. The common folk were dancing in cheery glee, and the other royals were each being escorted from their fancy carriages into the magnificent palace covered in ivy and the most vibrant of pink roses. It seemed that the sun had finally shined its glorious light upon the Rose Kingdom, so it only seemed fitting that the celebrated princess be named after the dawn, Princess Aurora.

And so, they came, one and all, but as in any kingdom, there were those who spoke in jealousy. And from their lips, spilled the envious resentment they bore towards the king. "What a ridiculous spectacle this celebration has become," said one of the older ladies of the court.

"Indeed, but I must say I am looking forward to the three magical fairies responsible for our land's restored fortune," said a plump man with a curly waxed mustache and a large hat.

"Yes, yes. Had they not cast their generous powers upon us, I fear we would have had to move away. I, myself, lost eight servants to the plague."

"Terrible business."

"Yes."

"But just imagine what power these fairies must possess to turn the winds of fate for the entire land. I cannot wait to see them."

"Well, yes, I think we all know the real reason everyone came to the celebration today. Everyone wants to see the three little fairies. It is said that they will be making an appearance."

"I heard they were going to be offering gifts upon the baby princess."

The woman smiled, fanning herself, "Well, that is nice."

"Oh, look, they are opening the doors. We should hurry. I don't want to be left sitting in the back."

The horns from the guard did then blow, and all that had eagerly waited, were now making their way through the open gates. And it was in that moment that the vision tunneled back into the darkness. When Maleficent opened her glowing emerald eyes, a surge of violent murderous anger suffused her. "They betrayed me! I cannot believe it! Me!" She screamed with rage, pacing the floor back and forth with thoughts racing through her mind. "Not only are they meddling in ways of magic again, but they are crediting the three fairies for all that I have done. They are to be celebrated, honored, and praised while I sit here in the dark alone. I think not!"

She stood from her throne and struck the ancient staff against the grey hard stone of her castle. "Come, my darling, I believe we have a celebration to attend. If these wretched humans want to see some magic, some *power...* Well, we wouldn't want to disappoint the people, now, *would we?*"

Grip squawked and flew to her shoulder, and with another hard strike of her staff, a raging swirl rapidly consumed them. Within mere seconds... the smoke faded away, and the castle that stood on the top of the cliffs of the Forbidden Mountain went as silent as an ancient tomb.

* * *

The day of the grand celebration was the first day in history that everyone in all the surrounding kingdoms gathered together to pay homage to a new heir. But it wasn't just the princess that had drawn the buzzing hive of both high and low estate to the castle. The truth was that most had become fearful of the king and his mysterious ties to the magic that had changed the land and brought riches to all. No one wanted to disrespect him, nor the fairies that had altered their fortune. Word of their upcoming appearance had spread like wildfire.

Little did everyone know that the fate of the entire kingdom rested in the hands of someone they didn't know existed... a fact that was about to dramatically change forever. Once inside the castle doors, the cheering crowds grew silent under the shining gold that glimmered by the vast hall of crystal chandeliers and flickering flames of candlelight. Banners of every coat of arms and vibrant colors hung down from the ceiling.

It was as if the entire world had come to the palace. Everyone had worn their best clothes, brought a gift, and many had even brought with them performers as tribute. Those of low birth that could not afford such offerings, brought food or hand-made cloths of exquisite designs. But through it all, there was only one present, one person that King Stefan cared about. It was the man everyone had believed would win the war, the man that everyone respected above all other princes of the world- King Hubert.

As promised, he and his only son, Prince Phillip, had come to the palace to show their loyalty and submission before asking for the princess's hand in marriage in front of all that stood beside them. King Stefan could hardly contain his smile as he watched his rival bend the knee.

The humbling gesture shocked all within the room. No one knew of the two king's arrangement, nor did they have any clue of what humiliation would strike down their most honored figure next. It was the little prince that held their gift. It was a small golden chest. Within it held the official jewels of a future queen. It was clever and showed the sort of confidence the people admired most about him.

King Stefan was not pleased, but his happy queen's grateful manner was quicker than his disagreeable notions.

After presenting his gift, King Hubert announced his proposal before the entire court, "I am here today in honor of you, your beautiful queen, and, of course, the little princess. We have brought you this gift in hopes that we might get one from you as well. I ask your most gracious Majesty to accept my proposal and unite our two kingdoms by means of marriage. My son and only heir could not hope for a more perfect match. Should you agree, I will also renounce my right to your daughter's dowry, as a sign of good will. Let us forget the past and love each other like brothers."

Not a single movement, nor even a breath could be heard then. Everyone within the crowd waited silently for King Stefan's official reply.

The moment was long, leaving only intensity to fill the air. But ultimately, it was the queen that reached out and held her husband's hand. With a sigh, King Stefan agreed.

King Hubert smiled, wiping the sweat from his brow with relief. "Thank you, Your Majesty. It takes a high king to forgive a former enemy. Your wisdom and generosity astound me, and I am so glad that all that have gathered here today had the privilege of seeing such a *noble* king. After all, victory in ways of war can change a man, thinking himself above all others in the world; a god amongst men, but I see now, as well as everyone else here today, that you are but a humble prince of this earth."

But everyone knew there was nothing *noble* about him. King Stefan had cheated to win the war. It wasn't the first time a king had the help of magic, but Stefan was nothing like King Arthur, nor would he ever have the same love from his people. He may have bullied every kingdom into coming to the grand celebration, but they all knew what he had done to take his glory...

What they didn't know was how low he had gone in his greed for power. Now that the two children were betrothed, it was time for the prince to see his future bride. The king and queen had hoped that the fairies would have come up first, to place their blessings upon the princess, but it was Prince Phillip that would first set his eyes upon her. Aurora had indeed been born with many afflictions, the three sisters and the Snow Queen had made sure of it.

The very sight of her made the young prince turn up his nose in disgust. It wasn't just the odd contorting of her weakened bones, or the bright marks that covered her skin; it was also the disturbing raspy sounds that came from her damaged vocal cords. Upon seeing his son's unsettling reaction, King Hubert decided to come over and investigate, but no sooner had he taken his first step- did the sudden sound of ten blowing trumpets stop him. It was then that a sparkling mist fell from above.

The moment that everyone within the palace had been waiting for had finally come— the arrival of the three good fairies. With a single flick of their wands, the fairies gave the official herald their desired announcement.

"Their most exalted and revered excellencies, the three good fairies— Mistress Flora, Mistress Fauna, and Mistress Merryweather!"

As the three sisters slowly floated to the floor and the herald covered his mouth in utter surprise, all within the vibrant castle gasped in awe. For while many found magic to be a source of evil, frightening, or even heresy, there was something rather sweet and comforting about their glowing appearance.

Each were wearing their usual formal attire that matched the shine that illuminate from their essence of magic; with sparkling gowns and glittering veils that flowed from the top of their beautiful hennins. But like all fae, especially those of noble birth, the most extravagant part of their wardrobe was their shoes. Covered in gems and tied by ribbons and twine, such fashion could only be seen as ridiculous by a mortal, but in the magical realms that lied beyond the seven veils, their shoes were in every way magnificent. In any case, whether in admiration or judgement, the three fairies had the courts full attention as they approached King Stefan and the lovely Queen Leah.

Even though the three sisters were being honored, they humbly bowed before the royal couple and spoke in perfect unison, "Your Majesties, each of us have come here today to bestow upon the princess a single gift. We offer no more, and no less, but rest assured, she will be the most treasured monarch since the beloved King Arthur ruled Camelot."

Queen Leah smiled, "Thank you, Your Excellencies. We are both eternally grateful for everything."

King Stefan on the other hand was silent, too consumed with the overwhelming wonderment on everyone's faces to show any proper gratitude.

With everyone at ease, the time had come for the three sisters to work their magic. Flora of course was first to approach the baby. Fauna and Merryweather promptly followed. They each gazed down at the child. How odd things had become. For the first time since the dawn of the first age, it was a human that could give a fairy what it wished for. She was the key they needed to get them back their home... and more importantly- their *mother.*

Flora raised her wand above the cradle, and all within the room held their breath and glued their eyes upon her every movement.

"Princess, my gift will be the gift of eternal beauty." At that, Flora slowly waved her wand in a circle, casting from its end a glowing red spell.

"I call upon the splendor
Reserved for the light
A rose untouched
By the darkness of night
Make her skin
As white as milk

And let her touch
Be as soft as silk
Give her two lips
That shame the red rose
And let sunshine follow her
Wherever she goes
Make her hair
Shine like gold
Though her blood be warm
Let her soul run cold
Magic please
Hear my call
Make her the fairest
Of them all."

At that, Flora lowered her wand, allowing the swirling mist of magic to descend upon the baby. The king and queen were most anxious to see their fae-touched child, to see her beautiful new form, but the fairies were not done yet. Flora backed away, now having fulfilled her part. Next was Fauna, the fairy covered in green. She approached the cradle, floating quietly. With a single glance upon the enchanted princess, she knew there was no turning back now. She lifted her wand and took a deep breath. Though she had always been the most twitchy and nervous of the three, Fauna did have an undeniable flair when it came to magic. She started slow, but within a few moments, the wand in her hand moved as if she were conducting the perfect symphony. Then suddenly, from the tip of her wand, a glowing swirl of green appeared. The crowd of everyone within the court gasped as the sound of whimsical music and echoes of a vast choir filled the air. "Dear Princess, my gift to you is that of our song...

Enchant this princess
With the fae melody
From her lips of scarlet
So, shall it be
Let no one resist
Her troubadour
Not even the animals
Can help but adore
Make each tone
Pure poetry
Let all who hear her
Need to see
Magic please
Let your chorus soar
Give her the song
That brings all to her door."

Just as her sister before her, Fauna lowered her wand and the swirling choir of glittering stars slowly fell, twinkling upon the tiny cradle. They had done it. They had given her every trait she would need to be the perfect vessel for the Snow Queen's daughter. There was only one thing left to do, one part left of the sister's clever plan to steal the baby. The Snow Queen had given each of them a tap of her essence, and Merryweather was going to use hers to put everyone in the palace into a deep sleep. It had always been a skill of hers, but today she was going to have to go farther than she had ever gone before. Afterwards, while everyone within the Rose Kingdom was in a deep slumber, they would take the baby to the queen and return later to leave a changeling made by her dark magic in its place. No one would ever know what they had done. As Fauna turned away and Merryweather made her way towards the child, all three sisters took an eager breath. This was it. With one last spell, they could finally have everything they had wished for since that terrible night in the woods. And so, with a racing heart, Merryweather rose her wand. But just as she opened her mouth to cast her spell... A rumble of powerful thunder burst through the tall castle doors, blowing each open with incredible force. A frightful chill of electricity and fear tingled upon every spine then. Everyone scattered in terror as a crash of lightning hit the castle floor, and a tall dark silhouette with horns appeared within a bright sinister glow. The three sisters frantically looked at each. They were too late. She was here. The Dark Fairy was here... and she had brought all the powers of her wrath with her.

* * *

There is a moment in every person's life when they become horror stricken by the realization that they have been caught by the very person they have betrayed. The terrible anxiety that hits... like lightning. This feeling began on this very day; the day that Maleficent's wrath struck mortal ground. Her storm of fury blew through the castle, harshly whipping many to the floor. King

Stefan and Queen Leah each rose to their feet, shock and fear filling their eyes. But nothing could compare to the terror that suffused the three sisters. For only *they* truly understood what she was— and what she could do.

"Oh, no, it's Maleficent," Flora whispered.

"What are we going to do?" Fauna asked with a trembling voice.

"We have to leave. Now," Merryweather cried out.

"We can't. If we try to leave, she'll kill us for sure. Besides, even if we did make it out, the king and queen would never allow us back inside," Flora reasoned.

"She's right. I'm afraid we are stuck here. But how did she even know we were here? About the ceremony?" Fauna asked.

It was then that the green glow from Maleficent's magic faded away and her large raven emerged from the green flames. With a single glance of his dark onyx eyes, they knew the answer. He flew to his mistress's shoulder with a wicked grin cornering his long beak. He knew they were looking at him, and he looked right back.

"Of course. It was her crows! Nasty little beast!" Merryweather scoffed.

"*Shush!*" Flora whispered. "This is *not* the time to draw attention to ourselves."

"Quite the glittering masquerade of a celebration, King Stefan," Maleficent said looking around. "Such riches, beautiful colors, wonderful music, and a mountain of gifts from every surrounding kingdom. And here I thought that I had given you everything you wished for. Still, I suppose it is only fitting that the princess of the glorious king be given such a grand ceremony. Isn't that right, my pet."

Grip squawked, flying to the top of her staff, perching himself upon the magical orb.

"We really felt quite distressed that we hadn't received an invitation to your celebration," Maleficent said, calmly petting her raven's dark feathers. It was then that she heard a familiar voice; one she had hoped to never hear again.

"Once again, Maleficent, you come where you're not wanted."

The Dark Fairy's glowing gaze rapidly traced the source of such disrespect, though it did not take her long. It was the fussy little fairy dressed all in blue. For the first time in her life, a surge of overwhelming anger brought frightening laughter to thunder from her lips.

But just as she took in the deep breath and lifted the staff a mere inch off the floor, it was the queen that spoke next. "Please, Your Excellency, do not be cross. We never meant to offend you."

"Offended? Why, no, Your Majesty. Why should I be offended? Having been the one to give your kingdom its glory, I merely found it strange that it was only *I* that was not given an invitation. After all, I see around me the *nobles, royalty,* the *gentry,* and of course the *real* reason they are all here, this throng of *useless* fairies you've given all the credit to. Is that why I wasn't invited? Because you did not want the world to know your *lies?* King Stefan, they say that even humans have the ability to know when they are being looked at. Tell me, do you feel the eyes on you now?"

Of course, he did. The staring of all those within the court felt as if they were burning through his skin. His heart began to race within his tight chest as he scraped through the depths of his inner courage to answer: "Yes, I do. But..." he stammered, looking out at the sea of judgment around him. "Good people, please forgive my..."

"Them! You want forgiveness from *them!?*" Maleficent screamed with wild rage. Her anger whipped through the air, knocking many off their feet. The sight of it was enough to bring a sinister chuckle from her throat. She scanned the room, soaking in their fear before returning her gaze to the king's throne. "I stand now in a palace full of liars. Your riches, your glory, even the people that came to this extravagant assemblage did so, not to pay homage to the little princess, but rather to loom over the three good fairies that brought you such fortune. Good fairies indeed! Well, that's the biggest lie of all!" She declared, moving in on the three fae in a most intimidating manner. The scars they had inflicted upon her body all those years ago began to burn as she drew closer to the woodland sisters. But Maleficent was far too angry to give way to old wounds. "I hate lies! I was lied to my whole life, and now, it seems I have no patience for such wretched deception!"

"Stop this, Maleficent!" Flora shouted fearfully. "After all, everything that is happening within this kingdom wouldn't be happening if it weren't for your own spells of deception. You started all of this!"

Maleficent shook suffused with rage. "You're right. I did. And now, I will atone for my mistake and bring this kingdom back to its most dreaded undoing!"

King Stefan felt as if his knees were buckling, "No, please. Have mercy, great one."

"*Mercy!* I came here, gave you everything you desired, and what did you do? You scheme behind my back with these nasty little creatures. I told you not to dabble in magic again, and you failed. Not only me, but yourselves, and your entire kingdom!"

"But the three fairies told us there was to be no deal for their magic. Only that they wanted to gift our daughter with the three blessings she would need to live her life. We had no choice!" Pleaded the queen.

"Fools! You had every choice. You made the wrong one. I gave you one chance. I gave the life of your daughter one chance, and you let magic come through your door. Well I cannot, I will not let her live the life they wish. You were promised three blessings, but now that I have seen your greed, I know all too well that you crave more. So, I too, will bestow a gift upon the princess..."

The three sisters slowly backed away, blocking the cradle with what little powers they had to protect her. But Maleficent didn't need to take a single step towards the cradle. Nor did she feel the need to set her gaze upon her victim, because to her, it wasn't the baby she was about to destroy, but rather every hope, wish,

191

or dream that the sisters and the Snow Queen so desperately desired.

With a squawk from her raven that flew up from her staff, a swirling darkness emerged within the magical orb. Maleficent twirled her hand in motion above the glass, staring with a glowing gaze at the coming curse she was about to cast. And from her lips did finally spill, the words that would change every one of their lives forever.

"The princess of frost will indeed be fairest in all the lands, unmatched by any other. Her song and grace will steal the love by all who know her. But... I swear now before the gods, the old and the new, that by the hour of sunset on her sixteenth birthday, she will prick her finger on the spindle of an ancient spinning wheel- and fall to the curse of the eternal death."

The three fairies gasped in shock, for not even they thought Maleficent would go so far. The queen rushed to her baby, scooping her up in terrible fright. It was then, as his wife held their newborn daughter, that King Stefan bravely stood from his throne. "Guards! Seize her! Seize the evil creature!"

His words brought more of her manic laughter to the air. But just as a large crowd of armed guards drew in with their weapons at the ready, the glowing flames that brought her appeared again, only this time, the ring of green fire burned them. The men screamed in agony. After all, the burn from the flames of magic can never be healed. But even in the swarm of painful cries, the sound of Maleficent's chilling laughter could still be heard within the disappearing fire. Then finally, she was gone, and all that remained within the palace was that of turmoil and utter despair. Not a single candle within the castle held even the smallest of flames. It was dark, grey, and dreary. The banners had been burned and torn by her fury. The feast was covered in the rot that dripped from her disdain. The music that was once so full of life now fell as silent as the dead. All the glory, all the joy, every color, and smile had been completely wiped away. King Stefan looked around at what his greed had wrought. There was nothing left, only the dreaded gloom that now shrouded their deprived world and weakened hearts.

Many believe, like most humans do, that they are the only living things with feelings. But this notion is nothing short of absurd. It is not just animals, plant life, or even otherworldly creatures that complete this puzzle either. No, the truth is simple, but far more unknown. It is not only living breathing things that have feelings, it is everything that has been created. So, it is no wonder that when a place, a town, or even a kingdom has been abandoned, destroyed, or cursed- it becomes a gloomy picture of despair. The vibrant colors of life fade to grey, and the very air fills with misery. And then, as with all deaths, the dust will come to let you know you have been forgotten.

King Stefan's castle may have still been full of living, breathing people, but the Rose Kingdom had indeed become nothing more than a dark, barren, ghost land. Maleficent had once given them a miracle, but now, she had taken it and more- away with a curse. All eyes then fell upon the three fairies. Being the only vision of glowing color left within the palace, the people gazed upon them as their last ray of hope.

Taking charge of the situation, Flora stepped forward, "Your Majesties, fear not, after all, Merryweather still has her gift to bestow upon the princess."

Her sisters didn't know what she was up to, but just as they had always done, they played along, and nodded in agreement.

"You must undo this wretched curse," King Stefan uttered miserably.

"I am afraid we cannot do that. We are merely three small fairies. Why, not even a thousand would be enough to overpower the magic of Maleficent," Flora replied.

"So, there is *no* hope?" Queen Leah asked, still cradling her baby in her arms.

It was then, as the three sisters saw the tears of her broken heart that they found the answer to their problems. "No, Your Majesty, there may be a ray of hope in this. You see, there is but one thing that is stronger than the Dark Fairy's magic... A true love's kiss. It has the power to break any curse- even Maleficent's. It's the rarest thing in the world. But with Merryweather's final gift, she can use her good magic to help the princess break the spell."

"But... *that means*-- the curse has to happen for it to be broken. Our daughter has to die?" The queen asked tearfully.

Flora stepped closer, "Think not of it as death, Your Majesties, but rather just a deep sleep; one that she can wake from with a single kiss."

King Stefan looked to his wife, "Sweetheart, put the princess back in her cradle."

Flora and Fauna then gave their nervous sister a little push. It wasn't in Merryweather's nature to be hesitant or shy, but this was a lot of pressure. Never in her worst nightmares, would the future of their fates rest upon her magic. This wasn't just about their mother, or even their home anymore. This was about securing their own survival. For if they did not succeed, the Snow Queen would surely rip out their souls, and add them to her collection.

The nervous fairy dressed all in blue, trembled, anxiety surging through her body. Fauna spoke out to her, encouraging her to do her best. *Easy for her to say,* Merryweather thought. She took a deep breath and rolled up her glittered sleeves. With a lift of her wand, a swirling blue fog full of sparkling stars appeared above.

"Magic please
Hear my call
Restore the hope
To one and all
A curse will come
On her sixteenth year
She'll prick her finger
But have no fear
She may fall
And her soul may sleep

But there is solace
To all that weep
Bring to her
A kiss to wake
And from true love
The spell will break."

At that, Merryweather lowered her hopeful gift upon the baby, and all within the palace let out a sigh of despair for the poor child. But it wasn't just the mortals of the Rose Kingdom that had seen the events of the tragic celebration; another fairy had as well.

After the ceremony was over, and the three sisters were given a room to recuperate after such an exhausting use of their magic, King Stefan used his own power to decree that every spinning wheel within both his and every surrounding kingdom be destroyed. Fearing that any one of them might be enchanted by Maleficent, each piece of wood was to be thrown in a pile and burned by the flames of a roaring fire.

The kingdom may have turned into a gloomy pit of despair, void of all color that illuminates from a hopeful spirit, but on this one night, the skies would be painted red by the fiery glow. From high above in the west wing of the castle, the three fairies watched the smoke fill the air.

"Do they not see how insulting this whole display is? To show such lack of faith in my spell?" Merryweather said, closing the windows with her wand.

"Do not blame them, sister. Maleficent stripped all hope from their souls. They cannot help it," Fauna replied sweetly.

"But why must they always use fire?" Merryweather asked in revulsion.

"Because they believe it to be the only way of purging evil magic from their world," Flora answered.

"I hate humans! All they know is destruction! And fire... The gods should have never given it to them!" Merryweather huffed with frustration.

"None of that matters now, dear sister. What we need to concern ourselves with now is how to get the princess out," Fauna said sweetly.

"Well, I cannot possibly put everyone in a deep sleep now. It will take years to restore enough magic to do something that big. I cannot bear this any longer. From the day we met her, Maleficent has ruined everything. Because of her, we lost our home, our mother, and today, she managed to steal it all away again."

"I am haunted by the events that took place that dreadful night as well, but in the time since, I must say that I found our behavior to also be a cause in mother's terrible fate, and our beloved home that now rest upon the scorched earth. Maybe we should try something different. I mean, if we cannot beat her, then maybe we should try reasoning with her. After all, we met Maleficent when she was nothing more than a lost, scared little creature that had wandered into our veil. We know that she wasn't always so... So evil," Fauna said timidly.

"Well, she certainly is now! But you are right, Fauna, we cannot beat her. We can only use our magic for good things. But maybe it doesn't have to be a matter of battling power. Maybe we could simply *outsmart* her," Flora stated.

"How?" Merryweather asked.

"I think we should..." Suddenly, Flora felt nervous that someone might hear them. After looking around in every direction, she whispered, "Follow me." She whipped her wand, making herself as small as a flea. Fauna and Merryweather did as she said and followed her into a golden trinket box that locked with a key. Once they were all inside, Flora excitedly shared her poetic idea. "I think we should simply turn her into a rose. No one would see us leaving with her and keeping a flower safe for sixteen years would be a lot easier than a roaming child."

At first, both of her sisters were on board, but the idea turned to foolery in mere seconds. "We cannot have the entire kingdom out looking for us and the baby. Maleficent showed no intention of kidnapping the princess; she didn't even look at her. The king and queen will know it was us. That would make matters far more difficult after the curse is broken. And besides, a rose may not be able to prick its finger, but I have no desire to see what Maleficent would do to a flower."

"Oh, my, you are right. I suppose she would expect us to do something like that anyways," Flora said with a pitiful sigh.

Merryweather went red with anger, "Well then, what should we do, sisters? What would Maleficent not expect? She knew about the celebration. She knew what we were up to. She has spies everywhere. She knows everything!"

"No, no, don't you see? She has turned into this monster because she doesn't know what it is to love and be loved in return. She feels no joy or happiness in her life. She never has. Didn't you hear what she said about liars? All those years she spent in the cottage with the Wood Witch is what did this to her," Fauna said sadly.

Suddenly, Flora was suffused with excitement. "That's it! You are right, sweet sister, it is the one thing she cannot understand, the one thing she would never expect us to do. It's too daring, too brazen, too bold! It is perfect!"

Merryweather and Fauna looked at each other in confusion. "What is?" They asked in unison.

"The story of three peasant women that raise a foundling child- deep in the Forbidden Forest." Flora said, eager for her sisters to catch on to her little scheme. But from the looks on their faces, she could see they had not.

"That is a sweet-sounding story, but what does...?" Fauna started before Flora turned her and Merryweather around to face their reflection upon a gold candle snuffer. As the two sisters turned around, Flora used her wand to enchant their appearance. The sisters gasped upon such a vision. They appeared like two middle-aged mortals.

"I do not understand. Why do you want us to look like this?" Merryweather asked. "I hate it!"

"The king and queen are clearly still in fear of their daughter's fate. We will go to them and offer to hide her away until her sixteenth birthday. They will object at first, but we will tell them it is the only way. Don't you both understand? We will not only take the baby, but it will be with their blessing. We will take the child into the forest with us, into the hidden cottage. Being woodland fairies, we can find it easily now that the witch's powers are not hiding it. Maleficent believes the ancient cabin has moved. She will never suspect we have done something so bold. No one will find us there. We will all be safe."

"So, you want us to live like mortals, like humans! Taking care of a mortal child for sixteen years?!" Merryweather asked as if horrified by such an idea.

Flora couldn't help but feel agitated by her sister's reaction. "I haven't heard you come up with any bright ideas, Merryweather! At least I am trying. Besides, it is not as if we can leave her here. She is fae-touched. The mortals will notice how different she is."

"Why can't we take the princess to the Snow Queen. Why should it be our responsibility to take care of the baby? She is the one who really wants it. And I, for one, really don't," Merryweather spouted.

"You know better than that! She is still partially mortal. The child cannot live within the Nine Realms; not until we find the spell the queen seeks. I know it doesn't sound glamourous, but it will give us time to find the witch's spell books. It is the right thing, the *only* thing. You agree with me, right, Fauna?" Flora asked, desperately seeking some support.

"Oh, yes, I think its brilliant. After everything we have been through, I would love nothing more than living in the silent woods, raising a baby. We can feed it, sing to it, rock her to sleep. Yes, Flora, I think it sounds wonderful."

Merryweather scoffed, "Raising a mortal baby! Why me?" She pouted. But upon seeing Flora's stern expression, she let out a sigh of defeat. It was two against one now, and Flora was right, she didn't have a better idea. "Alright, alright. I suppose it's not such a bad plan. At least we will have our magic to take care of the little rose princess."

"Actually, using our magic might draw attention. Maleficent knows our powers. If we use them in our everyday life, she is sure to find out and find us! We must refrain from magic, entirely if possible. I am sorry, sisters, but it is just too dangerous otherwise," said Flora.

"Wait! You mean you not only want us to appear like mortals but live like them as well. We couldn't possibly. No! We have never done anything without our powers. I have lost everything because of Maleficent. I refuse to lose my magic too!" Merryweather barked, flying all around the trinket box to avoid Flora snatching her wand from her hands. But there was very little room in the trinket box, so despite her best efforts, ultimately, Flora chased her down and ripped her wand from her grip. Fauna, on the other hand, didn't feel the need for such dramatics. She handed over hers to her sister willingly.

Once Flora had all three within her grasp, there was but only one thing left to do to finish their little meeting. With a flick of their wands, Flora took away their wings, and the three sisters then left the golden trinket box, no longer as fairies, but as common mortals.

CHAPTER SEVEN
NO REST FOR THE WICKED

There have been times throughout the historic ages, that an impossible force of nature has been witnessed within the mortal world; moments when the elements came together to display the very power of godly wraths. But what the human world doesn't know about is the deadly storm that struck the Forbidden Mountain on the night of Aurora's celebration. The roars of monstrous thunder and veins of electricity spread violently across the darkest of skies that overlooked the towering castle that stood upon the rocky cliffs. Each flash of lightning met its glorious reflection on the raging sea below. It seemed that Maleficent's anger had stirred every element of the mortal world. The ancient rocks began to crack and even break apart, falling into the thrashing waves of black water. But even as the very picture of danger rumbled outside, the real chaos was what lied inside the Dark Fairy's castle. The bright green flames could be seen from the same window she used to gaze at the stars. And inside were the wailing screams of such fury, one would half expect a banshee was living there. But even the strongest of fires will ultimately burn out. Maleficent had in truth worn herself out; not only by her extreme performance of magic, but emotionally drained as well. Luckily, her loving Grip was there to console her, just like he had always been.

She crumbled to her lonely throne. "Oh, I am sorry, my pet. I am just so, so... I don't know. I know I have won. I took revenge on those that betrayed me. But even as their kingdom suffers and the vessel of the rose is cursed by my own power, I feel as though I have lost something too. I know it sounds strange. I cannot explain it."

Grip squawked, rubbing his feathered head under the soft touch of her hand. Maleficent could barely bring herself to smile in that moment. It wasn't that she didn't appreciate her companion's loyalty; she did, but he just couldn't fill the void growing in her heart. It was a hole that had been there for as long as she could remember. Her years with Jack made her feel special, hopeful, and connected. But now the only thing that was filling the hole within her heart was the spreading darkness of evil forces fighting to consume her soul.

All of the sudden, a flash of blue came over the sky, and the storm faded away, leaving only the stars to glitter the sky. Their twinkling beauty set a calm over her. And the memory of her thoughts before the news of the traitors came back into her mind. Her desperate breath touched the air as she thought of what would heal her bitter heart. There had only been one that had the power to possess her with happiness. *Him.* But the Snow Queen would never relinquish her power over him. He was hers; possibly forever.

The thought hitched a lump in her throat. It was painful, too painful to think about. Yet somehow, in the darkness of that hopeless night, the stars twinkled upon her like a beacon of hope. As if he had heard her thoughts, Grip squawked sweetly with an encouraging gaze from his onyx eyes. Somehow, his support made the idea not so silly, and with a gentle nod, Maleficent looked up into the sky and made a wish upon a star.

"I wish, I wish that my true love will appear before me; out of the Icy Citadel that imprisons him. Please, bring him here to be with me. Bring back the cold moon to light up my dark and lonely world. Come before me, my love. I wish that you appear before me."

It was then that the night sky went dark. The stars that had whispered hope stopped twinkling, and a feeling of terrible despair came through the salty breeze. Maleficent looked around, searching high and low within the stone walls of her palace, but her love was not there. She was still alone.

I don't understand. Why didn't it work? Why would the voice tell me to make a wish if it wasn't ever going to come true?

Like all loyal companions, Grip could feel her sadness. He flew to her shoulder and caressed her cheek in time to catch a falling tear. With a sad sigh, she reached up and pet his soft feathers, "Oh, Grip... How cruel it all is. The mortal world betrays me, those of the Nine Realms loath me, and now I find that even the stars are cruel to me." *Why?*

Suddenly, the star on the left began to move. Both Maleficent and Grip watched in awe as the glowing ball of light moved closer and closer towards the castle. And through the open window that she loved, she watched as the star came through.

The murder of crows screeched, flapping away to the top of the palace beams, trying to get away from the blinding light. Maleficent too, covered her hand over her eyes. That is, until what appeared to be a glittering silver burst within the room, and all went dark again. She slowly dropped her hand and set her sight upon the sparkling figure that emerged.

It was a fairy, but she didn't look anything at all like the others she had seen in the past. She was beautiful. Not in the intimidating way that the Snow Queen was, but rather held a sweet presence. Her eyes were not black, but rather blue and purple. Her turquoise hair was long and flowed in the air as if swept up in a gentle breeze. The gown that dressed her thin frame shined from what seemed like a million baby blue diamonds. She had a pretty face, and a look in her eyes that was both teary and hopeful.

"Who are you?" Maleficent asked.

Ainsel looked down, unable to shake off the sharp cut of disappointment. For though she knew better, she couldn't help but hope that somehow, someway, Maleficent would recognize her, remember her. But she could sadly see from her expression that she had no idea who she was.

"I... I am your- My name is Ainsel."

Maleficent scaled her with a blazing stare of suspicion. "What are you doing here? Who sent you?"

"I came here because you called me. It was my star you wished upon just now, my dear. Not *his.*"

His? "How do you-?"

"I know a great many things about you," Ainsel interrupted, unable to suppress her lip from curling up into a small smile. Her expression was not a welcome one, however. Too often had Maleficent been the target of ridicule. She couldn't fathom any other cause for the fairy's gleeful urge.

"You dare to smirk at me! Why? Was my wish amusing to you?!" Maleficent scowled harshly.

Ainsel flinched under her glowing fury, "No, no, please, Maleficent. You misunderstand me. I am not here to mock you. I wouldn't dare. Please, do not be angry."

Maleficent cocked her head in confusion. She didn't know what to make of this odd creature before her. It wasn't just that she believed her plea, but also felt a strange sensation of guilt for scolding her so. Her tone, so sweet and nurturing, seemed to soften her hardened expression. "It is I who should be apologizing. It is just that I haven't exactly met another fairy who... Well, let us just forget the matter. It was I who summoned you here, but that was a mistake. Please- leave."

Her words halted Ainsel's breath. "Leave? But I came to help you."

Maleficent's brow raised intrigued, "Help me? How? Can you give me my love back? Can you save him from the Icy Citadel?"

"Is that what you really want, Maleficent?"

Her question burned into her stomach, "What else could I..."

"As I said before, my dear, I know a great many things about you. I know you feel like something is missing, something deep inside you. I know that you feel that this boy can help to heal the hole in your heart, but I fear you are mistaken. He is not the answer you have spent your whole life searching for. I can help you, but you must be honest with yourself and ask the right question. It is the question that is growing like a black hole inside you. Your actions, I fear, will only drag you farther into the darkness that threatens to consume you. Coming here tonight may cause grave consequences, but after what I saw you do in the Rose Kingdom, I realized I could not watch another night go by with this distance between us."

Maleficent felt her mouth go dry, and her blood sing as she said her next words, "Who are you?"

Ainsel's beautiful eyes quickly pooled with tears. Still she steeled herself and answered with a calm tone, "I already told you. My name is Ainsel. I came from the-."

"No!" Maleficent halted, locking her gaze as she stepped closer. "Who are you— *to me*?"

Ainsel closed her eyes, feeling herself come undone under Maleficent's fervent determination. Her will was palpable, strong, and resilient. Her face was breathtakingly beautiful, but her intimidating stare felt as if it had the power to burn right through you. Ainsel tried to hold back the second urge to smile. *Well she definitely got that from her father.*

The thought was a sweet and bitter one. Oh, how she missed him. If only he could see her now, their tall and radiant daughter. She herself had been able to watch her from afar all these years, but even that was agonizing. It was hard to think about James. She couldn't help him. But maybe, just maybe, she could help her daughter— *whatever the cost.*

"Answer me!" Maleficent demanded, aggravated; not only by the fairy's silence, but also by her secretive smile she had tried to hide.

Ainsel's sweet expression then turned into something desperate and painful. Maleficent held her breath, waiting for her answer. The answer that she already knew deep down.

"Say it! Say the words!" Maleficent cried out.

Ainsel could hear the pain in Maleficent's voice. She had spent her whole life getting hurt, and now even she had caused her heart ache. She feared what danger or havoc the truth may wrought, but she could not deny this. Not anymore. She locked her gaze upon the emerald eyes of her young, and bravely let the words fall from her lips. "Your mother. I am your mother."

Maleficent gasped quietly, parting her quivering lips for breath. Time seemed to stop, allowing what felt like a million thoughts to rage against her mind. A stir of anger, pain, and even a strange sort of comfort swelled inside her. There were things to say, too many things. And yet, she could not utter a single word. Here she was, her mother, her *real* mother. She was beautiful and radiated kindness. Maleficent could see the longing in the fairy's two bright eyes. She wanted to reach out to her, and a part of Maleficent wanted her to, to be held and cared for, but a stronger part of her wouldn't allow it. It was the darkness that all the years of abandonment and lies had created. Too many things had happened. Things that wouldn't have happened if it weren't for her parent's absence.

The pause between them had become torturous, agonizing even. Ainsel locked her gaze upon her daughter's big emerald eyes, searching for any glimmer of what she might be thinking. But Maleficent kept her expression cold and fixed like stone.

"Please say something, Maleficent," Ainsel pleaded, taking a step towards her.

But Maleficent merely took another step back, announcing silently that her space was not to be invaded further. Ainsel felt her harsh demand, and though it pained her to do so, she kept herself within the aching distance between them.

"I know this must be hard to hear, but I had to..."

"You had to what!?" Maleficent shouted, finally breaking her silence. "Why are you here? Why now?"

Ainsel felt the sting of each word as if they had hit her. "I told you. I had to come see you. After what happened in King Stefen's castle, seeing what you had become, what you were willing to do, even to an innocent child. I knew I couldn't stay away any longer."

It was then that Maleficent's face went hot from the boiling blood that coursed through her veins. The fire in her eyes blazed with enough fury to melt a mortal's bones. "So! You say that you have been watching over me all my life! Meaning you have seen everything I have been through. You watched the lying hag raise me as her pupil, to be a lonely outcast forever locked away in the Forbidden Forest! You watched her lie to me year after year, about who I really was, who *she* really was! You watched as the woodland fairies struck every painful blow that left me covered in hideous scars! You watched as the Snow Queen's monster dragged my true love and I through the burning snow and into the Icy Citadel to exact upon me the revenge for my father's evil sins! You watched me beg Mim for the spell that could give me back the one I love— and *fail*. You watched those mortals betray me, giving my enemies the fame and glory! You watched them treat me like a monster, undeserving of their loyalty and respect! How sweet it is- that I've lived my pitiful life suffering alone and hated by all— *all* under the watchful eyes of my *mother!*"

Her words were full of rage, but the tear of sadness that fell from her right eye is what hurt Ainsel the most.

"Oh, darling, please..."

"I cannot believe that you have the nerve, the boldness to come here, invade my home, to appear before me after all these years. Not for *me*, but for a *mortal child!*"

Ainsel quickly jumped in objection, "No, Maleficent! You misunderstand me. I wanted to come for you. I came close so many times. But I couldn't! For your protection!"

Maleficent scoffed at the very thought, "If you truly saw everything that has happened in my life, you know full well that you didn't protect me from *anything!*"

Ainsel sighed sadly, tears free-falling down her perfect skin. "I know that is what you think, but I have, Maleficent. I am sorry for all the things I couldn't protect you from, for all the things that have brought you sadness. Believe me when I say that being kept from you and your father has been the worst torture imaginable. I haven't been happy since the day you were stolen from us. We both tried to get you back, but the one that took you is far more powerful than we could hope to fight. He gave me a way to always see you but warned that if I ever made contact with you, he would kill not only your father, but you as well."

Maleficent felt the lump in her throat grow and her chest tighten with pained curiosity. "If the thief wanted to keep us apart, as you say, why would he allow you to know where I was?"

Ainsel sighed, "I don't know. I have spent years wondering why myself. But as each day that I had to watch you from a distance passed, the more painful my agony became. I think that is what he wanted. For me to always be able to see you, but never have you."

"The Wood Witch said I was with her because of a deal she made with my grandfather. Is that true?"

Ainsel nodded, happy that they were finally starting to communicate. "Yes, that is true. Your grandfather was cursed, and he sought her help to rid him of the ghosts that haunted him. In turn, she was to gain his first- born child."

Maleficent squinted in question, "If that were true, why didn't she take him? *My father.* How did she come to possess me instead?"

"Your grandfather is a pirate, a notorious pirate in fact. The curse that was cast upon him made him immortal. Over the years he remained careful not have any children, but time ultimately made him careless. After he discovered that he was going to have a child, he told the woman he loved about what he had done. The woman ran off and left your father on a doorstep of an orphanage after he was born."

Maleficent's face turned up with frustration, "What is an orphanage?"

Ainsel frowned, "It is a place for- children without parents."

Maleficent looked down at the ground, knowing full well the burden of such a fate. Unloved, unwanted, and forgotten by the world, she knew the feelings all too well, and they sat alive as ever in the pit of her stomach. Afraid of her vulnerable expression, she turned. "Go on."

"The poor woman's efforts were noble but feeble in the eyes of the fae. Your grandfather's curse left the mark of magic on his son. It didn't take too long for a fairy to find him. But your father, unlike most lonely children, didn't want to go with the fairy willingly. He wasn't easily lured away with magical promises. This was... Well, to be honest, such a situation is highly unusual."

Maleficent sat in her throne as the lump in her throat finally gulped down painfully. The memory of the night of the party under the calling moon was all too vivid. The colors, the food, the music, not even she was able to resist its alluring enchantment. But unlike other children, even her own father, the reason she had escaped such a fate wasn't because she resisted them, it was because she simply wasn't wanted. The sting of their rejection suddenly burned her scars like fresh cuts under the waves of the salty sea. The pain made her wince, but still, she kept her expression hard, listening intently to the soothing sound of the Blue Fairy's voice.

"The Scarlet Fairy grew angry and resorted to torturing him within his dreams. He was saved by a kind mortal who gave up her own life and soul to protect him from the likes of our kind forever."

Our kind? Two words that nearly stole her breath. It was a wonderful feeling. Melting even.

No. Maybe she didn't mean 'our' as in 'me and her.' Maybe she was just speaking for fairies in general. Yes. Don't be foolish, Maleficent. You don't have a kind. The fairies didn't want you. You're not even welcome in the Nine Realms. You're alone.

"I do not wish to hear anymore. None of this makes any difference now, does it? Please leave," Maleficent said with a cold tone.

Ainsel felt stunned. *Had she said something wrong?* "I did not mean to upset you. I do not want to leave you. I came to help you."

214

Maleficent turned up her gaze, huffing in mild amusement, "Oh, yes. You came to save the child I cursed. How could I have forgotten?"

Ainsel couldn't help but feel her legs weaken as her eyes fell in disappointment.

Maleficent laughed cruelly at her pitiful state, "Hmmm... Well, *Mother*, the woman you left to raise me did teach me the art of a deal. So, I'll tell you what. If you can give me back my true love from the likes of the Snow Queen, I will remove the curse on the little rose."

Ainsel sighed again, disheveled by what she was about to say, "I am sorry, darling, but I cannot do that."

Maleficent's lips curled. "You need not look so miserable. After all, I didn't expect you to be able to do something that I myself wasn't able to do. Now that we agree you cannot give me my happiness; however, I ask that you leave and not look upon me in the future."

"I did not say that I cannot grant your wish because I do not have the power to do so. I said that I cannot because..."

Maleficent's eyes went wide, rage filling to the brink, "Because of what?!"

"Because... the one you love is not who you think he is. I'm sorry." Ainsel lifted her eyes with bravery, "He doesn't love you."

"What- did- you- just- say?"

"I'm sorry, darling, but..."

"You can't say that! You have no right! You think you know everything that has happened in my life, but you don't. He and I have spent years together in my dreams. It was our secret. He is the only one who has ever treated me like..."

"He lied." The words of the Wood Witch suddenly echoed through the very tunnel of her memories.

The memory was an unwelcome one, and only managed to infuriate her further. "I am going to tell you the same thing I told the old hag. I cast a spell that would ensure he was telling me the truth. I did not give up my heart so easily. I was careful. But even as my unyielding doubt and suspicion rained down upon him, he never gave up on me. He never left me *alone.*"

Ainsel flushed under the attack of her last words.

"He has never given me any reason to think he would betray my heart. Why would he spend years trying to win my love? What is there to gain from such a cruel act? Your accusation just doesn't make any sense! He was there for me when you weren't, and he told me the truth while Mim fed me only lies. There is nothing you can say that would change my mind. Nothing!"

Ainsel nodded slowly, "I can see that."

In that bittersweet moment, Ainsel could see James' stubbornness in her. But the thought was fleeting as she realized what was going to happen next.

"You are right, dear. I haven't given you any reason to trust me, and the witch... well, I think you might find that she had reasons for her deceit. I can see now that you no longer have the ability to believe something solely on faith alone, but rather can only derive the truth from discovering it yourself. Only then will you see through the love that blinds you. But believe me, the truth will become clear soon. I only wish that you realize who really loves you before it's too late. Not only for the mortal you have cursed, but also the soul that I love that is darkening within you."

A tense pause filled the air between them in that moment; the room suffused with both love and hate. Finally, Maleficent stood. "Get. Out." She commanded in an eerily cold tone. "Consider our ties broken. Do not look in on my life again, or I will happily burn out the star that twinkles with your presence in the sky, proving once and for all, that in the end- there is only darkness."

Ainsel wiped a tear from her cheek and she turned to face the open window from once she came. But just before she began to flutter her wings, she heard Maleficent ask one last question.

"Wait! You said that I would soon discover the witch's reasons. How? She is dead." Caught within a quiet whimper, she found her mother's sad voice. "Sleep well, my darling. *Sleep well.*"

And then she was gone. Gone from the dark palace that stood upon the Forbidden Mountain, maybe even gone from the world. Maleficent couldn't resist the urge to saunter over to the open window, the very frame that has so often in life been the gateway for the fae. And this time, it had been her own mother who had come through. If only she had done so all those years ago. All the years she had looked up at the stars and the moon, searching for anything to not feel so lonely. But now, the knowing of her mother looking down at her all those times didn't fill her with the love or longing that it would have then. Now, knowing that her mother had always been there, just out of the reach of comfort, the idea swelled her being with fury.

Grip sleepily flew over to her, interrupting her overwhelming thoughts. His dark precious face made her lips curl into a slight smile. "Did you hear all that, my pet?" She asked as he nuzzled his head into her palm.

"I mean, even if this being, this thief did threaten her... She should have tried harder. She shouldn't have been so weak. Or maybe this wasn't about protecting me at all. Maybe this performance was purely in hopes of saving her beloved mortal. True, there are still so many things I do not understand, so many things I still do not know. But every time I discover the truth of something that I didn't know... I wind up wishing I could go back to the blissful ignorance. She left me alone, to survive on my own, to face my enemies alone. Well, I did. And I did it all without her!"

The storm that stirred wildly inside her had brought her to an erratic pace across the cold stone floor of the darkening castle. Grip could hardly keep up with her, yet his focus remained, listening intently to every word of her rage.

"Coming here to help me! Me! The Mistress of all Evil needing the help of one weak little fairy that couldn't even protect her own baby. Help me! Ha! And sleep well? Why did she say that? Sleep well. Did she somehow know of my recent night terrors? No, she couldn't possibly. She said she had been watching over me my whole life. She didn't say she could see what happens in my head. I suppose she merely took notice of my lack of sleep, not that she knew the cause. Still, such a strange departure."

The adrenaline that had been surging through her body for days was finally burnt out. Maybe it was the emotional draining of the Blue Fairy, or maybe it was the curse she had inflicted upon the little rose. In truth, she was exhausted before she went to King Stefen's castle. Sleep. The very idea sickened her. It wasn't out of fear. It wasn't even about the nightmares. It was simply because of her. *"Sleep well."*

Maleficent shook her head, feeling the heaviness of her eyes and body. The thought of lying down upon a comfortable bed was unbearably inviting. Still, she couldn't stand the thought that she might be being watched. With a wave of her hand, long woven tapestries of exquisite designs hung before the windows; the largest covering the window of the two twinkling stars. The thickness of each hanging left the castle in complete darkness. Maleficent then stood, using the glowing glass orb upon her staff to light her way through the castle to her bedroom.

Once inside her somber chambers, Maleficent surrendered to the massive black four-poster bed covered in thick blankets and pillows. No sooner had she carefully laid her horned crown upon her pillow; did she drift off to sleep.

* * *

Just as Flora had predicted, the broken minds of the king and queen were only too easily convinced to hand

219

over their newborn daughter in hopes that the three fairies could keep her hidden for the next sixteen years. In truth, all the fairies had to do was shine the light on the very real possibility that Maleficent would come to the kingdom again, this time to find and kill the child. The thought of Maleficent returning was not only terrifying but crippling as well. Whether it was truly for their daughter's protection or for their own, the sisters did not know, but in the end, it didn't matter. The child was handed over to their care, and the three fairies discreetly made their way out into the dark night under their heavy cloaks.

The journey into the Forbidden Forest wasn't only a most exhausting venture for magical creatures having to travel as mortals on foot, it was also a painful reminder of everything they had lost that terrible night of the woodland party. None of them had anticipated the agonizing memory would affect them so harshly. The darkness of the night hid the tears that trickled down their strained faces. No one said a word as they made their way through the knotted trees and virgin brush. But then suddenly, the feeling in the cool air changed. It was tense and full of such profound misery that it crept upon every inch of their skin.

They were *here.* Standing upon the edge of the scorched grounds cursed by the old witch. Fauna couldn't help but twitch and tremble in that moment.

"No. I can't. We can't. We can't walk through there. There must be another way to the witch's cottage," Fauna whimpered quietly.

"Get ahold of yourself, sister. Don't forget *you* are the one holding the baby," Flora scolded.

Fauna looked down at the sleeping child in her trembling arms. Only after seeing the calm serene breathing of her unknowing innocence did Fauna notice her own erratic breaths racing against her panicked pulse.

"Stop, Fauna, stop. You are going to wake it up," Merryweather said sternly.

Fauna nodded but couldn't bring herself to take another step. She tried to will herself forward, but the weight of her anxiety left her frozen. Tears streamed down her cheeks as she parted her lips in an unrelenting sob, "I can't move. I just can't."

Merryweather sighed in irritation, "Oh, for the love of the gods. Let's just use our magic and fly to the cabin."

"No," Flora said in a scolding tone. "Have you two lost your senses? We cannot use our magic. Not now. Not here. Anyone could be watching, or even listening."

Merryweather and Fauna looked around fearfully.

"This is the only way. Now, I hate this as much as you two do, but if we want to get to the cabin, then we are going to have to cross the... We have to cross our home," Flora whispered, trying to keep her strong composure. "Not another word. I want you two to get behind me and follow my lead. And no matter what happens, keep your feet moving."

Fauna took in a deep breath, conceding defeat to her sister's command. And though Merryweather hated when her sister told her what to do, she followed suit for the sake of their mission.

Flora turned her back, giving them a moment to get behind her. She had been strong. Strong for them, her younger sisters. She had done her duty as the oldest and taken charge. The woods had become eerily silent, leaving only the sound of the two sister's feet to shuffle behind her.

But even with her back turned, Flora could feel her sister's fear and dread. As the silence was torn by the whimpering sobs of Fauna, and the pounding heartbeat of Merryweather, she knew she had to remain calm and quiet. Now they were ready, *ready* and waiting for her. But there, upon the edge of their former home, Flora took the first step across the threshold, unleashing the silent teardrop of her inner torture to fall secretly upon the ground. Step by step, the three fairies made their way into the sacred part of the woods. Never had the three sisters been more grateful for the illusion of magic. But even as they walked through what appeared to be a majestic forest full of green and thriving life, they couldn't bring themselves to look up into the swaying branches that chimed from the hanging shadows of their family. The misery and sadness twitched upon every nerve of their spines as they passed under their invisible dancing forms, reminding each of the three fairies of the immortal sorrow that hovered above them.

The sisters felt the crushing weight of the sadness that flooded the scorched grounds, but they pressed onward, putting each foot in front of the other. They finally made their way to the hill, and for the first time in what felt like the longest stretch of agonizing hours, the three fairies looked up. The cottage was invisible, but they knew it was there. Like so many parts of the world, they merely needed to cross its barrier. The veil that had kept the witch's home a secret place, hidden to everyone but the lost had now, by some strange twist of fate, the home of the one who had destroyed their own... now belonged to them. The hill was steep, and the sisters were beyond exhausted. But the idea of escaping the haunted that lay behind them was enough to push them through the invisible veil and into the cottage where they would hide for the next sixteen years... Three mortal maidens raising a baby.

* * *

For most, the idea of being watched over by their loved ones above, is a comforted one that is welcome. But to the Dark Fairy, sleeping deeply within her castle upon the Forbidden Mountain, it was her greatest hope that no one was looking down upon her. Little did Maleficent know, however, that her mother wasn't the only one. True, the Forbidden Mountain was hidden to most of the world, but for magical creatures, tracking the source of such explosive power wasn't going to take long. Maleficent had been too preoccupied with the storming chaos of her own life. She hadn't used the proper control needed to hide the powers she had taken from Mim.

Hunted. You'll be hunted. The words of such dire caution seemed so far away now. Too far. To be fair, Maleficent's own list of long enemies seemed to grow by the day and had left her utterly exhausted. The idea of having to deal with Mim's enemies felt like an impossible task. Or maybe— the reasons for Maleficent's complete disregard for such threats was simply because she no longer feared anyone. Yes, she was cold, hard, and consumed with darkness, but it was how she had survived. It was what she needed to be. She not only hated the idea of being weak but was also repulsed by those she thought were. Mim may have been powerful, but to Maleficent, she was nothing but a liar and a coward who had spent her long life hidden away in the woods, too afraid to confront her enemies. The fairies, the Snow Queen, the mortals, even her own mother and father were weak in her eyes. Too weak to fight and win. But not her. She wasn't afraid of anyone or anything. She was alone, yes, but such a fate had left her strong. With Jack, she had love. And though it had broken her heart to lose him, the Snow Queen's wrath had cured her from the burden of weakness. There was nothing left to take from her, to use against her.

But a different kind of burden was about to declare war against Maleficent. Only this time, there wasn't the threat of loss, it was a flood of memories that were going to swarm her dreams. She hadn't given much thought as to why Mim's powers had possessed her after her death, but she was going to find out. She was going to find out soon.

As Maleficent lay sound asleep in her dark bed, Ainsel decided to go against her daughter's wishes and came back to the window. The tapestry was thick and kept the narrow passageways into Maleficent's chambers almost impossible to see. But that wasn't the biggest problem. What made sneaking into Maleficent's castle impossible was the crows. One inch into the darkened palace, and her black-feathered darlings were sure to sound the alarm. No, Ainsel was going to have to cast her spell from the cracks of the bedroom window.

Quieter than air, and more graceful than an angel, the Blue Fairy floated her way before her daughter. And from the cracks between stone and woven cloth, she uttered a quiet spell to help her:

"In the darkness
Where you sleep
Slow the memories
You have to keep
Through her ancient eyes
Let the truth become clear
Answer the questions
You know you fear
Course through the years
Burdened by second sight
And through your darkness
Let our love be your light
You think you're alone
But I'm always right here
Once you give up your pain

It will all become clear."

Like a nursery rhyme spoken with love, Ainsel released her spell and let it fall silently upon her lost love. Maybe Maleficent was right. Maybe she was too late, but she couldn't give up. She would never give up. One way or another, she would find a way to get her daughter back, get James back; one day. Until then, she would have to wait; wait from a distance that had become an endless stretch of torture.

*　　*　*　*

Meanwhile, across the mortal world in a forest far away, the three fairies were suffering their own kind of hell. After enduring a most strenuous journey, full of emotional agony and physical exertion all they wanted was to surrender to the bliss of peaceful sleep. But they were about to learn just how difficult being mortal mothers was going to be.

Maybe it was the strange aura that lingered within the cabin. Maybe it was the dusty, stifling air, or maybe it happened for no reason at all, but the little princess had awoken, crying and screaming beyond any measure of their tolerance.

Fauna tried to console the little baby, patting and bouncing her gently in her arms, but nothing she did seemed to work. She was too tense, too anxious after the journey through the scorched grounds. Flora ran about the cabin, looking for milk and linen to help, while Merryweather stood with her hands over her ears, glaring hatefully at all of them.

"Don't just stand there and scowl at us, sister! Help us!"

"Merryweather scoffed, "This was a terrible idea! Taking our magic away! How are we supposed to nurse it, give her a cradle, give her clothes? We need our magic for all of these things if we are to truly stay in this cabin for the next sixteen years!"

Something about her angered tone managed to make things worse. Princess Aurora erupted into the most horrific wails and cries they had ever heard. Putting her hands back over her ears, Merryweather gave in to her anger, and used what little magic she had mastered without her wand. She reached out her arms, and before Flora or Fauna could say a single word, Merryweather put the little baby into the realm of Slumberland.

"Merryweather! What did you do?" Fauna asked frantically concerned.

"Oh, calm down, sister. I merely placed her into a state of magical sleep. It is perfectly harmless," Merryweather hissed.

Flora stepped towards her, fury blazing in her darkened eyes. "Why. Did. You. Do. That?" She asked seething through her teeth. "I told you that..."

"Well, nothing you two were doing was helping. I told you that we weren't properly prepared. We have nothing we need to care for this- this *thing!*"

"I told you that we couldn't use magic! You're too impulsive! Acting purely out of selfishness! We agreed we had to live like mortals for the next sixteen years! And you cannot handle one single night?!

227

Honestly, sister, you are absolutely infuriating!" Flora scolded.

"Are we in danger? Do you think she will find us? Should we leave?" Fauna asked, her voice covered in panic.

Merryweather rolled her eyes in that moment, "My gods, Fauna! Must you always be so dramatic?"

Fauna flushed under her harsh words.

Then Merryweather turned her frustrated gaze back towards Flora. "You said we couldn't use our wands! I didn't want to give mine up. You took it! I didn't want to live like a mortal for sixteen years! You insisted on it! I might be selfish. That might be true, but I did not cast this little spell impulsively."

Flora squinted her eyes and pressed her lips into a firm line, unsure of what to think. "What do you mean?"

"I meant it when I said we don't have what it takes to take care of the child, stuck in this dreary cabin. We don't have the knowledge, nor the necessary equipment to raise her. Somewhere, deep down, you know that I am right. If we try to handle this with only what we have in the old hag's house, we won't have to wait for Maleficent's curse. The baby will die before she even reaches her first birthday!"

Flora felt her blood boiling, but it was true. They hadn't the faintest idea of how to take care of a baby. With a sigh, she gave in, "Alright, Merryweather. Enlighten us of your *little* plan."

Merryweather couldn't help but sneer at her sister's rude tone. "As a matter of fact— I *do* have a

228

plan! And it's a lot better than the three of us racing around this horrid shack, hoping to find a single thing for the crying creature." Merryweather then looked down at the sleeping baby, unable to remove the disgust from her face. "Horrible, *irritating* cries."

Fauna then turned her arms away from her as if the words might hurt the child somehow. "Sister, please. She cannot help it. She is a baby. Crying is what they do. Especially when they hear angry shouting," she said in a harsh whisper.

Again, Merryweather rolled her eyes and shook her head.

Flora sighed in frustration, "Would you two stop this nonsense! Merryweather, get to the point. What is your idea?"

"No. Forget it," Merryweather mumbled under her breath, crossing her arms in a fuss.

Flora huffed, trying desperately to suppress her growing rage, "Merryweather! You are either going to tell us your plan— or so help me, I will wake that baby up!"

Merryweather looked up at her in horror. She could see that Flora meant it. They were sisters. They knew each other better than any siblings ever could. She was not sure what kind of toll it would take to wake the baby without their wands, but if anyone could- it was Flora.

Merryweather's pride and temper wanted to hold her ground. But somehow, the idea of the child waking up, screaming, and wailing, managed to crumble her mountain of rigidity completely. "Alright!" She shouted in defeat. "It is no secret that the idea of raising this baby, or any baby for that matter, sickens me."

"Well, despite your selfish needs, we cannot just keep her asleep," Fauna hissed.

Merryweather couldn't help but smile slyly at her sister's brazen tone. "Well, actually, sister, we *can*."

Flora and Fauna looked at each other in confusion, but from a single glance, they could each see that neither of them had a clue what she meant.

"What do you mean, Merryweather?" Flora asked.

"I did not just send the child into the Dream Realm. I sent her to Slumberland," Merryweather answered, as if that were enough to answer their question. But after a long pause of their blank stares, she explained further, "Don't you see, sisters? We can manipulate her reality this way. She will grow thinking we fed her, clothed her— *cared* for her. She is already fae touched. She will be absorbed into the illusion we give to her. She will see this cabin. She will see us. She will live happily and healthy. All because that is the dream that we will kindly give her. We are woodland fairies. Only we have the ability to enchant the food and drinks within Slumberland. We can do this. We *should* do this. Otherwise..." Merryweather paused, looking around the dreary old cottage. "*Otherwise,* I fear we will fail her. The baby, our family, our mother, the king and queen, all of them are depending on us."

Flora and Fauna too, looked around the shabby cabin. It was dreadful. Without the illusion enchanted by the witch herself, there was only the truth of time left behind. And in every wall covered in dust, every corner filled with elaborate spider webs, and creaky old furniture, they saw that Merryweather was right. They had all been so caught up in fulfilling the Snow Queen's wishes, that they hadn't thought to prepare properly.

Fairies hate admitting they forgot something. *This is why people think we can only hold one thought at a time. Some even believe that fairies can only have enough room for one feeling at a time. Ridiculous.* Flora thought to herself, though she knew her sisters were thinking the same thing. Still, it simply wasn't something one said out loud, especially when they are already feeling foolish.

Instead, she decided to say something else to them. With a sigh of defeat, she uttered the words her youngest sister loved to hear. "You. Are. Right, Merryweather. This is the only way."

Fauna's hope collapsed. Unlike her sisters, she was excited about nurturing the child. Tears welled up in her eyes. She wanted desperately to change their minds; to fight for her chance to be a mother, but there was nothing. There was no hope at all. Her sisters were right. This place was not suitable for a baby; not even for them. It was going to take some serious fixing up, and without magic... The whole notion seemed all together impossible.

It was then as Fauna looked down at the infant's angelic face that she thought of something. Glee gleamed in her wide eyes then, getting the immediate attention of her sisters.

"What, Fauna? What is it?" Flora asked with wonder.

"The child has to stay in Slumberland. That is true. But the illusion must be dealt with carefully. For though it is a dream, there are still dangers. She could wander too far from the cabin. She could eat poisonous berries in the woods. She could come across some of the witch's books, maybe even some of her magic. We all know of what menacing creatures lie beyond the veil of dreams. They are the worst sort... such hungry shadows. She cannot ever discover the magical illusion that surrounds her, for if she starts to question things, any things... Then it will shatter the dream completely," Fauna answered with a cautionary tone.

"Oh." Flora's expression turned to frightful anxiety at the thought. "Well, we certainly cannot let that happen. That would indeed be awful."

Fauna could suddenly feel herself filling with joy, holding a hidden smile in the corner of her lips. "Yes, it *would* be awful! And I think that the only way to make sure nothing like that ever happens is for us to absorb ourselves into her illusion. We would teach her how to dress, how to dance, how to read, and of course, to explain what dangers lie beyond our part of the forest. And most importantly, as it is a dream of our own creation, what we need and the surroundings we find ourselves living within can manifest by our most clever design. It is the only way. We cannot survive here in this terrible place without magic. We would be fools to think otherwise. In the dream world, our powers could go undetected. Besides, I just think one should handle some of her raising with a personal touch. Just for the important moments, of course."

Merryweather had squinted her gaze, shaking her head ever so slightly as she caught on to her sister's cleverly worded suggestion. "Ah, ha. And just who were you thinking this *one* should be, Fauna? You, perhaps?"

Flora smiled, understanding now what was going on. Fauna flushed under their gaze.

"I think that is a great idea, Fauna. And since it was your idea, I think it only proper that you be given the charge of creating such a design; for the good of the child, and for us as well," Flora said kindly.

Merryweather rolled her eyes. *Like there was any chance of me doing it. What do I care if the child can dance or not?* Still, seeing the utter joy in her sister's big eyes made it impossible not to smile. "So, it is all settled then?"

"Yes," Flora said firmly. Then suddenly she realized something. "No, wait. There is one more thing. A name. She will need a name. As she will be in Slumberland and may accidentally come across another creature. They cannot know who she really is. For they might surrender such information if questioned by Maleficent. Loyalty has a way of being bought by fear. Yes, we have to be really extra careful."

Flora and Merryweather turned their gaze back towards their beaming sister, only to find her nuzzling her nose against the baby's. With closed eyes, and a smile that nearly reached her ears, it was clear how blissfully happy she had become. They had never seen her so content; so calm. She had always been so shaky, so riddled with anxiety. But right now, in this one moment, none of the other stuff mattered. All that mattered now was this little sleeping creature. The baby. Her baby.

"Fauna?" Flora imposed.

Fauna looked over to her as if pulled away from a heavenly daze. "Hmm?"

"We need a name for the baby. Well, I mean she will need a name. What would *you* like to name her?" Flora asked sweetly.

Fauna was stumped. She hadn't thought of that. She had never named anything before. Enormous pressure suddenly suffused her as her mind raced with possibilities. "Should it be a fairy name? Or should it be a mortal name? Should we name her after a jewel, a flower, or something of ancient beauty? It has to be something worthy of her, something as beautiful as she is! But what?" She asked out loud, feeling utterly overwhelmed.

Merryweather was starting to get annoyed again. *Enough with this baby.* "Really, sister, you need not make this so complicated. It does not matter what you name her. She is merely the princess from the Rose Kingdom."

Fauna gasped, looking at the baby in her arms. The answer was written upon her face. The pale perfection of her skin. Her floral scent. And her dark pink lips. "Rose. That is her name. *Briar Rose.*"

* * *

Sleep. For some, it is peaceful. For others, it can be utterly exhausting. A place where imaginations run wild with your subconscious; each inspired by your natural life. But for those that have lived their lives in fear, subdued by the living nightmares of their cruel existence, the dream world can be torturous. For Maleficent, her dreams used to be a wonderous escape. It was a place of beauty, love, and magic. But that all seemed so far away now. So long ago, a past painfully unforgotten. But it wasn't *her* past that swarmed through her chaotic mind. It was another's.

Before this night, it was a racing flood of flashes that coursed through her dreams; each piece mere fragments, slicing through the darkness of her brain like millions of tiny shards of a broken mirror; each piece reflecting a torrid life that seemed to have gone on for centuries. But for some reason unknown, the tiny bits and pieces that had only appeared in an unbearable, disturbing frequency, started to come together like a puzzle; one that would ultimately bring together a whole existence. *But who's was it? Where did they come from?*

"Don't fight it, Maleficent. Open your eyes. See what I saw. Feel what I felt. Open. Open!"

The strange voice jolted her, pulling her out of the darkness, into the binding pieces. It was tense and almost painful.

The first sight of such a collision was somewhere in the woods. *The woods.* How she hated them. The vision brought with it a most uncomfortable sensation. It was calm and almost peaceful. Her eyes felt as if they had been ripped open. She tried to close them but couldn't. In fact, she didn't have control over her body at all. *What's happening?*

"*It is not your body. It was mine... a long time ago. Don't give in to your fear. Be calm. This is just a memory. It has already happened. You cannot change it. To gain control, you need only to give in.*"

"*Who are you?*" Maleficent thought frantically. But no answer came. Instead, the only voice she heard came from *there*. Out there.

"Nimueh— Nimueh, where are you?"

"*Who is that?*" *Maleficent whispered.*

"*My sisters.*" *The voice within answered.*

She began to walk, unwillingly forward. Feelings of both dread and resistance suffused her. It was incredibly strange; feeling things that were not your own, not being able to control your every movement. It was unbearable to have zero control.

"*Where am I going? Where are you taking me?*"

Everything began to get fuzzy, like fading in and out between life and death. It was the most frightening feeling she had ever endured.

"*You're fighting it, Maleficent. Do not let your fear take control. It is just a memory. It has already happened. Let yourself see...*"

Maleficent did as the voice told her. She didn't know why, but it felt comforting, like the sort of protection you get from hiding under your blanket as a child in a room filled with scary noises.

"You're not alone. I am here with you."

After hearing the voice's last words, all started to become clear again. She was still walking, but her legs... they were shaking. *Why do I feel so afraid?* She stopped, feeling her dread mounting.

"We're here. This is where it all started. The crossroads."

Maleficent looked around. She was deep within the entangled woods now. But down, on the forest floor— was a four-way yellow brick road.

Suddenly, three young women emerged from the distance of each surrounding direction, causing goosebumps to rise upon her alien form. It was fear. A *terrible* sensation of fear. The women came towards her with a most predatory expression on their faces. *How could three sisters that are visibly the same age appear so dramatically different from one another?* Maleficent thought. It was then that she wondered what the body controlling her looked like. She tried to dismiss the thought before she was heard, but the faint sound of laughter made her think otherwise.

Coming from the east was a young maiden with dark red hair. Her lips were the shade of a ripe plum, and her eyes shined like a fierce sunset within the shadow of her garland of everlasting roses. She wore a long-woven dress as striking and vibrant as fresh blood. It was split in seven different slits that rose to her thighs, and rippled behind her like ribbons on a breeze, revealing her slender legs and dainty bare feet. Her skin was dark and golden, looking as if every inch of her had

237

been touched by a desert sun. Her glorious beauty was only overshadowed by her obsessive vanity.

"Who is that?" Maleficent wondered.

"That is Crimson. She is the wicked witch of the east. She is heartless, merciless, and rules the element of fire. She has the power to burn anyone or anything that crosses her path, leaving only ash and scorched earth behind her."

Scorched?

Maleficent's thought rapidly evaporated as she turned to see the next sister coming down the southern path. Instantly, the vision of her repulsed Maleficent, yet for some reason, she also felt herself relax in her presence. She was short, pretty, and irritatingly covered in sparkling pink. She wore what appeared to be a tall glittered crown atop her long peachy hair that hung in waves down to her hips. The dress she wore, unlike her sister's, puffed out from her waistline like a fluffy cloud. Her creamy skin was so white that she almost appeared as livid as a corpse. It was as if there was no blood in her veins at all. To Maleficent, it was eerie and unsettling. There was no color in her lips, and her eyes were bright and clear. If it weren't for the fluttering of her long lashes and the overwhelming blush painted upon her cheeks, one would think she was a fancy animated dessert. As she came closer, Maleficent couldn't help but notice that the sparkly woman wasn't walking towards her, but rather floated as graceful as a river.

Ugh. *"Who. Is. That?" Maleficent asked with utter disdain.*

A cackle of laughter echoed in the distance then. *"That is Glinda. She is the good witch of the south. The image of her may leave a sour taste in your mouth, but her soul was as sweet as sugar. She brought hope and happiness to all around her. She rules the element of water, but like any sea, just because the waves can be calm and serene, that does not mean they do not have the power to drown you. This was the last time I saw her this way. And though her appearance was always ridiculous, I always cherished her true heart. The heart she had before..."*

"Before what?"

"Well, well, look what we have here sisters. The half-ling runt!" The third sister said with a most malicious tone before bending her head back with cackling laughter. It was a sound that made you feel sick and fearful. It was the kind of sound nightmares are made of. But it wasn't just her raspy voice or her terrifying laugh that made her the thing of utter horror. It was her appearance. The sight of her was one most foul indeed. She wore a long black dress and a charcoal colored hat that came up to a sharp point. She had green skin that stretched like leather across her long-curved nose and pointed chin. Her eyes were black and yet they looked to be hungering for power, for everything. She carried with her the scent of death itself. Her sharp shoulders appeared like horns for her wicked body. She wore long-laced boots that had small curled heels and pointed at the toes in a way that looked as if they would be absolutely agonizing to wear. Her hands looked skeletal, with gnarled fingers that longed to be around your throat. It was then that Maleficent noticed something else. At first, it looked like she held a wooden staff in her grasp, but upon a closer glance, she was surprised to find it wasn't a staff at all. It was a broom.

"That is Delora, the wicked witch of the west. She is ruthless, vile, the epidemy of evil itself. There is nothing good inside of her. Her heart is darker than the black on her dress. She rules the element of air. It is an incredible power to possess, but she wants more. So much more."

"Why is she green?"

"Envy, greed, her sour heart... You may not see it, but everything has a color, an aura. You cannot see them because they are hidden by the living vessel that surrounds them. Well in this land, let's just say that colors are a little more vibrant than they are in any other. Who you are, what you are— is far more exposed. You need not wait to discover one's true colors. Not here. Here, your spirit is always revealed. Things on the other hand, like the forest, the food, the clothes... I always found them to be overwhelmingly colorful."

"What color are you?"

Maleficent could almost feel a smile as the voice answered, *"I suppose I was mostly purple."*

Before Maleficent could say another word, Delora spoke again: "Do you know why we are here, Nimueh? Why we are *all* here?"

"No." Maleficent felt her mouth say the word, but it wasn't her own. It was so strange. She felt possessed somehow, and yet, this wasn't that at all.

"We are all so tired of your ways, your failures. We all do our biding, our duties given to us. But you, you just run off into your part of the woods, never delivering, never..." Delora huffed, seething through her dark teeth.

Suddenly, Glinda floated forward. "Nimueh dear, what Delora is trying to say is that... Well, after our mothers heard of your sudden rebellion, they charged the three of us to find the root of your disobedience. So, we..."

"You've been spying on me? Even you, Glinda?"

"She didn't have the nerve!" Crimson stated sharply. "It was Delora and I that discovered your little secret."

Maleficent felt the heart drop within her body and an intense battle of tears fighting to reach her eyes as Delora slithered up to her face, heaving her rancid breath upon her skin. Maleficent wanted to push her, to *end* her, but she couldn't. She couldn't do anything—anything but watch.

"We know you have been helping the lost travelers out of our woods! Freeing the souls that belong here! To us! To Oz!" Delora screamed, unleashing an odor most foul to smother Maleficent's scent.

"Why would you do that, Nimueh?" Glinda asked sounding deeply concerned. "You were the best at getting them. Out of all of us, you have always been our mothers' greatest weapon. The greatest hope for

Oz. With you, our possibilities will become endless. We were all created to rule the world. The four of us. North, south, east, and west. Why would you want to take that away?"

"Because she is a traitor. Because she only cares about herself. Not us. Not even her own sisters!" Crimson yelled in fury, her skin getting as red as her dress.

"We know something else as well, runt!" Delora hissed. "We know you have created some hidden little place in your part of the forest. You think you are so clever, that I won't find out what you have been up to! Well, my pretty, you are dead wrong! I'll find a way into your hidden little nook, and I'll be the one to expose your secrets!"

"And to think, we always treated you as our equal, as our dear little sister. But now, we see who you truly are!" Crimson declared.

"Oh, I always knew. She is not our equal. She is nothing but a defiant half-ling," Delora whispered harshly before slowly withdrawing her up-close invasion. "Oh, well. It is of no matter now. Our mothers will take care of everything, even you!"

"What do you mean? They wouldn't, you wouldn't hurt me?"

A chill crawled up her spine as the witch's cackling laughter erupted again. "Oh, Nimueh, I would love nothing more! But no, our mothers have something else in mind. Something that will make you one of us. Well, a much weaker version of us, but that is just a punishment you will have to endure. Maybe if you are lucky, our mothers will still allow you to rule the north. Even after they kill him."

"Him?" Her voice shuttered with terror.

"Your father," Crimson said, unable to suppress her pleasure.

Suddenly, she felt seized with horror.

"What, Nimueh? Were you thinking we meant someone else?" She asked with a sinister twinkle in her eyes before she straddled her magical broom and rose into the sky. "Remember what I said, *runt!* You won't be able to keep your secrets forever! I'll find them out! And when I do, I won't be coming back with another warning." At that, the green witch flew away into the ever-changing sky.

Maleficent turned to find that Crimson, too, had left her. Now, there was only Glinda floating before her. "Poor sister, I know it seems harsh, but I am sure it is for the best. Killing the Erlking will rid you of your mischievous fae afflictions. You will be just like us, and I will help you. I promise."

"No! You cannot do this. He is my father. I love him. He has been so good to me. It is not his fault. Do not punish him for my defiance!"

"Nimueh, we cannot go against our mothers, and you shouldn't go against us in this way. We are sisters. Our bond is one made of magic. You may never be our equal, but you are still our sister. Please, Nimueh, just accept our mother's decree. Obey, and do not interfere," Glinda said sounding sweetly authoritative. Then, from a flick of her hand, a thin bar of power emerged in her grasp. She whipped it like a wand, and a massive pink bubble suddenly appeared around her and after one last sympathetic smile, the bubble carried her away.

Maleficent suddenly felt suffused with sadness and terrible grief that rose with guilt because of her relief. It was a storm of emotions. She couldn't take on her sisters. She couldn't take on her mothers. Still, she had to try. It was the right thing.

Suddenly, she was running, running fast upon the yellow brick road. *"No! Stop! Turn back! There is nothing you can do!"* Maleficent thought. But it was no use. She sped through the trees, bursting into a city full of green, everything green.

"Where am I?"

"This is Emerald City."

She raced with inhuman force up to a gigantic palace. It was her father's home, her home. It was the home that she and she alone could roam. Her sisters had always hated this, even Glinda was known to give in to jealousy when it came to the castle. She looked up, at the top where she knew her father was, reading his favorite story within his vast library of magical books. It was a collection he was most proud of. He had even read some of them to her. He wanted her to learn fae magic, to impart his wisdom upon her. He treated her with love, the kind of love only a parent can give. And now, because of her, they were going to kill him, killing the best part of her in the process.

She tried to run inside, but the guards were under her sister's spell. "Let me pass! This is my home! Father!"

But the guards wouldn't budge. Their eyes were empty, their minds blank. They were mere puppets now. Maleficent felt her body turn back, and a desperate scream pierce the air. "Father!"

The Erlking came to his balcony, looking down to her with concern. The sight of him let a single breath of relief to escape. But then suddenly... he was struck with blasts. Not just one, but six. She could see them. Her sister's magic, her mother's magic, all of it- slicing and burning through him. All the while, through every strike, his eyes never left her gaze. And in the end, she watched the life leave his eyes.

"Father! No!" She cried, crumbling to the ground.

"I thought it was over then, but I was wrong. Things were about it get worse... a lot worse."

Maleficent couldn't bear to see more, but as her eyes looked back up to the father's dead body, she realized she was going to have to watch something else happen. She was going to watch the mother's plan unravel. Like the very core of dark magic, the broken vessel of the Erlking came undone, unleashing a toxic evil that rose into the air like a black storm. The vision was absolutely horrifying.

"What is that?" Maleficent asked.

"That, Maleficent, is the beginning."

"Of what?"

"Of me."

"But if your father died, didn't you lose half your powers?"

"You never asked what my powers were?"

Hadn't she? She thought back to all she had said, all that she had seen, but the sight of the darkness swelling the sky made it hard to think. *"Well, I know you have half the powers of a witch and half the powers of the fae. Your sisters each have the power of an element. Fire, water, air... I know you were the one that was meant to rule the north, but what element do you rule?"*

"My mothers and sisters had always underestimated my powers, but that was nothing compared to how much I had underestimated myself. I was meant to rule earth, but after this terrible night, the night that all the dark magic of the worlds was spilled out upon the land of Oz... I would come to rule them all."

"All?"

"Yes. And soon, you are going to find out how."

"But I..."

"Hush now. You did well, Maleficent. Now open your eyes. Open them."

* * *

Lost between two worlds, two lifetimes, and two dreams, two souls were caught within a beautiful lie and a painful truth.

Night after night, the three sisters desperately searched for the Wood Witch's hidden spell books. For though they were behind the veil of dreams, no magical item could be removed. And by day, they pursued in their course, lovingly upbringing the child they had taken while Maleficent waited alone within her dark palace on the Forbidden Mountain. Questions and fear fought side by side to consume her. She didn't know what was happening. *Where did this voice come from? Why was she showing her these memories? Was she going mad or was this some sort of trick?* Her mother's last words to her echoed in her head... *"Sleep well."*

Mim had warned her about the powers the fairies menacing influence within the dream realm. *But why now? What was to gain by forcing her to possess a memory? And whose voice was it that controlled her so wretchedly? It sounds both strange and yet familiar somehow. But that is impossible. I do not know anyone from that place... from Oz.*

It was all so invasive, so confusing. Afraid of the time, never quite knowing the hour due to the everlasting darkness outside her windows, Maleficent's tension only grew. Dreading the weariness of the upcoming night, Maleficent fought hard to stay awake, but it seemed not even a sorceress as powerful as herself could ward off sleep forever.

Luckily for her, one of her faraway crows came through the window squawking just as she was about to nod off upon her throne. What *was* unlucky, however, was the reason for her little darling's visit.

"Hello, my pet. Come here, let me look at you," she whispered in a sweet and drowsy tone. The crow obeyed and flew to her welcoming hand, perching himself upon her fingers. After a gentle stoke through his feathers, she lifted his long beak to look into his beautiful onyx eyes. "I've fought for hours not to look through another's eyes," she chuckled to herself. "Let's hope you have some good news to share. Show me."

A tunnel twisted and turned through darkness into a vortex of spinning colors. All too fast, the vision stilled, revealing the massive flames that towered over the gloomy Rose Kingdom, desperately burning what appeared to be a towering mountain of spinning wheels. At first, the sight made Maleficent smile inside. *Pathetic fools. "You needn't worry, my pet, their efforts are laughable."*

Maleficent waited for the vision to end, thinking that the fire was all there was to see— but it wasn't over. Suddenly, she felt as if she were flying, moving closer to the windows of King Stefan's dreary castle. *"What is this? What are you trying to show me?"*

The answer came quietly as her vision came to an open window. There within the new princess's chambers, she found only an empty cradle. She could feel the sadness that flooded the lonely room. Then with a quick glance to the left, she found the only sound to break such silence. It was the queen. She was in a most wretched way. It wasn't just the effects of her spell; this was a different kind of sorrow. The king came into the room then, kneeling to her in hopes he might offer her some sort of comfort. "Please, dear, do not weep. She will be safe now. I am assured of it."

"But what if Maleficent..."

"Oh, damn that miserable creature! I will hear no more on the matter. You must trust me. I have done and will do everything within my power to destroy her, and then... our beloved daughter will come back home where she belongs. With her beauty and title, she will join together the two kingdoms, and all will be well again. My reign will be glorious again! Every kingdom across the lands have heard our cry. Vast armies are out there now, hunting her down."

"But I..."

"Hush now!" He commanded harshly. But after a great breath of composer, he set upon her a small token of affection. "Come now, it is late. Let me help you to bed. There is nothing in this room for us anymore; nothing but sadness."

The queen looked around at the dark empty room, holding her gaze for a moment too long upon the cradle that painfully stood still. A heavy tear fell down her cheek as she whispered, "Wishes."

"What was that, my dear?" He asked sweetly

"It was the wishes that brought us here. Do you think it strange?"

"I do not understand. What do you mean?"

"We already had everything before we wished for more. We wished for glory, for wealth, for beauty, but the more we wished for, the more we lost. And now, I find that I have never wished for anything, nor longed for anything as much as to see her cradle rock; to hear her precious coos that fill me with such joy. For now that I am without them, I see that I will never feel happiness again until she is in my arms."

"Leah, it is not your fault. *This*— is not our fault."

She turned her sad gaze to his, "I neither know who is to blame, nor who I should trust any longer. I know that I feel tricked, but I am not sure by whom."

The king scoffed at her words, "It was that devil! It was Maleficent!"

"Was it?" She replied in a calm tone, too weak from sadness to match his. "We made a promise; a promise we broke, however misguided. Our intention does not change, nor correct our error. And now, our daughter's life is in the hands of magic once more. You say that you are assured, well, I am not. I think I would be a fool to feel assured by anything or anyone at this moment. I will not rest easy, sir. Every breath I breathe will be full of dread and every day that passes without my child is another day I pray for death."

"Leah! You must not say such things! You are the queen."

She shook her head and huffed quietly as she made her way towards the chamber door, "Queen of what, husband? Our kingdom is in ruin, and I am just a mother— without a baby."

Her words stilled him, rendering him speechless. She opened the door and without properly lifting her dress from the floor, she walked out into the darkness that shadowed over the gloomy castle, and into her bed chambers to sleep, hoping, praying, but never wishing that she might get to see her sweet little princess in a faraway dream. Little did she know, it was the closest she was ever going to get.

* * *

After the king left the room, closing the door and all hope away, the vision from the open window closed, tunneling away back to Maleficent. She opened her eyes, burning with fury. "Damn me?! Destroy me?! Ha! What an insolent fool. Thinking he could destroy me! By the gods above and below, he can send thousands to hunt me down, but they will not succeed. My curse is absolute. There is nothing they can do. Hiding the child was a mistake since it was just another arrogant act against me. I half expected a vision of remorse, desperation, a cry for my forgiveness, and what do I see instead?"

"But what about the poor mother? Did you not see her remorse? Her suffering?"

The question came like a sharp pain to the head, unwanted and intrusive. It was so quick, so sudden, that Maleficent was not completely sure where it came from. *Did the voice come from someone else or was it simply the sharp cut of her conscience?* She shook her head, refusing such pity. "I care nothing for *mothers,* nor their sufferings! Why should I? No one, including their royal highness care for mine. No, instead they plot to hunt me down, to kill me. A mountain of spinning wheels burning to ashes as they try to hide their precious princess. And with those three little minions no doubt."

Suddenly, as if out of thin air, she was struck with an idea. *Minions. Hmmm.* "Maybe it is about time I have some servitude to do my every bidding as well," She said calmly sauntering towards the window that looked out to the black sea. "Come, Grip, let us call an army of our own. I shall not be destroyed! Not by the three sisters, not by an army of mortals, not even by an arrogant king! No, *I*—will be their suffering, and I will be their end.

* * *

Determination is quite a weapon, especially if it is a dark heart that drives it, and Maleficent seemed to always feel determined in every choice she made. She could not be bothered to concern herself with minor trifles, such as fear of her dreams, confusion over whom it was that possessed her thoughts, nor a sliver of empathy towards the sad queen that spent her days and sleepless nights wallowing around her castle like a ghost, living but not quite alive. No, Maleficent could only think of one thing, one purpose— to find the baby that her enemies tried to hide from her, and to destroy all of those who stood in her way. Everything else offered her little ease. Remorse, mercy, doubt, fear, all of them had to be eliminated. She could count on no other emotion but one: hatred. It was strong. It has given her purpose, and in each and every moment that she gave in to its darkness, she found that she felt more powerful than ever. It was the only real thing she could control, so why should she possibly desire anything else?

But even with great power, Maleficent could not stop the time from ticking onward. For immortals, sixteen years feels like days; she was going to need some help. *But who? Or rather what?* She thought back to all of the Wood Witch's teachings, all of her studies and the countless books she had read.

Who could she count on? They would need to be subservient, but also loyal. She closed her eyes and dashed through the ancient pages held within her memories; some it seemed were not even her own. But like so many other things in life, the answer is too often the most obvious one.

"You are thinking about it too hard, Maleficent. You know of whom you need. Tap into your inner knowledge and call upon those you seek." Whispered the unwelcome voice that haunted her.

The words came quick and soft like that of an ominous breeze passing in the night; Maleficent hadn't more than a mere moment before she could feel whatever presence vanish from her thoughts. Maybe it was because there were more pressing matters at hand, but it seemed she didn't feel the slightest bit resistant.

Instead, she did as the voice said. She took a deep breath, expelling all the scattered pages from her mind; all but one. A single parchment remained aglow amongst those that faded to darkness. And from the blurred image of black and red ink, the written words came into focus, the top reading:

Goblins! Of course.

The fact of the matter was that these diminutive foot soldiers could prove to not be as perfect as she thought. Yes, they would both fear and respect her, but the only thing smaller than their brain was their sense of sanity. More like unruly children, these creatures delighted in destruction and causing havoc. Still, they were the best choice during this great moment.

Not wanting to waste another second, Maleficent sat upon her throne and with a whip of her hand, the heavy drapes she had placed upon her windows slowly moved aside, revealing the wonderous moon that shined upon the black sea below. With a tall and powerful posture, it seemed like her new mission had driven away her weary heart. She felt energized and though she would never have admitted it, not even to herself, her lonely isolation within her dark castle had begun to feel like a prison.

There was a tinge of excitement that should the goblins come to serve her; she would no longer be so alone. With the ghost of a smile upon her face, she twisted her glorious staff and made her daring call:

"Come not one,
But rather all
To those born of chaos
Let thou turmoil fall
Come serve your mistress
Paint your evil my way
Do what I will
And do as I say
On pain of death

Betray me not
Or I condemn you
All to rot
But please me well
And rewarded you'll be
I call to all goblins
Come out for me."

With a flash or green light, her summoning was cast. Now all she had to do was wait for her princes of mischief, her new little children.

It did not take long, not long at all. They came from each corner of the worlds beyond. Through each veil torn asunder, they shifted and scrambled to make their way towards the Forbidden Mountain. They came by high air and slithered up from the sea, and one by one, they transformed into their true horrifying form. Eager and afraid, the goblins crawled up the slippery rocks that led to her dark castle. The ominous aura of her power lured them in like blood in the water. They couldn't resist such magic. The closer they came towards her door, the taste of her wickedness came thicker through the cold air, causing them to pant like dogs with each and every huffing breath.

At last, they arrived. As the first goblin took his final step upon the last stone, he looked up in awe as the towering doors opened, slowly creaking with a most wretched pitch that the impish creatures desperately reached to cover their ears. It wasn't that the door was old, for this wasn't an ancient castle at all. It had been made by her own design and thus so was this particular painful screech that scratched its way into their brains. True, it was a cruel welcome, but to Maleficent, it was an important one. She needed their first entrance to be a submissive one. Writhing and skittish upon the moment of their arrival was exactly what she desired for her grand introduction.

By the final count, it seemed more than a few hundred goblins had come by her call. And just as she had wished, they came crawling in awe. Each gazed upon her as if she were more wonderous and fearsome than the gods. It was not by any lack of encounters, for the goblins were older than any fairy. Time had passed them in so many ages that they were ultimately fogged, leaving their very own origin a mystery— even to them. But that should never suggest that they are naïve in matters of the other magical creatures of the past and present. But this— *her...* They had never witnessed such profound power. Being of little brain, they could not detect the multiple sources within her that caused her presence to be so magical.

It wasn't in a goblin's nature to question things; sense, remorse, and even one's motives were nothing more than unnecessary complications. They didn't trouble themselves with such trifles. They had never served anyone before, only their malicious desire to cause mayhem.

Luckily for Maleficent, they couldn't comprehend why they had come, nor would they spare a single moment wondering why. All they understood was how powerful she was, and that she had both threatened and bribed them. Goblins didn't usually meddle with fairy affairs, nor any witches for that matter. They knew what kind of pain and misery they could cause, but they had never been offered a reward before, and by one glance upon Maleficent, they knew they never had a choice in the matter. They belonged to her now. And as she stood from the seat of her throne, they bowed before her dark majesty.

She looked down upon their impish stature, with skin like a crocodile and squished up faces of disproportion. Each appeared more hideous than the last. With greasy hair that hung low around their head, with big ugly ears that erected outward like horns. Their eyes seemed to glow yellow, both too big and round. Their hog-like nose snorted, and the snarling sounds that came from their throats could be heard echoing off the walls. But what made these creatures so incredibly wretched was the smell of death that came from the breath beyond their jagged teeth. One could almost see the rotting flesh between them as they drooled naked upon the floor. She smiled at them before erupting in a fit of laughter so wicked, it made each of their bones tremble before her. At last, she had her army. They were there to serve her— their beautiful Mistress of all Evil.

After a moment delighting in her elated euphoria, Maleficent tried to compose herself, after all, if she was to be their leader, their queen, then she should behave as such, and not allow herself to show such joy for petty pleasures. If she was going to be able to control the uncontrollable, then she would have to do it the way of the Wood Witch. She would have to control them with fear. Little did she grasp that her fit of manic laughter, however gleeful, had struck more than enough fear in the goblins. In the realms of magic, even the goblins understood that fear was the recipe of respect. Though how long one could keep the respect of such chaotic little minds, none of them knew. With goblins, all one could expect is one moment. That is as long as you have to catch their eyes, and if they feel even a whiff of boredom, they would surely leave, but not before performing a masterpiece of destruction upon whomever dared to be so dreadfully dull in their presence.

"Thank you for coming! All of you are welcome, here in my castle, my home. Some of you are here in hopes of rewards, tokens of magic with powers you've never known possible. Others came here terrorized by my threats, but I tell you all here and now that I am not a difficult creature to please, nor will your charge be anything too difficult for you. Not only do I think you will find my request reasonable, but also horribly fun!"

The goblins heard little of what she said, in fact, they found her proper words of introduction to be dry and dismal, but her last words sent a spark of electricity up their crooked spines.

"What is it you want?"

"What do we do?

"Tell us, Dark Mistress."

"Tell us. Tell us. Tell us." The goblins cried out to her.

Maleficent smiled at their excitement. "I want you to find a child. Not just *any* child; I need the princess born to the Rose Kingdom. She has been taken from King Stefan's castle. They mean to keep her hidden from me."

"Who, Mistress?"

"Who would dare?" The Goblins shouted.

"The babe has been touched by three meddlesome fairies. They have bestowed a great deal of magic upon her. They are my bitter enemies."

"The fairies?" A small goblin asked.

"But aren't you..."

"I am *nothing* like those vermin!" Maleficent roared, knocking the nearest off their feet. "I am so much more than any mere fairy or witch alike. You needn't concern yourself with defining me. Keep your limited focus on your given task— the baby!"

"The baby. The baby. The baby," the goblins whispered to each other, snickering back and forth like that of mischievous children. The words spread, filling the cold damp castle with an ominous air.

"How do we find her?"

"Where do we look, Mistress?"

Maleficent rolled her emerald eyes, "If I knew how or where to find the wretched creature, I would not be asking you to search, would I? Idiots! Search the lands far and wide, leave no home, no corner, no sea, nor any shadow unseen. I may not know where to look, but I can tell you this— the princess will not appear like any other babe you have seen. The fairy's gifts upon the brat will prove to be more useful to me than to them. The baby will be more beautiful than humanly possible. Listen for a mystical voice that shames even the most

259

talented of angels. Her hair will shine like golden wheat and her violet eyes will have the sweetness to sway anyone who come across her."

The gathering of goblins scrunched their faces and winced at such an image. To them, she sounded absolutely horrid. "What do you want us to do when we find the baby?" The front goblin asked.

"Can we eat it?"

"Oh, yes, I love babies."

"No!" Maleficent declared sternly. "You may not. I have plans for her; plans I wish to go unspoiled. I want you to bring the child to me! Alive and well!"

The goblins grumbled like a thunderous tantrum of disappointment.

Suddenly, the clash of Maleficent's staff struck the ground, silencing them instantly. "Be quiet!" She screamed, slowly turning her burning gaze through the crowd of unruly monsters. "I promised you all a reward and I swear to you now, that you can count on my words. I might be evil, and my soul might be black, but I have never lied! I do not lie! Do you all understand?"

The goblins looked towards each other, unable to vanquish all doubt and suspicion from their simple minds. After all, if there was one thing to know about a magical creature, any magical creature, it was that you should not ever trust them. If what the Dark Fairy said was true, then it would only further the divide between her and those in the Nine Realms. But the goblins could not dwell on such deep thoughts and questions. Instead, they focused on the important things: the baby and the rewards. But there was one last matter, or rather three.

"What about the fairies?" The front goblin asked, drool dripping slowly from his crooked jaw of jagged teeth.

Maleficent smiled. "Do whatever you like with them. Kill them. Beat them. Drown them with their own blood... I do not care."

"But what if they use their magic?"

"They are crippled in ways of dark magic. They cannot cast it. They couldn't do anything to harm you, even if they wanted to do so. They are good fairies, forcibly as it were. You need not fear them. They are but three insignificant pawns in this game. But they stole the weapon I need to win this battle of love and queens: the baby. Every hour, every minute cannot go wasted. I need the child to win this war, and you all will be my soldiers," she announced, tapping her staff against the floor once again.

The goblins suddenly looked around. They were all now wearing armor. It was dark and heavy, each piece fitting their individual frames. But that wasn't all. They also had a deadly weapon in their hands. The sight of them lit up their ugly faces.

Maleficent smiled at their menacing glee. "Go now. Go into the many lands and kingdoms of the mortal world, and by my right of wrath, wreak havoc upon them all. No one will be able to stop you. Your armor will protect you from all earthly things, and magic of any kind. You need not hide in the forest and shadows so long as you work for me. Set your chaos free upon them all, but do not forget your charge. I am happy to give such gifts and rights, but be warned... I am not patient. For every full moon that comes and goes, one of your kind will turn to stone by the following dawn. So, make haste! Go forth and find the stolen baby. Go!" She roared, sending the vast crowd of goblins to shift and race out of the castle, into the air and others into the sea, each excited and fearful of their purpose, but one thing was certain— they weren't going to be bored.

CHAPTER EIGHT

SCORN

The trouble with chaos is how quickly it can spread. The acts of the goblins swarmed the earth, searching through each and every kingdom. No village was safe, no corner of land left unturned. But word too had spread like wildfire throughout the many realms. The scars upon the mortal world ridden by catastrophes could only be done by goblins. *But why?* Magical creatures tried to intervene, not on behalf of the mortals or the ruin of their vain world, but rather the critical need to regain control. The goblins had never wrought their art of disaster so openly before. They had always been a hidden race, keeping their mischievous ways in the shadows and that of their shapeshifted design. They were too dangerous and unruly for such freedom. There were those within the Nine Realms that dealt with such matters, but one by one, ten by ten, more and more attempted to vanquish the goblin's reign of terror, but they quickly realized by ways of Maleficent's gift of armor, they hadn't even a glimmer of hope.

The magical enforcers may not have been able to harm the goblins, but they did manage to capture one. They took him to the great room of dread and iron. The goblin was young and very small in stature. With long thin limbs and bulging eyes, the little monster of mischief was chained and locked, to be questioned, and on pain of death— they would get their answers.

"What is going on?"

"Why are the goblins destroying the lands?" The enforcers asked sternly.

At first, the young goblin was silent, appearing almost like that of a frightened child. And in that moment, the enforcers felt pity for the young monster chained before them. The goblin then whimpered pitifully as if the restraints were too much to bear. Like all magical creatures, the enforcers knew the torture that the ancient iron could inflict. No doubt it would be most agonizing to something so small. But even a flinch of empathy from one of the enforcers would prove to be a dreadful mistake.

Among the four enforcers were a shimmering white Kelpie, an ancient Kitsune in its true form of a beautiful fox, Jenny Green-Tooth, a nasty water witch covered with the scales of a crocodile, and finally the oldest of Fachans, a massive bird-like creature whose terrifying gaze is as lethal as its seething hatred. Having some of the same powers as the goblins, the Kitsune transformed into a beautiful woman. Sympathetic to the goblin's mischievous nature and its youth, the Kitsune inched her way towards him.

"What do you think you are doing?" Asked the Fachan in an eerie whisper.

"The chains; they are too tight. Can't you see the little thing is in pain," answered the Kitsune. But not a moment before she reached too close, the whimpering goblin suddenly snapped, biting deeply into her milky skin. After a screeching wail of instant pain, the Kitsune broke free. Jenny Green-tooth and the Kelpie snickered with wicked mockery.

"Land creatures have no depth of mind, it seems," said the white Kelpie.

"Indeed," replied Jenny.

"Enough!" Declared the Fachan. Its anger lifted its dark blue feathers like spikes that swelled around its legendary club. "Tell us what you and your kind are up to? What gives you the right to come out into the clear of the mortal realm? How is it that you are in your true form, yet you do not turn to stone by the light of dawn? The rest of us have not changed. Why do the rules of our kind on earth not apply to you as they always have— for all of us that dwell and hunt in the shadows?"

The goblin laughed insanely before answering with a smug grin that spread widely across his small face, so much in fact, that his olive-green skin looked as if it might rip from such a stretch. "The sun cannot hurt us. Your rules cannot control us. We were chosen. We are free."

"Who chose you? Chose you for what?" Asked the Fachan.

"What would anyone want with goblins? What could anyone gain from such a plague of infestation?" Jenny Green-Tooth grumbled.

"My mistress. My queen, she has more evil than you've ever seen. On her great throne is where she sits, with two tall horns as sharp as her wits. Waiting for she who was recently born, the rose with no petals, but only thorns. Our armor protects us from all in our way, this was amusing, but I'll be on my way. The rules have changed, accept her will, for those who do not, are the ones she will kill."

"Who?! Who is your mistress?" Asked the Kitsune.

The goblin smiled as if smitten at the thought, *"I will not tell her name, for your unworthy of the sound, but you will find out once the child is found. Do not try to stop her, or she'll come for you too, but for my entertainment, I hope that you do. Once I flee, I hope you will see, we serve only— the Dark Fairy."*

All at once, the creature disappeared, leaving only his rhythmic hints and echoing laugher to pacify the enforcers.

Much like within the mortal world, word travels fast. The enforcers did not know exactly who this threat was. Only those within the Unseelie court knew of the power's origin. But even *they* were not keen to her plans. The problem for Maleficent however, was the questions. It was the questions of *who* and *what* and *why* that stirred the realms with fear and confusion. News of goblins searching for a child normally wouldn't be cause for concern, but the words the young monster

266

had revealed were more than enough to gain the attention of the three fairies hiding within the Dream Realm.

* * *

"Goblins! Really?!" Merryweather grumbled.

"Yes. That is what I heard. She has gained the service of all of them, sisters. This is serious. Goblins venture into the Dream Realm. It is one of their favorites, actually, due to it being the only realm where they can really get creative," Flora replied.

"You don't think they will find us? Do you? And Rose? Goblins delight in killing children..." Fauna stuttered.

"I heard they *eat* them," Merryweather chimed in, to her sister's horror.

"Merryweather! Have you lost your senses? Look at dear Fauna. She looks absolutely petrified." Flora scolded.

Merryweather and Flora then set their gaze firmly on their frozen sister. But she didn't move. She didn't blink. Her breath was quiet but shook with her fear. That was the bad thing about being in the Dream Realm, your thoughts could get vivid, too vivid. How quickly a dream can become a nightmare. Only for them, waking up was not an option.

"Fauna! Fauna! Listen to me! It is going to be alright. I have an idea," Flora shouted, slapping her across the face trying to snap her sister back from her imagined torment. It worked. Fauna moved her eyes, swelling with tears, but the fragile fairy would need to hear more. Seeing that she had given her younger sister a glimmer of hope, Flora smiled and caressed her cheek. "There. There, sister. Hear my voice and calm your mind. Flee thou nightmare and peace you'll find," she whispered softly in her ear.

"Must you always need that incantation, sister? We are going to face many dangers now that we have taken the one weapon each side needs to win this war. The Snow Queen, Maleficent, and saving our home in the Woodlands, our mother... all of them rely on this child, and we have her. We cannot have you falling apart every time a threat arises, because there are going to be many!" Merryweather stated firmly.

"Merryweather!" Flora screamed in frustration.

Merryweather rose her hands to silence her, "I am sorry to be so harsh, sister, I am. But there will be. We must be able to count on you, like you count on us."

Flora sighed and turned her gaze to Fauna, "It is true, love. We must all be strong; for the baby... and for our family that hovers in the cursed woods that used to be our home. We are fairies, immortals! Sixteen years will fly by."

"Ugh. Don't say fly, sister. I needn't be reminded of our most wretched status," Merryweather huffed, lifting her ragged skirt from the floor, revealing her most hated shoes. The shoes were the worst to Merryweather; plain, boring, uncomfortable, and above all, they stated clearly what they had become. In the fairy world, it was your shoes that defined how important, how powerful you were. But here they were, dressed like that of three poor peasant women. Merryweather avoided looking at herself at any cost. It was just too dreadful.

Flora had spent her time not consumed with vanity, but rather with the obsession of finding the witch's books they need to satisfy the Snow Queen. But night after night, as the little child slept, she searched high and low within the glamoured cabin, but to no avail. As far as Fauna was concerned, when she wasn't suffused with worry, spent her every waking hour taking care of the little princess. They may not have had their proper magic, but she could charm every moment of the child's life within their dream. Every meal she ate was perfect. Every dress she wore, though fit for any handmaiden, still managed to flatter the girl's angelic features. Her beauty seemed to grow with each passing day. One needed only to set a mere glance upon her to realize she was not just any human. Yes, the girl's image was likely the most dangerous threat to the sisters, for it wasn't Maleficent alone that was looking for the child. Now she had an army.

"You said you had an idea, Flora. What is it? You must tell me. Will our Rose be safe?" Fauna asked with a tone of mustered bravery.

Both of her sisters smiled upon seeing her effort to remain calm. "Yes, I believe my idea just might do the trick." Flora winked.

"Well? Well?" Merryweather pressed on, impatiently circling her hands. "Go on. Tell us. Must you drag everything out as if performing a show? Get on with it!"

Flora sneered at her rude sister, "You know, Merryweather, my idea..."

"-if you ever get to it."

"My idea! Is one that might just protect you too, you infernal brat!" Flora twitched with rage.

"Sister?" Fauna interceded. "Please."

Flora grumbled in a much-needed fit, but after a moment to digress, she told them of her plan... "Well, as you both know, we cannot use magic. Not in front of the child, nor for fear of drawing attention. But we must keep Rose away from any other magical creatures as well. She must not know magic even exist. But there is a way that all of us, especially Rose, could ward off those that seek her."

"The goblins?" Fauna asked.

"Precisely." Flora replied with enthusiasm.

"How?" Merryweather asked suspiciously.

"Come on sisters! We were born of the Woodlands, the daughters of Titana herself. We know the woods better than them all. It does not take magic to make a goblin flee. All one needs to do is..."

"Sing!" Shouted Merryweather with her finger in the air.

"Exactly!" Flora replied, the three sisters each looking at each other with understanding. And with that understanding, a wave of relief swept over them.

"The goblins find the power of a song to be absolutely unbearable. They cannot stand to be anywhere near it. Even a mortal could do it. We gave the child the gift of song. Can you imagine the range of protection she could give us just by singing?"

"Wow, sister. I must admit— that is a very clever idea." Merryweather admitted. "Should we ever need a shield of protection or when the child does go out into the woods, we will tell her to sing."

"But we mustn't tell her why," Flora warned.

"Then what do we tell her?" Fauna asked.

"Simple," Merryweather stated plainly. "She is a girl after all. Humans are romantic creatures. They seek love and affection. We will tell her that her song will bring her good fortune, that her voice will help the flowers bloom and calm the streams of running water. We will tell her the animals will hear from her tranquil song that she is no threat to the forest, as so many humans are, but rather a friend amongst them; someone they can trust. And if she sings loud and with all her heart, her song just might bring her love."

Flora and Merryweather nodded together, but upon one glance at Fauna in her romanticized state with her hands together by her cheek, they could do nothing else but shake their heads.

"Good grief," Merryweather mumbled as she walked down the corridor. The sun was rising. "Wake up the girl. The next day is upon us."

At that, Fauna leapt from her footing and raced off to her Rose, eager to spend another day as her mother.

Off in the distant corner, Flora and Merryweather watched her skip in glee to the child's room. "I just don't get it," Merryweather whispered.

"Well, for us it is just an act, but for her... well, it seems to be the only thing that brings her pure joy," Flora replied quietly.

"The girl is also now bringing us goblins. Gods only know what she will bring upon us next."

* * *

Just as Maleficent had promised, the goblins had free reign over the earth, but with each sunrise after a full moon, another goblin was turned to stone and left as an ornament upon her castle; to watch and caution those that dared waste another night. But even as their count continued to grow, so did Maleficent's frustration. It wasn't just that the child hadn't been found yet, it was the nighty torture of possessed dreams. It felt as if her exhaustion might drive her into utter madness. She struggled for a thought she could be sure was her own. The sisters of Oz had become all too real. She could hear them even when she was awake. The black storm of the Erl King's darkness did not swarm the land for long. It was looking for a vessel, a source. But the power itself would not be consumed by any that sought to abuse it. The magic felt but one tie, and until the door it needed to cross was open, it would continue to poison the lands. The three fates and each of their pure-blooded daughters fell low, both in power and corrupt in wickedness. If there was ever a glimmer of goodness between them, it had turned rotten. Even Glinda's bubbly soul had darkened. Crimson and Delora had become more deadly than ever, willing to spill any and all blood necessary to take the full force of such power unto themselves to rule all. The only one that did not crave to hold such a crown was Nimueh. It was she and only she who could open the door the magic wanted so badly to enter: the door to her own soul. And so, to save the lands, and her one true love before the darkness changed him forever, Nimueh opened her arms and cast her spell to summon her father's power into her heart.

It was a feeling Maleficent knew all too well and having to experience such an event was almost enough to vanquish her sanity. Many believe that taking in another's power, from that of their soul, would be a wonderous feeling, but it was not. It was painful. How could it not be? It wasn't just a physical transformation, like that of a shifter or a werewolf, this was the soul being torn and forced to consume more than it was ever intended to. It was the kind of agony that could never be understood to someone who hasn't experienced it themselves. And now, she had somehow come to feel such wretched torture twice. The following morning, Maleficent couldn't even bear to get up from her bed. She just lied there for days; not speaking, not moving, just awake.

"I don't know if I can keep doing this," whispered Ainsel from the hidden corner of the Dark Fairy's mind, a place neither Maleficent's hearing nor understanding could reach; at least, not yet.

"We must, dearie. It is the only way. You and I both know it to be true," said Mim.

"I keep thinking of her father, his childhood. The things that made him... I mean, is this right? After all, James too suffered the agony of nightmares and the torturous dread of time. Now I find that I am helping do the very same to our own daughter. What would he think of me?"

"None of us wished this for your daughter. But the cards have fallen, and however cruel their design, we must keep trying. This pain she suffers will only grow as long as her hatred grows. She will come to see the light."

"How can you be so sure?"

"...Faith, child. Faith. It isn't just a tool to worship the gods, it is a power, a marvelous wonder all on it's on. I believe in our daughter, as should you."

"But for how long must we make her suffer this way. It breaks my heart to see her in such misery. After all, sixteen years will be exceptionally cruel if she has to endure two lives at once, and two terrible fates."

The ancient witch cackled in the distance, "Every creature thinks its cruel to wait for time to pass, but when the truth is learned, they will find it is far crueler that time passed and did not wait for them. Time does not wait for anyone. And do not forget, sweet Ainsel, if we succeed... she need never suffer again."

"You're right. I know you are right."

"I love her too, dearie. Trust me."

"I do."

Maleficent may not have been suffering alone, but after what would come next, she would never feel lonelier. The saying goes... when you meet the right one, you'll know. But what people do not like to admit is the terrible heartbreak that comes from losing the one. It is a pain of such a loss and the loneliness that comes after is so powerful, many have died from it. Fully aware of the danger, both Mim and Ainsel watched with great sadness as Maleficent succumbed to the agony of a second heartbreak.

His name was Merlin. He was young, wise, and beautiful, with long dark hair and eyes the color of heavens. Born of two worlds, he too was a half-ling. Not a fairy, but half god. He had the greatest powers of all wizards despite his human essence. But no matter how strong his magic was, the love he bore her was even greater. He had stayed in Oz for her, ignoring Nimueh' s pleas. But once the black storm began to spread, there would be no escape, no body nor soul could leave. The only way to save him from the darkness that would surely consume the land, was to sacrifice her own soul to the Erl King's wickedness. Once the storm had gone, however, the true danger upon them became all too clear. The three sisters of the south, east, and west came for their half-born sibling, with nothing left inside them but jealousy and murderous hatred. When they discovered that it was *she*—who had absorbed the dark power, the three sisters began their hunt, a deadly game that would go on for ages, and one that would ultimately cost Nimueh everything.

* * *

Oz may have been an extraordinary realm, full of life and great distance of measure, but when you are being hunted by three of the most dangerous witches, the darkened land suddenly felt incredibly small. Though the two lovers went to incredible lengths to stay hidden, it didn't take long before the blood-thirsty sisters discovered their whereabouts, learned by their mothers, the three fates. Not only had Nimueh been abandoned by her mothers, but she now knew that they wished for her death. Only then, could their *pure-blood* daughters rise to true power.

Among many other majestic abilities, Merlin could see the future. It was a talent that wasn't always under his control, but in this case, it may have very well saved their lives.

"They know of me and will use our love against you. We haven't much time, for they are on their way here now. The fates, in their cruel intentions, have spilled the truth of us, and mean for your sisters to kill me for the power you took, that in their eyes, was meant to be their own. We must act now!" Merlin declared urgently.

"What must I do? What can I do?" Maleficent felt the words fall unwillingly from her mouth. "Am I to fight my sisters?"

"No, you mustn't. The darkness you have taken fights desperately to claim your heart completely. I fear if you kill your own blood, you will no longer hold the light inside you that I love so dearly. You would become pure evil, incapable of love and care. You must hide the magic and ourselves from them— at *all* cost."

"How can I? My mothers..."

"The fates may have the great bird's eye, but with your power and the distance given by other realms, their skills with sight will prove harder to reach."

"Where?"

"My world, the mortal world. You must use your new magic to take us there, into the deepest of woods, and there we will take refuge."

"But the magic... It's changing me. I can feel it."

"I know. I know. I have a plan, but we have to move— Now! Take my hand and repeat after me:

Beyond these borders
Sweep us away
Not by broom
But what I say
Into the woods
Hidden away
Not by wand
But what I say
Give us shelter
Never touched by day
Not by the moon
But what I say
Only by the lost
Will I be found
Not by sight
Nor by sound
To live amongst mortals
To live amongst fae
Take us there
Do what I say!"

Then, like the massive jolt that occurs often in dreams, usually before a death, the lover's rapid transportation sprung Maleficent from her slumber and in a moment of sweating clarity, the answer to her burning question was finally answered; the mysterious voice of her exhausting possession was... "Mim."

* * *

Maleficent quickly emerged from her bed, looking back at its feathered pillows and sheets soaked with her sweat as if it were a wretched prison she had just escaped. With heavy breaths, she left the room, slamming her chamber doors behind her. The echoing sound of Grip's flapping wings grew louder as he raced to her side. Feeling the overwhelming storm of sadness and fury stirring within the castle. The loyal raven squawked quietly, trying to understand her abrupt discontent, but his offer of comfort was to no avail. Maleficent had been pushed beyond any and all reason or patience. Her mind swelled with memories; each piecing together like a puzzle: the woods, her hiding, the night of her death, the magic she had absorbed against her will, the caution of those who would hunt her... "Why did you do this?" Maleficent screamed aloud, startling poor Grip right off her shoulder. "I know it is you! I *know* you can hear me! Why?!"

But there was no answer, no voice, just a deafening silence.

"I am not going mad. I am *not* going mad! Answer me, Mim! You needn't hide behind nightmares, haunting me so wretchedly!" Suddenly, another crow came into the room, alerting her. She turned towards it with fuming irritation, "What is it now?!"

The black feathered creature flitted uneasily under her anger, reporting that once again a full moon was upon them and the goblins had still not found the princess.

"Useless imbeciles! What is taking them so long? It's been five years already!"

The frightened crow lingered, flitting his feathers once more.

"What? What *else* ails you enough to bother me at such a time as this?!" She screamed.

The crow screeched in reply, telling of the poor status of the human world, of the utter chaos of ruin that the goblins had caused.

"I am on the brink of insanity here! Do you all not see my misery! I sit here night after night, waiting in this infernal prison, haunted by a horrid witch I had thought I rid myself of years ago. And you speak to me of human feelings! Well fine! They want to be *happy,* to feel *joy* again. I'll cast upon them a dancing curse!

Let them die from absolute glee! And like me, let time offer no peace, no relief despite exhaustion! Dance, fools! Dance even when your feet are soaked by blood. Dance even when your muscles burn with agony. And when your breath weakens and your sweat drips down your mortal flesh, I desire you to dance faster, until you breathe no longer! And for each human that sets their eyes upon this festivity, let them then join the dance, a joyous bunch they'll be." With that, she slammed her staff against the stone beneath her feet,

unleashing a most malevolent curse upon the mortals—
again.

The crows were shocked, not by the spell or the
cruelty of it, but rather her by her manner towards
them, which had always been one of love and
endearment. Grip, too, couldn't help but be feel
concerned, not for his own safety, for he knew of the
great love she bore him even in anger, but rather for
her. He had never seen her so out of control, and he so
out of tune with her emotions. With a sigh to digress,
Maleficent sauntered into the throne room, to sit and
wait as she always did. Seeing that she had somewhat
calmed herself, Grip flew to her once again. With a
mere glance upon his worried face, Maleficent softened.
"Oh, darling, I am sorry. It's just these *nightmares.*
They are really getting to me. Its Mim. The voice that
has been guiding me and subjecting me to endure her
horrible past. As if any of that is going to change
anything between us. I just do not understand why.
What do these dreams mean and why does she want
me to see them?"

Grip squawked in reply, widening his glowing
gaze.

"Oh, my pet, I know. I wish you could help me
too, but unless you can visit me in my dreams, I do not
see how."

The dark raven fluffed his feathers, lighting
Maleficent's spirt like a freshly lit candlewick.

"That's it! Oh, my darling, would you? Really?"

Grip brought his head to her cold cheek, giving
her the only answer that could truly offer her a moment

280

of comfort, but however small the gesture, it was one that she heartily treasured.

"You've always been there for me. I know if you are with me, I won't feel so alone during these strange memories that I am forced to endure. Thank you, my pet. Thank you."

* * *

After the source of her dreams had been revealed, Maleficent fought them harder and harder with every night that passed, but as strong as she was, it seemed that these haunting memories had entered through a door that could now not be closed. She had let too much of Mim in to deny her influence now. At least, that is what Maleficent told herself. But maybe, the truth was that she wanted to know more, to uncover all the answers to the Wood Witch's past. *What did they all mean? And why wouldn't she speak to her now?* It was all so maddening. And that is exactly what the nightmares were doing... driving her mad.

Luckily for the mortals within the human world, the dancing curse had been lifted with the help of the red shoes designed by the saints, soaked in holy water. Only then, were the mortals able to stop their bloody feet from moving to the silent song of their death. Those that did survive the dancing plague did not dare complain of their misfortune or the goblins again. They would suffer their poverty and destruction of all their earthly goods in silence. It wasn't by a single prayer whispered out into the night, but rather the ticking of the clock that would bring the earth relief from Maleficent's unruly children. Day after day, year after year, not a single one of the goblins had found the missing princess; a failure that would cost one of their lives after each dawn that followed a full moon.

The three fairy's caution had paid off, for while the goblins continued their search throughout the Nine Realms, many had indeed attempted to look through Slumberland. But the poor dim-witted creatures did not think twice about the beautiful voice that sung from the forest, nor did any of them think it wise to bring such bothers to Maleficent. After all, they had their armor. If it was a matter of great defense or an attack, then they would surely be immune. Yes, the three sisters had been very clever, but there was still one matter they had forgotten; one that could ruin everything they had worked so hard for.

The little princess was growing nicely. She was beautiful, sweet, and obeyed her three aunties in all matters. But there was one dark cloud that hovered over the little rose, her loneliness. And like so many children before her, she drew the attention of the Snow Queen's court, and that of Jack Frost himself. The visit of the ominous winter came over the enchanted cabin like a quiet secret whispering into the ears of the three sisters. The cold woke each of them suddenly, though it was his presence at the center of their room that sent chills up their spines.

"What the devil?" Flora snapped out of fright as each of the sisters rose their blankets over their ruffled nightgowns in embarrassment.

"How dare you burst in on us like this?" Scolded Merryweather.

"My apologizes, ladies," answered the dark silhoette. All at once, as the figure tapped his staff, casting itself away, along with all the frost of winter. The lad then stepped into the moonlight that shined through their open window. It was Pan, in his image before he had turned cold.

"How? How are doing this?" Flora whimpered.

Pan chuckled, enjoying their fear. "I can appear as I desire. We are in Slumberland after all. Do not worry, the child will not wake whilst I am here."

"Why *are* you here?" Flora asked with authority.

Pan smiled at her with his old crooked smile, "I have always admired a creature with a little spunk... but don't piss me off."

"Well!" Flora huffed, bringing a hand to her chest in awe.

"How dare you speak to us like that!" Merryweather shouted, forgetting her volume.

"Hush, sisters. We do not want to wake Rose," Fauna whispered.

"Fine, Fauna," Merryweather grumbled in frustration. "*What- do- you- want?*" She whispered hatefully.

"Everything is going according to plan. The Dark Fairy does not know where we or the princess are. Surely the Snow Queen is pleased with our progress." Flora said.

"She is, and yes, you have done well, but do not flatter yourselves too hard. After all, you were not able

283

to hide the child from me. I could sense her loneliness."

"Nonsense!" Fauna spouted, offended at such a notion.

"Oh, yes, ladies. I felt it from afar. I could practically taste it." Pan insisted arrogantly.

"Well, what are we supposed to do? Without our powers, we couldn't make her a changeling friend. Even Slumberland has its limits. Dreams are a tricky business. One can only manifest the image of someone with a face that they have already seen somewhere at some point in their lifetime. And the princess has none." Flora pointed out.

"Yes, and it stands to reason that if we did manage to mold a figure into this vision, that figure would likely be faceless and it would send her into a panic; a fact that would likely break our sleeping spell and ruin everything!" Merryweather snapped.

Once again, she was met with the sharp glares from her sisters, reminding her of her temperate volume.

"Oh, for the god's sake. I cannot help it. He comes in here, uninvited, intruding upon us in our bedroom, complaining about the child's loneliness. So, excuse me for being annoyed," Merryweather huffed with a scrunched-up expression.

"I think your time spent without magic has somehow hindered your ladies' imagination. How horrid it must be to live like mortals for so long, and with so much more to go. Alas, you three have not seen to every matter of your charge." Pan said smugly.

"Whatever do you mean?" Fauna said with concern. "We have seen to her every need. I have cared for her in every way a true mother can. It saddens me to hear that she is lonely. But what can we do? My sisters are right. She hasn't seen any faces but our own."

"Well, she has seen her real mother's face. And dreams are not limited by time. There is no expiration on memories here," Flora said.

"Do not be daft, sister! The queen's face is a mother's after all. What good would that do for the child's loneliness? If a mother's love or company was good enough, then surely the three of us should suffice. What she lacks is not a mother, but a friend. And she hasn't seen a child's face! So, I say again... this is pointless!" Merryweather whispered sarcastically, before throwing herself down upon her bed, and lifting her blankets over her in a fit. With her back facing all of them, it was clear that Merryweather was done with the conversation.

"Sister?" Fauna whispered.

"No! I've heard enough. Goodnight to you all!" Merryweather said sternly.

"I fear I must tell you... well, actually, I am only too happy to tell the three of you- that you are wrong again," Pan said with a little too much joy in his tone.

Just then, the lamp that sat upon one of the bedside tables smashed to the ground by Merryweather's hand. "I said goodnight!"

"Sister please!" Fauna cried out before turning back to Pan, now standing completely in the dark. "Please, tell us. What have we forgotten?"

From the darkness came their answer, one that would strike them all wide awake: "The princess *has* laid her eyes upon a child's face, the very same face she will need to fall in love with if you have any hope in breaking Maleficent's curse."

All three sisters widened their eyes, whispering in perfect unison— "Prince Phillip."

Merryweather jumped from her bed, racing around the dark room trying to find a lantern to light, only to trip and fall on her face. The loud thud made Flora shake her head. She reached to her own bedside table for the lantern she usually used to read while her sisters slept. It was not very big, nor did it offer very much light, but on that night, in that darkness, it was more than enough. Once lit, Flora, Fauna, and Pan watched in awkward silence as Merryweather peeled herself off the floor. She looked up to find all eyes on her. "Yes, yes. I fell. You do not all need to stare! Get on with it," she said dusting off her hands, wishing she could also shake off the embarrassment. In one of those silent moments of shame that seemed to drag on forever, Merryweather made her way back to her little bed, only for the silence to be broken by Pan's cruel laughter. Merryweather felt her blood boil in that moment. She hated him. But she hated Maleficent more, for if not for her, she could use her magic to hurt him. Instead, she had to sit there and endure Pan's vexing.

Feeling sorry for her sister, Fauna tried to quickly intercept, speaking just loud enough to talk over his laughter. "Excuse me. Excuse me? You were speaking to us about Prince Phillip, were you not?"

Pan's manic glee slowly subsided, after all, he wasn't going to cut his fun short if it meant easing the blue one's shame. Still, there was more fun to be had. After all, who doesn't enjoy making others feel foolish? "Yes, yes," he said, collecting his breath. "I did... Or was it not plain enough to you?"

Now Fauna felt small. "Yes, I just meant that... Well, what should we do?"

Pan smiled that damned crooked smile, "Well, it is clear that the three of you are unfit to handle this matter, but have no fear... Pan is here," he said playfully.

Flora's expression went cold, "I do not appreciate you mocking me or my sisters! We have been doing our best. What have you or your queen been doing? Nothing. Meanwhile, we are here taking care of the child day after day..."

"Yes, but your efforts count for nothing in the matter of breaking the curse she will come to endure. It isn't enough for her to simply survive until her sixteenth birthday. She needs to be in love if true love's kiss is to wake her from death."

"And how do you purpose we do that? We cannot simply kidnap the prince!" Merryweather spouted.

"I already told you, I will handle this," Pan said with pride.

"But how?" Asked Fauna quietly, afraid the answer would be obvious, and she would be left feeling foolish again.

"How? By possessing the prince, of course," he answered.

The three sisters gasped in unison.

He chuckled at their astonished expressions. "Don't you see how clever it is?" But their faces proved to be nothing short of stunned. He sighed with irritation, "Of course you don't... It is really quite simple. I will possess the prince and guide him during each slumber towards the forest where the princess dwells. They will meet. I will befriend her, charm her, and gain her love. The prince will think his lack of control as just another part of dreaming but will also be falling in love with the girl. That way, when the princess pricks her finger on the enchanted spindle, I will leave the prince, and he will race to save her."

"But if he does not think her real?" Fauna started.

"Leave that to me. I will be in control of his thoughts, remember. I will be the link in connecting the dots for the lad."

"But how can you be sure she will fall in love with him?" Fauna asked.

Pan chuckled at the thought, "Let's just say, it's not my first time. Collecting hearts is no hard task for me. She won't be able to resist my charm. Let the girl roam the woods, let her sing her songs and grace the forest with her beauty. *Leave- the- rest- to- me.*" He said in a chilling whisper that blew out the flame within the lantern, leaving the room dark again; only this time, his ominous silhouette had vanished.

Just as he had said, Pan waited outside the young prince's window for the right moment. It was a nostalgic feeling for him. Beautiful frost collected on the glass as he watched the boy fall asleep under his thick covers. Then he slithered in like a winter breeze and with one cold breath, Pan swept inside the boy's vessel, taking control of every string of his new puppet.

But Prince Phillip wasn't the only one who was having possessed dreams, for across the lands to the one most secret was the Dark Fairy, fighting the raging storm of memories that were not her own. The only thing more unbearable than letting Mim take over, was fighting her. The dreams would swarm over her like a blur of chaos, full of sadness, heartbreak, and loneliness. With only pieces of answers, Maleficent watched as Mim said goodbye to her only love, Merlin, in fear that her sisters would find him. Merlin assured her of his love and though they would have to live as enemies, he saw a future that would bring them back together. He didn't know how yet, but he had seen a vision of a women that would lock him away in a tree that stood tall within a deep forest, and that one day, when she found the power to change fate for herself, she would be the one to free him, and they would return to Oz as king and queen.

"You must divide the Erl Kings power, for if you do not, it will poison your soul, he said.

"But how and where?" Maleficent felt herself ask by force.

"I can help you remove it, but where you put the magic will have to be a secret you cannot share with anyone, not even me. The magic is too powerful to be placed within one object. You will have to divide the power into three different items. That way, its aura won't be so easy to locate. Once you have placed them, you must hide each object away, as well as..."

"What?" Mim asked.

"As well as yourself."

"For how long?"

"I fear I do not know the answer to that question. But do not worry, for I have cast a shield over this cabin. Those that would seek you will not find you. But it is my hope that you continue to help the lost. Will you do that?"

"Yes. I will."

"Good. But whatever you do— Do not leave the cabin. For if you do, my shield will be broken and can never be remade. I don't want anything to happen to you. Promise me."

"But what if I..."

"Promise me, Nimueh!"

Dismayed, she gave in to a life full of isolation, "I promise."

After what felt like her insides being ripped away by a blade of scorching hot iron, the pain painted the world with darkness. Maleficent couldn't see what happened next. It was as if Mim had fainted or maybe even had died. If Maleficent had ever thought of what death would feel like, that was it.

It was the screeching caw of her raven that finally woke her. Her skin felt as cold as a corpse. Once again, Mim's agony left her feeling utterly weak and exhausted. She had been able to bring him into a few nightmares, but there were just too many times that she couldn't muster the strength to do so. But no matter what, it was Grip that was there to greet her and comfort her when she awakened.

"Thank you, my pet," she whispered faintly. Grip squawked quietly. She sighed, "I know. I wish you had been there too. It was awful. I'm so tired. Why won't she answer me? Why won't she give me some peace? I haven't rested in years. She is draining my soul. I can feel it. I just need to..." Maleficent drifted back off to sleep then. Only this time, though it wouldn't be for long, Ainsel soothed her mind into a deep sleep; one completely *empty.*

"What are you doing?" Asked Mim.

"Can't you see? If you keep pushing her like this, she could die. Even fairies need to sleep, not to dream, but to rest. Let her rest. Please." Ainsel asked sweetly.

"Very well, but after this..."

"Be reasonable, Mim. She cannot go on like this. Not every night."

"Ainsel, there is still much to show her, and so little time."

"Then we must press ahead. I think it is time to show her the lost ones, and her father."

"But what about the hidden three?"

"She is not ready. I fear what she might do with all that power. No, she must not know where they are yet."

"Yes, I believe you are right."

"So, we agree?"

"We do. It is time for her to see who her father really was, not the murderous monster the Snow Queen portrayed... but rather the man behind the hook."

Ainsel felt a gripping clutch on her heart... "James."

"Indeed, but in order to understand how your love came to meet me, she must see the three that brought him to my door."

"You mean..."

"That is correct: Blackbeard, The Scarlet Fairy, and yes, Peter Pan."

"But what if she recognizes him and begins to doubt all of this?"

"She won't. He was very different then, not just in appearance and youth, but also in soul. He did not keep his evil heart so hidden then. She will realize he is Jack, but not for some time. Believe me. Her love for him may be blind, but I plan to obliterate every lie he ever told her. She will see him for who he is... when the time is right."

"It is strange."

"What is?"

"That I should desire and dread such a day. She is going to be devastated. What if it breaks her?"

"Oh, dearie. I do not dread it at all, in fact, I'm longing for it. You don't know Maleficent like I do. The

292

truth about Pan is not going to break her, it is going to restore her! And by all the gods, I swear to you, hell hath no fury like the Dark Fairy scorn."

* * *

Maleficent had finally gotten her wish, though it may not have been the one she was expecting. Her true mother had granted her a deep and peaceful sleep. And even though she refused to wake for nearly eighteen hours, Mim could see now how badly her little witch needed it. The Dark Fairy awoke feeling rejuvenated and eager to check the status on her wicked plan. It had been too long since she had spoken to her unruly children. After all, one tends to lose track of time when they are enduring the torture of two lives and no rest. Grip flew to her in urgent haste, having spent many hours in terrible worry. His sweet concern brought a smile to her face; something that he hadn't seen in quite some time. There was color back in her sharp cheeks and a powerful vibrance that shined in her brightly rested eyes. "It is true, my darling, though I don't know why it happened, but I finally got some regenerating sleep. I feel great. Now, tell me, what have my naughty goblins been up to, for I think it too long since I've seen them?" Grip lowered his feathered head, not wanting to spoil her good mood, but his silence said it all. Still, she wasn't going to allow herself to be consumed by anger, not on this blissful morning. No, she would simply just call upon them for answers herself. And so, with her body reenergized, she rose from her bed and went to the great window of her throne room. With a grace of her hand, she pulled aside the heavy curtain she used to keep out prying eyes and stood proudly before the raging waters below.

> *"Come to me, minions*
> *Hear your mistress' call*
> *Will you bring me the babe?*
> *Or watch another of you fall*
> *Come to me, goblins*
> *Your mistress calls*
> *Bring me victory*
> *Or join those on the walls.*
> *I summon your leaders*
> *To come forth now*
> *To face your dark queen*
> *And take your bow."*

And sure enough, within mere minutes, the leaders of all the goblins were well on their way to the Forbidden Mountain, though they were in little hurry to arrive. For they had no good news to share. Still, the leaders had a plan to pacify their terrifying mistress. They would bring her a baby, but it was not the princess at all. No, what the goblins were going to do was give her a hobgoblin that had shifted itself to look like a beautiful mortal baby. With as much detail as they could remember, they were sure this glamoured illusion would be enough to escape the Dark Fairy's wrath. Right?

Making Maleficent wait was hardly going to work in the little monster's favor, this they all knew, but they needed to brace themselves. It was difficult for a goblin to lie, mostly due to their lacking the cunning wit that one needs for strategy. Still, the leaders were the most capable amongst the rest of their kind. They were older, more experienced, and therefore, they were the ones others came to for guidance.

One by one, the leaders made their way from the sea and air towards her towering castle upon the mountain. The path of stones that led to her massive doorway was decorated with those of their kind. It was chilling and quiet there, too quiet. Each step forward felt as if they were walking upon a piece made by a friend, family, or even a stranger. It was more than unnerving. After all these years, the Forbidden Mountain had somehow become even more horrifying. No longer would the dark queen and her castle be without a kingdom. Instead, the air was full of the thick fog of an ancient cemetery. But the feeling of dread that suffused them would only grow with each step they took up the stairway towards the palace that could only ever be seen by the eternal storm of thunder and lightning that stuck above the castle. And by the looks of the calm downpour illuminated by the subtle flashes of blue, it appeared the Dark Fairy was in good humor.

The leaders came to the door and knocked, both eagerness and dread smothering their thought process. Then by the creaking door that screeched painfully through their ears, the leaders grabbed their bleeding heads and raced inside so the door would close, and the pain would fade. It was not the first, second, or even third time this has happened. After all, they had been looking for the princess for years. But if hope prevailed, this would be the last time they would have to endure this horrible place. Goblins were mischievous tricksters. It was probably the one thing they were good at, though it only ever caused destruction or harm on others. But this, here tonight, the wisest of their kind would attempt the *trick* that would triumph over all the tricks in the past.

They each took a deep breath before entering the great throne room with a baby wrapped up in a thick rag that lied quietly in one of their arms.

No sooner had they approached Maleficent and quickly dropped to take their bow, did she spot the infant wiggling around inside its itchy blanket. She stood from her chair and slowly set her malevolent stare over them. She tapped her staff against the floor, ordering them to rise at once.

"What- is- that?" She asked in a crisp tone.

The leaders each rose slowly, pushing forth the one holding the baby. The poor goblin stood there, shaking and speechless. She looked at the paralyzed monster with irritation, waiting for an answer. But the harder she looked at him, the more he froze.

"One of you better tell me what is going on, and I mean— *now!"* She demanded.

The oldest amongst the leaders finally braved a reply, "We brought you the baby," he said looking to the others for support.

The leaders joined together in agreement. There was no turning back now. "Yes, yes, we found it."

"We brought her to you."

"Our search is over."'

"Are you pleased, mistress?"

"Yes, yes, we hope you are pleased."

Once they got started, there was no shutting them up. Their voices began stacking on top of each other. And as annoyed as Maleficent had been by their silence, this was far worse.

"Enough!" She shouted with the power to echo off the stone walls and silence them all once again. After the huff of an angry dragon, she spoke again: "So you brought me the babe?"

The goblins eagerly nodded together.

"Yes. Yes. Yes." They all said repeatedly, thinking their plan was not only going well; it was succeeding.

"Really? You have brought me the princess, have you?" Maleficent said with an ominous smile that made them a little uneasy.

Still the leaders did not faulter and continued on with their not-so-dubious deception. "Yes, we did! We have. Take her. Take her." They said as the one goblin lifted the glamoured babe up for her to grasp. And she did. She grabbed the baby, but what happened next— none of them was prepared for. Maleficent unwrapped the tattered rag from the small creature. She smiled and cooed sweetly at the little babe, confusing the leaders. Within seconds, Maleficent slammed her glorious staff against the stone beneath her, instantly removing the enchanted glamour they had cast upon the hobgoblin. The little creature screeched and squirmed within her tightening grasp. To each of the leader's horror,

Maleficent erupted in manic laughter as she crushed every bone and squeezed every breath of air from its little body. Once it was dead, she dropped its corpse to the floor like a ragdoll. Even after the creature's terrible demise, her laughter didn't cease. Each of the goblins frantically panicked, racing towards any open window or doorway, but without so much as an incantation or a flick of her wrist, each and every window and doorway within the dark palace slammed shut, locking each of the terrified goblins there within the room.

"Leaving so soon, my pets? Don't you want your rewards for bringing me the babe? Your— *just* rewards?" She said with a tone so chilling, it danced on their spines like fire and ice.

"Mercy, mistress! Please grant us mercy!"

"We did not mean..."

"What?!" She howled. "Are you telling me you did not *mean* to bring me that— that disgusting imposter?! Did you really think you could fool me? Me! How dare all of you! Not only have you not managed to find the real princess, but you also came here in hopes to deceive me. And to add insult to injury, you have managed to completely ruin my perfectly good morning. Isn't that right, darling?" She asked her dark beloved companion. Grip squawked and screeched at the goblins aggressively as he perched himself upon the orb of her staff, causing it to glow. "I think you are right. But how do we make them suffer for this traitorous act?"

The goblins dropped to the ground, each pleading and begging for mercy. "Forgive us, our queen."

"Yes, we are so sorry for this heinous treachery!"

"Let us go and we will find the real princess!"

"We swear by the gods, we will not fail you again, mistress!"

But Maleficent was in no mood for mercy. "We are upon the dawn of the tenth year! And all you have to show for it, despite my wonderous gifts and generosity... is this deceitful betrayal! How dare you beg for mercy! Have I not given you everything? For ten long years, you have had every realm at your feet, to unleash your most devastating of mayhem upon them all! And for what? I just asked for one little thing! That you bring me the one child I seek. You are the leaders of your kind. You have survived the ages of time and countless threats. But not anymore. Your time has come, my naughty children. You are never going to leave this castle again." Before even one goblin could utter another plea, she tapped her staff and the glowing power within unleashed upon them all... and turned them into the greatest of decorative stone, each to forever adorn every doorway and window to the dark palace, to be telltales to all who came to the Forbidden Mountain, as a warning to all: that those who cross the Dark Fairy will have to pay a terrible price.

CHAPTER NINE

RESEMBLANCE

𝕴n life, there are three questions that every living soul seeks to answer:

Where do I come from?
What am I meant to be?
And how will I meet my end?

For most people, these tormenting mysteries are left unanswered until it is too late. But surely life offers something besides suffering. At least, that is the great hope. For Maleficent, it was the mysteries that had fueled the fire to her lifetime of anguish. *But would the answers to her questions bring her solace... or more misery?* It was a riddle that neither Ainsel nor Mim could answer; that is, not yet. But it was their hope that if Maleficent knew where she truly came from, and the truth about he who holds her heart, then maybe, just maybe, her soul could find its way out of the darkness, and into the light. And it was this hope that would not only save a princess, a cursed kingdom, but herself. But should they fail, the entire realms, both magic and mortal alike, would surely suffer her wrath of fiery hatred. All worlds hung in the balance— all on a single desperate hope.

As they had planned, Mim sped up the clock, stirring up a chaotic whirlwind of flashing visions, voices, and feelings. All racing and ending with a knock on the cabin door. Taking in a deep breath, Maleficent looked through the Wood Witch's eyes to find herself in her old home. It looked exactly the same as it did the night that she returned. It was dreary, dark, and gloomy. The air was filled with sadness and inner turmoil. And in that moment, all she could feel was Mim's loneliness. But all that was about to change. For once that knock struck the door, the cabin began to change. The glamour was that of a charming little cottage. There were shelves full of knick-knacks, and crisp leather-bound books, all without a single speck of dust upon them. The walls were covered in vibrant ornate patterns, and the quaint furniture appeared polished and inviting. Maleficent had seen this homey illusion before. Mim had always said that it was for them, the mortals. She wanted the cabin to be the drawing welcome that would properly allure those that were lost in the forest.

And it was.

But unlike most weary travelers that came upon the cottage by accident, this visitor knew exactly who he had come to find.

She opened the door to discover a wretched looking soul. He was a pirate, and a horribly haunted pirate at that. One only needed to lay a single glance upon his blackened eyes to see the cursed veil that shrouded him unrelentingly. But it was not just any curse that had been cast. It was fae, and it was eternal. It was the sort of punishment that was normally given to those that dared to cross one of the ancient fairies. The removal of such great power was simply too dangerous to bestow. It might draw attention, and although many knew of the notorious witch in the woods, she wasn't about to unleash her boundless potential for the sake of a brut like Blackbeard.

"Well, what *can* you do for me?!" He blurted out, suffused with frustration. "They are everywhere! I can't stop the screaming, the howling! That damned howling! Please! If you cannot rid me of these ghosts, then I beg of you to use your powers to at least end my suffering and just kill me!"

Maleficent could see how desperate he was, how desperate he would have to be to beg for death. She ached trying to speak to him. She wanted to call out, *"Grandfather! Grandfather!"* But she couldn't.

Instead, she let out the involuntary cackle of Mim, "Now, dearie, we need not rush matters. Sure, I could kill you, but why be such a bore? Nah, I think your fate lies elsewhere."

Blackbeard looked instantly confused. "What der ya' mean? I have sealed my fate with this blasted curse!"

"Aye, that ya' have, dearie. What I am offering is not the removal of your curse, nor the dullness of your death. What I am offering is to break the seal and change your fate."

"How? How?" He asked with a glimmer of hope in his eyes.

Again, Maleficent felt herself let out a choking cackle, "I will offer you a deal, young man, a trade."

"Name whatever it is you desire, gold, lands, slaves— I do not care what it takes. I will give you anything you want if you can rid me of my torment."

"*Anything*, you say?" She responded with a tone both menacing and eager.

"Yes! Anything!"

"Good. Then I'll be wanting your first-born child."

"But I don't have..."

"And in return I will blind you to those who lost their lives by your arrogance and greed, and furthermore, I will deafen you from all of their suffering and the one that howls from the isle. They will still be there, and you will still be immortal, but you will no longer be living in terror. You may choose to live your everlasting life however you please. And all I ask is the claim to your first-born. Do we have a deal?"

Having no children, nor any plans to, the haughty pirate agreed: "Yes, we have an accord."

"Good," she replied with a sheepish smile. And with a mere snap of her fingers, her appearance and that of the cottage changed into their true forms. Blackbeard slowly circled, eyeing in unease the gloomy cabin, and the haggard old witch he had just struck a deal with. She cackled harshly at his sudden discomfort. "Don't stare, boyle, it's not polite."

Blackbeard tried to shake off the horror from his face, but the best he could do was to avoid looking her in the eye. "Pardon me. I just didn't expect..."

"Well, let's see," she said strolling over towards her vast book and potion collection, as if she didn't hear him at all. She looked around for a few seconds, wiping the thickened dust and countless webs from the spines, before suddenly finding the one she was looking for. "Ah, here is the one we need."

Blackbeard squinted his eyes, trying to see what it was, but it was too dark now without all the gentle flames lit within the decorative lanterns of her glamour. She sauntered over to her old rickety table, pulling out an unusual bowl and a small black blade. A chill crawled up Blackbeard's spine then.

"Come over here, laddy," she said pouring something dreadful into the bowl from one of the cloudy potions she had grabbed from her shelves. Its contents smelt dreadful, even from across the room. She turned to find Blackbeard trying to cover his face from the toxic stench. "Well come on. No use being shy now. Come to me."

"But how will you..." His words were stolen by fear as she picked up the black blade and grabbed his hand with incredible strength. Blackbeard instantly tried to break free from her grasp, but her grip was too strong.

His struggle angered her, "Give me your hand, pirate! Give it to me or leave my cabin with your ghosts!"

Blackbeard huffed, knowing this was it. It was this or go on suffering. He gave her his hand and watched as she took the black blade and sliced into the flesh of his palm. Without missing a single drop, she caught his spilling blood with the bowl. Once the bowl was completely full, she let him go, and gazed upon the magic that was about to unfold with glee.

Blackbeard pulled back his hand and fumbled backward, not knowing what was come next. He didn't know how, but he knew there was no turning back. Too late to turn away. Too late to walk out the door. This was happening. Mim placed her boney hand just above the bowl, whispering ancient dialect in a sinister hiss. Upon her last uttered word, the contents within the bowl began to stir. Blackbeard leaned forward, quietly trying to see what was happening. The dark potion and the red of his blood came together like a storm. And once it was finished, she called out to him again.

"Come back here, Blackbeard. We must do this while it's still warm and fresh. Come. Come," she urged harshly.

He did as she commanded, unable to hesitate even a moment. Once he was close enough, she reached up and grabbed his chin, "Bend down now. Let me see your face," she said coldly.

He did as she said once again, growing more regretful by the second. Then suddenly, to his great surprise, she dipped her fingers into the bowl and wiped it across his forehead.

He wanted nothing more than to wipe it off, to get the wretched muck off of him, but by the look in

305

her emerald eyes, he dared not move an inch. A sudden stir of wind and force erupted within the cabin. She turned up her gaze and placed her hand in front of his face. She cleared her raspy throat and said the words that would change all of their fates forever:

"I stand here now
To strike a deal
Forgive my mercy
In breaking his seal
Let he see no spirits
From the realm of the dead
Let me deafen him from those
That would toy with his head
Let the howling return to its place
On the isle of man
Have pity on he who survived
And ran
I bestow these gifts
In hopes not to offend
Yet I take pleasure knowing
What reward he will send
Blood to own
Blood that's owed
And from your seed
The reap that you sowed
His first-born will be mine
For his debt to be paid
In return of my help
The child he'll trade
Say the words, Blackbeard
Speak them loud and true

Do we have a bargain?"

"Yes, we do."

At that, she brought her boney fingers towards his head again, only this time it was to wipe away the bloody muck, leaving behind the mark of the raven on his forehead, fading away from sight. She looked at her slowly moving hand like a wild animal as she brought her hand to the book she had taken from the dusty shelves. She opened the book and without pen or ink, she used her long bloody nail to write his name in the book. Blackbeard watched in wonder as his born name, Edward Teach, was written precisely and permanently on the page within the book. Once the last letter had been marked in blood, the spell was complete. A calm came over him then. The haunting torture he had endured for so long now faded away like a distant memory. He didn't feel their gaze, nor hear his crew's screams.

"The howling! The howling is gone too. All of it, everything... It's all gone. I can't believe it. Thank you, ma'am. Thank you for this." He praised, overwhelmed with the fresh breath of a life void of sorrow.

"No need to thank me. Just remember our bargain. Your first-born child belongs to me."

Blackbeard let out a small arrogant chuckle, "Right. Right. If I ever have a child, it is yours." But no sooner had he said the words did a question suddenly dig its way into his conscience. "Uh, say that I do..."

"Have a baby?"

"Yes. What about the mother? How will she?"

"Don't worry about that, dearie. I have no desire to make a mother suffer such a terrible loss. Trust me, pirate. This is not the first child I have claimed. And I have never broken a mother's heart. It will happen while she is asleep, and in the babe's place, I will put a changeling. The mother need never know of our private arrangement."

"Ah, I see," he replied with a nod of discontent. "And who would come for the baby?"

"A fairy, of course. A *red* fairy."

* * *

When Maleficent woke up the following day, she was instantly relieved to be out of the cabin. For her, it was a place full of bad memories and lingering resentment. But seeing her Grandfather, not only a part of her family, but also the first of many dominos that were doomed to fall. It was surreal and emotional to see the beginning of all that would soon unravel and not be able to do anything but watch. She wanted to blame him, to hate him, but just like her father before him, she couldn't deny the torturous suffering he had so long endured. "How could you do that? He came to you for help! You didn't have to make that trade! Why didn't you just help him?!" She cried out, hearing her voice echo off the stone walls around her. She circled in sadness, hoping for an answer, and suddenly, as if lost in her echoes, she heard a voice that was not her own.

"Maleficent," the voice whispered.

Maleficent looked around in all directions, but she didn't see anything... or anyone. She realized now that it was in her head. "I know you are there. I know what you did. I just do not know why! Did you know, Mim? Did you know what was going to happen?"

No answer.

Determined to get an answer, she screamed again, "Did you?! At least tell me that! Did-you-know?!"

And just as before, caught between her echoing voice in the castle, she heard Mim's whispering voice answer, "No."

Maleficent dropped to the floor, not knowing what to believe, or what she hoped to gain from the answer. It was done. It was done years ago. She felt helpless and emotionally drained. With a last whimper, she cried, "I hate you. You hear me? I hate you all."

Having raised the willful child herself, Mim was used to Maleficent's dramatic emotions. And she expected nothing less when it came to unleashing the past, but for Ainsel, watching her daughter in such pain was almost too much to bear. But sadly, this was just the beginning.

"I know you cannot hear me, but I pray you might feel me. You're not alone, my sweet love. I'm here. Your mother is here. I'm not going to leave you." Ainsel whispered to the depths of Maleficent's soul. And suddenly, Maleficent's tears ceased to fall. She wasn't sure why, but she felt as if she was being held. She reached her hands to her shoulders, feeling a soothing warmth upon them. She lifted herself up, and calmly strolled to her throne, where she and her dark

beloved watched the black waves of the night sea from her window. Tonight, the storm of Maleficent's rage would not divide her from the stars. Tonight, the blanket of twinkling lights above was welcome.

It's amazing how many hours can pass when one is lost in their thoughts. Silence is crucial when diving into the depth of a tortured mind. And Maleficent was nothing if not completely surrounded by silence. Not even Grip dared disturb her. He simply waited for her to speak to him once she was ready. But no matter how hard she tried, Maleficent couldn't dig deep enough to find the answers that suffused her. Only Mim could do that. Finally, it was with great frustration that the quiet air of the castle was broken.

"I need to go back to sleep, darling. But tonight, I feel I will need you," she said to the dark raven.

He squawked and rubbed his feathered head against her.

"I don't know what lies in store for me tonight, but I fear the mounting anticipation will weaken my resolve. It must be now, when I'm strong and ready. That way, I can bring you in with me. I can't be sure, but I don't want to be alone for fear of what might come next. Will you join me?"

It was a question she never needed to ask. Grip was always there when she needed. He perched himself upon the branches of her bed, letting her know he was ready. She smiled and with a heavy sigh, she grabbed her staff and the long train of her tattered black gown and made her way back to her dark chambers. As she left through each room, the drapes to each open window fell, leaving all in darkness behind her.

Once she reached the bed, she laid flat on her back and crossed her arms upon her chest. Grip flew down to them, waiting for her to say the words that would bring them together in the dreaded Slumberland. Little did they know that the blossoming rose was never too far away, nor was the man she had given everything for.

> *"Now I lay my head to sleep*
> *I call upon*
> *The shadows that creep*
> *Take this raven*
> *Into the deep*
> *For it's his company*
> *I wish to keep."*

With her last words, she drifted away, and those that lived in the shadows granted him passage to the doors of her slumber. When Maleficent opened her eyes, she found herself in another tunnel of time, and enduring all the agony within those passing years. But to her great relief, flying next to her was Grip, flapping desperately in effort to remain at her side and not get lost in the old witch's dashing memories. The flashes of lights and visions were nearly impossible to follow, but through it all, as if intended to be so, tinkering music followed by a single voice could be heard like a distant echo in a cave. Grip listened ever carefully, trying not to break his stride in his urgent flight.

"I fear I have not been able to collect the boy. He has been willful and continues in his disrespect towards me. But there is another amongst them that reeks with wickedness. I've heard his villainous thoughts and know that he means to kill the boy tonight."

"You must be sure that does not happen," said a familiar voice.

"As you wish, old one, but surely if he dies, I could simply take his soul and deliver it to you."

"No! I want the child alive."

"Of course."

It was then that the tunnel of lights tightened and shined with only one color. It was red. There were no voices then, just cries. It sounded like a child, but it was strange. It wasn't just the shrill cry of fear, but also the very depth of pain. It felt as if it would go on forever, and the blood red tunnel appeared as if it might just close in on them, crushing them. Grip flapped his wings in a frantic haze, but soon the inner tube in which they passed had already begun to squeeze him, rendering his ability to fly at all. *What was happening?* He wondered. This had never happened before. He had made the journey into Slumberland before, but he had never endured the intense and dangerous strain of keeping up with the Wood Witch's flashes of time. He screeched out to Maleficent, but she too looked panicked.

"No, I don't know what this is! Who is that? Who is crying?" She screamed out in desperate fear, feeling the pressure of all his pain and torture slowly squeezing the very life out of her. This was it. She didn't understand why, but it seemed that everything—

everything would not in end in pitch black of darkness, but in *red.*

Just when all felt lost, and the surrounding cries of terror was leading them straight to death's door, a light appeared. They didn't know if it was the fact that the screaming had ceased, or the fact that the red was fading away, but a soothing calm came like a gentle wave over them. All the pain, all the fear... it was just gone. They each took in a deep breath of relief, thinking it was over, but they were wrong. The voices, they returned, and now the tension of mounting anger filled each and every breath.

"How could you fail me?"

"It was not my fault. This child, this boy... He is different somehow. I've never seen anything like him. I watched as the other boy nearly beat him to death, leaving him in mess of blood and broken bones. He was succumbed to long stretches of sleep, and I used each and every opportunity to break him. He should have begged to come with me, but someone else interfered just as I was about to ring out the last drop of his courage."

"And just who was this *intruder?*"

"She was... Well, she was one of them. A woman clothed in black and white, but both her soul and body are married to the one of light."

"That is impossible. No mortal has dared interfered in our matters before. To do so is to dabble in the very thing they deem evil. How could you have been so sloppy! To catch the eye of a mortal of light, honestly!"

"It wasn't me! It was him! I don't know how, but the mortal formed some bond with the chosen child. I've been taking the lost and unloved from orphanages since the first one was built, and I have never encountered something like this. Every time I get him close to the edge, this wretched woman is there to lift him back up again. I feared that with her being a woman of light, her love for the boy might be too strong for me to destroy, and I was right."

"What do you mean, you were right. What did the woman do?"

"I'm sorry, old one, but I cannot bring you the child you so desired. It is done."

"How dare you! How could you fail me?! I don't care what happened or what foolish havoc you have wrought upon my plan, but I want the boy brought to me. Do you hear me?!"

"Even if I could, Madam Mim, I daresay he is no longer the prize you once desired. After what this boy has endured is beyond that of any other victim. His body, scared as it might be, is still that of a child, but believe me when I say that any youth that once resonated in his damaged mind— is now dead. I may not have broken him enough to bring him across the veil, but he is most definitely a broken soul. You don't want him. I can get you another child. Any other child."

"No, you foolish fairy! He is the one, only he has the blood I need. I could smell it the second his father stepped foot in my cottage. It is prophesied that the blood of the cursed will come to my door, and from that blood a half-ling will be born. A life to love and a hate to cause my end. But in my death, the truth will unfold the sin, and by this half-born's power, I will find my love again... So, you see, this boy is *mine*. He is everything."

"Oh, no, she is talking about me. She thought it was meant to be my father, but the prophecy is about me." Maleficent said in what felt like an emotional revelation.

"I don't care how damaged he is, come to him in his next slumber, and do not leave until you have him firm in hand. Do you understand what will happen if you should fail me?"

"How dare you caution me! Don't you know who my mother is?"

A cackle thundered throughout the portal then, with only blurred images of those that spoke around them. "I care nothing for the Snow Queen, or any other. So, by all means, tell her what I have said. For she knows my threats are not idle. She should have taught you better. *Clearly* you were not ready for such an important task. Suppose I should be the one to inform her of her dreadful mistake in overestimating your abilities, your competence, and your importance. What do you think?"

"No, ma'am," the other voice answered humbly.

"Good. Then go, and don't come back empty handed again, or I'll make the torture you so wretchedly inflicted upon my child... look like a cheery game. And in case your mother also forgot to mention... I am not only more powerful than the lot of you, I am also really quite vicious. Now, off you go, little red."

And that was it.

The Scarlet Fairy left; a fact made clear by the sudden absence of red light around the tunnel. Maleficent wanted so badly to hear what happened within the next encounter between her father and the fairy? But it was a question that even Mim could not answer, because as it turned out, the Scarlet Fairy made one more terrible mistake that she cowardly failed to mention; that she made a deal with the loving nun in hopes to be rid of them both. The boy was making a fool out of her, and the old hag was protecting him at every turn. Soon, he would be on his feet again, and no longer vulnerable to her torturous nightmares. James was living breathing proof that whatever doesn't kill you, only makes you stronger, because that is exactly what happened. She had lost her chance, and together, the woman and boy could have proved to be a great danger. She had seen from afar the vast books of their kind. She didn't want to be a part of it any longer. *So yeah, the nun wanted him protected from all fae magic in the future. Sounds simple enough. What is the worst thing that could happen, right?*

Finally, after one more thrust through the rushing portal, they came to a jolting stop that left Grip feeling breathless.

Was it over?

After a brief moment to collect himself, he looked up to find that he was once again in their old home. But Mim was nowhere to be seen. It was quiet. Too quiet. Suddenly, the awful sound of someone purging came from the front patio. He found it strange, but then again, it wasn't completely unusual to find Mim sitting on her porch to admire the surrounding trees. She always seemed to be looking for something in them, squinting and counting as she peered out into the shaded land. But Grip had never seen or heard of Mim being ill, not once. With his curiosity mounting, the sudden bump on the door was enough to startle him. Then, as if out of nowhere, she appeared. It was her walking towards the door, Madam Mim, with Maleficent inside her.

Then suddenly, as if somehow triggered by the knock on the door, the cabin changed into its charming glamour. Mim turned the knob and opened the door.

* * *

There is a moment in every child's life where they try to see a part of them in their parent's image. A dimple, the shape of their smile, or even the quirky sound of their laugh. It's like finding the puzzle pieces of your creation. They can be hard to find. It may only be seen like a glimmer of the soul, but if you look hard enough, you can see where you came from. It was a moment that Maleficent had never truly experienced. She was too suffused by her anger to take such a moment with her mother. But now, right here, in Mim's body, where she couldn't turn away or even close her eyes, she would finally face such an encounter with he that stood on the other side of the doorway.

He was tall, broad, and dark. He had long brown hair and a pirate hat that cast a shaded shadow over his piercing blue eyes. His face was clean and shaven, though he smelt like alcohol and the sickness he had just purged upon the porch. Still, there was something determined in his eyes, a purpose. He was dressed in ornate silks and regal cloths, mirroring that of royalty. She could see that he was not this low-life scoundrel that behaved like a blood-thirsty animal. He was quiet, proper, and had the appearance of someone important. Maleficent could hear the distant blur of whatever Mim was saying to him, but it was as if her voice was a million miles away. All Maleficent could do was look at him, unable to resist studying him. She knew who he was from the glassy image shown to her by the Snow Queen, and while he still appeared intimidating and maybe even terrifying, he seemed different somehow.

She walked over towards the fireplace, offering him a seat in the chair that sat next to hers, but as she spoke in her welcoming tone, the expression on his face changed. He knew who she was, where he was, and the glamour faded away, revealing the dreary cabin as it truly was. He announced that he was not there due to her deal with Blackbeard, but rather for his own purpose. He wanted answers, the secrets that could lead him to the hidden veils.

Initially amused by his arrogance, Mim suggested they come to some arrangement, but he was not like the others. With brazen disrespect, he declared that there will be no cost for what he came to seek. Maleficent had never seen someone so confident and disrespectful to Mim before, and from the feelings swelling inside her body in that moment of feverish anger, it seemed neither had Mim.

Mim quickly answered with rage, calling him a foolish child, and threatened him with her wrath. But when he told her that her life depended on her corporation, Mim lost it. She rose up her arms and cursed with all her might, igniting enough energy to completely obliterate him. The walls, the shelves, the furniture, the crows— everything shook and shattered in the cabin. Everything but *him.*

He stood with a bored expression, staring at her as if waiting for her poor attempt to be finished. Maleficent could feel Mim's skin cracking under the pressure of her own power. She didn't know how much longer she could hold on, but the stubborn old witch continued her wicked efforts until her vessel was about the break. Heaving with exhaustion, she sat herself down into the creaking rocking chair, now broken and on the other side of the room. Maleficent couldn't believe what she had just witnessed. No one had ever spoken to Mim that way. She was not a creature of tolerance. All respected her, feared her. This simply didn't make any sense. And yet, somehow, Maleficent couldn't help but feel a sense of pride. He may have been just a mortal man, but he had done what no one else dared to and lived. He had bested the best, and he was her *father.* But it wasn't his threats that made him impressive, it was his calm manner, that aura of certainty that radiated with his unrelenting confidence.

Finally, after Mim collected herself, he came and sat at her table, and revealed the cause of his immunity to fae magic. At first, Mim denied being fae, and would only accept the title of witch, but the pirate seemed to know more than she thought. He explained the telltale of her emerald eyes and what they meant. Once she realized she would have to cower to his demands, a feeling of madness flooded through her. Maleficent felt the seeping insanity crawl over her. It was a terrible affliction to endure; one that Maleficent never knew she suffered. It was like adrenaline and heavy defeat were at war within her mind. There was no room for any other thought or feeling. She wanted to rush out into the woods as if it were possible to escape the fear coursing through her body, but she couldn't. She was stuck inside the cabin, alone with a man that had proved himself to be a terrible threat. Maleficent felt Mim give in to the madness then. She could no longer fight it anymore, and so, by ways of rabbling rhymes and silly songs, she gave the pirate the answers he needed. Through poems or just random spurts of knowledge, she told him of the seven veils that led to the Nine Realms. He pressed her for information on the Scarlet Fairy, but she truly didn't know where she was. The fact was that the last time she saw or heard from her was the night she claimed a woman's interference was hindering her ability to capture him.

She told him that while she didn't know at the time, she believed that when the Scarlet fairy told her this, she had actually already made the deal with the nun. "She seemed skittish when I told her that no other child would do. She left on the promise that she wouldn't return without you, and well, she didn't."

"Why did it have to be me? Why didn't you just accept her proposal to take another child? Why me?" He asked.

"You know why," was all she could manage to reply in her frantic state. It seemed that her panic was mounting. It was a sensation both erratic, and deathly draining. Maleficent had never wanted to escape Mim's body more than she did in this moment.

The panic felt like a poison that was spreading to every inch of her body. She could feel it in her hands and feet. She could feel the pounding of her racing heart, and the quickening of her breaths. Everything felt wrong, and all she wanted was for him to go away.

He must have sensed her mind breaking, or maybe he could just see how afraid she was, but something sparked a glimmer of compassion within him. He withdrew a sword from the bridge of her neck, relieving a pain she hadn't noticed was even there. He had asked what her name was, and while Maleficent knew many, it was his spiteful reply that sent a sting in her heart.

"You don't deserve to be called the mother of anything."

This was all starting to be too much. The stir of so many emotions were unbearable. *Am I really feeling pity for Mim and admiring the man who ruined my life? "Stop this! Stop this! I want to wake up!"*

Grip squawked loudly, letting her know he was there, that she wasn't alone. It was exactly what she needed to hear in that desperate moment. And while it did not stop the story unfolding before her, hearing his unique caw was enough to distract her from the storm raging in her mind.

Suddenly, as if Hook had heard Grip, he asked Mim about her connection to the crows. It was odd, like Grip had somehow tapped into their conversation. *Could it be?* The question picked at her as the two continued their conversations about animals, but then something happened that changed everything Maleficent was feeling.

The moment hit her like a strike of lightning, and it happened just as fast. While Mim was trying to explain the evil nature of humans, Hook began to paint his passionate hatred towards the fae, and the vengeful wrath he would soon unleash upon them.

And there it was.

The moment every child looks for. The first piece of her puzzled creation had been hiding behind his passion, his vengeful heart, his desire for revenge against those that wrought such pain upon his soul. All of it appeared in his eyes like a fiercely glowing fire; the same fire that burned inside her. A surge of connection and belonging came over her. Her father might be a frightening man consumed with revenge, but so was she. His passion, his power, and will had been passed on to her, and though she knew he had done terrible things, a part of her felt like she understood him now.

He kept his word to spare Mim's life and said his goodbyes. To Mim's great relief, he walked out the door, leaving her cottage forever, but for Maleficent, the second that door closed behind him, she felt the terrible ache that only comes from the heart. Just when she felt she knew him, when that wonderous moment she didn't even know she was waiting for had finally come.

It was gone.

* * *

Maleficent woke with dazzling tears of sadness filling her tired emerald eyes, leaving her gaze quite flooded with emotion, and she wasn't alone. Unfair as it was, Ainsel's own suffering from the sight of her love too mounted within the hidden depths of the Dark Fairy's mind. She had thought herself prepared for the old witch's memory, but not even those of great power can withstand the turmoil of seeing a lost love, and not be able to speak to them, touch them, hold them... Yes, it was truly terrible, and for no one more than Maleficent herself. Ainsel, at least, had known what vision was to appear, whereas poor Maleficent never knew what horror or sadness awaited her in the shadows of her slumber. But to her amazement, and that of her frazzled familiar, she was no longer dreading the night's unveiling... In fact, she anxiously, even desperately desired to dream again. Days and nights soon intertwined within her world of darkened rooms of long thick drapes, void of even the smallest shimmer of moonlight, and the lulling song of the black sea outside her walls. Under the covers of ornate designs and feathered fluff, she lied in bed waiting with burning impatience for the darkness behind her closed eyes to claim her and bring forth the past sight of Madam Mim.

Time seemed to pass her by this way, the memories taking her to that of their own. For most, it is the unforeseeable future that holds the most mysterious possibilities, but for Maleficent, it was the vast encounters of the past that allured her so intensely. But in the hours when she laid dreadfully awake, the pieces of the grand puzzle stacked in her mind, each coming together at such a violent pace that at times would leave her head busy with painful aches. The silence of the Forbidden Mountain seemed to make the wild stirrings of questions echo more loudly with each and every thought.

The boy, the screaming, the pain... it had all been her father. And the red-lighted tunnel that had nearly swallowed the life out of her and her pet had been the force of the very fairy that wreaked havoc on all their lives. Maleficent had felt every moment of the suffering that suffused him as a boy, and the flame of vengeance that then did ignite. The same fire that still burned within her. If only she had known that it was the Scarlet Fairy that had awaken the dragon with writhing hatred roaring within their blood, she would have never pitied the snowy realm her father painted red. But as much as Maleficent had quickly come to hate the late fairy, it was clear that someone else was at the core of this story. She could feel it whilst coursing through the tunnel of his torture. His agony, his sorrow, his murderous rage, everything that had swelled his vengeful ambition— it had all started with him.

"But there is another amongst them that reeks with wickedness."

"He means to kill the boy tonight."
"I watched as the other boy nearly beat him to death."
"I used each and every opportunity to break him."

Who was this boy? Did the Scarlet Fairy mention his name? ...No, she didn't. So, who was he? Why was he so important to my father? I hate not knowing the answers. Every night that I drift off to sleep, I hope for even one piece of solace, just one answer to help me understand. Instead, I am met with more mysteries and thus left with more questions. How much longer is this going to go on?

The answer to that however was not going to be the one she was hoping for. For what was to come next was the night Mim wrought her winter curse. At least, that was the plan. But before the Wood Witch could reveal her final truth, Ainsel had a few memories of her own to share first. And so, the following evening, when Maleficent slid under her covers and lied her crown of horns upon the bed, she closed her eyes as she always did, but this time, when she opened them in Slumberland, it would be through her *true* mother's eyes. The feeling that came over her almost instantly was far different than the emotions Mim carried. Even the magic coursing through her was strange. It felt loving, forgiving, and oddly generous. To Maleficent, such kindness felt weak. *What is this? Who is this? This doesn't feel like Mim. And then it hit her... the Blue Fairy. How dare you violate me this way!* She screamed within the imprisoned memory. Squirming

325

and fighting with all her might, she tried to free herself from her dream, but it was no use. She was stuck. With less power to enforce her influence, Ainsel could only manage to reveal mere flashes against Maleficent's resistance. Voices began to emerge within their battle, and though she had heard it once before, Maleficent withdrew her struggle when she heard the voice of her father.

All at once, his image painted vividly in her mind. She was there, sitting across from him, and she couldn't tell if it was her or her mother's feelings that wanted to get closer to him, to understand him, to help him. Lost in the sea of his blue eyes, she listened to the story of his painful past, and whom he needed to destroy next. It didn't take long before Maleficent knew that he still sought the death of the boy who had nearly killed him as a child, but what had only now become clear is his reason for such deadly devotion.

"Ainsel, please understand; if I do not stop him, then he will take the lives of the innocent for all time. But once I kill him, all the guilt I carry from each soul he takes will be lifted from my shoulders. I created Peter Pan! And it must be me that destroys him!"

Peter Pan. Wait...

"But he is only a child? You cannot kill a little boy! There must be another way!"
"... There is no hope for him."
"But maybe he can change!" Maleficent said *unwillingly, hearing her mother's desperation cry out.*

"No! This sadistic child will never change! He was born evil!"

I know what you are doing! This isn't going to work. But no sooner had her thought echoed, did she feel the painful thrust of time passing. It wasn't like Mim's vast spur of years. No, this was clearly a mere jolt ahead. Short as it was, the push was still enough to rob her of a true breath. All was fuzzy for a moment, but when her vision finally returned, she found herself in what appeared to be inside a collapsed cave. Wreckage and broken debris surrounded her. At first, she could barely see beyond the dust of dirt in the air, but as she floated forward, the image before was that of a young boy and the fresh corpse of a green pixie.

The sight pierced Maleficent's heart, remembering the words of the cruel yellow fairy in the Snow Queen's realm. *"Do you think me a fool- like that little green one of yours? Ha! And just where is that treacherous friend of yours now? — Oh, that's right! She is dead!"*

No. It's not true. It's not true. That's not Jack. No. That boy looks nothing like him. Her thoughts rumbled like mayhem within her dream, making everything stir violently out of control. It was then that somehow, someway, she tapped into the hidden corner where her host dwelled.

"I told you this was not the way. She is too powerful to be contained by your past," Mim whispered harshly.

"No, she has to know! I need her to know what he did to us! Please, help me. Help me, I beg you."

Hearing the pain of a mother's loss was enough to soften the old witch and brought to light exactly what they needed to do. "Alright then, together," she said, reaching out to Ainsel to join her. "I know now where to go. Speak with me, and with our united power, she will be forced to see. Ready?"

Ainsel took a deep breath of desperation before answering, "Yes."

"Good, then let's begin...
Hand in hand, Soul to soul
Answers to questions, let us fill the hole
Take her back, to that dreadful night
To the beginning, of all our plight
Show her the face, of the thief that came
Show her his wickedness, who's evil to blame
Mother to Mother, From us to you
Open your eyes and see what's true."

It was then that Maleficent was forced to see what was before her. The image was shocking and sad, though she didn't know quite which room she was in or where she was at all, she recognized both her mother and her father within the room. They both looked so blissfully happy. It was a wonderful picture, one that any child would love to have seen. But she would soon see a most tragic twist as their precious moment was suddenly interrupted. A dark shaded man came out of a mirror that stood in the corner of the room. He was quiet and menacing. Immediately, it seemed like there was something familiar about him. He didn't look like Jack, of that she was very certain, but to Ainsel and her father, this figure seemed to be someone they knew,

,someone they feared, but above all, their dread meant he was somewhat expected. Within a mere moment, she was ripped away from the loving cradle of her father's arms, mere minutes after being delivered from her mother's womb. How small she was, how weak and helpless. Rage shot through her then. *Why didn't they fight for her? After everything she had seen them do, why were they so easily defeated now? Maybe they didn't love her enough to fight for her, for surely if they did...*

Her thoughts were suddenly suffused with the most horrific pain Ainsel felt in that moment. Strange that a memory, something that happened so long ago, could still be felt that strongly. It was beyond anything she had ever felt before. It was stronger than any rage. It was stronger than any sadness. It was even more powerful than that of a heartbreaking romance. It felt like an unbearable force was crushing in on her soul and then ripping her heart in two. It was crippling, absolutely crippling. For most, it was the sort of pain that makes one beg for a limb to be severed, anything to make it stop. But you can't amputate the soul. You must endure, for a mother's loss will never fade. Instead, the body and mind will slowly deteriorate around it, leaving her a miserable shell waiting for death.

Just when she thought it couldn't get any worse, her eyes dashed to the sight of her father jumping into the portal after the cloaked man that had snatched her away. She wanted to jump after them, to follow them, to see where they went, but the portal to the land of everlasting shadows tragically closed behind them, the timing ever so calculated. The man knew her father would jump, he counted on it. A small round man within the room instantly rushed to her, but despite his most kindly efforts of comfort, there was not a single thing he could say or do to console her. Then, they realized something else. Someone else had made it through the mirror in time. Catcher, too, was gone. And though Maleficent didn't know her father's creature, she could see then and there that he was to him what Grip was to her. And as sad as it all most certainly was, she found a glimmer of relief knowing he was with him.

But what happened then? Where did they go? How did she end up with Mim? Was this all Mim's doing? Had she simply sent him to collect her? She was marked by a blood oath, after all. It was easy to place blame on Mim, as she had done with many other things over the years. But something, something dark and haunting deep inside her knew she was wrong. And in that moment, when she gave way to her anger and resistance, however small it was, was enough to carry her towards the final answer. And though she had fought hard and desired it for so long, she couldn't help but feel the weight of dread and fear when the moment finally arrived.

Her vision was then thrusted once more. But she was not to go far. When she arrived, she could see right away that she was in the damned cabin again. The feelings that came with the new vision were unfortunately familiar. It was Mim who possessed her every movement now. And in a way, Maleficent preferred it that way. For it seemed that the agony that suffused her mother was a storm of suffering that would never fade away, and for Maleficent, it was unbearable. Mim's, however, was consumed with bitter anger, feelings she was far more comfortable with. When the cloaked man came to the door, Maleficent could feel the witch's spark of curiosity. She hadn't had a lost traveler in a few years, and she wasn't expecting anyone. After all, no one who knew of her would know where she was. But for a woman who heard so many knocks upon the ancient doorway, the fact that someone had the boldness to go straight for her doorknob, as if hoping to force their way in... well, it most certainly wasn't that of the lost, desperate, and in need of some help. In fact, it was foolishly aggressive. Eager to meet this brazen figure, she whipped open the door to find it was Pan standing on her very own porch.

It wasn't long before she realized who he was, despite his drastic change in appearance, from a boy to the heart-breaking Gancanagh. The slow lift of his wide hood was like that of the unveiling of a painted masterpiece. There was not a single feature flawed, nothing that could be changed for the better. No, he was in every way- perfection. But it wasn't just his beauty that could leave you breathless, it was the intoxicating charm that coursed through his blood. Maleficent was both struck with awe and mounting relief. This man was extraordinary, and he had taken her away from her parents, and even lured her father away to a world unknown, but he was a stranger. This was not Jack Frost. This was Pan, and though he was no longer a young boy, his boundless arrogance had never ceased; a fact that would rapidly cost him a great deal. It was obvious that he knew who and what she was, so it was absolutely horrifying to watch as he dared disrespect her. It wasn't like the way her father had addressed her. For in his tone, there was both respect and purpose. He had the upper hand, and even though he knew this going in, he never stooped to act without proper manner. There wasn't an evil air about him like there was with this enchanting man.

When he revealed that he had taken Hook's child, ripping her out of his arms, the witch scoffed in disbelief. But once the truth of what he had done came into the clear, that he had just stolen a newborn baby in front of its mother, Maleficent felt Mim's fury erupt. Mere seconds after he had asked permission to come visit the baby, did the Wood Witch strike him with a spark of her magic, rendering him helpless, twitching in pain, and seized with a most horrendous illness. It was so horrible, in fact, that he collapsed to the floor, barely breathing. He should have died, but there was something else keeping him alive, a power that wasn't his. Mim reached down and with a tiny blade within her hand, she cut his arm. The blood that spilled was cold and glittered with frosted magic.

"Ah, so you are here doing the Snow Queen's bidding, are ya? But your cold blood cannot compare to your cold heart. The wickedness of all that you have done is a poison brewing. I do not know what you and your queen have planned for the babe, but you will not have her. I can feel the vast sea of souls you contain for your own desire for power. I fear what you might do if I let you leave untouched, powerful, and suffused with deadly ambition. For I have seen what you are capable of, stealing a child away from its mother. And as if that weren't cruel enough, you lock away her love. Poor fairy. *Tisk-Tisk-Tisk.*" She whispered, pacing back and forth with her long purple dress dragging behind her. She appeared to be thinking, but to Maleficent, it felt as if she were agonizing. She took her gaze and turned it towards the baby. And as she rocked her in an ancient cradle, she couldn't help but smile at the infant's sleeping breaths. But when the baby began to mouth the expression of suckling, like a child does when it wants its mother's milk, Mim's heart sunk, and another spark of fire began to enflame within. "I'm sorry, little one. I would take you to your mother if I could. Alas, I am stuck in this cabin, and by your mark of the raven, you are as well. I vow to you now to protect you from those that would harm you, and I vow to devote all the love I have to offer to that of being your other mother. I will find a way for your mother to find you, and I'm sure if she can, she will come to collect you. Prophecy be damned, I want nothing to do with the infinite turmoil they have wrought upon your family. You have my word, for every day you are in my care, I will love you like you are mine, and when the day comes that your parents find you, I will sacrifice all that I have desired for so long, if it means you are where you belong." After bestowing one more smile upon the dreaming baby, she turned her attention back upon the villain that laid unconscious on her floor. With a most sinister gleam in her eye, she came down close to his face. "You are beautiful, yes, indeed. But that is not who you are. There is no warmth, no kindness, no light inside you. You measure your power by the souls you have stolen, but now you have stolen a living child, right out of her father's arms. Such a crime I fear cannot go unpunished. No, no, it most certainly cannot." Then she placed her hands above his chest.

> *I call upon the true reflection*
> *For he who has no light*
> *Take the sun away from him*
> *And leave him to the night*
> *I call the staff and talisman*
> *Of the great Joan the Wad*
> *I charge him to guide the lost*
> *The helpless and the sad*
> *For every soul he passes*
> *Who breathes the deathful cry*
> *I call upon the chains of burden*
> *Make him carry those that die*
> *Bitter, cold, and cruel*
> *Such evil has a cost*
> *I shall take the souls he's stolen*
> *And leave him to the frost.*"

And then it happened. Pan began to change. His hair went white, his skin went pale, his lips turned blue, and the air that stirred around him carried the cold chill of winter. *It was him.*

"This isn't real! This isn't true! I tested him! I cast a spell! He could not lie. Not to me. But both of

334

you have lied, and you are lying now! Admit it! Admit it!" She screamed, waking herself in burst of fury and tears.

* * *

Denial. If it is true that belief and that of faith itself holds enough power to manifest the unnatural, heal the sick, or even shroud the fearful with the blind blanket to all the mysteries and doubt of the unknown in exchange for the certainty that all living creatures long for. To give one's faith in the hands of an unseen force may seem foolish, but the truth is— doing so for the sake of one's own blissful ignorance is not faith at all. It is denial. And if the power of belief, *pure* belief, can create that which would not have been without it, then it stands to reason that denial has the power to damage, delusion, or even destroy not only the soul of the source, but those that would dare challenge their fantasy as well.

It was this destructive force that would bring two dark soul's together. Maleficent knew the pieces of all she had come to discover, pointed to a heartbreaking truth, but she couldn't, she wouldn't accept that. The final dream she had endured, had pushed her over the edge. The Forbidden Mountain was now rumbling with such powerful force, the storm her rage had released then exploded with magic. It was just as Mim had feared. For though Maleficent had been kept hidden in her dark castle by the sea, such an eruption was bound to catch an evil eye. "Stop, Maleficent!" Shouted Mim within her head. But she couldn't. She couldn't even hear her through the chaos of every thought, every word, every vision flashed like thunder and lightning around her. All the years of hate, isolation, possession, anticipation, exhaustion, and mounting questions had come to a conclusion that felt worse than death. And she wasn't ready for that. She needed more proof.

Despite the power of Madam Mim's pleas, the storm of Maleficent's rage had caught someone's attention. But it was not the sisters of Oz that dwelled within another world. It was someone within the mortal world. And they had a message for her. The Dark Fairy's chaotic mind was suddenly silenced as a knock came on the castle doors. The sound echoed its way towards her, bouncing off the old stone walls. Full of aggression, Maleficent whipped open the doorway, almost hoping for a worthy confrontation. It would be nice to unleash some of her anger, on an innocent or not. But to her dismay, it was just another one of her goblins. "If you do not have the princess with you, then just go away. I am not in the mood for visitors!" She huffed, turning her back to him and proceeded to storm back to her throne to think. But the little goblin waddled in after her urgently. His armor clanked so loudly when he moved, Maleficent could feel her irritation turning murderous.

"No. No, Dark Mistress. I must deliver it. I must. I must. Please," he cried out desperately from under his heavy helmet.

"Deliver what? What are talking about?!" She asked harshly.

"The letter! The letter! It is for you! You must take it. I must give it. For if I don't, she will surely kill me."

"She? She who?"

"Pretty, so pretty."

It was moments like this that made Maleficent wish she had charged her desires to creatures with even half a brain. "Oh, just give it to me!" She screamed, snatching the letter from his sweaty hands. The poor frightened goblin remained standing before her as if frozen in fear. "What is it?"

"What do I do now?" He said in a pitiful whisper.

Rolling her emerald eyes, she replied, "You have given me the letter. You have done as this woman has wished. So, why do you stand here so consumed with terror? —I'll tell you why. Because while you were supposed to be finding the princess— I need to cast my curse, you have been off serving someone else. And that, my little monster, makes me angry!" At that, she pointed her staff at his head and hissed, "I have had it with the lot of you! This final act of foolery is the last straw! Come, my little naughty children! Appear before your mistress— Now!" She commanded, slamming her staff to the floor, instantly conjuring each and every surviving goblin to appear before her.

She hadn't used such harsh methods with them before, but she was not in a patient mood. Sure, the forceful jolt would be nothing short of painful, but in her eyes, they deserved it. Then it happened. One by one, two by two, the goblins appeared like flashes of lightning, both swift and severe. The thrashing journey proved to be too much for the little monsters. Maleficent rolled her eyes in disgust as they vomited, falling to the floor, gasping for air.

"Pathetic fools! Get up!"

Her commanding voice stole their breath, leaving the room as silent as a tomb. The truth was that the transportation had happened so quickly, they didn't even have a moment to think about what was occurring, let alone who had caused their torturous voyage. But now they knew. Her commanding voice was unmistakable. They knew why she had brought them to her. They had run out of time. With beady eyes filled with terror, they looked around to see if anyone of them had the princess, wishing it were so, but alas, they had again come back empty-handed; a dreaded fact that would likely end all of their lives tonight.

"I said get up! All of you! Now!"

The goblins took a deep breath and rose themselves up from the stone floor. The oldest leader was the first to answer as was their custom. Due to his utter fear however, all the poor goblin could muster was a grumble under his quickening breath. Seeing their leader speechless was enough to send the rest into an all-out frenzy. Maleficent was then met with a chaotic mess of-

"It is his fault!"

"No, it was him!"

"I could have found her, but then..."

"Enough!" She screamed, silencing them all. "I have had enough of your excuses! Your time is up! Have-you-found-the-princess?" She asked in a slow harsh tone that made them tremble beneath her.

This time, the leader did muster up a reply, "We tried, Mistress, but she is just nowhere to be found."

"That's impossible!" She roared. "She didn't just disappear, you fools! You have had fifteen years to search every kingdom, every forest, every mountain..."

"We did! We did! We searched for her everywhere!" Cried out the little goblins.

The leader looked behind him with a scolding glare to silence them before turning his gaze back to her. "It is true, Mistress. We left no stone unturned. We searched every town, every wood, every home, the mountains, all the cradles..."

Maleficent's eyes went wide then. His last words planted the seed of shock that would soon detonate into a deadly rage. Like the calm before a dreaded storm, Maleficent giggled, reaching her hand out for Grip. The dark raven perched himself upon her long fingers as she spoke sweetly, "My darling, did you hear what these naughty children said? All of these years, fifteen in all- they have been searching for— a baby! Hmmm, a baby," she said again, with the last ounce of calm she had left. And then it happened; Maleficent's rage erupted like a fiery volcano. "Fools! Idiots! Useless imbeciles!" She screamed, striking them with lighting with each and every word. The pain she struck was

339

severe, but not deadly. The armor they wore fell to the ground. Burned and bleeding, the goblins rushed to escape her wrath, and to their surprise- she let them. Their failure had been so defeating, so agonizing, and yet, she could not bring herself to obliterate the last of their kind. She had killed so many already, each calcified into the very stone of her dark castle. Those that were left were gone, as was the magic she had gifted them all those years ago.

CHAPTER TEN
THE MAGIC MIRROR

𝔄s Maleficent sat down upon her throne feeling drained and dismayed. "I suppose the fault is mine, my pet. I should not have trusted such an important task to a bunch of mindless monsters. If I want to find the little wretch, then I am going to have to do so myself," she muttered solemnly, bringing her head down into her hands. It was then that she felt the envelope the little goblin had brought her earlier, crinkling under her dress. Having forgotten the matter, she lifted it up with mild interest. She opened the mysterious letter, eager to uncover the identity of the writer. But as her eyes observed the message, she found herself fascinated. Delicately hand-written upon the fine parchment were the most exquisite markings of the written word. One could see the drive for absolute perfection in each and every stroke. Maleficent had never seen such precision, for even magic had its flaws. There were no scratches of ink, nor a single drop misplaced. The paper even seemed to carry the magnificent scent of perfume.

Who was this mysterious writer? And what did they want with her?

341

Your Excellence,

It has come to my attention that you have bestowed a curse upon the Rose Kingdom and that of the princess born to King Stefan and his Queen. Others, like myself, cannot deny admiring the glorious masterpiece you have cast, brazen as it was. Most like us, me above all, must keep our wicked ways hidden, which is why I have need to ask for your help. You see, I too have a princess in my kingdom. I am the queen, the fairest in the land, but with each passing year, the king's brat grows more beautiful. I want nothing more than to hold her bloodied heart in my hands and keep it as a trophy. As queen, I find myself unable to do with her as I would like. I want her tortured, slashed, and left an ugly mess. As our kingdom isn't far from King Stefan's, many have heard of your dark magic. I ask you to kill the princess to restore my rightful vanity. No one will trace her death back to me. I need someone I can trust and in exchange, I offer you my most prized possession, my magic mirror. It can show you anything you desire. There is no question it cannot answer, but be warned, for it will only reflect the truth. I hate that. Should you wish to comply, please send to me one of your ravens with your written answer.

Ever fairest,
The Evil Queen

"How very interesting. Very interesting indeed. It seems we may have another way to settle all of this,

342

darling. What do you think?" Grip squawked with an excited flutter of his feathers, mirroring her sinister enthusiasm. She laughed wickedly, petting his head sweetly as she made her way towards her room of Mim's ancient spell books. They had been all too easy to conjure them with the witch's staff. Grip watched with intense curiosity as she quickly selected one. She sat down with a thrill, and without a feather or a drop of ink, she uttered her words, delivering them in perfect form upon the paper...

Fairest Queen,

I am honored by Your Majesty's humbled admiration and sympathize your grave plight. But I fear while I appreciate your murderous desire, I cannot kill your stepdaughter. A curse is only as powerful as the hate you bear towards your enemy. But I can help you accomplish her demise, and the beauty of my plan, is that you will be able to do so however you wish. Get creative. I understand your concern about the girl's death being traced to you, but should you agree with my terms, I vow to you that the magic I offer will come with a full transformation spell to disguise yourself, so you can spill blood without suspicion. I offer to you one of my ancient spell books, containing all you need to fulfill your darkest wish. And in return, I ask that you send me your Magic Mirror. I feel as though I might have some use for it. I hope we can help each other and bring to the darkness the deserved end to all of those who dared try to destroy our happiness. I am sending one of my finest ravens, if you are content with my terms, read the following incantation and our magical offerings will then exchange.

Your darkest sister,
Maleficent

And then upon a second page, she shared the spell that could turn the winds of change in their favor.

Recite these words.

Magic for Magic
Witch to Witch
Possessions with powers
Let us summon a switch
Give the Dark Fairy
The Mirror on the Wall
And give me the book
To make me fairest of all
Give her all truth
And give me a disguise
Power for Power
Let our wickedness rise

Bell, book, and candle
Spells and potion
Sisters of darkness
Put our evil in motion.

And that was that. Maleficent sent her trusted friend and companion to deliver her most delicate of correspondence to the Evil Queen. She wasn't sure how long she would have to wait for a response, or if she would get one at all. For the queen had asked quite specifically for it to be her that murders the king's stepdaughter. But alas, it had to be this way. *What if she does not find my offering fitting to her own? What will I do if she does not send the mirror? How will I find the rotten brat that evades me? I feel as though everything is falling apart. And above all else, the boy that started all of this could possibly be... No. No. I refuse to believe any of their lies.* Just as she had finished her final thought, she knew that she had done so for her host to hear. Or maybe, she truly needed to reassure herself. For to think otherwise would mean something so tragic, she couldn't possibly go on. The heartbreak, the guilt, the shame, the loss, the years wasted, the lies, everything she was, everything she had done— *Had it really all been for a lie?*

Thankfully, Maleficent's thoughts that had all but drowned her, were suddenly interrupted by the first glimmer of hope she had received in ages. It was here. The mirror. It hung upon the stone wall next to her glorious throne. The room instantly felt different. It was the feeling one gets when you feel someone is watching you, only this was different. It was far more intense. It was as if the mirror's eyes were not only watching you, spying on you, it was looking inside you. And not just for this particular moment, but rather like it could see everything about you, past, present, and future. It was an eerie feeling, yet somehow, she couldn't bring herself to do anything but come closer and closer towards the black glass that appeared like a window to a pitch-black world. She almost succumb to the desire to put her hand through the hole of the frame to see if she could, but just as she reached out her hand, an eruption of smoke appeared within the void. It was green, like her own. *How odd.* And then, a sudden face appeared on the mirror, not her own, it was someone or something else. As she looked closer, she could see that it wasn't in fact a face at all, but rather what looked like a mask. A terrifying mascaraed mask that glowed and came up to two sharp corners, like that of horns. The eyes, or the lack there of was what made him so horrifying.

"Good Evening, Your Excellence." The Man in the mirror said, in an ominous tone that seemed to fit his image perfectly.

"Um, hello Mr.—"

"I have no name, Miss. I am but an oracle created and born from the darkest of magic."

"Oh. Well, who created you? And why do you appear with a mask?" She asked, feeling that her questions would burn right through her if she didn't ask.

"I will answer your questions, if that is your wish, but I must warn you of your limits."

"Limits? The Queen didn't write to me anything about limits."

"That is because Her Majesty only has one desire, only one question. It is the same question she asks of me every day. For every soul that comes to possess me, they may ask me three *different* questions. No more, no less, no second chances. So, choose wisely, Mistress. I can tell you anything, anything but a lie. Just say the words, though be careful how you place them. For like I said, you will not get another chance."

Anything but a lie.

"I know what I need. What I need to know. How does your magic work? What do I do?"

He hovered for a moment, staring at her with a blank expression. She squirmed with anticipation but dared not vent her frustration. Luckily, the mirror finally replied: "Her Majesty needed a powerful incantation, but you do not need to invoke any magic to help. You possess more than enough to summon me to you. Ask your first question, but remember, the truth is all I can give, and I fear any truth you seek will not be what you desire to hear. A lie can be believed, no matter how false, but the truth— the truth reveals all. You must take it as you will. Do you still wish to proceed?" He asked with a tone of certain doom.

In all honesty, Maleficent *wasn't* sure if she was ready to accept the truth, but she had to know. She wanted to inquire about the princess, but the itching agony about Jack felt like it was about to burst out of her mouth. Not wanting to appear with any less stature than the queen, she collected her composure and firmly stated in reply, "I do."

"As you wish. Ask your first question."

Wanting to word her question precisely, she took a moment to piece it together. Suddenly she realized that her hesitation was just a stall. A fact obnoxiously made by her pounding heart and racing breath.

"Do you wish for more time, Miss?"

"No! I know what I want to know, but you have got me all scrabbled about how to put things, that I only have one chance! It is a lot of pressure. And I do not appreciate your queen's omission on such matters as this. She *should* have told me."

"Her Majesty did not share these limitations because she knew exactly what she wanted to know. Questions may at first appear deep and complicated, but this really isn't so. I think you will find that your question can be asked successfully with less than ten words. You are pushing yourself into a senseless scatter. Let it be simple. If you truly understand what you seek to know, you need only to ask."

Maleficent huffed with irritation. "What good did it do me to hear of the Evil Queen's ease with such things! Are you trying to make me feel foolish?!"

"Is that a question?" he replied plainly.

Maleficent's eyes flashed green with a fierce glow. But it was in her fit of anger that she came to realize how she would handle her dilemma. And as always, the wicked thought brought a burst of volcanic laughter to bellow throughout the castle. It was the kind of disturbing madness that had always struck her audience with fear, but the fixed expression of the mirror's mask never wavered. Which could only make one wonder what sort of evil he had served in the past; the things he must have seen to be so calm now. Maleficent wondered at it all. His mysteriousness. There was so much about him she wanted to know. The mask, his creator, his limitations, his past, his age, and what destinies he has cheated... but alas, to ask him a question about himself would mean sacrificing one of the answers she sought for herself. Why, even to ask him if anyone else has asked him for a glimpse of his history would be a question wasted. Limitations. Though her entire childhood in the cabin had been nothing but limitations, she had never hated them more than right now.

"Has my Mistress had a change of heart?" He asked in a monotone.

Maleficent smiled, "No, Mirror, not at all. I was just thinking about what you said about the queen. How she handled acquiring the answers or answer she has sought. And well, I feel that while I respect her ways, as they have clearly served her well, I fear I cannot follow her path with the same ease. And so, I have decided that I would go about this my way. The way I was always taught."

"What way, your Excellence?"

"Well, I am afraid you are going to find it unpleasant, but you see... I do not let *anyone* pressure me, nor rule any matter with which involves me. I am in charge now. I have three questions, just as you said, but

I will not be burdened by perfection. If I need to explain or see the truth for myself, I demand that you do so. And if you deny me, I will crack your glass. It will be small at first, but I promise that I *will* grow more volatile with each and every disappointment you bring me. The queen may need you, but *I* can smash you into a million pieces and go to sleep with a smile on my face. I do not seek your guidance for the sake of my vanity, like your former master. My matters are grave, and I will not allow your precious limitations to ruin my plans. Now, *do- you-* understand?" She said with a threatening nod.

After a long pause, the Magic Mirror on the wall agreed with a most grim voice, "Very well... Proceed."

* * *

Maleficent may have known what questions she wanted to ask, but which would come first was the one she wanted answered the most, and the one she dreaded to hear. But she had come too far now to cower before the truth, wretched as it might be. She took a deep breath, the kind you take so you can conjure courage instead of tears. And once she could finally bring the words to her lips, she opened her mouth, and let them spill into the air to catch the mirror's hearing...

"The man I love, the one from my dreams, is Jack Frost my father's enemy? Is he *Peter Pan?*" No sooner had the question expelled from her heart, did she start silently wishing for her wanted answer over and over again in her head, not caring if Mim or Ainsel were listening or not. *Say no. Say no. He loves me. He is not*

Pan. He isn't. Say no. Say it. She knew how strong belief could be, and maybe, if she could just will it so, then the answer might be...

"Yes. The mortal boy once known by Peter has changed much over the course of such a vast amount of years, but a name cannot hide the soul from me. They are indeed, one and the same. Though it was by the Wood Witch's power and not by that of Father Time that ripped his image of the shining sun into the cold reflection of winter, his heart has remained as it always was- black."

"Black?" She whimpered in a whisper.

"Black as poison
Black as pitch
Cruel as death
Fouler than witch
Was born evil
And will die the same
His wicked soul
Love cannot tame
Trickster to all
Stealer of souls
Breaker of hearts
Guide from the cold
His charm is a glamour
But only skin deep
A nightmare disguised
In the dreams where you sleep."

His deep voice, void of any compassion or the hesitance one usually has when delivering a heartbreaking truth, seemed to be even more brutal. The complete absence of expression on the masked mirror's face seemed to burn her to the core, yet there was a fair amount of relief that came from knowing the mirror didn't care about her affairs. There was no judgement, no humiliation, no pity, the mirror spoke his unsugared words as if they were simply just facts. She didn't have to worry about what he thought.

But... that didn't mean she didn't. For even as a mirror hung on the wall before her, she didn't need to look upon the enchanted glass to reflect on all the choices she had made because she thought he loved her. But it had all been a lie. All of it.

"How is this possible? He might be powerful, but my spell should have worked. How could he lie to me? I was so careful." She uttered in raging whispers as she paced back and forth upon the stone beneath her feet.

"It's true your power is absolute and unflawed. I'm afraid it was his trickery in the art of such delicate wording that his deception proved powerful enough to blind you from the truth. For it was through your besotted vision that believed that it was you he was describing that night. The lad is clever. He did not lie."

"But he said it was my blood that brought him there night after night. That I was the one he..."

"It was not you to which he was referring, in his dark depth, but rather your father. So, you see, the blood that keeps him coming back is the blood that now courses through you."

The crushing blow hit her ever harder in that moment. "But why? Why make me think that he loves me? Why did he take me to the third realm? Was the Snow Queen in on this the whole time? The attack, the abduction, the charge she gave me... Was this all really just a heinous act of revenge against me because of their hatred towards my father? I know that my father killed the queen's daughter, but why should Jack... I mean Peter Pan go to such bitter lengths as this. Did my father kill the green pixie of his? Is that what this is about? I just do not understand..."

"It is true that the pixie would still be alive if it were not for your father, but their history is far more complicated than the death of one. Your father took away the one that Pan loved, an Indian girl by the name of Tiger Lily."

"Tiger Lily— *ugh,*" Maleficent scoffed as if repulsed by the name, when it was if fact what the girl represented. Suddenly, she found herself hoping that it *was* her father that killed the girl. "Is my father responsible for her death as well?"

"No. The girl lived a long and happy life here within the mortal world because of your father. He struck a deal that freed the entire Indian tribe of stolen souls back to the mortal world with their spirits intact. The loss of Tiger Lily changed Pan forever. He has spent all this time trying to find the kind of love to fill the darkest void in his heart, but he never has. That is, until the Snow Queen divulged a devious plan to change both their fates; a wish that could only come true with your help. They need the late witch's magic, and the child born from the kingdom of roses to conjure enough magic to bring back all that they have lost."

"The princess! It all comes down to King Stefan's mortal brat! Damn her! Damn them all! When I think of all that I have done... I killed my mother for him- I mean Mim. She tried to tell me. Both she and my true mother did. But I didn't believe them. All these years, the guilt I felt for the Snow Queen's wrath, the pain of her taking away my own true love... But I was just a pawn in their cruel manipulating game. They have made a fool out of me!"

"Their actions were that of cruelty indeed, but now that you are enlightened to the truth, maybe now you could lift the curse you have placed on the princess. For she too has been used as a pawn, living a life full of lies and deception. Take pity on the girl who mirrors the tragic story of your life. It is not too late. The child's sixteenth year of age dawns tomorrow morn. She still has a chance, and you are the only one who can give it to her."

Maleficent huffed, each breath angrier than the last. Her entire world had just come crashing down, and yet again, the only care seemed to fall upon that wretched girl. *Why did everyone care about her so much?* Even the magic mirror who was supposed to be void of any judgement or personal feelings was now pitying her.

"What about me? Does no one care what cruel fate has befallen me? My life has been nothing but a sequence of tragic events... Born a half-ling, hated by those that live in the Nine Realms, and feared by the

354

mortals that share half my blood. I spent my entire childhood isolated and hidden from the world, only to discover that the woman I had always believed was my mother- was nothing more than an ancient witch who was collecting a blood debt. The only light in my sad dark world was the man of my dreams. But it was all just a lie! All of it! I have been tricked and deceived my entire life. Despite all of that, I did try to be merciful to the humans. I was kind and used my powers to give them everything they wanted. And all I asked in return was that they not meddle with magic again. And they did! Not only did they strike another deal with the fae, they did so with those blasted sisters that hate me!"

"Yes, Mistress, but you only sought out the princess in an act of revenge for the queen taking your love from you. Now you know that there is no cause for revenge."

Maleficent turned to the mirror with her green eyes glowing so intensely that it seemed to burn the glass. "Oh, yes there is! All of this happened because they wanted their precious princess! All the lies, all the pain, it has all been about her. My enemies have hidden her from me, but all that is over now! They are all going to pay for what they have done to me!

Magic Mirror on the wall,
Let them pay one and all
Show me where
The princess hides
Remove the glamour
Of their lies

Let her see
Those meddlesome three
Her sixteenth year
is the last she'll be
The king and queen
Will pay for their deal
When she pricks her finger
On the spinning wheel."

With a fixed expression of a blank stare, the mirror faded away to reveal the image of what she sought upon the glass. But what vision emerged then before her was more shocking and infuriating than she could have possibly imagined. They were all asleep, deep asleep— *But where were they?* Suddenly she could see the cloudy frame that surrounded them. *They were in Slumberland. Of course! They had been hiding within the lie of their designed illusion. But wait! The room where they slept. The windows. The floor. The walls! Oh- my- god!*

"The cabin! All these years... they have been hiding her in my mother's cabin!" It was then that Maleficent's fury exploded into the air with a soul-ripping scream that rumbled the entire castle and shattered the magic mirror into a thousand pieces.

After her scorching breath of rage, Maleficent crumbled to the ground. Feeling as though her anger had been torn from her, all there was left was the sobbing tears of sadness that had been suppressed by the force of her fury. But now, as she gazed down upon the broken glass beneath her, all she could see were the shattered pieces of her dark heart, each shard reflecting the agony and pain wrought upon her by her enemies; her dreams with Jack, the dance they shared, the night of the woodland party, the blank dolls that still dangled on an everlasting chain that hovered above the grounds scorched by the witch she had believed was her mother; and then there was the three fairies. *Why did it seem like they had always been there?* They were there the night her darkness was born, the night her horns rose from her head, officially transforming her from the image of a mere child into that of a creature. She remembered how ugly they made her feel, a fact made more brutal by the thousand scars they had left upon her skin. They had sought out the king and queen, no doubt as some revenge against her. Truth be told, it *wasn't* just the mortal's betrayal that had scorned her so wretchedly, it was why they had done so. It wasn't just about their precious princess, or even their glutenous greed; it was about her appearance. She was tall, dark, with striking features that struck fear in those around her, while the three sisters wore their light fluffy dresses and glittered hats, each glowing like little balls of light. They appeared like small good fairies— of course, the mortals turned to them instead of her. Of course, they would gather all the kingdoms together to celebrate *them*, keeping her a dark hidden secret. After all, that is what she had always been. Even Mim kept her hidden away. She had been told she was beautiful, but then again— so had Pan. But they lied. *I'm not loved. I'm not beautiful.* She thought, picking up a jagged piece of the mirror, setting her sight upon her reflection.

They say that love blinds you from seeing the bad in others, even yourself. So, it stands to reason that hatred has the power to blind you from seeing the good. Maleficent should have seen the astounding beauty of her reflection, the kind that made others writhe in envy, but she didn't. All of her hatred, however strong against those she despised, were nothing compared to how much she hated herself. All she could see was— a *monster.*

A sudden surge of anger then brought Maleficent out of her depressed state. She wiped away her unwelcomed tears of weakness and rose herself up from the floor, throwing the broken glass from her bloodied hand and lifting her arms to raise the rest of the shattered pieces of the magic mirror and put them back together. One by one, the glimmering shards of glass returned to its united object of reflection. The mirror was whole again. And there, with the given vision of her image, Maleficent smiled wickedly. "They all think of me as a monster. Well, fine! I'll be the monster."

The Mask that came from the magic mirror then emerged with the surrounding image of smoke to frame its ominous expression. It didn't speak a word; it just stared its cold stare. *Did it even know that she had broken its glass? Was it mad at her? Maybe it didn't even work anymore...* There was only one way to find out. "Magic mirror of mended glass, I know the question I need to ask."

But there was nothing. The mirror said not a word. After a long-held breath of hope, Maleficent let go, turning away in despair. But just when all seemed lost, she heard the word that brought it all back; the voice that proved one important thing. She may have broken the glass, but the magic of the mirror remained.

"Proceed."

One of the good things about making mistakes, is they make you think much harder before you make another decision. Yes, the question Maleficent wanted so badly to ask was where *he* was. *Where was Pan? Was the Snow Queen hiding him? Were they laughing at her? The first time I saw him was the night I met the three sisters. Now I find that they have been living in the cabin, protecting the same princess that Pan and the Snow Queen desire. I can't help feeling that they are all laughing at me. Much has gone against me, favoring their driven plot. They may have the princess, and the passed time of fifteen years behind them, but there is still one thing they don't have, the one thing they need to make their wishes come true...* "They haven't found the book. Well they can have the last fifteen years with the little brat! I hope their time hidden in the woods, isolated in my mother's cabin were as wonderful as they were for me. The fairies may have given her a lovely dream full of lies, but it's time to wake up and face the Dark Fairy's nightmare."

Grip screeched with flitting thrill. How he loved to see her so devious, so passionate. He had been with her through it all, every tragic heartbreak after another.

"What is it you wish to know?" The magic mirror asked in a deep menacing tone. It seemed the

359

villainous energy within the room had even coursed its way into the smokey glass.

This was it. The final question... "Where within Madam Mim's cottage dwells the hidden spellbook of her darkest power?"

The face within the enchanted mirror then faded away, revealing the vision of her desired answer. The rooms of the ancient cabin did then emerge upon the glass. Maleficent drew closer as the image began to move like a person walking down the halls. Upon the long curves of shelves that lined either side, hung many portraits of people and creatures, all unknown. As a child, she enjoyed making up little stories about them. She had passed these halls too many times to count. There was no book there. "This cannot be right. There is no door, no window, nothing. Where is the book?" She screamed in frustration. Then just as she was beginning to think she had been tricked, she saw it. There were frames of all sorts of colors, sizes, and shapes among the paintings, but the vision had brought her to one. The frame was red, and the painting was that of a haunting scarecrow that was hung beyond what appeared to be a yellow brick road. The vision sent a chill up Maleficent's spine. She had seen that road before, not just in the hall, surrounded by a delicate frame, but in the memories of her dreams. But there was something far more disturbing about the painting. Things that had been there before were gone now. How strange it is that all it takes is a mere picture to remember something you had long forgotten. She looked closely through the mirror, trying to see every detail. The painting was indeed old, but its colors were as vibrant as a freshly painted landscape. Before, it had been full of wonderous things... A field of lollypops and bubbles, an exquisite hourglass half full of red sand, and a pair of ruby slippers that glittered so brightly, they seemed to glimmer off the paint. There used to be monkeys that flew in the sky and crooked trees that held a vast forest of shining apples. Mim used to say that it was a place where people go when they are desperately trying to find something, a place where treasures are hidden. Not just material treasures, but those that people believe they lack. They come looking for a magical wizard that can grant them whatever it is that they desire most. But magic doesn't work that way. That's what Mim would always say. When Maleficent asked why she kept the painting, Mim had told her that it was a reminder; that whether you are seeking knowledge, heart, courage, or even a place to call home- you must look deep inside yourself and not to magic to discover what you really need and how to find it. Bad things happen to people who come to see the wizard. Maleficent never asked about the painting again, nor any others. Instead, she just made up her own stories about them. It was less scary that way. She had tried to avoid its image ever since, but now, here it was again. Upon the landscape, hidden in dark corner surrounded by fog was a small book.

   With a light touch upon the book from an unseen force, a secret doorway then opened within the wall, revealing the exact location of the most hunted of treasures. It was the third and final piece of the

Erlking's dark magic. The wood wrapped with skin that covered its ancient pages were the sharpest shade of red, bright, and vibrant, even under the blanket of dust that had collected upon it over the years.

"That is why she wouldn't give me the book; why she didn't want it in the hands of the Snow Queen or Pan. But how did I not see this before? I know that I have touched all of these paintings before. Why did the door not open then?"

"The door will not emerge for those that seek it."

Maleficent smiled, "Ah, yes, that is indeed Mim's style."

"The magic you need to retrieve the book now lives inside you. With Mim's power, the door will open."

"But how can I find the cabin. It is lost to me now. I know that it is in the Forbidden Forest, but its woods are vast, and the cottage will likely be invisible to my eyes. How do I know for certain that they have not already found the book?"

"I am sorry, Mistress, but I'm afraid you have run out of questions. I have given you all the answers I can. It is now up to you to choose your destiny."

Maleficent let out a single breath of disappointment but accepted the fact that he was right. She had asked her questions, and due to her threats, she had received more than any other in the past. "Very well." At that, Maleficent sat upon her throne and tried to think of her next move. Then it hit her. The morning was to come soon, very soon. She had already removed the glamour of the three, and the princess would be waking in less than four hours. If those little pixies want to keep up their charade, then they are going to have use their magic. All three of them. And once they do, we will find the hidden cottage and take what is rightfully ours... The princess and the spellbook.

* * *

Grip wasted no time in his journey to the Forbidden Forest, but no matter how hard he flapped his wings, he could not beat the dawn. The three fairies were the first to wake up on that dreadful morning. It was the day they had longed to see, but none of them were prepared for the dawn that greeted them. Their illusion was gone. The cabin where they dwelled was horrid, dirty, and smelled foul. Morning panic is the worst, and on this frantic occasion, panic was too little a word. The sisters looked at each other for a second, each realizing what was happening. Dashing out of their little beds, the three tried desperately to clean what they could before the princess woke. Yes, they had made it to her sixteenth birthday, but there was still time for it to all go wrong. They didn't know who was responsible for their awakening, but if they were not in Slumberland anymore, then that meant that they could be found, even in the hidden cabin of the Wood Witch. And it seemed, though none of them wished to admit it out loud or even to themselves, that someone or *something* already knew where they were.

By the time Briar Rose woke up, she found her home in quite a different state. It was incredibly dark, like no sunshine existed at all. It was murky, making it difficult to breathe. When she came out of her room, she found her three aunties cleaning the cottage, each sweating from their efforts. As soon as they saw her, they urgently rushed her out the door, asking for her to pick some berries, the best she could find. Rose found this a little odd, since her aunties knew that the berries they desired were far off into the woods. Such a task seemed unfitting for her birthday. Still, something about their uneasiness made her think twice about their need to distract her. They were up to something. A birthday event no doubt. They had always gone so overboard on her birthdays. It was almost as if they were celebrating her age for themselves as well. Suspicious as the whole situation was, in truth, Rose was more than eager to get out of the dark murky cabin. The sisters called out their usual warnings to her on her way out; two of which were the most important. One, sing. Two, do not talk to strangers. And as always, Rose heartily agreed like a perfect daughter should.

As Rose made her way out into the distant woods, she found that they too somehow looked different. She had lived within the Forbidden Forest her entire life and yet the woods appeared completely new to her. Her aunties had been telling her for a while that strange things were going to happen on her sixteenth birthday, though they didn't exactly explain what. It sounded quite cryptic now that she looked back on it. Feeling a little uneasy, she began to sing. It didn't take more than a few notes for the animals within the woods to come to her: each loving her instantly. Rose always adored meeting new animals, but the soul she so desperately wanted to see was *him.*

Just as he did every day, Prince Phillip took his loyal horse out into the woods. It was a good way to escape the boredom of royal politics of King Hubert's castle. He and King Stefan had waited years for this day; they were both so eager to end the gloomy fate they have so long endured. But just as the possessed prince riding the disguised kelpie heard the voice he had come to love, a distant raven also overheard the wandering beauty, and came to lurk.

Perching upon a low hanging branch, he turned his leering gaze upon the princess. She was wearing peasant clothes and wore her hair down with no ornaments to glamour her appearance. Still, this girl was anything but a plain sight to behold. To say she was beautiful would be a fool's poetry. With golden hair, skin as fair as porcelain, and lips the color of a blooming pink rose, she appeared to be more enchanting than humanly possible. To see her was to know that she was different, not only in sight, but with the magical sound of her song. He had found her. Little did he know who else he was going to find.

CHAPTER ELEVEN
TOUCH THE SPINDLE

Back at the cabin, the three fairies were in quite a mess. For years, the princess had seen them sew, cook, and clean. But now, they were forced to keep up the charade with nothing but a lie of experience. But in the midst of utter chaos, it was Merryweather that was the first to crack!

"We can't do this! Fauna's cake is sixteen tiers of a disaster, and this dress looks absolutely horrid, Flora!" She screamed, looking down at the hideously pink fabric her sister had draped over her.

Fauna was too busy using a broom to hold up her bizarre bakery to pay mind to her sister's outburst. Flora, on the other hand, stopped everything to set her furious glare upon her fussy sibling. Feeling utterly offended, she scoffed, "How dare you be so rude!"

"Me!? You're the one that said it was me that made this dress look so awful! How rude was that?! Besides, I am only speaking the truth. We are running out of time. Rose will be back soon, and the truth she will find couldn't possibly be any uglier. We don't know what will happen if she uncovers our secret; what she might do. And I for one have not endured the last

366

fifteen years just to see it all fall apart on the last day. And let us not forget what might happen if things *do* go wrong. Are the two of you ready to be hunted by the Snow Queen, Jack Frost, the king and queen, and the worst- Maleficent!? No! No! Something has already happened this morning that should not have happened. I do not know what is going on, but I have a terrible feeling. Oh god!"

"Merryweather, calm down!" Flora spouted, but it was too late. Merryweather jumped down from the stool where she stood and ran up the creaking staircase that led to their room. Flora and Fauna looked to each other with confusion and concern.

"Should we go after her? I've never seen her so scared," Fauna whispered.

But before Flora could say another word, Merryweather came hopping back down the steps, this time with a smile and three wands in her hands.
"Oh— no," Flora objected.

But Merryweather had made up her mind, and not even her older sister was going to change that. "It is the only way, sisters! Please. Take your wand and let's do this right. We can still make this work, but we need our magic. What is the worst thing that can happen?"

Flora and Fauna knew the danger of such a decision, but she was right. Things couldn't be as they were when Rose returned from the woods. So, with great reluctance, they took their wands and used their magic to create a magnificent cake, a clean cabin, and a dress worthy of a princess.

Out in the deepest part of the forest, Prince Phillip and his unknowing betrothed were blissfully lost within a magical waltz, each staring deeply into each other's eyes. Too bad neither of them noticed the lurking gaze from the Dark Fairy's raven, hiding in the shadows of the thickest trees. But it wasn't the princess that had stopped the crow frozen in a state of disbelief, it was the telling gleam of a familiar evil in the prince's eye. It was him. He was certain of it. Familiars of magic can see right through the veil of possession. He knew what to do next, though he really didn't want to. He closed his eyes, calling forth Maleficent's sight, a moment between them to unite. When he opened them again, his view would be hers, and thus revealed a most dreaded betrayal.

Maleficent opened her eyes. There he was. Dancing with the princess the way he did with her- once upon a dream. The vision was cruel, but instead of feeling any pity for the girl he was bewitching now, Maleficent found herself angered by the foolish princess, because all she could see was *herself.* "Stupid, pathetic child! Why can't you see past that wretched mask of poisonous charm?"

Then suddenly, a question emerged... Why is Pan using this young man's body? Who was he? "Get closer, my pet. Find out who he is?"

Grip did as she said, sneaking ever quietly down towards the dancing couple. But the answer was not on the man at all, it was on the horse he had brought with him. The saddle of the finest leather, the cut of the hair, and the shine of its coat... This was a horse fit for royalty- a prince. Maleficent gasped as it all became brutally clear. Pan had possessed the prince so that he would fall in love with the princess, and she with him. And by the looks of it, his trickery had once again worked perfectly. She looked disgustingly smitten.

It was then that the prince slowed their pace, bringing her towards a lovely gully of water that reflected their sickening image of true love. "I have a gift for you on this special day," he said in a smooth voice that made her swoon.

"You didn't have to get me anything. All I wanted was to see you. Things seem a little off today. I was a little afraid you weren't going to show. Not after what I told you the last time we met."

"You should never fear my devotion, or the measure of my love..."

Maleficent scoffed, "Oh, god."

"—I meant what I said. I want to come and meet your family. Did you tell your aunts about what you found?" He asked.

"About the hidden doorway? No, of course not. It must be a secret they didn't want to share with me. I don't want them to be upset. After all, I wasn't snooping. I came upon the passageway by accident."

"But you said it was behind the painting with the red frame, right?"

"Yes, why?"

In truth, Pan had snuck into the true cabin many times, doing exactly as she described, but nothing ever happened. It needed to be her. She didn't seek or desire what lied beyond the portrait. She was the only one that could deliver him what he wanted.

"So, what gift have you gotten me?" She asked sweetly.

"It's a surprise. I want to come to the cabin tonight. I want to attend your birthday with you and your aunts. I don't want our love to be a secret anymore."

"But what if they don't approve?"

"Don't worry, my heart. I promise after tonight, we'll all have cause to celebrate. *Everyone* will be happy."

Maleficent tightly closed her eyes with rage, "We'll see about that! Grip, do whatever you must! Find the cabin!"

* * *

Inside the witch's cottage, the three sisters had managed to pull together the ultimate last-minute illusion. The cake looked incredible, as did the cabin itself. All that was left was the finishing touches of the dress; a decision that had caused quite the ruckus in the cabin. Flora and Merryweather were completely enthralled in a battle of pink and blue color. With shots of magic upon the dress, the fabric switched back and forth in shade. Soon, with the matter escalating, the burst of forceful magic proved to be more than the little cottage could contain. With every window and door locked, the magic had nowhere else to go but up the chimney. And like so many lost travelers that had found a glimmer of hope in the sight of smoke coming from the witch's warm fire, it didn't take long at all for Grip to spot the sparkles and glowing dust bursting out from the top of the ancient stone chimney. He instantly flapped his wings in urgent haste towards the magic, fearing that they would stop casting before he got there. And in any case, the prince was saying his goodbyes to the princess. He needed to hurry.

The princess was now on her way home, and she had never been more excited in her life. By the sound of his words, she just knew he was going to propose marriage. He had said as much before. *"We will all have cause to celebrate."* But now, he would finally ask her to be his forever. The thrill of such an evening seemed to lift her bare feet off the ground as she ran back to the cottage. She had completely forgotten the strange morning with her aunties. All she wanted to do was finally tell them about him, the man she had fallen in love with and who would be coming over to supper with them in honor of her birthday. When she arrived at the door, it was just as she expected. Her three aunties rushing to her, screaming their birthday cheers of surprise. Little did she know just how much of a surprise she was going to get.

The final cast of magic had come from Merryweather, finalizing the color of the royal gown. It was blue, of course. Blue and dazzling. Rose was in absolute awe. Not only was it unlike anything she had ever worn, but the design seemed far beyond the skills of her aunts, even on their best day. The cake, however, was entirely ridiculous. Every year, her aunt Fauna added another tier to her birthday cake. It was sweet, yes, but now it just seemed silly. *How were they even going to eat all that cake?* Despite her questions about the gown, Rose couldn't contain her joyous news. The fairies listened to her ramble on about the true love she met in the woods. And then it happened... The truth spilled out. They tried to explain that she couldn't possibly marry a commoner because she was betrothed to Prince Phillip. They were hoping she would be thrilled, but they were wrong. Even the truth about who she was and what life had in store for her didn't bring her joy. Instead, she crumbled in disbelief and ran off to her room.

Outside of her room, the three sisters gathered, wondering what to do. "Shouldn't we tell her that the man she loves *is* the prince? Then she wouldn't be so sad," asked Fauna.

"No. We can't do that without basically telling her that we have all been in on a lie and the visits from him weren't sincere, but rather just another lie," answered Flora.

"I don't know why she is making us feel so terrible... I mean, we went through a lot for her, more than she could possibly understand," said Merryweather in an annoyed tone.

"That's it! We will just explain that we were just trying to protect her," Fauna interjected.

"Yes, Fauna, that is a brilliant idea! Let's tell her that she has been cursed and hunted her whole life by a dark fairy. That ought to make her feel better. Happy birthday to you— *tra-la-la,*"Merryweather mocked.

But while the sisters were arguing back and forth, Rose tried to understand her crushing reality. How had everything changed so dramatically in one day? Why, even her name was a lie. "They called me Princess Aurora, the daughter of King Stefan and Queen Leah. She had parents and her aunts were... Well, she really didn't know who they truly were or why it had been them that raised her. Then suddenly, as she wiped the tears from her eyes, she spotted something, something utterly bizarre. There, within her room, was a little mop swishing soapy water back and forth upon her floor, moving entirely on its own. She wiped her eyes again, thinking she must just be seeing things, but upon a second, third, and even fourth glance, she found that what she was seeing was real.

A scream cried out from upstairs, striking alarm in the three sisters that were still arguing below. They quickly dashed up the steps and when they entered the room, they saw it. The one thing they had forgotten. The mop. There it was— The truth staring them all in the face. Rose was absolutely petrified as she watched Fauna use her wand to stop the mop, allowing it to fall to the wet floor.

"I can't believe this! Who are you? What are you? What is happening?" Aurora screamed in fright. The sisters tried to calm her, tried to explain, but it was no use. She was completely frantic. Finally, when nothing else worked— one of the fairies had to do something that they wished they would never have to do. Taking charge of their volcanic situation, Flora used her wand to put their withering rose in an almost catatonic state of hypnosis. Void of any expression or words, the sisters placed the enchanting gown that sparkled like sapphire upon her. Once the dusk began to fall, they all put on their cloaks, and headed out of the cabin, to make their way towards King Stefan's castle.

Once they arrived, the castle and all of its guards were on high alert, each fully prepared for their arrival. The three sisters and the stupefied princess made their way into the dark and dreary castle. They had thought to meet with the king and queen, but the king merely sent them a messenger with a letter telling them that they did not want to see their daughter until the following morning. So, it seemed the three fairies were going to be babysitting the princess for one last night. Merryweather was annoyed, Fauna was sobbing in sadness, and Flora had to put all of her energy into stopping Merryweather from going off on the royal couple. They sat Aurora down before a mirror, allowing her to see the new and truthful vision of herself in its refection. The gown she wore was indeed exquisite, and to signify her new identity, Flora used her magic to create the perfect crown for a princess. But once she placed the heavy burden upon her golden hair, the last bit of self-awareness came to the edge of the girl's mind. Tears fell from her cheeks as she sobbed into the comfort of her own arms folded on the vanity before her. Flora used her wand again to calm her before the three fairies left the dark room, each hoping she would simply drift off to sleep. They had a key to her door. Nothing or no one was going to be able to get through the chamber door.

Fauna fell to her knees. We cannot do this. How do we know Prince Phillip's kiss will work? We do not even know if he truly loves her. He has merely been possessed. We don't truly know what's in his heart. What if..."

"Calm yourself, sister. I have thought and feared the same thing. And I think it may not come to that. We haven't heard or seen anything from Maleficent in all these years. She doesn't know where the princess is or if she is even still alive. All we need to do is guard this door until sunrise. If our Rose can just last one more day without touching the spindle of a spinning wheel, then we won't need Prince Phillip at all. She will be safe, and the Snow Queen will have her wish. We may not have found the book she wanted, but the payment of the girl should buy us our lives, or at least some more time."

Fauna and Merryweather were both thrilled with the idea. Flora always seemed so wise and well guiding, so in moments like this, they always trusted her judgement. "Yes." They both replied.

"So, we all agree then? We will stay here and guard the door?" Flora asked.

Her sisters turned to each other and returned to her gaze with smiles and a nod. They were going to protect her, at all cost.

* * *

As the three fairies talked frantically amongst themselves, each battling the other with opinions and ideas, Princess Aurora had been left quite alone within the grandest room of the castle's tower. They thought they had left her in perfect conditions. With the drapes closed and a nice warm fire burning in a large fireplace, offering heat within the cold and dreary room. But despite their efforts, the chamber felt like a prison, one that now contained a prisoner. Aurora continued crying. It seemed to be the only thing her body could do at her will. The hypnosis was in every way terrifying. She felt like screaming, running, but she couldn't. The fairies had thought this would keep her, at least until she could see for herself that the man she loved was the prince she was going to marry. But the sister's temporary fix had made her a perfect target; one that wouldn't be able to fight her doomed fate.

Suddenly, the flames within the fireplace began to dance, now glowing bright and green. With the power of the elements that dwelled inside the Wood Witch's magic, the doorway had been all too easy to enter. Maleficent emerged from the darkness behind the flames, collecting the fire into a single orb, beckoning the princess with the ominous sound of a most haunting music. Then from the darkness where Maleficent stood, the bricks faded away, and with the powers of all willow-the-wisp, the hypnotized princess followed its lead through the very doorway that would take her to her death.

In a mere moment of shared silence due to their frustration, the three fairies felt the chill of absolute evil crawl up their spines. The music. It had a distant element, and it wasn't quite fae, and yet they knew exactly to whom it belonged. In perfect unison, they uttered her name and barged into the dark chamber, only to arrive a moment too late. The wall of bricks returned, blocking them from their rose. One by one, room by room, staircase by staircase, the sisters urgently raced through the dreary tower, each screaming out for the princess they had promised to protect. It felt like a maze, a labyrinth with no real end. They knew Maleficent's magic was toying with them, but they couldn't bring themselves to stop. They couldn't give up. They had come too far.

Finally, the girl had reached a hidden room of stone and old rusty pieces of metal that once had been used as torture devices. The medieval clamps and spikes still painted with the blood of countless victims that died by order of the king and those before him. The room was walled with nothing but old stone, cracked and even scratched by those that tried to escape. To Maleficent, it was perfect. The green orb floated to the center of the room from its flashing glow, it spread lines of black wood, each piece connecting until it formed into a glowing spinning wheel. The spindle shinned brightly, calling her forward with the gentle hum of the Dark Fairy's song.

"Touch the spindle. I command you. Touch it. Touch it," Maleficent whispered from her magic, each word making the spindle flash brighter. The princess didn't want to. She was scared, beyond scared, but the fairies had left her defenseless. She reached out her hand and pricked her finger.

Maleficent laughed as the three sisters finally entered the torture chamber, lifting her long dark gown to reveal the dead body of Princess Aurora.

The three gasped in utter horror at the sight of her corpse lying on the cold stone stained with blood. Merryweather and Flora had to keep Fauna from collapsing, swallowed away by her screams. Maleficent savored such a moment. "You poor fools! You've lost! All of you! I've killed your precious princess and I would kill you three as well, but I think I will leave you to face the Snow Queen with your failure. Enjoy being hunted. Enjoy living in fear. Enjoy being hated. Enjoy being alone. And don't think that you are going to hide in Mim's cabin again!"

A look of utter shock flashed upon their faces then. "You... You..." Flora stuttered.

"Oh, yes, I know where you have been, hiding like cowards in Slumberland, leaving your worthless bodies in my mother's cottage. The nerve! Why, I wish she were still alive to see what you have done!"

Merryweather hissed, "Too bad you killed her too. That is all you do. Tragedy and disaster follow you wherever you go. You *are* a curse, Maleficent. And this story is not over yet!"

The Dark Fairy bellowed with laughter then, mocking the three. "Oh, yes... Your plan with the prince. True loves kiss." She bent back with laughter, nearly robbing her of breath. The three sisters looked at her with hatred and confusion. *Had she known all along?* They thought. She seemed to know everything, and they had no idea what she had been doing the last fifteen years. Maleficent knew what they had prepared, but what had she? Maybe they *had* lost. The princess was dead, and maybe the prince was too. All they had left was the book. They needed it now more than ever. It was their only hope.

Maleficent smiled at them, taking one last moment to enjoy their suffering. "Well, I must be going. I have other matters to attend to. I have never attended a birthday party before. It was *quite* fun," she giggled wickedly before vanishing in a blaze of glory, leaving the three sisters with their dead flower.

* * *

For the first time in her life, Maleficent felt incredible, unstoppable. And next came the best part... The Forbidden Forest was especially quiet on this night. One could almost feel the malice in the crisp air. The branches upon the trees swayed slowly, the cold breeze moaning like ghosts with the clanking sound of the chain that hovered the scorched grounds. Grip had led her to the cabin. It was a place she had hoped to never enter again, but somehow, with the smell of the ancient wood and the endless shelves of her mother's trinkets, she couldn't help but feel at home. When she looked to the fireplace where they had spent so many nights reading and sewing, practicing magic, she was absolutely furious to discover Mim's rocking chair was gone. Something about its absence stung her, reminding her of all the loving moments they had shared and the tragic death she had caused her. How she wished she could take it all back. She slowly made her way down the great hall where the witch's sea of portraits hung. There it was. The painting with the red frame and the creepy scarecrow that hanged grimly beyond the yellow brick road. The shadowed corner hiding the book emerged, feeling its master nearby. In this moment, she was glad Mim was with her- that she had *always* been with her. She knew now why Mim let her kill her that terrible night. It was the only way she could protect her from *them*— Pan, the Snow Queen, and herself. The witch that had survived the ages, hiding in isolation to protect the wizard that she loved and the lands from her wicked sisters, had died for her. Maleficent felt a tear fall down her cheek as the vision of her death flashed in her mind. She had cruelly murdered her mother... And she had done it for *him*. But no matter, for he would be dealt with soon enough. She wiped away the drop of weakness from her cheek, composing herself back to her fierce devotion. "Come, Grip darling, we must hurry and move the book before our company arrives."

* * *

After two simple spells cast by the Dark Fairy, everything was prepared. All she needed to do now was wait. Once the sun had completely disappeared and the moon had risen high into the darkness, she felt the chill of frost come through the cracks of the doorway. A knock tapped on the wood. It was him.

"Come in," she said with the sweet tone of a young maiden. Then he opened the door. It was dark in the cabin, but she could still see the sparkle of winter frost in his eyes. Once he had come inside, the door slammed shut behind him, and it wasn't going to open until *she* wanted it to. With a snap of her fingers, a swarm of goblins, her ugly children, ambushed the prince with magical rope. He fought hard, but there was just too many of them. In fact, Maleficent had released all of those who had turned to stone to come and collect her prey. It all happened so fast. He was trapped, tied, and gagged in the darkness. Out of breath and out of strength, the prince fell to his knees. Out from the shadows of the great hall, a spark lit the wick of a single candle. The flame was no ordinary art of mortal fire; it was the burning glow from the fires of hell. Maleficent then stepped forward, raising the candle to illuminate his face. And then their eyes met, each finally seeing exactly who they truly were— and a smile spread across her sharp face as the sound of his thumping heart began to race.

"Well... What have we here, my pets? I came here to catch a peasant, a mortal, a prince, and low and behold— I capture he who held my heart..." She said, before leaning in close so he could feel the warmth of the flickering flame. "...And *broke* it."

His eyes went wide then. He struggled harder, but the mortal vessel that contained him left him utterly powerless; a fact that made Maleficent laugh.

"There are some downfalls to possession, Pan! But do not worry, my *love*. I will separate you. But I can't promise it won't be excruciatingly painful."

The rope tightened harder as he struggled to his feet, his angered words muffled by his gag. The goblins chuckled at his helpless efforts.

"Come, children. I have great plans for our royal guest at the Forbidden Mountain."

The door opened then, and the swarm of monsters dragged him out of the cabin with their mistress and her darling raven behind them. She took one last glance at her former home and said goodbye. Then once again, the cabin door closed, leaving only the prince's hat that had fallen during his struggle, and within the fold of the royal fabric was a single feather— old, withered, and *red.*

CHAPTER TWELVE

LET EVIL DIE

an had said that the night would be one of celebration for everyone, but it seemed that there was but one among them all that had cause to celebrate. The goblins had indeed taken the prince and the fairy that dwelled inside him to the Forbidden Mountain. The castle was a work of horror, with crumbling stones, gargoyles, and a fog-covered cemetery full of the creatures that had died at the Dark Fairy's hand. The rocky cliffs that overlooked the impossibly black sea, shined from the crashing waves that threatened to swallow anyone or anything that dared to venture too close. The ocean seemed alive there, dangerous and wild, but nothing was as fearsome as the storm that raged above the dark palace. Pan may have once brought the sun, and even carried the frost of winter, but the storm that struck the night sky wrought by the wrath of Maleficent's fury was enough to frighten even the gods. Not even the stars wished to share the night with the deadly clashes of her thunder and lightning. It was a display of power with the likes of which Pan hadn't laid eyes on since the night he met the Wood Witch. But this wasn't just Mim's magic that stirred in the darkness— it was the manifestation of Maleficent's inner turmoil. All the pain, loss, and betrayal; it had finally erupted, and the fairy lad that had caused her so much misery was about to suffer. This time— the *piper* was going to pay.

Once they had entered the castle and the prince was chained before her throne, Maleficent raised her hand to silence the rioting monsters, picking and kicking their struggling prisoner. It was the most fun they had enjoyed in years. But now, it was her turn to deal with the prince, and he who possessed within. The dreaded pause was stiff, tense, and palpable. And though the room was full of monsters and crows, the moment was entirely theirs.

Pan tried to break free, not only from his shackles and rope, but the vessel that held him. With the light taps of her nails upon the orb of her staff, Maleficent smiled at his feeble attempts. "You needn't rip the poor prince apart with your desperation. I told you that I would separate you, and I will. But I have a few things to say first..." She said, standing up from her throne, slowly sauntering towards him. "I want you to know— that *I* know who you are and what you have done. To me. To my father. To my mother, and all the tragic events that were led by your devious design! I know who you were as a mortal, and the boy who once ruled Neverland. I know of your little green friend and even your beloved Indian princess."

Pan squirmed with rage, causing the robes to tighten past the point of his ribs and into the flesh of his wrists and ankles. The prince screamed in agony inside, his cries screeching like scratch marks against Pan's mind, bringing the body to its knees.

"I know it was my father that took away your love, your eternal childhood, and the lost island, your bloody playground. I also know that my mother, the Blue Fairy, rid the worlds of your pixie. But neither of them, despite their greatest efforts, could do what I am about to do. I am going to kill you, Jack, once and for all! But first... the separation. You need to know that this is not an act of mercy for the prince, for he too has no future; this is so you know that I did not beat you because of such a disadvantage. This is about you and me— the great Peter Pan and the Dark Fairy. They say you are the best there ever was— Well, let's see how you do up against me!" She declared, slamming her staff to the floor, igniting the roaring cheers from her monsters. "Now, what do you say we remove the young Phillip from our affairs?" She asked with a sly smirk.

Pan huffed in fury but remained completely bound. And though he had fought profusely to separate from the prince, he would soon learn that for a possession to be removed by force, like that of an exorcism for a demon, it is quite painful for both sides if not done carefully— and Maleficent had no interest in being careful.

With a raise of her hand, she called upon the magic of division.

"Thou within

Come undone
Split the two
That once was one
Control no longer
Nor possess the stride
Let thouest reveal
What the vessel may hide
Take the soul
That doesn't belong
Divide this imposter
Who's invaded too long."

At that, she struck the staff to the floor, blasting a strike of her green magic to the prince in the center of the room. The goblins quickly scattered away to the safe distance of the walls. The hit knocked Phillip to the floor. Then, as he slowly lifted his head, the chocolate-brown color of the boy's eyes flashed to the winter blue of frost-covered ponds, and his hair went as white as snow. Pan growled from the pain, looking up at her with bitter hatred. The freezing cold that came from each of his huffing breaths froze the cloth that gagged him, and with a final blow, it cracked and fell to the floor in pieces, freeing his first words since his capture, "Maleficent... stop! Please, do not do this. I don't want to fight you. I love y——"

Blast! Maleficent struck the staff to the floor again, blasting him hard in the chest, knocking all breath from him and blood to spill from his mouth. "Do not dare try to charm me with your trickery again. Haven't you been listening? I know everything! The

orphanage, my father's vendetta, my mother's agony—
One way or another, it all comes back to you. From the
very beginning... Well, there was that red fairy that took
her cruel pleasure in tormenting my father when you
weren't. I am pleased by her death. She deserved it.
The day that you took me into the Snow Queen's
realm; when she showed me the massacre he had
wrought upon her world; I was suffocated by guilt. I
hated him for that; for causing such suffering upon
innocent creatures, simply because they were magical.
But that wasn't why my father went to that realm, was it?

Pan looked down, spitting the blood from his
mouth, answering lowly, "No."

"Right! It was a lie, as was your terrific
performance. But the truth has emerged now, and I will
not let my father's triumphs be undone by you, the
queen, or the rose vessel. My father killed the Scarlet
Fairy, and I am going to honor his death by making
sure she stays dead!"

Stretching the sore muscles of the prince's jaws,
Pan forced him to smile through the pain, "Hook is still
alive. Your father— is still alive."

His words stopped Maleficent cold. She hadn't
been sure if it were true or not, but now she did. He
was alive. But where? "Where is he?" She asked in a
calm tone.

"Let me go and I'll release him back into this
world. Your mother can have her true love back. You
can finally have a family. I promise I will never bother
any of you again."

Maleficent giggled as if amused by his proposed bargain. "And the princess? What of her?"

"Well... I cannot speak for her Majesty, but I can swear for myself that I will not go near the mortal again."

"But don't you love her, Jack? All those years of sweetened words and dancing in the moonlight... How are you *ever* going to part with a love so *pure?* That kind of heartbreak— It can really change a person."

Pan inhaled deeply, "I feel nothing for the princess. I just needed the book. I just— I need the book."

"Ah, yes. The book, the book... The same reason you tricked me into thinking you loved me all those years ago. Why, Jack? Why did you do that to me?"

Pan coughed, feeling the vessel draining of life, "It was nothing personal, Maleficent. It was the only way."

"The only way to what?!"

"To get back everything that I have lost."

Maleficent bent backward with laughter then. "And because of your ruthless ambition, I have lost everything too. You took my parents away from me. You tricked me into loving you, into killing Mim in a desperate attempt to save you. Of course, that was also a lie. I declared revenge for you. I cursed a baby for you. Well, all of that is over. Now I do what serves me, and no one else. You are never getting the book. You don't have a future beyond this night; here in my castle!"

Blast! The prince was struck again.

"That was for my mother; for taking her wand, her love, and her child, me."

The prince and Pan writhed in torment, feeling themselves being literally ripped apart, their screams stacked in frightening echoes, never knowing which was which. But just as his body began to go still...

Blast!

"That is for my father; for his childhood, his darkness, his sufferings."

Now the division was manifesting; the prince's body looked as if a ghost was emerging from his skin. "Maleficent, stop! Now! If this prince dies, I will kill you! Stop!"

Blast!

"That is for Mim, for ever making me doubt her love. For making me chose between you when you knew you felt nothing for me in return. And for her death, that would have never happened if I had never met you. And finally—"

Blast! The separation was complete. The prince lied unconscious on the bloodied stone, badly hurt but still alive. Jack alone stood before her.

"And that— was for me; for taking away everything I could have had and for making me the way I am now. You said once to my father that your life of magic was because of him; that he made you who are. Well, now I am saying the same to you. I may be dark, evil, and wicked, but it was *you* that created the monster."

"Ah, Maleficent... always the poor blame-less victim. You know, you and your father are so much alike. You both blame your personal tragedies for the darkness within you, but the truth is... No one made you do any of the wicked things you have done. No one forced you to kill the Wood Witch, though I still don't know how you managed to do... Well, it doesn't matter anymore. You did it. Not me. Not the Snow Queen. You. The princess, the doomed kingdoms, even those you call your children- that was all you! So, I broke your heart. I lied. I tricked you. I have done it to countless others. Get over it. Your father took away the girl I loved, and your mother took away my friend, the companion of the soul. They took them from me. Revenge... It's a poison. But Hook, you, and me— We love the taste of it. At least I can admit it. I own my darkness. I do not blame others for the evil things I do. I do the things I do because... Well, its fun. I enjoyed toying with you. You were so pathetic. It was too easy. And the death of the witch— that was just the icing on the cake. I wish I had been there; to see the old hag die. I think that might be my only regret. Was she surprised? Did she know you were doing it for me? Did she cry?" The thought made his sinister laugh erupt, each breath bringing the chill of winter into the room. Maleficent stood still, her eyes fixed with their demonic glow. The surrounding goblins however began to shake and tremble from the cold. The room quickly echoed with the sound of their chattering teeth. Pan smirked as he saw the frosted air expel from the huffing breaths through her nose. "What's the matter, Maleficent?

Can't handle the cold? Or can you just not handle the truth?"

The tense moment of pause between them added fuel to his arrogance. But then something happened. Something he didn't expect.

She smiled.

His expression fell as she opened her mouth to answer, "On the contrary, Jack. I find that your bitter means have given me much to think about. And I have to admit... You are right."

"I am?"

"Yes. *I* made the choices that led me here. I chose to walk down the path of darkness, as did my father. But here is where my father and I are different... he failed to kill you due to a certain disadvantage, a weakness."

"You didn't have the pleasure of knowing him like I did. James Hook was many things— *weak* was not one of them. Do not think to put yourself above him."

Maleficent giggled, "Such the flatterer. But you are wrong. You see, my father lost his battle against you because of one simple thing— love. He loved my mother, and he walked the plank for her. That is why you won then, and this is why I will win now... I have already lost everyone I love. There is nothing for you to take, no last-minute weapon to unleash. So go, unleash your finest snowflakes, Jack. Let's see how your frost holds up against my fire."

Pan felt a lump fall down his throat, "Fire? You are going to set me on fire?"

Maleficent smiled again, "I am."

Pan swallowed the sharp rock of breath, but just as fear began to suffuse his body, a realization struck him. "Even if you do manage to kill me... There will *always* be ways for me to return. And besides, I am the only one who can release your father from his eternal torment. Are you really ready to leave him there forever just to indulge your own vengeance? Are you truly that heartless, that cruel?"

"Oh, I will find a way to free him, and as far as your delusions of a future return— I'm afraid that just won't be possible. You see, I am not just going to kill you, I am going to completely destroy your eternal existence by ways of Hell fire! You're never going to return. Not even the gods will be able to bring you back. No turn of fate, nor any power will be able to undo what I am about to bestow."

"No. No. That's not possible. Not even you possess the dark magic it would take to do that."

Maleficent bent back her head with chilling laughter, igniting terrible fear within him. "Ah, I do now," she said, slowly turning over her hand with a graceful twist of the wrist. The hidden book emerged in her palm. The sight struck him like lightning.

There was only one thing left to do now, one last hope remaining... escape. Wasting not a second more, he turned and made a run for the grand window. But just as he reached the ledge, the thunderous clap of her staff struck the ground, and the floor beneath his feet began to crumble, dragging him down into a deep pit of broken stones.

He was trapped. He tried to climb. He tried to fly, but nothing worked. One after the other, his feeble attempts left him scraped, bloodied, and breathless. But each time he fell, the sound of the Dark Fairy's cackling brought him closer to tears.

Finally, she approached the edge above, looking down at him with a most sinister gleam. "What's the matter, Peter Pan? No happy thoughts?" She said, looking to her darling raven with snickering laughter.

"Let me out, Maleficent! Release me and I'll do anything. You can have anything you wish!" He screamed.

"No!" She roared with glowing eyes. "No more wishes! No more deals! Not anymore! It ends here! Right—now!"

"No, Maleficent, don't! Let me out! Please let me out!" He cried as she rose the book before her eyes... But no one— Not Mim nor even the Blue Fairy could stop her. She was too powerful for any of them.

"I call on the Fates
And the Erl King as well
Let their powers be mine
For this one single spell
The death of all deaths
Is my grandest desire
I summon destruction
By the purge of Hell Fire!
In the pit of ancient stone
Is where my enemy lies
I call upon the underworld
Let your burning flames rise!"

393

At first, nothing happened, giving Pan a mere moment of relief, but then he heard it. The stones around him began to crack and break. The pit rumbled with such force that he thought to be knocked to the ground, but he wasn't. No, what happened next was far more terrifying. Something held him up, locked upon an invisible stake, so he could have the petrifying view of the rocks fall beneath him to give way to the rising green flames that rose to burn him alive. Maleficent smiled, turning to walk back to her throne, to sit and enjoy the show. The goblins then roared with cheers, dancing around the glorious fire, and the crows watched from above on the pillars, each staring their ominous stare at the pleasing sight of scorching evil below. All but one, that is, for Grip was not like the others. He was hers. And he took his rightful place next to her, perching himself upon the top of her stretched finger. When the screams ceased to cry, she turned to him with a chuckle... "You know, darling, I do believe he was right. I do enjoy the sweet taste of revenge. And how delicious this one turned out to be," she said with a sparkle in her eye.

But the party was far from over. For there was still the real prince to deal with, and the three small fairies that were already on their way to save him.

* * *

The three sisters had made their way to the cabin, but not before using their magic to put the entire kingdom into a deep sleep. They didn't want King Stefan or King

Hubert to know that both of their children were now gone. For if they did, then who knows what kind of catastrophe would befall them. No, they still had a chance to make things right. For them, for the princess, the prince, and maybe— even the Dark Fairy herself. When they saw the prince's hat upon the floor of the ancient cabin, they knew where she had taken him. The magical power of Pan's possession had left a trail to her castle, but were they really brave enough to infiltrate the dark palace of Maleficent? Could they really survive the Forbidden Mountain?

If they had any hope at all, they had to try.

Maleficent quickly grew bored, and felt the need keep the fiery celebration going. She and Grip took the quiet stroll to the dungeon to visit the real Prince Phillip. He was in quite a dreary state. His body was weak, too broken to stand. The death of Pan had lifted her spirits and somehow left her feeling a bit merciful. Looking upon his mangled body on the very verge of death, she couldn't help but pity him. In a way, she saw him as another unfortunate victim of Pan's. She had only experienced possession in her dreams, and by those that love her; nevertheless, it had been absolutely torturous to endure. She couldn't imagine Pan had dealt with the prince as delicately. In a flash of generosity, she pointed her staff towards him, unleashing a slow-moving smoke that circled him before finally going up his nose into the wreckage of his insides.

Then it began. Piece by piece, limb by limb, and each rip and tear of his innards and those upon the surface of his skin began to heal. Within a few moments, every wound that threatened to take his life had now vanished. The blood he had spilled was now nothing more than old stains. There wasn't so much as a scar left behind as the magic expelled from him, coming back to the staff from once it came. From the moment his crushed bones repaired, his breath returned to him. He opened his eyes to find his savior was none other than the one who had nearly killed him. It was dark in the dungeon, terribly dark. But he could see her glowing eyes, as bright as emeralds staring down at him, followed by her white smile, spread eerily wide across her sharp-boned face. The silhoette of her tall curved horns made her look like a tall devil in the doorway. She then brought forth a single candle, held by a golden swivel frame as if out of nowhere. Its flickering glow illuminated her terrifyingly beautiful image. Her perfect face seemed to surpass even the princess's in the candlelight. The long dark gown that covered the rest of her person was tattered, the edges and train were singed, no doubt by the enormous fire. It was then, as the smell of burning flesh filled the air and the scent of smoke suffocated her black fabric, that he understood what had happened to his possessor.

"Poor Prince Phillip. Why so melancholy? I have freed you from your captor, your prison," she said as if surprised by his lack of gratitude.

"Yet, I find myself in another," he replied glumly.

"I'm sorry it has come to this. It was not my wish to hold you captive in my castle, but it had to be done. I cannot free you without freeing her."

"The princess?"

"Yes."

"Please, let me go. The cold man took me to where the Snow Queen dwells. If you let me go, I will go there and kill her. She is evil and she too threatens to take my Rose away. Once she is dead, you need not fear the transfer of souls. You have the book, and I can give you her death. Please. Just release me from these chains and I'll serve only you."

Maleficent scoffed in amusement, "You— You'll serve me?"

"I swear it," he said with fierce devotion.

Maleficent smiled at his bravery, "I'm sorry, dear prince. If it weren't for all the times my trust was betrayed, I might have believed you. But the fact is, you are mortal. A mortal man. I have no conviction left for such matters."

Phillip dropped his head in dismay, his arms weakening from the chains that held them high behind his back.

She squinted at his stance, pitying his discomfort. With a quick snap of her fingers, the chains broke from the stone wall and locked to the floor, allowing him to sit or stand with ease. He looked up at her then, with a look in his eyes she had never seen before. Was it sincerity? She shook her head as if telling herself no. "I accede your proposal. But I will say— you bring up a good point of fact. I do not need you or anyone to do my killing for me. I had thought to let the Snow Queen live, to suffer her great loss for the rest of her eternal days."

"But with her death, two innocents may live without suffering..."

"I said I would think about it! I will not be well-handled if rushed. After all, we have all the time in the world. You will just have to await my decision. It could be today. It could be tomorrow. It could be another fifteen years. True, you will age, and she will not; not if those meddlesome three have anything to do with it."

"But if I age..."

"What's the matter, young Phillip? Is your love not true?"

"It is. I love her."

"Then what's a little thing like age against the power of true love?" Then she saw it, that flicker of anger behind his mortal eyes. She smiled. "You look upset. Are you suddenly uncertain? Feeling that sting of doubt?"

He glared at her but did not reply. But he didn't have to. It was written on his chiseled face. The devotion he had promised only moments ago had disappeared in his expression. He looked at her then the way that they all had— like a monster.

Grip began to squawk, angered by his snare and the message behind it. But Maleficent wasn't upset. She pat his head, calming his fluffing feathers, "It's alright, my pet. We cannot blame the prince for being dismayed. He is just a human after all. They say have faith, but when they have to rely on it, turns out— they don't believe their own hype. Or maybe he just lacks the imagination and needs us to show him. What do you think, darling?" She asked the dark raven. He screeched in reply, almost eager in response. "Without our late Jack to guide his mind, it falls to us to show him..." She tapped her staff lightly, igniting the green glow of the orb. Bringing it close to her face, she swirled her hand above its shine to reveal a vivid image within; a story unfolding with the ominous voice of the Dark Fairy, narrating sweetly as if telling a bedtime tale. In the end, Prince Phillip watched as the vision of his older self rode away on a white horse, finally free to leave the tall iron gate of the Forbidden Mountain. "There he goes, like a knight on a white horse, to prove that true love conquers all!"

Prince Phillip charged, furious at her mocking illusion. But his fury just made her laugh.

"Come, Grip. Let's leave our guest to watch the magic of imagination coming to life."

* * *

Maleficent sauntered away, back to the throne room where the flames of the celebration still burned. But as her shadow followed behind her upon the ancient stone, neither she nor her beloved raven saw the three small shadows that floated nearby. It was the three sisters in their smallest form. They had made it past the goblin guards that littered throughout the castle. And now they had found him; not Pan, but the prince, chained in iron, sitting alone on the floor. They were instantly struck with surprise to find him in one piece, perfectly intact. They had expected they would have to heal him, and the dangers of someone or something detecting their magic.

"I don't understand. Did Maleficent heal him?" Fauna asked in a quiet whisper.

"I suppose—but why?" Flora wondered.

"It doesn't matter why! We need to hurry up and get out of here!" Merryweather whispered harshly.

At that, the three fairies sprung to their normal size. The prince was startled, but the sisters didn't have time to explain. With the magic in their wands, they freed him from his chains and melted away the lock on the chamber door. Phillip raced to his feet, ready to dash out of the dungeon, but Flora quickly stopped him in caution. "Hold on, Prince Phillip, beyond these walls of stone and this castle of great evil, we have set in place a magical bridge that will take you and your noble steed straight to the Rose Kingdom where your true love awaits your kiss. But such a path will bring forth many more dangers. Maleficent will not let you go so easily. You will have to face her alone. Our magic cannot be used to fight her... But we *can* give you what you will need to survive the journey," she said with a flick of her wand. Suddenly, a strong silver shield appeared strapped to his arm. This is a shield of the greatest virtue, made by the same magic that once protected the Dark Fairy's father. No fae magic will be able to penetrate it. And now..." She flicked her wand again, "This is the sword of all truth. The powers these weapons contain are all you need to triumph over evil. Use them wisely, for they are all you have."

Prince Phillip was in awe at their gifts, but there was no time to waste.

"Come on! We have to go!" Huffed Merryweather, hopping with impatience by the door.

They dashed out of the dungeon with the prince, but they were too late. For just as they feared, someone did feel the presence of their magic— and it was none other than Maleficent's darling raven. Face to face with the creature, Grip squawked and screeched in alarm. He turned to alert the others. They had to hurry. Following the prince, they turned down the other corridor to a nearby staircase, but just as they reached the middle steps, they were confronted by a full wave of Maleficent's army with her raven at the head. The goblins came in swinging their weapons and chomping at the bit to kill their running prey, eager to please their wanton mistress.

Turn by turn, each corner they dashed through was another trap full of monsters led by her pet. The one that had been her eyes and ears for years. It was *he* who had alerted the Wood Witch the night of their party. It was *he* who had found the princess and told Maleficent where they were. He had always been there. The fairies heard the magical call he made to his master. If Maleficent came, they could all die. The squawking grew louder, finally bringing one of the sisters to the boiling point. Merryweather couldn't stand it anymore. The meddlesome bird had interfered one time too many. She turned away from her sisters, chasing after him. Flora and Fauna begged her to stop, to come back, but she couldn't. She hated him. She wanted him gone. He screeched in panic, trying to get away, calling out to Maleficent for help, and then it happened... The little blue pixie whipped her wand, zapping a blast of magic upon him, instantly turning him into stone— just as the Dark Fairy emerged from the balcony above. Her eyes went wide as the worst horror imaginable filled inside her. "No! —— She screamed, rushing to him. But it was too late, the withered stone began to crack. She wrapped her arms around him, begging it to stop, "No— no— no— Don't leave me. Grip! Grip!" She wailed as the rock crumbled away, the pieces of her beloved companion falling to dust. She was robbed of breath. Her face and vision were completely covered by the tears of her most heart-wrenching sorrow. The world seemed to stop in that moment. In a life full of tragedy and soul-crushing blows, this was the most painful of them all. He was gone. Grip— was gone.

Her haze of agony was suddenly struck by the sound of hooves clip-clapping out the gates of the palace. Then she saw them, the three fairies and the prince escaping; off to save the cursed princess. Something happened in that moment. The loss of her raven seemed to have stripped away the last shred of light in her heart. All there was now— was the pitch black of darkness.

* * *

The skies roared with the thunder and lightning of her rage, the storm spreading over the world. Blue strikes of blazing light struck the ground as she spiraled above, each hit springing a massive bush of deadly thorns. Within seconds, the Rose Kingdom was covered in the towering vines with spikes as sharp as blades. The prince and fairies were blocked. The horse could barely move, too terrified to go further. But Prince Phillip wouldn't give up. He and the fairies did all they could to cut their way through. Despite her wicked efforts, the fairies and prince had nearly reached King Stefan's castle.

"Enough of this!" She declared, rapidly coursing through the air like a glowing hurricane, landing upon the ground that lay just beyond her enemies.

They all halted in utter terror. It was as if the presence of all evil stood before them. It was Maleficent, but something else too, something more. They didn't know what it was but it—was—petrifying.

"I call on the gods, the north, east, and west, I call on the fates to do my behest, I call on all souls—taken by the fae, visit me now and do as I say. Forces of darkness and all powers of Hell, I summon you here. Come serve me well! The three sisters and Phillip froze in panic as the vision of the Dark Fairy reached out her arms, allowing all the evil in all the worlds to swallow her up, evolving her into something else. The fairies watched as Maleficent faded away. Everything she once was gone now. And from the flames of wickedness, she rose into the sky in the form of a massive black dragon. Prince Phillip could hardly breathe in the presence of such horror.

"Oh my—god... What do I do now?" He stammered fearfully.

But the three sisters were suffused with the overwhelming pain that filled the smoky air. "I can't believe it," Fauna whispered. "What have we done? Maleficent... I can't even feel her anymore. She had nothing left."

"We have to stop this!" Merryweather declared, on the verge of flying forward, but Flora quickly grabbed her and pulled her back.

"Wait! There is one thing... Yes, one more thing we can try."

"Use your magic!" Prince Phillip yelled as the black dragon locked its glowing gaze upon him. Then suddenly... a blaze of fire shot at him with her powerful roar. He quickly rose his shield, protecting him and the fairies from the flames. "Do something now!" He screamed as she roared again, this time setting the entire ground in a green inferno.

The sisters rushed him to one of the tall rocky cliffs, "Come on! Prince! Up this way!" Flora screamed.

"Use your wands! Put out the fire! Fight her! I can't do this alone!" He shouted, climbing to the top.

"We can't! We're good fairies! We can only cast good magic!" Fauna cried out.

Flora stopped, "That's it! We can fix this! Only *we* can fix this!" She said to herself.

"What?" Her sisters asked, barely able to hear her through the roaring flames.

"Our magic! That's the answer."

The moment was now. The dragon chomped its jagged teeth, threatening to eat the prince whole. He swung the sword back and forth, but it couldn't reach, and now he had backed his way to the very end of the cliff.

Flora called for her sisters to grab her hand and rushed to his side. The dragon's fire blasted the shield away. This was their last chance. She rose her wand and reached deep into the core of their true magic. "We are the daughters of the Woodland Queen, together we can do this...

Let this sword of truth,
Fly swift and sure,
Let all evil die,
And let the good endure!"

The sword lit up with all the power of righteousness, everything good they could conjure.

"Now, Phillip! Now!" Flora commanded.

With one last hope, the prince threw the sword with all his might, and the four watched as the magical blade pierced through the dragon's chest. A wailing scream burst through the air as the malevolent monster crashed to the fiery ground.

"Is she dead?" Prince Phillip asked, nearly out of breath.

"I hope not," whispered Fauna.

Flora's eyes teared up. "If there was anything good left in her— then maybe... The sword was enchanted to destroy evil. Now we have to wait and see if there was anything good left in Maleficent's heart."

* * *

The flames of evil and the black dragon each began to fade away, leaving only the scorched grounds and the Dark Fairy that laid upon them. On the verge of death, too weak to move or speak a word, Maleficent was left with her last thoughts. She thought of Mim and all their special moments together in the cabin she called home. She thought of everything that her loved one's had done for her, what kind of sacrifices they had made for her. For the first time, she was able to see beyond the lies and betrayal. It was strange, wonderfully strange. Even as she laid there, slipping away into the cold embrace of death, she couldn't bring herself to be angry— not anymore. She thought of everything her ravenous rage had wrought upon her. Her revenge had cost her more than any glory could have rewarded. She had been blinded by it. She had let her obsession consume her and had taken the lives of many others. It all led her here, to die upon the ashes of the burned Forbidden Forest. No doubt even the hidden cabin had been engulfed by her flames of evil. Yes, her darkness had destroyed everything. And though she didn't understand how, she knew it was gone. It felt good. She was happy to die, to be erased from it all. For in death, she could be reunited with her dear Grip. She didn't deserve to live, maybe she never did, but if there were one piece of solace to hold and keep, it was that she had rid the realms of Peter Pan. No one could take that away. It was the one good thing she had done, and even if she had to go through hell to destroy him, she was glad she did. The evil. The pain. The torment... It would all end with her last breath.

She could feel the cold coming over her then. She began to feel tired and the pain from the sword had become numb. It was time now. The smoky air faded away, and through its gray blanket that hid the sky, the vision of life could finally be seen on the other side. There they were— the stars. They were beautiful. And there were so many. Twinkling brightly in all kinds of shapes and sizes, she had never taken the time to really admire their radiance. Then suddenly, she saw the blue twinkle of her mother's star. She didn't know if she was looking down on her, or what she must be thinking after the heinous acts she had done, but she hoped she was. With the last bit of strength, she brought the words she needed to say to her mouth, and let them go with a weak breath, "I wish..." She coughed, feeling the warm blood in her mouth choking her. "I wish— my mother was here."

Almost instantly, a flash of blue appeared. Maleficent weakly moved her eyes to look, but Ainsel was already rushing to her. "I'm here, sweet love. I'm here," she said stroking her daughter's face.

"I— I just didn't want to die before..."

"What is it, darling?"

Maleficent looked down at the sword that went through her. She could barely feel anything anymore. She wanted so badly to close her eyes, to give in to this drowsy pull, but she had to fight it, just a little bit longer. "I wish I could fix all the evil things that I have done.

Can you do that? I could die in peace if I knew such a miracle could be done."

"Oh, Maleficent," The Blue Fairy cried, seeing the light leaving her eyes.

"I'm sorry for it. I'm sorry I couldn't free my father. I am sorry I was cruel to you. I am sorry for the curse and for killing Mim. And..." She teared up, barely able to say the words— "I'm sorry I got my beloved Grip killed. Do you think anything I've done can be forgiven?"

"Yes, Maleficent, I do. But darling," she said loudly, trying to keep her awake, "Listen to me. Listen. I won't let you go! I won't. We can fix this! Together, you and me.

Magic, please
Hear my call
I need your power
One and all
I summon the book
That conjured Hell's fire
Come and grant me
My one true desire
Bring her back
Healed by my vow
That the darkness is gone
Only light is here now
May I burn forever
In the underworld
If I should ever fail
To do as I've told

I swear she'll never falter
Or break her stance
Please give my daughter
Her second chance."

At that, the hidden book that had been left within the dark castle appeared in her hand, and the bright glow of glittering blue came over Maleficent as her heart beat its last. For a moment, nothing happened. There was no breath, no color, no life. She was dead. Ainsel threw herself on top of her, sobbing harder than any fairy ever had. It was the kind of sadness no heart could endure. But without Maleficent, without James, she didn't want to live another day. She would stay there for as long as takes, at her daughter's side, the very place she had wished to be all along.

The black tunnel of death is a portal one may only enter through their end, never knowing where it might take them, what door will open for their soul. Suddenly, through the silence of her passing, she heard a voice, one that spoke from the realm of the dead. "Maleficent. You need to wake up. You have to keep fighting."

It was Mim. *How was this possible?*

"You're strong, Maleficent! It's only the darkness that is dying. My powers still live inside you. If you give up, the power and the book will return to Oz. If my sisters should get their hands on them... all the worlds would be doomed. It's up to you, little witch. Wake up, Maleficent! Open your eyes—right... Now!"

Like a clap of lightning, Maleficent's bright green eyes opened and a heartbeat thumped in her chest. Ainsel looked up to find her daughter alive. "Oh my god! You're alive! My baby is alive." She said with streaming tears falling down her face as she hugged her daughter tightly. Maleficent felt a bit uneasy under such unfamiliar affection, but she rose her hands to return her mother's embrace.

"Thank you for saving me, mother, but it was not my wish to escape death. I wanted to erase all the..."

"I know, my love. I know your wish. And together, I think we can make it come true."

"How?" Maleficent asked with eager intrigue. "I'll do anything."

Ainsel smiled and caressed her cheek, loving every second of contact between them. "I will too."

"So, what do we have to do?"

"Well, we have the book and we have our powers, and the essence of Mim that still lives inside you. I think by our triangle of magic, we can—"

"What?"

"Maleficent, I think we can change our fate."

"What? That's impossible. It hasn't been done. It cannot be done."

"It can. But you must be ready to pay the cost. You must let go of your power. The good, the bad, all of it. You have to be ready to give it all up. If you do, then we will have enough to cast the spell. Can you do that? Can you give it all up?"

Maleficent suddenly felt scared. Giving it all up. What would that mean? Where would that leave her?

410

What if she did and then the spell didn't work? How would she protect herself? Still, a life alone within her castle on the Forbidden Mountain seemed to be the worst thing that could possibly happen. After all, what has all her power done for her? With one last look upon the dark castle on top of the rocky cliffs above the black sea. It was a grim view. And with that one glance, she knew she never wanted to return. She took a deep breath and placed the crooked staff of power on the ground between them. Ainsel smiled, understanding her answer.

"You're sure?"

"Yes, I just need to do one more thing," she replied lifting the orb to gaze within. "Show me the princess." Her words frightened Ainsel. She didn't know what was going to happen. After all, the prince and the three sisters had already arrived at the gloomy castle. The image of a room decorated in fine silks of purple and blue emerged, and there upon a thin bed, was the princess. The prince hurried up the steps to her chambers, eager to awaken his future queen. He gazed at her beauty. She was breath-taking, even in death.

He leaned down carefully and gently kissed her cold lips. And as he rose to look upon her face once more, he saw the color of life return to her. Her lips went red, and her porcelain complexion appeared too fair to be real. She opened her long-lashed eyes and smiled at him. The moment was enchanting, like something out of a dream, but as Maleficent looked closer, she saw them— the lavender shade of the Snow Queen's eyes.

Ainsel too saw the mark of her Majesty's vessel and urgently pleaded for Maleficent's focus. "It is going to be okay, dear. After we cast our spell, everything will be different. We will take care of the Snow Queen. You must trust me."

"Alright."

Ainsel nodded in happy relief. "Yes, let's. The book says that we must say the words in perfect unison, then tap the top of the orb three times. The power of fate will then appear within the glass."

"And then what does it say to do?"

Ainsel's face fell, "We must smash the glass to set the changed fate free."

"Smash it? You mean break Mim's staff?!"

"It is the only way, Maleficent."

The thought brought the Dark Fairy to tears. She couldn't help feeling that such an act was to kill the last piece of Mim there was. The cabin was gone because of her, and now she would be forced to break the staff...

"Sweetheart, do not worry. Everything will be done for the best. Come now, it's time."

"What will happen? Where will we go?"

"There is no way of knowing exactly what fate has in store for you. The spell merely guides it to a moment— a moment that if done differently, it could change everything. It's a leap of faith. But it's a chance I am willing to take. Are you?" Ainsel asked in a sweet naturing tone.

Maleficent was afraid, but maybe it was time to take the path of light and that of faith. After all, it was what her mother, the brightest star in the dark sky, wished...

"Yes."

Together they put their hands on the staff and turned their hopeful gaze upon the chosen page of the red spellbook.

"Sisters of all
Fate of the Past
I summon thee
With this spell we cast
The thread you hold
Pull back the string
Rewrite the stars
A new tale to sing
We marvel at your power
For whom nothing is too late
Take us to the moment
That could forever change our fate!"

They screamed to the skies. Then they tapped the orb together, whispering, "One... Two... Three."

A small blue vortex then appeared within the glass. There it was. Their change of fate. All they had to do now was set it free. With a mutual nod and a deep breath, they rose the staff high and after one more glance into each other's eyes, they brought the staff down with great force, breaking the wood and smashing the glass.

* * *

In a single flash, Ainsel opened her eyes. She was aboard James' ship, lying in her bed. Then she saw them. Standing in the corner, humming a sweet song, was her handsome pirate, holding their newborn daughter, cradled carefully in his arms. The beautiful baby looked up at her father with her innocent emerald eyes. She cooed happily.

Ainsel smiled. She knew why fate had brought them here. Pan was gone. Nothing could bring him back, not even the fates. They were free to be happy now. Ainsel wasn't sure if Maleficent would ever remember anything that happened before, but someone else did. A sudden click came on a small window in the room. She looked over to find— it was a crow.

James turned to it in alarm. Ainsel waved her hand, opening the frame to let the dark creature in. He carried with him a basket, and within it was a heavy cloth with a letter on top. It was addressed to Ainsel. Once she held it in her hand, the crow quickly flapped his wings and took his leave. Hook was suspicious, "That was one of the Wood Witch's creatures. Why would she be sending you a letter? And on this day of all days? What does she want?" He spouted in his typical protective tone.

Ainsel smiled at him. It seemed she had even missed his temper. "It is alright, my love. The witch and I... Well, it's a long story. But you needn't worry about her. I assure you," she said sweetly.

414

He looked at her with confusion. What did she mean? He thought. His attention was quickly recaptured with the heart—melting sight of a baby's smile. Hook caressed her cheek with the spark of love in his blue eyes.

Ainsel felt blissfully happy. They were all together again. She opened the small parchment sealed by magic. The hand-written letter then appeared on the paper.

Dearest Ainsel,

I want to congratulate you on your new—born child. I have a present for the green—eyed beauty. It belongs with her, and always has. I know she will love it with all of her heart. Tell the girl who was once my daughter, that I shall love her forever and will look upon her sweetly, if only in a dream.

Hidden, but never lost,
The magnificent, marvelous, Madam Mim

Ainsel placed the parchment down beside her and looked into the basket. She curiously lifted the cloth to see what was inside. The sight was one that made her smile. There had never been a more perfect gift...

It was a baby raven.

The End

† But if I know you †
I know what you'll do
You'll love me at once
The way you did once
Upon a Dream.

Printed in Great Britain
by Amazon